Jessica Fletcher Presents...

MURDER, THEY WROTE

18 All-New Stories From
Today's Most Popular Mystery Authors

FEATURING:

Janet Laurence ❦ Mary Daheim ❦ Jane Dentinger

Marlys Millhiser ❦ Nancy Pickard ❦ Marjorie Eccles

Sally Gunning ❦ Jean Hager ❦ Kate Kingsbury

Ellen Hart ❦ Sarah J. Mason ❦ Charlaine Harris

Janet LaPierre ❦ Margaret Lawrence ❦ Betty Rowlands

D. R. Meredith ❦ Katherine Hall Page ❦ Gillian Linscott

MURDER, THEY WROTE

EDITED BY

Martin H. Greenberg
and Elizabeth Foxwell

BOULEVARD BOOKS, NEW YORK

MURDER, THEY WROTE

A Boulevard Book / published by arrangement with
MCA Publishing Rights, a Division of MCA, Inc.

PRINTING HISTORY
Boulevard edition / February 1997

All rights reserved.
Copyright © 1997 by MCA Publishing Rights, a Division of MCA, Inc.
Book design by Casey Hampton.
This book may not be reproduced in whole or in part,
by mimeograph or any other means, without permission.
For information address: The Berkley Publishing Group,
200 Madison Avenue, New York, New York 10016.

The Putnam Berkley World Wide Web site address is
http://www.berkley.com/berkley

ISBN: 1-57297-194-0

BOULEVARD
Boulevard Books are published by The Berkley Publishing Group,
200 Madison Avenue, New York, New York 10016.
BOULEVARD and its logo
are trademarks belonging to Berkley Publishing Corporation.

PRINTED IN THE UNITED STATES OF AMERICA

10 9 8 7 6 5 4 3 2 1

CONTENTS

Introduction

By the time this book is published, *Murder, She Wrote* will have finished its twelfth and final television season, making it one of the all-time most successful shows of its kind. Every year, the program has consistently placed among the fifteen highest-rated shows of the season. *Murder, She Wrote* has also been picked up for syndication, ensuring us many more years of watching Jessica Fletcher solve various whodunits.

Of course, the idea of television mysteries has been around for years. From the venerable *Perry Mason* series to lesser-known programs, such as *The Father Dowling Mysteries* and *The Most Deadly Game,* many have tried to find the elusive formula for long-lasting success. *Perry Mason* found it, and the track record of *Murder, She Wrote* proves that it has as well.

There are many factors that contribute to the show's success. Rather than relying on manic action scenes or climactic shoot-outs, *Murder, She Wrote* prefers to keep the violence mainly offscreen and concentrates on solving the crime using old-fashioned deductive reasoning. With a generous cast in each episode, the tightly woven plots challenge the cleverest viewers.

Another big plus is the show's lead actress, veteran movie and stage star Angela Lansbury, who stars as Jessica Fletcher, the mystery writer/amateur detective. Her gracious charm, combined with common sense and a keen mind for clues and criminals, makes watching her solve the crime as much fun as trying to figure it out. The fact that her character is an ordinary person who often solves the

crime at the expense of the police and others doesn't hurt
either.

There is perhaps another, more subtle reason for the
show's longevity as well. *Murder, She Wrote* is an engaging study of a relatively ordinary cast of characters, living
ordinary lives, one of whom, for whatever motive, commits
a murder. Now the game begins, as Jessica attempts to
catch the culprit before he or she gets away with it. The
study of everyday people driven to commit murder is fascinating, and few shows do it better than *Murder, She Wrote*.
Even fewer shows give viewers a fair chance to solve the
murder themselves.

The authors collected in this anthology, too, place ordinary people in extraordinary circumstances, usually with
murder as the centerpiece. Unlikely people, forced into the
role of detective, are challenged to put the puzzle pieces together and find the wrongdoer. From D. R. Meredith's fic-
tional town of Highwater, Texas, to a living room in an
English cottage where tea is served with a deadly twist,
some of the top writers on both sides of the Atlantic serve
up their finest mysteries of manners in the best *Murder, She
Wrote* style.

Of course, no *Murder, They Wrote* anthology would be
complete without a visit from the renowned sleuth herself.
Jessica Fletcher guests in Charlaine Harris's "Deeply
Dead," where a library luncheon turns deadly for one of the
patrons. Jessica has also provided a short introduction to
each story, written in her own inimitable style.

Of course, Jessica Fletcher isn't the only fiction writer
who guest-stars. In "The Potluck Supper Murders," Nancy
Pickard dishes up a dinner with murder as the main course.
Margaret Lawrence proves that murder is as old as the
United States, with the crime in "The Cat-Whipper's Ap-
prentice" taking place just after the Revolutionary War.
Gillian Linscott combines fruit and felony in "Poison
Peach," a tale of honor lost and regained amongst the or-

chards of an English estate. These are just a few of the excellent stories that can be found here.

Like the long-running television series, the stories in
Murder, They Wrote are all exciting and challenging, and
could have been written by Jessica herself. So turn the page
and try your hand at catching the culprit in each of the eighteen cunning tales that follow.

—The Editors

Some matters of the heart can never be resolved, especially when more than two people are involved. Here, two women meet over afternoon tea to discuss the one thing they had in common, the man who had been, until recently, in both their lives. By the end of the afternoon, however, he isn't the only thing they share anymore.

Come to Tea

Janet Laurence

I'M WAITING FOR Julia Norman to arrive.

"Come to tea," I'd said on the phone. I hadn't really thought she would. Not all this way. But then, curiosity killed the cat, didn't it? And no doubt she wonders as much about me as I have about her.

I've got everything ready. There are the very special sandwiches, nicely laid out on the commemoration plate. I just have to remember when handing it to her to keep the royal monogram toward me. And there's one of my sponges. John always said no one could make them rise quite so high or taste quite so good. It's the butter, I told him; you've got to make them with butter and beat them till you drop. The cake's filled with homemade strawberry jam and whipped cream. And after she arrives I'll make two kinds of tea, Darjeeling and Lapsang souchong. I know how these things are done, you see; John taught me.

When John and I met, I was a typist. He was on his way up, spending a period of time in all the departments, being groomed for the top. During his stint on the sales side, he used to bring me his reports to type. He was supposed to give them to Mrs. Harris, who ran the pool. She would then hand them out to whoever was free. But from the very first, John used to bring them straight to me. Then he'd give Mrs. Harris his special smile and say, "Eileen can read my writing."

His writing was difficult, I'll grant you that. But I never had any trouble with it. Just as I never had any trouble with him. Until he died.

It was after he'd moved on from Sales that he first asked me out and I discovered that underneath all that intelligence and style he was really a very simple man. He said he could relax with me, not have to worry about remembering all he'd learned since clawing his way up from the same sort of deprived background I come from.

It's strange how things turn out. I've always been such a home-loving person. Never wished harm to no one, never expected harm from no one. Not clever, not particularly attractive, the sort who doesn't stick out in a crowd. The sort who sticks to her man.

If I'd been different, if I'd wanted to be a part of John's business life, had entertained for him, insisted on being taken around with him, would things have turned out different?

But I was happy to make him comfortable in our little cottage, happy he wanted to be there with me rather than racketing around. Of course, I understood when business drew him away so frequently, and having the head office in London meant he had to stay up there more often than I liked.

It was John's funeral, though, that opened my eyes to what had been going on.

I ordered the biggest wreath the florist could provide, but hers outdid it. "My heart will be forever yours—Julia," the card said, peeking out of a mound of white lilies as large as a compost heap. I knew who she must be as soon as I saw her but I pretended to ignore her and she ignored me. I suppose we were both too involved with saying good-bye to John.

It wasn't until afterward that the full truth of the situation was brought home to me. That's when I began planning.

There's the doorbell now. When I think of all I've gone through, I'm quite surprised I can be so calm.

I open the door and she's standing on the mat that says "Welcome," looking a little nervous. I saw at the funeral that she was beautiful. Now her looks strike me afresh. Blonde hair in a feathery cut that softens what I suppose you would call classical features, a lovely figure even though she must be well over forty, and such a smart navy blue suit in some sort of soft crepe. She has gray eyes, very large, with long, sooty-dark lashes.

For a moment we stare at one another, then she smiles. "Eileen, I'm so pleased to meet you at last. All these years we've had so much in common." She holds out her hand and all the time she's smiling this lovely smile. But her words reverberate inside my head. Even while I ask her in, my voice steady and pleasant, anger churns in my stomach. Like acid it is. It's been there ever since John's funeral. I thought I knew him, you see. I thought we shared everything, that I could trust him. Then to find out . . . well, it was too much.

She comes into the lounge, I excuse myself to make the tea. When I come back I can see she has been examining everything. "What a nice room," she says, but with a note in her voice that betrays what she actually thinks of the three-piece suite, the flowered wallpaper and carpet, my crochet mats on the back of the sofa and chairs, just like the ones my gran made. Shall I tell her that John helped choose almost everything? He said the powder blue flowers on the wallpaper matched my eyes and he searched everywhere to find a suite with the same shade of velvety upholstery. But I chose the red vase that sits on the windowsill. The bubbles in the glass catch the sun and I like to think fish are at the bottom, sending up streams of air. I loved it the moment I saw it that time we went to Venice.

It was the only time John took me abroad with him. I suppose I can't really blame him that the trip wasn't a success. Once I'd got over how Venice looked just like all its photographs, I couldn't wait to leave. The hotel was too smart; it made me uncomfortable. I hated the food, all that pasta and oil, and even riding in a gondola didn't make up for the boredom of being on my own so much in a damp and rotting city with only boring art galleries and churches to look at. I didn't have my garden, you see, or cupboards to turn out, and I'd forgotten to bring my crochet. But I did love that vase.

Julia Norman sits herself down in one of the armchairs, carefully arranging her long legs to one side. She puts her big navy blue leather handbag on the ground beside the neat, matching, high-heeled shoes.

"I'm glad you rang." She leans toward me, her expression frank. "The two halves of John's life should meet—we have so much in common."

How dare she! I want to pick up the teapot and throw it at her. Instead I say, "Would you prefer Indian or China?"

She looks amused. "China, please. And without milk."

The liquid looks anemic—cat's piss, John would have called it. The thought catches me under my heart, gives it a squeeze that's exquisitely painful.

I hand over the cup, one of my precious Minton set that John gave me for our fifth anniversary. "You should have the best," he'd said as he handed it over. That was just before he was appointed to the board. I suppose I knew then that I could never be the sort of wife he needed in his professional life.

Julia sips the tea, gives a relieved smile as she replaces cup and saucer on the little table I've placed beside her. "That's delicious," she says, and, damn her, she sounds surprised.

"Have a sandwich," I say, giving her a plate together with a tiny linen serviette—no doubt she'd call them napkins. I hold out the commemoration plate, keeping the royal monogram toward me. "My own special pâté, chicken liver with wild mushrooms, *trompettes de la mort.*" I pronounce the words carefully, the way John taught me. Trumpets of death, he said they were in English. Funny name for something that's quite harmless. John used to bring me packets of them, dried, from France. I'd suggested once he take me there. That was after our disastrous trip to Venice. I explained I'd be happy browsing around the food shops and this time I'd take my crochet. But he said it would be no fun for me, he was going to be so busy and he didn't want to be worrying about me. I told him I quite understood. Now I wonder if Julia went with him on those trips.

Julia eats one of the sandwiches. "Delicious," she says. "But then John told me you were a great cook."

"He mentioned me?" I ask, keeping my voice low, conveying nothing but a quiet interest. But inside I am seething. How dare he talk about me to this woman! I feel I never really knew him. But then, ever since his funeral I knew that the man I'd loved for so many years wasn't the man I'd thought him.

"Oh, yes." She gives me a queer little smile and takes another of the little sandwiches, places it on her plate. "I think he had to."

I suppose she means he felt a sense of guilt. And so he should have.

I watch while she eats the sandwich. Once more there's that expression of pleased surprise, and I hold out the plate again.

"Take two—you've come a long way," I say.

Julia Norman lives 120 miles away, in London, where the head office is. I live in Somerset, not far from the factory. It had been easy for John to keep us apart. She's driven down; her BMW is standing outside my cottage door now. No one else will have seen it—the cottage is nicely off the main road and my nearest neighbor is several miles away.

I take a sandwich myself, from the other side of the plate. The pâté is rich, with an unusual depth of flavor. That's the *trompettes de la mort;* amazing how those black, dried old bits of fungi revive when you pour boiling water on them. There's brandy in the pâté as well. It really was one of John's favorites.

"I didn't realize how hungry I was," Julia says, almost apologetically. "I should have stopped for lunch but, well, it was easier to keep driving." She doesn't need to apologize. Not for eating those sandwiches. With each one that goes down, some of the anger and acid in my stomach disappear.

Then it's as though she doesn't know what to say next. I'm not going to help her. She glances around the room and sees the photograph that lives on top of the cocktail cabinet. She rises, goes over and picks it up.

I want to tell her to put it down, that just by touching it she defiles my memories, but I push down the hasty words. I mustn't alert her to the depth of my feelings.

She looks at the alert face of the small boy in his first school uniform, so proud of the badge on his blazer. "Your son?" she asks. She looks shocked. This, then, is something she hadn't known about.

"Yes," I say proudly. "Mine and John's." I don't have to add that because she can surely see John's proud blue eyes, his determined chin and full, sensual mouth. My darling Mark had them all, but I say it just the same. Just for the pleasure of saying it. There is nothing else left for me.

"How old is he now?" Her eyes search the room as though looking for more photographs. She won't find them.

"He died—meningitis—two months after that photograph was taken."

She replaces it on the varnished cabinet, which mirrors back a shadowy reflection. "I'm so sorry," she says.

I hardly hear her. Mark's death still hurts. John wasn't with me at the time. I had to bear it all on my own. He'd said he had to go to France on business. But when I tried to ring the hotel, to tell him Mark had been taken into hospital, they said he wasn't there. Later, when I'd rung the office and got them to contact him and tell him to ring me, he said it must have been difficulties with the language, that he'd been there all the time. Those were the days I believed everything he said.

He'd been as devastated by Mark's death as I was. Something finished for both of us then. It was after that that I began to see less and less of him.

Julia picks up her handbag, opens it, takes out a wallet, and then hands me a photograph. "My girls," she says, and there is challenge in her look.

My heart seizes up. John's daughters! I don't really want to look but something compels me to take the photograph.

Pretty girls. They have John's smile. That smile that said he wanted nothing more in life right at this moment than to be with you. But their eyes are gray like hers and both are blonde while he was dark.

"Lovely," I say, and for the first time my voice is stiff.

She takes the photograph back. She doesn't need to say anything. Then she notices the little conservatory that leads off the cottage's main room. "What a wonderful display," she says, her eyes genuinely appreciating the gloriously colorful collection of plants and shrubs.

"One of my hobbies," I say without false modesty. My cymbidiums have won prizes, after all.

Her fingernails tap against the glass of the conservatory door and her thoughts seem miles away.

"Would you like some more tea?" I ask. "And do have another sandwich."

She sits down again. Her hand hovers over the commemoration plate, then she suggests she might have a slice of my delicious-looking cake. I cut the cake and give her a piece, than take a sandwich for myself, one from next to the monogram.

She wipes an odd cake crumb from her lips, holding the serviette daintily in her long fingers with their beautifully painted nails. She's left a smear of discreetly colored lipstick on the little linen square. I wonder if it will come out in the wash. "His death was such a shock," she says. "So sudden."

She can say that again. You don't expect a man of fifty with no history of heart disease suddenly to fall dead in the middle of a meeting. In Paris. Just when he was expecting to be made chairman.

I wonder how Julia heard the news. Who got in touch with her? How did she tell her girls they were never going to see their father again?

At the funeral there had been the width of the grave between us. We'd faced each other across the freshly piled earth as the priest intoned the final prayers. Around us I could hear the whispers, the shocked realization. I don't know how I managed to keep my composure. But, like today, I just knew I had to remain calm. I couldn't let myself down. But if Mark had been at my side, nothing would have hurt quite so much.

It was after the funeral that I'd had that talk with the lawyer and discovered John had left me nothing, that everything had gone to this woman and her daughters. Even the cottage wasn't mine. John had talked of putting it in my name but had never got round to it.

This cottage means everything to me. We'd chosen it together, furnished it and lived here together. This was where Mark had been born and had lived for his short life. I had created the garden and the conservatory.

It would be easy to say John had never expected to die so soon, that he really meant to take care of me. But it wouldn't be true. His will showed me just what I'd meant in his life compared with this woman now sitting opposite me.

Of course, I saw at the funeral that Julia is the sort of woman that John needed for his career. The sort of woman who could talk with directors, joke with the chairman, put the other wives at ease. Who knew which knives and forks to use at smart restaurants, how to dress, how to do her hair and makeup.

It hadn't taken much detection work on my part to discover her telephone number. I'd needed, though, considerable courage to ring up and suggest we meet. I thought it would be difficult to persuade her to come to tea, all the way down to Somerset, but it hadn't been. She'd sounded almost pleased, excited even.

And now she's here. And now I don't know what to say to her.

All I can feel is the burning injustice of it. I loved John with all my heart and he betrayed me. I wasn't the center of his world and I never had been.

She puts down her cup and says, "I came here to tell you that I shall be making arrangements for you to have the use of this cottage"—once again she glances around and once again she makes it clear in that subtle, low-key way of hers what she thinks of my home—"for the rest of your life. Together with a small income."

I am dumbfounded. "Is this because you think it is what John would have wanted?" I jerk out.

Her smile this time is wry with an edge of bitterness. "I think we both know he was a totally selfish man who thought of nothing beyond his own needs and pleasures," she says, and her tone is gentle. "I'm doing it because I think you deserve it. And because without you my life would have been very much more difficult than it was. You gave him something I couldn't."

I can see that all right. With her he'd have had to be on parade all the time.

She picks up her bag and rises. "We won't meet again, but I'm glad we've had this chat."

I follow her to the front door, unable to think. All my careful planning has suddenly been turned upside down.

Before she'd said that about the cottage, I'd have been only too glad she was leaving so soon, delighted she was going to be in her car driving back up to London. I'd wondered what I was going to do if she showed signs of wanting to stay. Now part of me would like her to. But then I will have to tell her what I've done and try and save her and then everyone will know everything. I can't do that. So I say good-bye. We shake hands awkwardly, as though neither of us is quite sure of the protocol. Already I think I can see a slight sheen of sweat on her forehead.

She gets into the steel gray BMW. I see her draw a hand across her eyes, as though she could be feeling unwell. Then she places the key in the starter motor, turns it, and drives away.

I go back into the lounge and ignore the clutter of the tea things. I open the door into the conservatory and breathe in the aroma of wet soil and green leaves. The honeyed fragrance of hoya carnosa, with its waxy white, star-shaped flowers, mingles with the tang of geranium leaves as I brush past them. The oleander is in the corner. It's in full flower, the deep, rich pink of the frilly petals is like a benison. Who could guess that every part of the plant—its spear-sharp leaves, the sappy wood, those lovely flowers— is so poisonous?

I wonder how long it will be before Julia Norman starts to feel really unwell. How long before she has to stop the car. But she'll keep going as long as she can, hoping to get home so she can go to bed. Then feelings of nausea will overtake her. Could she lose control of the car? More likely, she'll sit in the car with the door open, vomiting onto the grass verge until her heart goes into cardiac arrest.

But suppose she manages to get to a lavatory. Calls for help. It couldn't possibly be in time to save her. For even though she didn't eat them all, those sandwiches contained

more than enough poison for a fatal dose. I reckoned two
would do it, and she ate several.

I am confident that whatever happens she won't realize
who is to blame. Even if she receives help, there's no danger she will implicate me. Why should she?

John died young of a heart attack and so will she.

I leave the conservatory and sit in my chair, thinking
about Julia Norman.

I'd planned my revenge so carefully and now she's ruined everything.

Why did she say that about letting me have the cottage
and an income for life?

I remember what John said about her. A woman who
had a stranglehold on his life, that was his story. Look
after me, he'd said; I need you, he'd pleaded. She means
nothing to me, he'd promised, but he said he couldn't ditch
her until his daughters were grown up. Even Mark's birth
hadn't altered that. I'd hoped then, but nothing changed.
Then Mark died. But I still believed that one day John
would divorce his wife and marry me. I believed I really
was the love of his life, not just a convenient mistress.
Until I spoke to the lawyer after the funeral. Then I knew
he'd never really cared for me, only for what I could give
him. Had it been the same with her? Maybe she'd been
right and we were the two halves of his life, a life he could
never make whole.

How I'd hated her: Julia, Mrs. John Norman. And now
she was going to die. She was driving down the A303 with
a lethal dose of oleander cardiac glycosides in her blood.
And I'm sitting here realizing how much I've lost. Knowing that I've destroyed any future I might have had.

With a sudden surge of passion I dash the Minton china
to the floor. Cups and saucers, with their delicate pattern,
their graceful shapes, shatter. I take a deep breath and
reach for the sandwiches. Not the harmless little squares
placed around the royal monogram but the last two still sitting on the other side. The sandwiches I'd prepared for

her. Tears streaming down my face, tears as abundant as the waterfall I'd made at the bottom of the garden, I eat the squares of bread stuffed with pâté and relish the richness of their flavor.

I wonder sometimes which is the hardest thing about committing a murder: having the willpower to actually commit the act, or having the confidence to be able to compose oneself and answer questions about it later. Some of the people I've questioned have had nerves of steel. But sometimes even steel isn't strong enough, as the murderer in this story discovers.

Tippy Canoe

Mary Daheim

July 1979

Joseph Patrick Flynn loosened his tie, put his feet on the desk, and tossed a crumpled memo at his wastebasket. He missed. Joe sat back to review the Lenski case.

"Open and shut," Joe's superior had said. *Good,* thought Joe; it was too hot for leg work. As a native Pacific Northwesterner, Joe Flynn wasn't keen on heat.

Still, there were always loose ends. The defendant, Art Lenski, had no priors, which meant that the prosecutor needed a solid case to ensure conviction. Joe, who had transferred from Vice to Homicide the previous fall, didn't want to botch the case. So far, his record was good: nine arrests, five convictions, four pending trials. Six cases remained unsolved, but that was an occupational hazard.

The Lenski homicide wasn't one of them. In fact, it wasn't Joe's case. He had inherited the Lenski file from Carney Mitchell, who was recovering from an exploit on his son's skateboard. Joe lit a cigarette and started reading Carney's report.

The phone rang. Still scanning the page, Joe picked up the receiver.

"Joe-Joe, your ugly dog got under the front porch and ate my mushroom farm." The voice was loud and shrill. Everything about Mrs. Bliny, Joe's neighbor, was out of proportion. At seventy, she had birdlike limbs attached to a stocky body. Her manner was tough as nails; her heart was pure gold. "If you don't shoot that mutt, I will."

Joe was used to Mrs. Bliny's complaints about the Flynn dog, Harvey Wallbanger. The previous day, she had griped because Banger, as he was known, had chased her Manx cat, Petunia, up a tree.

"Now then, Mrs. B.," soothed Joe, laying on the Irish charm which she both loved and saw through, "it wouldn't be that you enticed the poor beastie with a bit o' leftover T-bone, would it now?"

"So he has to eat it with mushrooms?" Mrs. Bliny demanded. "I'm making plum pie. You want any?"

Joe was tempted, but he had work to do. And he was in no hurry to go home. He never was.

"Save me some, okay?" he begged, dropping the blarney. "If you see Banger, throw a net over him."

"If I see Banger, he'll be paws up."

Joe was still smiling when he heard a rap on his partition.

"Hey, Flynn—how you doing?" Herman "Cool Hand" Luke leaned into Joe's cubicle. "You got the Lenski case now?"

Joe pointed his cigarette at the file. "Yeah. Why me? Didn't you work with Carney on the original investigation?"

Luke wedged himself into the cubicle, popping chocolate-covered peanuts in his mouth. "I'm on vacation week after next, remember?" said Luke, easing into the vinyl chair next to Joe's desk. "What do you need to know, except that Lenski's a coldhearted killer?"

Joe arched his eyebrows. "He says he's innocent."

"Yeah, right, sure." Luke polished off the peanuts and dug a Snickers bar out of his shirt pocket. "His alibi didn't stand up, his wife was a lush, he got the insurance, and he had a girlfriend. We proved it wasn't an accident, and then some other woman says he tried to kill her, too. Listen, Flynn, some murderers who get caught standing over the body with a smoking gun still swear they're innocent. They may even believe it. You'll get used to it."

Joe knew that Luke, a ten-year Homicide veteran, was right. "Lenski might've gotten away with it if it hadn't been for Carney and that tub," Joe mused.

"The *imprint* of the tub, you mean." Deftly, Luke tossed the candy bar wrapper into the wastebasket. "It was put there before the fire started, but gone when the emergency guys arrived. So what did Carney figure? Karen Lenski didn't do it to herself. She may have been drunk, but she didn't start that fire." Reaching into his back pocket, Luke produced a bent Baby Ruth bar. "Want to go fishing this weekend? My brother-in-law says we can use his boat at Lake Lautrec."

"Luke." Joe shook his head with mock pity. "Lake Lautrec looks like a wading pool. It's not country anymore, it's a damned suburb. The only fish you'll see is if somebody spills an aquarium. Face it, Luke, there isn't a lake within thirty miles that has trout after the April opener. If you want fish, you go to Idaho or British Columbia or—"

"Hell!" Luke dropped the Baby Ruth on his beige bell-bottom pants. He stood up, gazing guiltily at the stain. "Have it your way, old buddy. I thought you'd want to get out of the house."

"Mmmm." Joe was noncommittal. Luke knew that Joe always wanted to get out of the house. House. Spouse. Souse. It was all the same. Joe felt a pang for Art Lenski. Vivian Flynn was an alcoholic, as deep into denial as she was into bourbon on the rocks. The marriage was on the rocks, too. It had gotten off to a bad start when Joe found

himself in a Las Vegas hotel room with a huge hangover
and a bride he hardly knew. That afternoon, Joe had put
two overdosed fifteen-year-olds in body bags, then gone off
to drown his sorrows at a nearby bar. A woman in a slit
skirt and plunging neckline had leaned over the piano and
suggested a "fun evening." Joe vaguely recalled the plane
ride; he remembered nothing of the wedding chapel. But he
definitely knew he was engaged to someone else. Judith
Grover, first-rate librarian and world-class female, had
been left virtually at the altar. Joe had never forgiven himself. Worse yet, Judith hadn't forgiven him, either.

But the union with Vivian—or Herself, as Joe called
her—had lasted fourteen years. Joe wasn't sure why, unless
it was because of Caitlin, his only child. Someday, Vivian
would kill herself, by ossifying her liver, ruining her kidneys, or burning down the house. Just as Karen Lenski supposedly had done.

Joe sketched the scenario in his head: Karen, thirty-one,
had died in a fire in her home north of the Ship Canal. Said
fire presumably had been started by a smoldering cigarette,
which had been dropped in a drunken stupor. A neighbor
had seen smoke and called 911. Karen was dead when the
firemen arrived. Police response had been delayed, due to a
reported rape six blocks away. Homicide had been called in
as a matter of routine. Damage to the $45,000 house was
estimated at $20,000. The fire had spread outside, destroy-
ing a portion of the garden area, but had been contained before harming the neighboring home. On the surface, it was
a typical, senseless tragedy.

But Carney Mitchell hadn't been willing to pass off
Karen Lenski's death as an accident. In the charred living
room where Karen's body had been found, Carney had noticed an area on the carpet that was barely touched by the
fire. The veteran homicide detective surmised that something had sat there while the fire burned, maybe almost up
to the time that the firefighters had arrived. A search of the
backyard had turned up an old-fashioned washtub, black-

ened by smoke and smelling of kerosene. Carney figured that someone had moved the tub next to the sofa, put kerosene-soaked rags into it, dropped a match, and removed the evidence after the fire had taken hold. Karen Lenski had died of smoke inhalation. No doubt she had passed out before the fire started. She never had a chance.

Clever killer, Joe thought, but not as clever as Carney, who had a knack for noticing things. He wasn't much for details, though. Joe was stuck with filling gaps.

Shortly before one o'clock, Joe wandered out of his cubicle in search of his partner. "J. J.," said Joe, poking his head around the partition, "you hungry?"

Jesus Jorge Martinez was thirty years old, average height, wiry, intense, nervous. His wife, Brigitta, was about to give birth. J. J. wasn't hungry, but decided that food would take his mind off waiting for the new arrival.

The two men headed out of the municipal building under a cloudless blue sky. Down the steep streets that led between skyscrapers, they caught glimpses of the bay, with the sun glinting off the water. Their destination was a venerable Japanese restaurant with efficient overhead fans.

"We've got to get cracking on this Lenski case," Joe said as they waited for their sushi.

J. J. squirmed in his straight-backed chair. "Got the file. Lenski shouldn't have lied about his alibi. Not smart." His staccato voice was strangely musical.

"Right." Despite the fans, Joe was perspiring under his thin polyester shirt. "Anybody who can't recall Game Four of an NBA playoff championship in this town should be in jail on general principles. Hell, it's the first professional championship ever around here."

Art Lenski had tickets to the second home game of the best four-out-of-seven playoff. Karen Lenski had died that same evening, around eight. Art had at first claimed to be in attendance, but when questioned about the contest, he couldn't remember anything, not even the tense overtime finish. Ironically, every other basketball fan could recall the game's progress down to the last time-out.

J. J. drummed his fingers. "Then comes that other alibi. Sure, the girlfriend backs him up. So what?" he loosened his string tie and ran his fingers through his wavy black hair. "Nobody knew about Angie Amato till Lenski mentioned her. Better to say he went for a walk."

Their orders were presented with formality by a middle-aged kimono-clad waitress. She was unfamiliar to Joe, and walked away with a weary, flat-footed gait. Joe went for the roe first. "Art didn't make bail. Let's pay him a visit."

J. J. nodded, wolfing down sushi, apparently having forgotten he wasn't hungry. "What about that other woman? Says he tried to drown her?"

Joe tasted the tuna. "Beverly Duncan? I read her statement. Did it strike you as incoherent?"

J. J. sat with his elbows resting lightly on the table. "Maybe," he admitted. "Canoe could have overturned by accident. But look what happened to the wife. You have to believe Beverly."

Joe recalled the young woman's formal statement. "Art Lenski and Beverly Duncan worked together at Coronet Books. She says he made a pass at her. He denies it, of course."

"We'll check Beverly out," Joe said, eating his last piece of sushi. "Maybe the neighbor, too. The guy next door swore he saw Lenski at the house that night."

"Bob Henson?" J. J. nodded, bouncing in his chair. "Is the guy a head case?"

Joe shrugged. "Maybe. Henson's divorced, bitter, retired Army. He's the kind who plays with his guns, and wishes he had the guts to try Russian roulette."

The waitress reappeared with the bill. In carefully phrased English, Joe asked if she was new.

"New, my butt," she snapped. "George and I own this place. Laurie's got cramps and Donna May fell off her water skis. Kids these days are wimps." The waitress-cum-owner flounced away, adding spring to her tired step. Joe added a healthy tip.

Art Lenski didn't look like a killer, but Joe knew better than to make snap judgments. In his brief career as a homicide detective, he had arrested a seventy-year-old retired timber buyer, a second-grade teacher, and a young man who could have posed for the Boy Next Door. Unfortunately, he had killed the Girl Next Door with a hatchet. Joe realized he couldn't go by looks alone.

At thirty-three, Art Lenski appeared older. He was almost six feet tall, but thin and pale. His blue eyes blinked behind wire-frame glasses, his prison uniform hung slackly, and his long jaw made him look vague. Yet Carney Mitchell's report stated that although Art was a college dropout, he was intelligent. The accused had managed a local Coronet Books outlet for the past three years and was highly regarded by his superiors.

Art Lenski related his story in the interrogation room at the city jail. Joe and J. J. already knew the gist of it: Art had sold his NBA playoff ticket to a stranger so that he could spend the evening with Angie Amato. Angie was a national publisher's rep. She was kind, she was smart, she was—maybe—in love with Art. And, he admitted, he was in love with her. But he hadn't killed his wife, and he certainly hadn't tried to drown Beverly Duncan.

"So who killed Karen?" Joe asked, assuming his most guileless manner.

Slowly, Art Lenski shook his head. "I don't know. Karen didn't have enemies. She stayed home and drank. I thought maybe it was that rapist who'd been terrorizing local women, but the autopsy showed Karen wasn't sexually molested." Art gave Joe and J. J. a helpless look.

J. J. was fidgeting in the chair next to Joe. "Karen had twenty-five grand worth of insurance, right? You're the beneficiary. You got the house, too."

But Art shook his head. "Not really. My mother owns it. We were renting. It was my folks' home until they divorced ten years ago."

Joe paused, fingering his round chin. "Where does your mother live?"

"She remarried and retired in Tucson." Art wore a pained expression. Joe could imagine that the son was suffering for the mother, as well as vice versa.

"Your father?" Joe asked, filling in gaps.

Art's eyes narrowed. "He's around. He remarried, too, but it didn't last. Nobody could put up with him. My mother was—is—a saint."

J. J. leaned forward in the chair, one leg jiggling up and down. "Your father abusive? Violent? That how you learned to tackle problems?"

Art Lenski blinked twice. He looked bewildered, then indignant. "My father wasn't above hitting my mother. Violence creates, rather than solves, problems." He spoke with bitterness.

J. J.'s question apparently had touched a raw nerve. Joe marveled at Art Lenski's acting ability. He also wondered, briefly, if Art wasn't acting. Denial, maybe, or the ability to convince himself that he really was innocent.

For the first time since getting the Lenski case, Joe had doubts.

Beverly Duncan lived in an apartment a half-mile from the shopping mall that housed Coronet Books. The building was about five years old, six stories with individual balconies, a swimming pool, and signs of premature decay. There was no evening breeze, and the heat of the day felt trapped in the small foyer. A philodendron drooped in a clay pot next to the elevator.

Beverly Duncan wore a persecuted air along with her white V-necked top and navy walking shorts. She was slim, almost boyish, yet without grace. On bare feet, Beverly led the detectives into her living room. "I hate talking to the police," she lamented in her wispy voice. "It makes me feel . . . tawdry."

"You're not," J. J. asserted. "We want to wind this up. Trial starts in September."

Beverly shuddered, her blonde hair hanging limply around her narrow shoulders. "Will I have to testify?"

"Probably," Joe answered with candor. His eyes scanned the living room, which was tidy, if uninviting. The brown sofa looked old, older than Beverly. A pseudo-Tiffany floor lamp leaned toward a wicker rocking chair. An end table held up a Princess telephone and a stack of romance novels.

Beverly had flopped onto the sofa, her feet tucked under her. She finally noticed that the detectives were still standing, and asked them to sit. "What do you need to know? I've gone over it so often."

"We'll be brief," Joe said, trying to get comfortable on an imitation-leather armchair. The sliding doors to the balcony were open, but there was no breeze. "You met Art Lenski a year ago?"

"Y-e-s." Beverly Duncan stretched the word into three syllables. "I used to work at the Coronet store downtown, then I got transferred last June to the North End."

J. J. was all but writhing in an ugly plaid chair. "How did Mr. Lenski treat you?"

Beverly frowned. "He was fine, at first. But then . . ." She lowered her eyes and twisted her hands in her lap.

J. J. stopped writhing. "Then what?" His own eyes were glued on the telephone.

"We-l-l . . ." Beverly cleared her throat. "We had coffee a couple of times. He told me about his wife, and how she drank. Art—Mr. Lenski—seemed miserable. The least I could do was listen."

Joe nodded. "Did he mention divorce?"

Beverly's eyes grew wide. Joe noticed that they were gray, almost colorless. "Oh, no. He's Catholic, you see. They don't divorce."

"Not usually." Joe bit the words off. *He* could divorce, though. Herself had been married three times before the Las Vegas elopement. In the eyes of the Church, Joe didn't need an annulment. . . .

Joe forced an encouraging smile. "Did Mr. Lenski have any other solutions to his marital dilemma?"

Clearly, it was a new question for Beverly. "You mean— like killing her?" She seemed aghast.

Joe's smile faded. "No, like counseling or AA." He'd thought of both; Herself had refused outright.

"Oh-h-h. No, I don't think so." Beverly toyed with a small gold heart on a chain around her neck. "He was very frustrated—and lonely."

J. J. gave Joe an appealing look. "I should call home. What if Brigitta has gone into . . ."

Joe rolled his eyes. "Ms. Duncan—have you got another phone?"

Ms. Duncan did, in the bedroom. J. J. rushed out with Beverly's directions bouncing off his back.

"When did Art begin making advances?" The expression sounded old-fashioned, yet suited the shrinking violet on the sofa.

Beverly hung her head. "At work. We were in the back room, unpacking new books. It was the first week of April, and a lot of May titles had come in." She stopped and pushed the limp hair off her face. "I was shocked."

Joe studied Beverly Duncan. According to Carney's file, she was twenty-nine, but she looked more like nineteen. Was it a lack of worldliness or the plain, unmarked face that made her seem younger? Joe sensed that Beverly had spent three decades without truly having lived.

"Yes," Joe said hastily, aware that he'd been caught up in his musings. "But you saw him outside of the store anyway?"

Close to tears, Beverly nodded. "He apologized, over and over. I think he was afraid I'd report him to the regional office. He offered to make it up to me." She leaned back on the sofa, staring at the ceiling. "Mr. Lenski said we'd go on a picnic. He'd bring everything—sandwiches, chips, cookies, wine." Beverly's teeth clamped over her lower lip. "I was naive. I should have known when he said there would be wine that his intentions weren't honorable."

Joe inclined his head, indicating that Beverly should continue. He didn't trust himself to speak; the apartment was in a time warp, and he was being sucked back into the Victorian Age.

"We drove to Lake McCall the next Sunday," Beverly went on. "It took about twenty minutes to get there, and he was very nice, polite and proper, the whole time. There's a little park on the lake, so we ate our lunch and talked. I had one cup of wine, but he had three." Beverly looked away, toward the balcony. "Then he started touching me. I jumped up and said we should get in the canoe."

Joe had almost forgotten about the canoe. "Art's canoe, right?"

Beverly nodded. "He'd brought it on top of the car. It looked like rain, but I didn't care. I just wanted Art to stop touching me. So we put the canoe in the water. Lake McCall isn't very big, but it's deep. Art stopped paddling. And then . . ." Beverly put her face in her hands.

Joe waited. He could hear J. J.'s agitated voice from the bedroom.

Beverly removed her hands from her face, which was now blotchy. There were tears in her eyes. "I can't tell you the awful details. The canoe tipped over. He tried to hold me under, but I got away. I'm a good swimmer. I reached the far shore and hid. He climbed back in the canoe and started after me, but I guess he changed his mind. The last I saw, he was paddling for the park." She heaved a deep sigh.

"What did you do then?" Joe kept his voice even.

Now that the worst of the story was over, Beverly mustered her self-control. "I waited, then I walked out to the highway, where I caught a Metro bus and came home."

"What about witnesses?" Joe asked as J. J. returned to the living room. "A lot of people live on Lake McCall."

Beverly's forehead furrowed. "Y-e-s—that's true. But I didn't see anybody around. It was raining by then. Not that I cared—I was already soaked."

Even dry, Joe thought, Beverly Duncan looked like a drowned puppy. J. J. was dancing nervously at Joe's elbow.

"You've been very helpful," Joe said, standing up and giving Beverly a reassuring smile. "By the way, when was this picnic?"

Beverly blinked, then grimaced. "The date? I forget—it was the third Sunday in April."

In the corridor, J. J. practically ran for the elevator. Brigitta was in labor. Joe offered to take his partner home, collect the mother-to-be, and go to the hospital. He could use the siren, if birth was imminent.

But when they reached the Martinez bungalow, Brigitta hadn't finished packing. The tall, handsome blond's languid air contrasted with her husband's frenetic manner.

"We have at least an hour," she announced, offering Joe a beer. "J. J.—have you seen my new bedroom slippers?"

J. J. hadn't. Indeed, he looked as if he'd never heard of bedroom slippers. Joe declined the beer and headed home.

Mrs. Bliny was on the front porch, reading the newspaper. "Your wife's gone," she called out as Joe parked in the shared driveway. "The kids took her to see her brother's new RV."

Joe was mildly surprised. Herself rarely left the house these days. "Who drove?" he asked, feeling a momentary sense of alarm.

"The big kid," Mrs. Bliny replied. "The one who got his license last year."

Herself had two sons, fathered by her second and third husbands. The elder was just seventeen; the younger had recently turned fourteen. Caitlin was twelve, and, in Joe's opinion, too young and too precious to ride in a car driven by his wife's reckless offspring. Still, he told himself, it was probably safer than having Herself at the wheel.

"How long have they been gone?" Joe asked.

Mrs. Bliny shrugged. "Ten minutes, maybe? You hungry, Joe-Joe? I made piroshkis."

Mrs. Bliny made wonderful piroshkis, with a light, flaky crust and a moist beef filling. But Joe knew that if he stayed close to home, he'd spend the time watching for his family's safe return.

"I've got to see a man about a murder," he said with an apologetic smile. "Save me one, okay?"

With his stomach rumbling, Joe drove across town to the murder site. Three months after the tragedy, the Lenski house still lay in partial ruin. A blue tarp hung over the burned-out living room and dining area. Much of the adjacent shrubbery had died or looked blighted. Next to the split-rail fence, a cherry tree had been cut down and a smoke-scarred rose trellis lay on its side. Joe wandered around for a few minutes, reminding himself that a murder scene could speak volumes. However, he didn't hear anything interesting, and went next door to call on Bob Henson.

"It's after seven," Henson said in a sandpaper voice. "Why aren't you off-duty?"

"Homicide Division never rests," Joe replied. "We eat and sleep standing up. You like talking to the cops in front of the neighbors?"

"I don't give a rat's ass," Henson shot back. "Nobody can hear us now that the Lenskis aren't around." He waved a beefy bare arm, taking in his corner lot. Henson was an inch shorter than Joe's five-eleven, though he carried an extra thirty pounds.

Joe was about to suggest going inside when it occurred to him that the one-story, low-roofed building might feel like an oven. "You got a patio?" he asked instead.

Henson didn't, but there were two battered deck chairs in the shade of an old pear tree. Joe sat down gingerly. The Lenski house was at his back.

"You were lucky the fire didn't damage your place," Joe remarked in a conversational tone.

"Damned lucky," Henson agreed, propping his feet up on a neatly stacked pile of freshly cut firewood. He wore cheap rubber thongs with Bermuda shorts and a sleeveless undershirt. A tattoo on his left upper arm depicted a dripping dagger. "Yeah, it was lucky. The flames set off some of those shrubs on the other side of the fence, but the firemen put them out."

"Who called the fire department?" Joe asked.

"Mrs. Krueger, across the street. Old busybody. You know the type—always snooping at her window." Bob Henson sneered.

Joe did know the type—and was grateful. Old people, especially the ones who had all their marbles, were often a big help in a police investigation. "Mrs. Krueger, huh? Maybe I should see her."

Henson shook his head. "She took off last week to visit her daughter in California. That suits me fine."

Ignoring Henson's comment, Joe calculated the distance: thirty feet, maybe, between the houses. "What did you see that night?"

"You mean Lenski?" Henson gave Joe a dark look. "Yeah, he'd gone off earlier, but came back around eight, at halftime of the big game. He didn't stay long. I figured he forgot something."

The gnats were congregating in front of Joe. "Did you talk to him?"

Henson shook his head, which sported a graying brown crew cut. "Naw, I just saw him go into the house. The front door is—was—right over there." He gestured at the fence and the blackened shrubbery. "He wasn't there more than ten minutes. Then he drove off."

"You knew the Lenskis well?"

"So-so. He's a snob. Always got his nose in a book. What do you call 'em? An egghead?"

"Or," Joe responded quietly, "a reader."

"Yeah, right. She was okay, though." Henson's tough features softened. "Sure, I know she drank. So what? I'd drink, too, if I was married to a stuffed shirt like Lenski. In fact, I could use a little drink right now. You want something?"

Joe stood up. "I'm on duty, but thanks anyway. Did you see anybody else come to the Lenski house that evening?"

"Naw," Henson replied, also on his feet. "Not till the firemen showed up. You sure you won't go for a short one?"

"I've got another call to make," Joe replied. "Did the Lenskis fight?"

Henson strolled alongside Joe to the sidewalk. "I guess. Karen bitched about how all Art could think of was the store and books and crap like that. He never wanted to party or go dancing or hit the bars. She had a pretty miserable life with that guy, if you ask me. I figure he finally got tired of her wanting to have fun."

The scenario sounded familiar to Joe: the husband with a job; the wife who wanted the party to last forever. Joe thanked Henson for his time and drove away.

His notes revealed that Angela Amato lived in a condominium east of downtown, near the hospital district. Angie wasn't in. Joe had no choice but to go home.

Tristan Olaf Martinez was born at one-ten A.M. Thursday. Mother and baby were doing fine. So was the father, who sounded uncharacteristically calm. His request to take the day off was granted. Joe could wind up the Lenski case by himself.

Angie Amato was home when Joe called early Thursday morning, but heading downtown to meet a bookseller. The store was three blocks from police headquarters. Joe asked if he could meet her for coffee at ten-thirty.

Angie was prompt. Joe assessed her with a practiced eye, taking in the shoulder-length black hair, the wide-set dark eyes, the sharp, yet feminine features. At thirty, Angie hadn't quite lost her bloom. She wasn't the type to stop men in their tracks, but Joe found her forthright manner and mobile face appealing. Somehow, she reminded him of Judith Grover. Despite Angie's hostility, he understood why Art Lenski had lost his head—and his heart.

"You think I'm lying," Angie said with an air of challenge. "I understand that. But I'll swear in court that Art was with me from six o'clock until almost eleven. I cooked dinner, we talked, we made love."

"The Lenskis' neighbor says otherwise," Joe noted quietly.

"That retired Army guy?" Angie gave a little sniff. "He'd say anything to make trouble for Art. If you ask me, Bob Henson had the hots for Karen Lenski. I don't know if they slept together, but they drank together."

"I wondered," Joe said in the same mild tone. "If you're telling the truth, who wanted Karen dead?"

Angie slumped in her chair. "I don't know. I can't imagine why Karen was killed. Maybe there's somebody out there that nobody knows about." She sat up straighter, then leaned forward, looking earnest. "I hope the police have done everything they can to find another suspect."

For just a beat, Joe had a sinking feeling. Carney Mitchell was a genius when it came to crime scenes. But he was also single-minded. Carney just might have overlooked someone who wished Karen Lenski ill. On the other hand, he had Bob Henson's eyewitness account and Beverly Duncan's evidence about the attempted drowning.

"You knew Art for what? A year?"

Angie considered. "More like two. But it was strictly business until about six months ago." She frowned, looking away from Joe to the busy lunch counter.

"Did he lose his temper easily?" Joe inquired.

Angie sniffed again. "Art? He was always on an even keel. Are you going to ask if he beat me?"

Joe grinned sheepishly. "I was, actually. Did he?"

"Of course not! And frankly, I'm not always easy to get along with. I'm the one with the hot temper." She sat back in the chair, hands at her hips, as if daring Joe to prove her point. "But I get over it in a hurry," she added, her voice softer.

"Did you ever meet Karen?" Joe asked.

"Once." Angie looked disgusted. "Art brought her to the booksellers' convention last year. She got smashed and fell into a university press display."

Joe had reached an impasse with Angie. As long as he couldn't shake her alibi for Art, there was nothing left to do or say. He hoped that the prosecutor could rattle her when she took the stand. Joe paid the bill and headed back to the Lenskis' neighborhood.

The house with its blue tarp looked as if it were wilting under the midday sun. Joe had long since shed his jacket and loosened his tie. He took another walk around the house, noting that Bob Henson's carport was empty. Glancing across the street, he wished that Mrs. Krueger hadn't gone to California. If anyone beside Art had stopped at the Lenski house on that fateful night in late May, Joe had a feeling Mrs. Krueger would have noticed. He wondered if Carney Mitchell had interviewed her. He should have, of course, but once again, Joe had to admit that Carney neglected details.

Five minutes later, he was a mile south of the Ship Canal in front of a run-down two-story house that stood out like a sore thumb among its tidy neighbors. Vern Lenski's stomach arrived on the porch about three seconds before the rest of him, or so it seemed to Joe. A big, balding bear of a man with bristling side-whiskers, Art's father had a growl to match his appearance.

"I already talked to the cops," Vern grumbled, barring the door with his girth. His seamed face suggested that he was in his mid-sixties. The striped overalls he wore hinted that he might be in his second childhood. "I got two things to say to you," Vern barked. " 'Get' and 'out.' "

Joe inclined his head from side to side. "Sure. Then I say, 'How about coming down to headquarters?' " Joe looked at his watch. "It's not quite noon. If we get busy and you get lucky, you can spend the night in one of our commodious cells. Okay, Vern?"

"Christ." Vern stood back, allowing Joe to slip inside. The house smelled rancid. A very old, mangy dog lay on the stained living room carpet. The animal didn't look up. Joe wondered if it was dead. The rest of the room didn't seem much livelier. The sagging drapes were closed, the TV picture flickered, and the furniture was dilapidated. Joe suddenly felt depressed.

"Look," said Vern Lenski, pointedly not offering Joe a chair, "I already made a statement. My son's no killer. He doesn't have it in him. Hell, he couldn't even make his high school football team! He went out for debate instead."

Joe leaned gingerly against a chipped bookcase that held a half-dozen tarnished sports trophies and a few old magazines. "Are you and your son on good terms, Mr. Lenski?"

Vern guffawed, revealing at least three missing teeth. "Hell, no! Art's a wimp. I got no time for wimps. I see him once, twice a year. That's enough. I eat steaks tougher than he is."

"Did you know his wife very well?" Joe's eyes strayed to the dog to see if it was breathing.

"Karen?" Vern Lenski rubbed his hairy forearms. "Sure. Cute broad. I'd chew the fat with her now and then when I stopped by to visit my train set."

Joe merely lifted his red eyebrows.

Vern jerked a thumb over his shoulder at a faded color photograph of a Great Northern passenger train. "See that? I was the engineer on that baby for twenty-four years. Then we got Amtrak, and a crock of bull it is. I been retired since '74. But I can still run a train—and I do, when I go to Art and Karen's to horse around with my model railroad. It's set up in the basement, on plywood. I don't have room for it here."

Joe nodded. At least he understood the striped overalls, if not the man who wore them. "So you saw Art and Karen then?"

"Karen," Vern corrected Joe. "Not Art. I'd go when he was at work. Art bugged me. Karen left me alone. Like I said, she was a good broad. Too bad she's dead."

"Did you ever meet their neighbor, Bob Henson?"

"Henson?" Vern chuckled. "Sure. The Sarge, I call him. Henson's a good guy, except he likes to shoot his face off. He gets a kick out of my train."

"When was the last time you saw Karen?"

Vern's small hazel eyes fixed on a lacquered wooden clock shaped like a guitar. It had stopped at two-oh-five, possibly years ago. "The day she got killed. I seen her that afternoon." He had lowered his voice to a mere rumble. "Spooky, huh?"

"How did she seem?" Joe glanced again at the dog. It still hadn't moved.

"Seem?" Vern's echo responses were beginning to annoy Joe, almost as much as the dreary living room and the rank odors. "She was in a good mood. I guess she'd had a few."

Joe resisted the urge to nudge the dog with his foot. "Do you think Karen was playing around?"

Vern gave Joe an exasperated stare. "Hell, no. She didn't go out much. Where would she meet anybody?"

Joe started to mention Henson's name again, thought better of it, and shrugged. Before he could pose another question, Vern broke in:

"Hey," he exclaimed, making a pushing motion with his hands, "I already told all this to those other cops. Karen was a sport. Too much of one for Art. Like I said, I don't think he has it in him. But maybe he does, underneath. You know, like a pot boiling over. It happens."

It did, as Joe well knew. Anxious to be out of the elder Lenski's house, Joe took his leave of Vern, his dreary house, and his almost-dead dog.

"So how's the happy father?" Cool Hand Luke inquired. He was sitting on the edge of Joe's cluttered desk, eating Gummy Bears.

"Great," Joe replied in semi-amazement. "Brigitta and the baby go home tomorrow. J. J. can't wait to start feeding and burping and changing little Tris."

Luke wrinkled his nose. "J. J.'s nuts. You coming tomorrow?"

Joe pushed some papers around on his desk, then leaned back in his chair. "Sure. I can use a day on the lake. I've talked to everybody connected with the Lenski case and can't find a single new lead. It's Friday, and come Monday, maybe I'll have a fresh viewpoint. But I doubt it. Carney was right the first time."

"Carney usually is." Luke slid off the desk, landing with a thud. "Seven okay? We can eat after we've limited." His grin was off-center.

"Oh, sure, Luke. We'll knock 'em dead." Joe shook his head. They'd be lucky to get a nibble.

"Good God Almighty." Joe rolled his eyes as Luke plied the oars of the ten-foot rowboat. The air was heavy; clouds were gathering; Joe was praying for rain. "This is your brother-in-law's idea of *fun*? What do we do when a water-skier gets tangled up in our lines?"

"The same thing we do when one of those kids runs into us with their inner tubes," Luke replied, giving a pair of ten-year-olds a baleful look. "Hey, I haven't been to Lake Lautrec for a while. How did *I* know it looks like Coney Island?"

A mere five years ago, Lake Lautrec had been inhabited only by summer people, with a few cabins along the shore and an occasional fisherman drifting on its waters. But in this summer of 1979, tract houses lined the lake, children cavorted everywhere, and pleasure craft zipped over the waves. A dozen other fishermen looked as beleaguered as Joe felt.

"Idaho," Joe declared, pulling at his shirt, which was sticking to his skin. "Next time, we go to Idaho. I told you, Luke, there isn't a lake on this side of the state that . . ." He stopped, then leaned forward so abruptly that the rowboat veered to starboard. "Luke—who's working those south Ship Canal rapes?"

Luke rested his arms on the oars. "Olson and Forbes? Why?"

Joe's green eyes danced. "Let's head in before we get rammed by a plastic turtle." He grinned at Luke as the first raindrops began to fall. "We're not going to get skunked. We're going to catch a killer. Row, dammit, row."

Back at headquarters, Luke worked with Joe to make phone calls. The State Fish and Game Department. The sports desk of the daily newspaper. Olson and Forbes from Assault. Shortly after noon, with rain beating against the cubicle's small window, Joe was using his two-fingered typing to fill out a report.

"You can't do much until Monday," Luke warned as he straddled a chair and munched a Three Musketeers bar.

"True," Joe admitted, not looking up. "Still, I'd like to check on our clever killer. I don't want the bird to fly away before I can show probable cause. And I have to start the ball rolling on Art Lenski's release." Joe resumed typing. Luke ate another candy bar. The rain kept streaming down, making a blur of the surrounding city.

At last, Joe was finished. "Okay," he declared, standing up. "Olson and Forbes can do their thing."

"I'll call Olson, you call Forbes," Luke said.

Ten minutes later, the partners from the Assault Unit had agreed to bring in Bob Henson for questioning.

*   *   *

"You son of a gun," said Carney Mitchell, leaning on his crutches and grinning at Joe Flynn. "You outfoxed me! Now I suppose the city will get sued for false arrest."

Momentarily, Joe looked grim. Then he shook his head. "I don't think so. Art Lenski's been through hell for the past few years. He's anxious to get on with his life. And with Angie Amato."

It was Wednesday afternoon, and Joe had put in long hours since Saturday morning. He made a final check for messages, found nothing pressing, and decided to go home.

The rain had finally stopped during the night. After four days, the air smelled fresh; the city sparkled. Getting out of his car, Joe noted that his house needed paint. The garden was overgrown. The lawn required mowing. But he was tired.

"Where've you been, Joe-Joe?" Mrs. Bliny demanded from her porch. She held Petunia under one arm. "I haven't seen you in days! I hear you've been righting wrongs and catching killers. Good work, Joe-Joe. Your dog's in the pound."

"What?" It took Joe a few seconds to realize Mrs. Bliny was kidding. "Oh—yeah, I feel good about this one. But it was just a matter of filling gaps. I'm learning."

Mrs. Bliny set Petunia down. The cat rubbed against her thin legs, then wandered off to sit at the edge of the porch. "So how did you do it? The TV and the newspapers don't always make things clear."

Joe strolled to the bottom of Mrs. Bliny's concrete steps. "Bob Henson said he'd seen Art Lenski come back home shortly before the fire started. He told the police that happened around eight, at halftime. It *did* happen around halftime—but the game started early, at six, because it was nationally telecast. That made me wonder. Then he mentioned a neighbor, Mrs. Krueger, who was always watching people. She was out of town, and he was glad, which implied that she wouldn't be watching *him*. I wondered what he was doing that made him not want to be watched. Then I remembered the rape that happened about the same time as the Lenski fire. I checked with Assault, and sure enough,

one of the earlier victims said the rapist had a tattoo." Joe
gave a little shrug.

"So this Henson was out raping women." Mrs. Bliny
looked disgusted. "But he didn't kill anybody."

"Right," Joe agreed. "Even if Henson had been home,
there was no way he could have seen Art Lenski from his
house. There was a big tree by the fence that would have
blocked his view. It must have been badly burned, because
it was cut down after the fire. Henson had some of the
wood stacked in his yard. His story to the police was created to give himself an alibi. In the process, he destroyed
Art Lenski's."

"And so did your murderer." Mrs. Bliny shook her head.
"It's sad, though. She must be crazy."

"Maybe." Joe was never sure how to define *crazy*. That
wasn't his job, though he always wondered. "Beverly Duncan was a lonely young woman who lived in a dreamworld
of romance novels and escapism. She became infatuated
with her boss. I suppose she thought she had a chance when
she found out his wife was an alcoholic. But she realized
Lenski wouldn't divorce Karen because they were
Catholic."

"So she liberated him. Death, not divorce." Mrs. Bliny's
thin lips set in a tight, disapproving line. "Beverly set the
fire. My! Did she think Art would turn to her instead of to
that Amato girl?"

"I don't think she knew Art was seeing Angie," Joe
replied. "When Beverly found out, she felt betrayed. She
made up that picnic story on Lake McCall. In fact, she
made up everything about Art pursuing her."

"She *wished*," Mrs. Bliny murmured.

"Right." Out of the corner of his eye, Joe saw Banger
wandering down the driveway. "The canoe incident couldn't
have happened, not on the third Sunday of April." Joe
reached down to pat Banger's shaggy head. "That was the
opening of lowland lake fishing season. Lake McCall
would have been so crowded that if Beverly Duncan had

fallen out of the canoe, she'd have landed in somebody's
six-pack."

Mrs. Bliny kept one eye on Banger, the other on Petunia.
"How did this Beverly react when you arrested her?" The
square face managed to convey both revulsion and pity.

Joe rolled his eyes. Banger loped up the stairs. Petunia
arched her back. "Beverly Duncan played the role of the
doomed heroine, sacrificing herself for love. I think she enjoyed it. She's finally in the limelight."

"I'm proud of you, Joe-Joe," Mrs. Bliny asserted, moving just enough to block Banger's passage. "By the way,
your wife's not home. She went to get her hair dyed."

"Oh." Joe's shoulders slumped in relief. The monthly
trip to the hairdresser was one of Herself's few regular out-
ings.

"I got peach cobbler," Mrs. Bliny said. "You want
some?"

Joe did. It was strange, he thought, how life's pleasures
grew smaller with time. Fifteen years earlier, he would
have aimed much higher: Judith Grover and a champagne
supper on an unfinished spur of the new freeway; Judith
and his classic MG racing up to Canada for a case of imported scotch; Judith and his new transistor radio, dancing
till dawn after sneaking into the mayor's empty office.

Times had changed. So had Joe. He heard Mrs. Bliny
rummaging in the kitchen.

"I could use some excitement," he called. "You got any
whipped cream?"

"The cat ate it," Mrs. Bliny called back. "How about
peach sherbet?"

Grinning, Joe entered Mrs. Bliny's cozy kitchen. "Peach
sherbet? Peach cobbler? Now that's exciting!"

Not only do murderers have to have the conviction to actually carry out their crime, but they must be determined enough to hide the knowledge that they are the guilty party, in essence by playing the part of one who is innocent. In this respect, criminals and actors have something in common. Our next story proves that it's not enough to have a calm face when it hides a jealous heart.

The Last of Laura Dane

Jane Dentinger

HAVE YOU HEARD that Laura Dane died? I'm speaking of Laura Dane, the Broadway legend. If not, let me be the first to inform you. She died on Monday, at least technically; i.e., she ceased to breathe on Monday. But for those of us in the theater community, Miss Dane had passed away years ago.

That's why I find this damned memorial dinner something of a farce. All the theatrical old guard gathered here at the Players Club to praise poor Laura and bury her a second time. I expect most of the speeches to be flagrantly fulsome and some downright maudlin. There's nothing like guilt to make people pull out the old eulogizing stops.

And they *all* feel guilty.

You can see it in their eyes, catch a sour whiff of it in their perfumes and colognes, hear it in scraps of conversation.

"I'm shattered, just shattered. I was going to call her this *week,"* I heard Nita Grey whisper to her former agent, Harv Shapiro. "See if she wanted to have lunch. And now she's—gone!" Tears filled Nita's eyes, threatening to wash away her false eyelashes. Harv, the old cheapskate, was not about to offer her his silk pocket handkerchief. He handed her a dry martini instead and that seemed to do the trick. Dabbing her eyes with the cocktail napkin, Nita took a swig and sighed, "Poor Laura . . . Do I look all right?"

Poor Laura, my arse! Nita spent the better part of her acting career toiling in Laura's shadow. And for those of you who don't recall, Laura Dane cast one hell of a shadow in her heyday. Casting-wise, Nita was always the bridesmaid, never the bride; that was Laura's role, every time. The idea of Nita, who married money with a big M and is now a merry society widow, taking time off from her whirlwind of hair, massage, and collagen injection appointments to treat her old nemesis to lunch made me smile. She'd sooner have the Hell's Angels over for sherry.

Of course, such observations I'll keep to myself. None of this will make it into my column tomorrow. Timothy, my new editor, a pink-cheeked tyro, wouldn't like it. Tiny Tim only wants the nice bits. He said as much before I left the office today. "Now, Wes, I want reporting, not opinion. No sniper fire, 'kay? Just get down what the folks *say* about Miss Dane. Not what you think they should say or your take on their subtext. Play nice, Wes, 'kay?"

He knows I hate being called Wes. The name is Wesley, Wesley Kincaid. You've probably seen my column—"Kincaid's Parade"—God knows I've been writing it long enough; long before Liz or Cindy or Joey came on the scene. Maybe too long for wee Timmy's taste, or lack thereof. Since my contract is coming up for renewal, it behooves me to follow his namby-pamby dictates, the little shit! But for now, for my own enjoyment, I'll call 'em as I sees 'em.

Ah, but hush! Solomon is about to speak and I must attend. Solomon, of course, is being played tonight by Frederick Revere, the elder statesman of the Players Club and, I suppose, the closest thing Broadway has to a wise man. Or a shrewd one, at least. You'd have to be shrewd to have a career as long and illustrious as Freddie's and still look that good. *Damn,* the old fox still has all his hair. And Christ, what style! Next to Revere, even Doug Fairbanks, Jr., looks seedy. Though I'm probably biased; like me, Frederick's a British import who made good in America.

Well, I'd better take down every golden word or Timmy will spank.

"Ladies and gentlemen, fellow actors, we all know why we're here tonight." (Nice pause; wistful smile.) "At least, I hope we do. We're here, quite simply, because we feel bad." (Shocking grammatical error!) "And not just because Laura Dane is gone—I could say 'gone but not forgotten' but that would be twaddle. The fact is we *did* forget Laura, long before she died." (My stars! Is he going to be *candid?*) "We forgot Laura when she ceased to be a star. Granted her early retirement was of her own choosing. Granted she went into seclusion after her unhappy experience. But Laura was no latter-day Garbo! She didn't *want* to be alone. Laura was a bird of bright plumage, whose wings were clipped by a sorry fluke. Still, she had enormous talent, guts, humor, and a gift for living. Laura was more than a great actor—she was a great lady—on stage and off. And *that* is what we forgot. And it's a shame. Out of sheer *gratitude* for the bounty she bestowed on us, we should've hammered on her doorstep daily. . . ."

Hell, why is my hand shaking? I need a drink. Where's that blasted waiter?

Well, Revere's done it. Shaken the house to its core. Who'd have thought the old devil still had the balls to do it? And, because Revere is who he is, they not only took it; they thanked him for it. He cleared the air like a crack of lightning.

Perhaps, I should explain. You may not know why Laura Dane retired from the stage at the height of her fame.

Laura had what I call Bernhardt Syndrome. The Divine Sarah was renowned for, uh, regurgitating in the wings; i.e., she threw up right before she went on stage. It's not all that uncommon, really. They used to keep a special bucket handy for Sarah. Bernhardt was perfectly fine once she hit the footlights, of course. The great ones always are. The lesser ones never get past it; they just go on and give sickly performances. Laura, needless to say, was one of the great ones, but she didn't care to follow Sarah's example. "What? And let the whole crew see what I had for lunch?" she once joked to me. "I'd rather *not.*"

Instead, thirty minutes before curtain, Laura always drank a cup of a special tea laced with anisette. This brew seemed to keep her nerves and stomach in abeyance until she got on stage and in gear. Though there were some nights, when she'd been absolutely on *fire,* when she'd take her curtain calls with supreme élan, then rush to her dressing room and just make it to the loo. But her public never knew about this, only those of us in her inner circle.

Until Laura did *Camille.*

I should say *La Dame aux Camélias*—that's the proper title of Dumas fils's classic tearjerker. It was gutsy of her to take the role. So many fine actresses, not just Garbo, had played the part before. And the play, really, is such an old chestnut; it only works if your leading lady does. Marguerite must be throbbing with charisma and romantic conviction or the whole house of cards caves in. Laura was absolutely electric, at least in the few rehearsals I was permitted to watch. She had the *best* tubercular cough I've ever heard. And I'm not ashamed to say I wept like a babe at her death scene.

But she overtaxed herself. Perhaps it was her subconscious way of getting to Marguerite's physical fragility.

Perhaps not. It was a grueling role, in any case, and right before opening night, Laura got a touch of flu. Not that she paid much heed to it; she was a warhorse at heart. But it seems she overestimated her stamina.

Opening night, she drank her tea, as always. Act One went well but she was still feeling queasy at intermission, so she had another cup. But, this time, it didn't do the trick. Whether it was nerves or illness or a combination of the two, we'll never know. But, at the end of the play, when a stricken Armand flew to her bedside, Laura's coughing became more than technique, I'm told. She couldn't stop; she started heaving. Just as Armand was proclaiming his undying love to the dying Marguerite, Laura Dane threw up all over her leading man, David Kell.

The curtain came down instantly, but not before the audience realized what had happened. Hell, how could they not realize; they *saw*. The reaction in the house, I hear, rivaled the night Lincoln was shot at the Ford Theater. Laura fled to her dressing room without taking her bow—and never appeared on stage again.

This may sound quite silly to you now, a tad farcical. But not to anyone who knows actors and acting. Anyone who knows about the nightmares. Actor nightmares. They *all* have them, even the ones who don't get nauseous before curtain. They've told me. Dreams of waiting in the wings for an entrance cue, then glancing down and seeing you've no pants on. Dreams of being on stage in a play you don't recognize and not knowing your part or your lines. Dreams of not being able to get a cab to the theater on opening night. It's hard for civilians to grasp how haunted stage folk are by such chimeras. But then, you've never had to deliver the goods on demand, in front of five hundred strangers, have you?

I think actors' nightmares are their way of knocking wood. Dream the disaster and it won't *happen*. I'm sure Laura felt that way, too. But then it *did* happen. Her worst nightmare came true. It destroyed her confidence completely, irrevocably. And for all time.

I need another drink.

Good lord, who's that frowsy old thing blubbering on Freddie's shoulder? It can't be . . . Christ, it *is*! It's Nelly O'Neal. I had no idea *she* was still around. But then, one doesn't keep track of such people. Nelly, in her youth—sometime during the Bronze Age, I imagine—was a dance hall girl. Then she developed a trick knee, couldn't do the high kicks anymore, and became a dresser. Eventually she became Laura's dresser. They were together for years, much to my dismay.

Nelly had the colorful vocabulary of a stevedore and the manners to match. And she used to keep a small flask tucked down her cleavage—"for emergencies," she would say. Apparently, each day was fraught with catastrophe, since I can't remember a time when she wasn't perfumed with the attar of Four Roses. I often told Laura she should hire someone a bit more respectable, but she would only laugh and say, "Pooh! Respectable's fine out front. Backstage I want someone like Nelly, who'll tell me the truth when I've hammed up a speech and make no bones about it. And, darling, she's a wonder with period costumes! Drunk or sober, Nell can do up a corset faster than anyone else living."

She was lying, of course. There was more to it than that. For all her acquired style and sophistication, Laura Dane was the child of poor Mick parents. She'd shortened her name from Delaney, and while she never played up her antecedents, she never forgot them, either. I believe, in some primal way, she identified with Nelly. And I know she trusted her completely. Nelly was always the one who prepared Laura's sacred cup of anisette tea.

Perhaps that's why Nelly dropped out of sight soon after Laura did. She might have felt she was to blame for the disaster; made the tea too strong that night or some such nonsense. The Irish are like that. All that Catholicism makes them comfortable with guilt, real or imagined.

Oh, no! Here comes David Kell to say a few words. Pray God they are few. Bet he's glad the podium is high enough to hide that paunch. Old Davy's let himself go and, right now, I'm sure he'd sell his soul for Revere's hairline. Dear, oh, dear, he's even resorted to combing his side hair up and across the balding dome. And there it lays like a piece of wilting, gray lettuce. Such a feeble ploy.

Time is cruel to all women and a few men like Davy, who was once an Adonis, I must admit, and a Don Juan as well. Kell was catnip to the ladies back then. And I'm sure he had eyes for Laura . . . well, who didn't?

"There were *two* Laura Danes, really, and I had the great joy of knowing both of them." (Good opening; I may steal it.) "One was a gorgeous girl with a wicked sense of humor, a lively curiosity and a—well, there's just no denying it—a very sexy way about her." (Knowing chuckles from the males.) "The other was a perfect—*nun*!" (Warm laughter all round now.) "Those of you who worked with her know what I mean. On stage, she was all work. A hard-nosed, nuts-and-bolts pro, completely focused on the play. And woe to the man who tried to get cute with her in a love scene! Believe me, I *know.*" (Big laugh.) "I remember one day, when she was working out a piece of blocking . . ."

Good for Davy, to admit in public, in so many words, that he never got to first base with her. I knew he hadn't, of course. That wasn't Laura's habit, to canoodle with costars during rehearsal, even during the run of the play. The nun analogy is quite accurate. Theater was Laura's religion, her church, and, as an Irish Catholic, she took it quite seriously—to extremes, if you ask me. However, *between* engagements, that was another matter, a very different, very *un*-Catholic thing altogether. Truth be told, Laura was a bit of a rake; she took her pleasure where she found it and took it with great zest. She threw herself into a love affair with an abandon that was intoxicating. That was her nature; she never did *anything* by halves. And she could make a man feel like he was the sun, the moon, and the stars in her universe—until she began another play. Then she became the good, the pure Sister Laura and the man became nothing but a dim and distant satellite.

Very selfish of her, very rough on the bloke, but she couldn't seem to help it. As she once told me: "It's like in the Bible, Wesky. You can't serve two masters. At least, *I* can't. And, be honest, most men *do* want to be masters. But, eventually, they'll take you for granted. An audience *never* does. . . . I know where I'm best loved."

"So I want to wish both my Lauras a fond farewell." (Oh, crap, Davy's tearing up. Somebody get the hook.) "I loved them both equally."

Well, that wasn't too god-awful. Damn, my glass is empty again. Oh, double damn—is Nelly heading my way? I was hoping she wouldn't recognize me.

"Why, it's Mr. Kincaid, ain't it? You remember me? It's been a while."

"Of course I do, Nelly. You've hardly changed at all." (I mean this in the most literal sense, as I seem to recall the faded gown she's wearing.)

"Ah, horse balls! I look like something the cat dragged in. But you, you seem to be keeping well."

"Thank you. I do it with mirrors."

"Go on with you now!" Nelly lets out a whiskey-laden laugh and grabs my arm with a gnarled hand. It's hard to believe those fingers were ever deft at undoing a corset. Then she drops her voice and leans close. "Hit it on the nose, didn't he? Mr. Kell. 'Bout Miss Laura's, uh, rehearsal habits. We both know how she got."

"Well, my memory's probably not as good as yours, Nell."

Where is that fool waiter? Nelly eyes my empty glass with a knowing smile. "They're getting a little stingy with the libations, ain't they? Now we're past the main course."

She winks and slips a hand down the front of her dress. Merciful heavens! It's the same damn flask. "Here, try a drop o' this, Mr. Kincaid." I shake my head but she pays no heed. "Don't worry. It's a damn sight better'n what I used to tipple, trust me."

I don't trust her but she's holding the glass right under my nose. I get a silky oaken sniff of something far superior to Four Roses. I sip, and she grins at my surprise. "Ain't exactly pigs' swill, eh?"

"No, not at all. What is it? Glenkeith?"

"Yeh, with something extra added. My own concoction." Nelly takes a short swig from the flask, wipes the top off, and says, "I always wanted to thank you for those columns you wrote—about Miss Laura."

"It was my pleasure. She was well worth writing about."

"True enough, but I always wondered—why'd you stop?"

"I think you've got it the wrong way round. *I* didn't stop. Laura did."

"No, no, I don't recall it that way." Nelly shakes her head, mule-like. "You never wrote a word about *Camille,* even after you came to rehearsal."

"Well, it wasn't my habit to write up a show *before* it opened."

"No?" She blinks at me like a woozy owl. "I could'a swore you—"

"Shh, Nell! Nita's going to speak."

"She *is*? Saints preserve us!" She squints up at the podium in disbelief, then chuckles, "Well, well, who sez money can't buy everything. Bought her that *chin* . . . Ah, poor Nettie." Nelly shakes her head with a sigh.

"Poor Nettie?" I can't help but laugh at Nell's volte-face. "My dear, she's hardly that!"

"Oh, I know she's got more money than God now," Nelly says, then adds softly, "But Nita never got what she really wanted."

I pick up my cue dutifully. "What's that?"

"Why, she wanted to be Laura, of course."

"To *be* Laura? You mean, she wanted to have Laura's career, don't you?"

"No, I don't. I'm not talking about roles and reviews." Nelly bristles slightly. "I mean just what I said. She wanted to *be* Miss Laura. More than anything."

I find this fascinating but Frederick is frowning at us, so I'll be silent.

Flustered to be in the limelight again, Nita fidgets for a moment, smoothing the front of her gown and patting her lacquered coif. Then she peers up at the light they've rigged over the podium, points to it, and grins. "Oh, thank God—it's *gelled*!" This gets a good laugh and Nita's back on home ground again. "I think the highest tribute I can pay Laura is to say how much I hated her *guts*." (Shocked gasp, which Nita cuts off with another grin.) "I'm not talking about personal animosity, folks, not at all, just pure *envy*." (My, my, seems Nita is going to follow in Revere's frank footsteps!) "And the hell of it was—Laura deserved every part she got. She was *that* good. No sugar daddies, patrons, or casting couches for our Laura, no. She never wanted or needed that kind of help. In fact, Laura took pains to make sure no one ever pulled strings for her." (Christ, that's all too true.) "Though, I *do* think her last name was a big advantage. It made it so easy for all those critics to write catchy headlines, like 'Great Dane!' Or, when she played Anna Christie, 'Melancholy Dane Dazzles.' Remember? And, really, what can you do with *Grey*? Hell, I did *Morning Glory* once and all I got was 'A Grey Dawn!'" (Howls of laughter—so why is Nita tearing up again?) "I suppose I could've changed my name, but it wouldn't have mattered. What Laura had couldn't be copied. Lord knows, I tried. I even tried drinking that anisette tea of hers before I went on once—but it just made me burp." (Nita smiles while tears stream down her cheeks, ruining her mascara, but she doesn't seem to give a damn now. She gulps for air.) "My career lasted longer than Laura's. But, so what? Better to be a bonfire than a—a sixty-watt bulb, if you ask me. . . . I hope Laura knew that, too."

As the audience applauds, Nita drops her head, shoulders heaving. Harv Shapiro finally does the chivalrous thing and gently leads her back to her seat. To my dismay, Nelly shouts out, "Attagirl!" then pours both of us another shot from the seemingly bottomless flask. I shake my head.

"Nelly, please! I've got a column to write tonight."

"Oh, go on with you now," she scoffs, pushing the glass toward me. "It never stopped you in the old days, as I recall."

"Well, I'm older now and, I hope, wiser."

"Are you?" She gives me an appraising look that is slightly unsettling. "Still, you've held up nicely, Mr. Kincaid. If you don't mind my sayin', you're a handsome devil yet."

"Why, that's very—thanks, Nelly."

"I wonder why it is you never married?"

"What? Well, I never—" The old girl's in rare form tonight. Thrown by her question, I down the shot and assume a blithe air. "I guess I just never fell in love."

"Never fell in love again, you mean." She gives me a nudge and a wink.

"What? What're you talk—" Nellie shoves back her chair and stands up. "Where are you going?"

"Mercy! Don't you know?" She nods toward the podium. "I'm up next. Here, keep this for me." Nell plunks the flask down on the table and walks toward the podium with a steady gait. The woman must have hollow legs! She seems sober as a judge and cool as a cucumber—oh, Christ, I'm sinking to mixed metaphors!

It must be the heat. It's gotten unbearably hot in here. Whose idea was it to have Nelly speak anyway? Good God!—was it Revere? Judging from the smile on his face, it must've been. But *why?*

The master of ceremonies is finishing his introduction. Nelly steps up to the podium, greeted by faint applause,

which fazes her not at all. I think they've dimmed the lights
some, or else my eyesight's failing. She looks rather blurry
from here. But her voice is loud and clear.

"Some of you know me, most of you don't, but that's not
important. What's important is that Miss Laura gets her due
tonight. I was her dresser for twelve years and it was the
finest job I ever had. You've all said what a great star she
was—and that's God's truth. But I knew her better than the
lot o' you put together, meaning no offense, and I'd like to
say she was also one of the sweetest souls that ever lived.
But Laura was human, too, don't forget. As human as you
or me. And she had her failings, so don't go making a myth
of her just yet.

"For one thing, Miss Laura was too trusting. She never
meant harm to no one, so she figured no one meant harm to
her. I knew better." (The natives are growing anxious.
There's something ominous in Nell's eyes.) "Like Miss
Nita said, there was a good deal of envy from some
women. That's to be expected. And resentment, too, from
some men. The beaux she'd drop when she started a new
play. I used to warn her about it—'There's nothing a man
hates more than a woman who treats sex . . . well, same as
they do.'" (Nervous titters. Ballocks! Why's she going on
like this?) "But Miss Laura'd always say, 'Nonsense, Nell.
They'll get over it. Broadway's littered with prettier actresses than li'l ole me.' She was right in a way. Miss Laura
wasn't the greatest beauty of her day. And most of the men
did get over it—but not all."

Shit, I've got a blinding headache from the heat. If the
old biddy doesn't wind up soon, I'll have to write the column in the morning. Blast! Might as well get properly
drunk. Nell's glass is still full. I grab it and toss the shot
back. . . . Why is that old sod Revere looking at me so
queerly, while everyone else is glued on Nelly?

"No one's really talked about it here—Miss Laura's last
night on stage, the night she retched. But I've been
mulling it over for *years*. Like I said, I knew her best, saw

her go on stage when she was running a fever or nearly
hoarse with cold—and she *always* made it through! She
would've made it through the opening night of *Camille*,
too . . . but somebody had it in for her. (Stunned silence.
Someone should stand up and protest this outrage; I would
but I can't seem to find my legs.) "I was too stupid to see
it, because I was the one who made her tea. I always
brewed a pot of strong Earl Grey, then laced it with
anisette that I kept in a glass bottle. I thought I was running low on it. But, that night, the bottle was nearly full, so
I thought Miss Laura had bought more. She hadn't."
(Nelly hits the podium with her fist, shaking the micro-
phone, creating a reverb.) "I didn't know! I didn't ask her
about it till . . . last month."

This is getting too surreal for words. Mercifully, I'm too
drunk to care much. But Frederick seems upset. He's just
slipped out of his chair and is heading down the long ban-
quet table, away from the podium and away from O'Neal's
ravings.

"Last month, my grandnephew was sick and I helped
nurse him. We had to give him an emetic, you know? To
make him vomit. Ipecac syrup in water. Now Ipecac's been
around for ages. But I forgot that it smells and tastes like
anisette. Just like I forgot that someone came to Miss
Laura's dressing room that night, before the curtain, to
bring a bouquet. But he didn't stay for the show. He was
Miss Laura's latest discard, you see. She was quite friendly
to him but it was real plain she'd done with him. So we left
him alone in the dressing room while we went on stage to
check the lights—that was our ritual. When we came back,
he was gone. Laura smiled and said, 'Poor Cady. I hope he
knows he's better off without me.' "

Oh, holy Jesus, seems I'm weeping now. I haven't heard
that name in years. Laura was the only one who ever called
me Cady. Laura, my love, my torment; the loveliest, cruelest woman who ever lived. I hated you that night and
meant to do you mischief—it was so easy, knowing your

habits as I did. And Nell's right—you were too trusting.
But I never meant to destroy you so utterly. I should say so
now, I suppose. Get up and make a clean breast of it,
only . . . I can't.

"Wesley, get up!" Frederick Revere is shaking my shoulder roughly. "Stand up, man! I think we need to get you to
hospital."

I push his hand away. "No, no, is all right. Let her finish.
I'm just a li'l drunk."

Nell is still speaking but eyes are drifting our way. Revere puts his hands under my armpits, attempting to haul
me up. My legs skitter away from me. Sensing the distur-
bance, Nelly looks over with a beatific smile and shakes
her head.

"Mr. Revere, I know you mean well, but—it's too late,
much too late."

From the wrong end of a telescope, I watch Freddie grab
the flask and sniff it. "Nelly! What the hell did you give
him?"

"Enough Seconal to drop a horse. But that's real fine
scotch I mixed it in, single malt, to soften the blow a bit."

From a long way off, I hear voices rising, footsteps rushing everywhere. Christ, won't Tiny Tim love this! It'll
make great copy. Too bad I won't get to write it. People
make feeble attempts to grab hold of Nelly, but she shrugs
them off like flies and saunters toward me. As she draws
near, Revere releases my arms. I sag back in my seat like a
bag of wet sawdust and look up into Nelly's eyes. I find
what's left of my voice.

"You knew it had to be me?"

"Oh, yes. Once I thought about it. You were the one who
couldn't bear to be thrown over, could you? She just
needed to act. You needed to be important."

I can't even nod my head now, so I just blink my eyes as
a "yes." Everything is drawing in on me, like a kaleido-
scope turning backwards. There's only one possible conso-
lation left to me now. I try hard to focus on Nelly's face

and manage to whisper, "At least—at least I'll get to see Laura again, won't I?"

Sirens are wailing way off in the distance, or maybe it's someone—Nita?—crying nearby. Either way, Nelly pays no heed as she studies my face, then says, "I wouldn't plan on it if I were you, Mr. Kincaid. See, Laura's in heaven."

"Oh, yes . . . right."

Birds never seem to have a care in the world, save for watching out for the occasional house cat on an evening prowl. People who watch birds, however, often have much more weighty matters on their minds. Like how to conceal a murder, for example.

Body in the Bosque

Marlys Millhiser

BETTY BEESOM ADJUSTED the binoculars for her bad eye, shifted her weight to relieve the stress on her bad hip, and leaned against the Posada de Pajaro Adobe van to sweep a claret sunset.

Sandhill cranes glided in groups of three or four toward the man-made lake along the Rio Grande River, lowered their landing gear, and came to a skimming halt among friends and relatives. Folding three-foot wings, the giant birds trumpeted rattling calls to incoming brethren. Hundreds already dotted the lake and still they came from grazing in surrounding fields planted just for them.

The crane clamor was deafening, but an unexpected crescendo from inside the van at her back startled Betty into jerking the binoculars. This forced her eyeglasses hard into the bony bridge of her nose, swept her vision from the magnificent birds to the barren black-barked trees at the marshy edge of the lake. She caught a glimpse of a duck perched on a gnarly limb and a human hand making a rude gesture closer in before righting herself.

"Now you listen to me, young lady. . . ." Mrs. Beesom yanked open the van door and rounded on the one passenger not standing out on the levee oohing and aahing over the fly-in at the Bosque del Apache. Only a teenager could ruin this paradise. Eve most certainly had been in her teens.

Libby Greene turned in her seat with that patrician stare Mrs. Beesom longed to shake until the girl's teeth rattled out of their metal braces. How Betty could have been so misled, so naive, so easily tricked into bringing this blonde disaster along on the trip of a lifetime she'd never understand.

"It's all right, Mrs. Beesom," came a gentle voice from a rough man reaching past her to switch off the radio, "we must have patience with the young." He was the only person on the crowded levee not wearing a coat. He puffed clouds into the air and even appeared to be perspiring. "Now, Libby-luv, I know you might think all this of no interest to such as yourself but let ol' Ian show you a mystery or two."

The girl gave Betty a venomous look, but slid out of the van to huddle deeper into her jacket when the chill hit. Mrs. Beesom had noticed how the creature responded more willingly to commands from men than to those of her own sex. Which did not bode well for Libby Greene or her single mother.

"He used to be a teacher, you know," said Ian's sister. They were the proprietors of the Posada de Pajaro Adobe, a bed-and-breakfast inn that catered to birders. It had been the second-place offering in a contest sponsored by *Bird-rapture,* a magazine distributed at Wild Bird Stores, Inc. Mrs. Beesom entered thousands of contests in her seventy years and never won a thing. She'd even tried to enter her bad-luck ratio in the *Guinness Book of World Records,* but lost there too.

So when word of her good fortune arrived, she couldn't believe she'd won an all-expenses-paid, five-day vacation for two to the Bosque del Apache National Wildlife Refuge.

Her best friend, Norma Tooney, fell and broke her hip at the last minute and couldn't come. Betty was too thrifty not to make use of both airline tickets or the free bed and board for two rather than one. This bed-and-breakfast served two hot meals and a sack lunch. With her luck it would be the only free lunch Betty would ever get.

She was in the process of a frantic canvass of her church group for another companion when Libby Greene decided to run away from home.

"Now, there. You see the snowy white flock at the other rim of the lake? That's snow geese." Ian stood close behind Libby to be sure she had the binoculars trained in the proper direction. "And look you to the left a little—them's Canada geese alighting."

Mrs. Beesom's travels had been mostly on PBS, the Discovery Channel, and the Christian networks, but she'd picked up enough on foreigners to decide he talked like a Scotsman raised by a poor family in Australia.

"Now you know about the grandeur and excitement out here, don't you, lass? Just a tad more to the left and what do you see?"

Libby turned a look of extreme disbelief upon their host and Betty moved quietly to intervene, but once again the girl obeyed and raised the binocs. She needed a father, no doubt about it. "A duck sitting in a tree."

"Ducks retire on the water, not in trees, luv. I think you're too far to the left."

"And some dork giving me the bird."

"No storks in the Bosque, dear," Sara Kertelstrup said. "Least I don't think so. Are there, Ian?"

But just then a shrill "ker loooo, ker lee loo" joined the rattling chorus of the sandhills and human cheers joined in from the levee. Sara had excited them all thinking she'd heard one earlier, but this time there was no mistaking the cry.

"It's the whoopers," Ian said. "Did I not tell you?"

With the sandhills rescued from extinction, an attempt was made to save the even more endangered whooping cranes by having the former hatch out the whoopers, hoping the adopted result would bond to their sandhill parents and learn migration routes. Birding books and stores were encouraged. But local rangers were worried for the whooping crane still.

Betty, searching the skies for incoming whoopers, couldn't help overhearing her dreaded charge insist, "That is so a duck. It's got webbed feet. We learned about them in—"

"That's merely the olivaceous cormorant you see. Look you upon the splendor of the whooper while you may."

Mrs. Beesom too had noticed a web-footed bird bedding down on a tree limb. She too had noticed what might have been the raised second finger on a human hand not far away. She swung her glasses back to the black-barked trees. "Mr. Kertelstrup, she's right. A man's laid out in the marsh there."

"There's been a murder, Mom."

Charlie Greene was disappointed to hear from her runaway so soon. She figured the kid couldn't get in much trouble birding with Mrs. Beesom and had planned the luxury of working late without guilt, sleeping through nights without worry, generally energizing—God forbid, maybe even having some social life.

But the voice on the other end of the line had only to sound shocked and frightened to put Charlie on the next available flight from LAX to Albuquerque. It went by way of Minneapolis, so that she didn't get there until midafternoon of the day after the murder. By the time she rented a car and drove south to Socorro, where she stopped for directions, it was late afternoon. Finally she pulled off a gravel road onto a long sandy lane.

The first thing she saw after rounding a curve was a two-story adobe building with an unlikely sunporch across its front. The second was Libby's hair.

Its silvery highlights caught the sun and the eye. She sat alone on a dusty picnic table, not bothering to move as Charlie stepped out of the car.

"Took you long enough."

"I'm glad to see you too."

"I'm still leaving home. I just thought you should know about the murder."

"Right."

A George Gelman had been found lying faceup in a flooded area of the bird sanctuary, his body caught by an outflung arm in the fork of a fallen tree limb, his neck and one index finger broken. He'd also suffered an awesome blow to the head that appeared a bit much to have come by way of an accidental tumble into the marsh. He and his wife, Shirley, were guests of the Posada de Pajaro Adobe and had ridden in the Posada's van with the other guests to see the fly-in at sunset at the Bosque, a few miles away.

"Know what Posada de Pajaro Adobe means?" asked Libby, who endured Spanish for her language requirement at Wilson High in Long Beach. "Inn of the adobe bird. Is that stupid or what? Like, the whole place is for the birds."

And it was. Birdbaths everywhere on the otherwise parched grounds, glass birds hanging among the plants on the sunporch, ceramic birds on tables and mantels in the massive lounge, bird paintings on the walls, bird books and magazines falling off the coffee tables.

"Some guest ranch—not a horse or a cute guy in sight," the kid groused. "Place needs a few hundred Tuxedos, that's what it needs."

Tuxedo was Libby's cat, the scourge of Charlie's life, and the Godzilla of Mrs. Beesom's bird stations next door.

Outside the windows flanking the dining room on two sides, birds of all sizes and colors frolicked at feeders and dripping water catchers hanging from the eaves, on pedestals and posts, flat on the ground, under and in scrawny bushes and trees.

"Let me compliment you on your daughter, Mrs. Greene," Mr. Goldfarb said at dinner, which occurred within minutes of Charlie's arrival. "She even pouts pretty."

"Prettily," his wife, Pearl, corrected.

"*Miss* Greene," Libby continued the correction, and stabbed a small drumstick from the passing plate. Watching the eyes upon her, she bit into it as if she were Tuxedo after a particularly succulent kill. "Tastes a little like robin."

Mr. and Mrs. Goldfarb had spent the last three weeks birding their way across the country from New Jersey with the Gelmans. They were astonished at the length of the interstates and highways between coasts and the fact that almost no one along the tortuous route read the *New York Times*.

Martin Goldfarb said of the murdered Mr. Gelman, "Only guy I know who uses cruise control in rush-hour traffic."

"Used," Pearl corrected.

"He was so relaxed, inattentive, slow. Know what I mean?" he tried again. "Can't figure how he made it in Jersey. Bet we didn't average more than two, three hundred miles a day all the way here."

Heads swiveled to Pearl for the rebuttal. She was a short, solid woman with thin, blackened hair. Her face looked a lot younger than her neck. She jerked, twitched, blinked rapidly when she spoke, as if somebody plugged her in when cued by her husband's voice. "That was only on days when we stopped to see something. If Marty had his way, we'd have driven past all the reasons for making the trip in the first place." She added unnecessarily, "We did Europe last summer."

The man next to Charlie applauded. "Oh, I'm so impressed." He handed Charlie the bowl of mushroom pilaf and introduced himself as Jim Mayo from Tucson and the woman beside him as his wife, Molly. "I'm glad you've come for the girl. She shouldn't be involved in this mess."

He was a stocky, balding man with heavy sunspots on his hands and forehead. Everyone at the table except the Greenes were well into their sixties or early seventies. Jim Mayo struck Charlie as perhaps the brightest light of the bunch until he shocked her by leaping to his feet and nearly striking her in the face as he swung his arm to point to the window. "Isn't that a pyrrhuloxia?"

Charlie and Libby found themselves alone at the table—two tables, actually, pushed together to make a square that could have seated six times their number. Everyone else let their meals cool while they grabbed binoculars hanging from pegs on the wall and stood before the windows.

"Getting any vibes?" Charlie's daughter whispered sideways.

"I do not get vibes. I'm here only to take you home."

"I'll just run away again."

"Promise you'll send for your goddamned cat when you get settled?"

Libby grabbed another drumstick and flounced off with narrowed eyes and an expletive. Charlie pushed her own plate away. Why did she let herself spark off the kid so?

No one mentioned Libby's absence when the crew returned to the tables. The proprietors, Ian and Sara Kertelstrup, looked amazingly similar for two people of such opposite construction. He was trim yet huge, the flesh still firm on a massive bone structure, his head of a size that made Charlie wonder how he found hats. He did, though, because the tan line ended evenly below the hairline. He wore baseball caps with the bill in front because his white hair had that telltale tail in back, accustomed to sticking through the hole between the fabric and the plastic adjustment band.

His sister, small-boned and frail, continually glanced at him for approval and nodded hers when he spoke. But the bones of the face, the eyes, the expressions clearly related the two.

Sounds of kitchen help came from a Dutch door with its top half left open, but Sara did most of the serving, while her imposing brother entertained. She cleared away Libby's place setting and Charlie's barely touched plate with the embarrassment of one who'd never suffered children.

The widow, Shirley Gelman, was sequestered upstairs with Mrs. Beesom, whom Charlie had not yet seen but would have been willing to wager was offering religious counsel along with the Kleenex.

So the Kertelstrups, the Mayos, the Goldfarbs, and Charlie were it at the moment. It was a great setup for the small-closed-group, cozy sort of murder she invariably rejected when they crossed her desk. For unless they were set in England, where it could still presumably happen, few but Jessica Fletcher could get away with that kind of thing now.

"You seem young to have a fifteen-year-old daughter," Ian repeated the second-most-repeated comment Charlie heard. Hey, no trick to it if you start at sixteen. The most repeated comment was a request to read someone's work.

"So where are the police? I mean, a man was murdered, right?" she asked.

"There's a deputy lurking somewhere," her host said, obviously embarrassed the subject had come up. How could he expect it wouldn't? "The county's a poor one and short-handed, but the sheriff will be back bright and early tomorrow. Meanwhile, two nights ago we observed a tradition at the Posada of introducing ourselves and our interests to each other over dinner. Would you not help us through a terrible evening?"

Charlie gave a minimal description of her work at Congdon and Morse Representation, a talent agency in Beverly Hills, where she served as literary agent. This set Martin Goldfarb to name-dropping publishing and writing types he'd read of in the *New York Times,* most of whom were too old for Charlie to have heard of but which set Pearl Goldfarb into a flurry of minimizing. Charlie wondered why Pearl hadn't been the one in this group to turn up dead in the Bosque.

And simply hearing the Goldfarbs seemed to set Jim Mayo's teeth on edge. He shifted in his chair, making light whimpering sounds. Molly jabbed him in the ribs twice that Charlie saw.

"Look, we heard how wonderful and brilliant you are the last two days, Joizey. It's just possible the rest of us are interested in hearing more about Charlie."

"Now, now, we're all under stress here," the soft-spoken Ian said. "In respect to the poor widow upstairs, let's put aside petty provincialism and keep—"

"Poor widow?" Pearl erupted, and then slapped her hand over her mouth.

Martin Goldfarb showed only confusion at Jim Mayo's attack but something quite different at his wife's outburst. Was it fear?

Charlie perked up. No, she was not getting mysterious vibes. She was merely a normally curious person. And the scene had changed rather suddenly here. So had the emotional charges feeding it.

Sara Kertelstrup rushed to the dessert cart and began serving precut pieces of apple pie. Her brother noticed she hadn't finished clearing the dinner plates and jumped up to do so.

The Mayos sat rigid with anger—at each other or the Goldfarbs, Charlie couldn't tell. But the six people with her at the table had changed. Or perhaps her vision had cleared of stereotypes. They'd gone from senior citizens too mature, settled, frail, or smug to commit murder to something else altogether.

"Can't sleep, huh?" Libby's hair cascaded upside down over the edge of the bunk bed above Charlie. Mrs. Beesom was still tending to the widow. "It's the vibes."

"Will you stop with the vibes? I notice you're not asleep."

"How could I be with you bouncing around down there?" The shimmery hair and the face from which it appeared to hang withdrew, to be replaced by an elegant leg swinging through a patch of moonlight cut in fourths by the panes of a window. The air smelled of parched wood and dust and Libby's shower gel. They had a room in the "bunkhouse" behind the main house, one far more lavish than any cowboy had ever known. "Why don't you open your mind to your psychic powers, Mom, solve the murder, and be able to sleep? You make perfectly simple stuff so damn hard."

Charlie knew her daughter had glommed on to this psychic business partly because of a series of coincidences and some misconceptions about recent events in their lives, and partly because Libby knew there were few better ways to aggravate her mother. "Well, as long as you're awake too, why don't you tell me about the introductory talks all the guests gave the first night at dinner."

They were soon sitting on the couch snuggled in quilts, drinking Cokes from the stock in their little drink refrigerator like two girls at a slumber party, Charlie enjoying the rare noncombat status more than anything.

Ian Kertelstrup had begun the self-introductions by explaining that he and his sister had managed hotels and restaurants in exotic places all over the world, but had settled here in semiretirement to do what they knew and loved on a smaller scale while indulging their attraction to birds. And of course finding themselves working harder than ever before. They had turned this old ranch house into a B & B about three years ago.

"Didn't Sara speak for herself at all?"

"I don't remember. Maybe . . . but Mrs. Goldfarb sure did." Pearl had spent her life working in Macy's and retired as floor supervisor in ladies' sportswear. Martin Goldfarb was retired from teaching political science and history in a private boys' school. He was writing a book on the hobbies of U.S. presidents since Washington.

"God, I hope he doesn't have his manuscript with him," Charlie said. "Did they say how they got into birds?"

The Goldfarbs became interested in birding because of the Gelmans, whom they'd met on a cruise to the Caribbean three years ago and discovered lived only about fifty miles from their home. Martin Goldfarb and his wife did not drive, so the Gelmans would come to their house and take them on weekend trips out in the country.

"They knew the dead man before they got here," Libby said, watching Charlie. Charlie was amazed her daughter had listened to the introductory speeches so closely. "They look like *it*, don't they? The Goldfarbs?"

At the moment they did, but Charlie asked, "What did the Gelmans say about themselves?"

George Gelman was a retired stockbroker, Shirley a retired mother of four—all grown, married, divorced, remarried. The grandmother of countless blood and appended children, her greatest sorrow was her children. One daughter-in-law had cut her off from her oldest son and his kids.

"She didn't come out and say all that to strangers on the first night?"

"She's a real bitch. Keeps right on talking to nobody when the rest of us start talking to each other, you know, like a teacher. I think she drinks."

Jim Mayo from Tucson was a retired accountant who loved golf but had picked up an interest in wild birds from his wife, Molly, who was retired from raising three daughters. The Mayos had moved to Tucson from Cleveland three years ago and made a big point of their children's successes. All had graduated from college and the two who were married still lived with their original spouses.

"She has hot flashes like Grandma," Libby explained, "doesn't go for Tucson, but likes looking at dumb birds, so he gets them out of there when she starts wigging."

Charlie nodded toward the ceramic tooth cup and Efferdent tablets on the bedside table next to the set of bunk beds across the room from theirs. "What did you and Mrs. Beesom have to say about yourselves?"

"I said they could sure use cheeseburgers and fries on the menu here. Good old Beesom went into public orgasm over how lucky she was to win a free trip to this excuse for a landfill. So what do you think? I can see your brain working in your eyes."

"I just find it interesting they're all retired except for the Kertelstrups, who, it seems, would like to be. They're all birders, and the phrase 'three years ago' keeps turning up." The Mayos retired to Tucson. The Kertelstrups bought the Posada and the Gelmans and Goldfarbs met on a cruise. More than likely, it didn't mean a thing.

"I heard Ian talking to Mrs. Gelman the first night. She wanted to know what Beesom and I were doing here. And he said the contest had been set up months ago and it couldn't be helped. Something about he'd keep us busy in the front seat. I was hiding in the shadows under the stairs after I snuck in looking for a TV. Mrs. Beesom was asleep; I figured the rest of the old farts would be too. But Sara was running the vacuum."

"She does the cleaning too? Who does the cooking? I heard someone in the kitchen tonight—there's some help."

"A lady comes in the morning, has the dinner ready before she leaves. Ian and Sara do the dishes after everybody else goes to bed." Libby had learned all this by typically going where she was told not to.

Another interesting point, Charlie mentioned, was that although there were a number of empty bedrooms in the main house, Libby and Mrs. Beesom were lodged outside it. "To keep you separated . . . I'm worried that I haven't seen Mrs. Beesom since I got here. You'd think she'd have time to run downstairs long enough to thank me for coming to take you off her hands."

• • •

"So how many ways did George Gelman die?" Libby Greene's mother asked Sheriff Ransom the minute he walked into the lounge of the Posada de Pajaro Adobe.

"You must have had your kids early," he said to establish more than an official rapport. Women liked the personal approach and he needed her cooperation.

"One was enough." Cool, crisp, cynical, and in command. She wore a bright green blazer, black skirt, and heels. The only informality she'd allowed herself was a green ribbon tying back a mass of copper-blonde curls. "And you haven't answered my question."

"Well now, we'll get to that. First, I need to know how you knew Shirley Gelman was holding Betty Beesom prisoner upstairs." This Charlie Greene and her daughter had wandered around the outside of the adobe ranch house last night until they'd stumbled into Deputy Hazelton and insisted he investigate Mrs. Gelman's room. Both women were asleep but the deputy couldn't get Mrs. Beesom awake. She was currently sleeping off a drug overdose in the infirmary at the School of Mines in Socorro.

"She hadn't come down to see me since I got here. Her nightgown, robe, slippers, and Bible were gone. But her tooth cup was still on the bedside table. And her Efferdent. Mrs. Beesom never sleeps with her teeth in. I figure she got suspicious and scared them. Somebody panicked and slipped her some of the medication that must be abundant upstairs. I don't know how long they figured they could get away with it but—"

"They? Mrs. Gelman and who else?"

"All of them. I just wondered if each one had to strike a blow or whatever to George Gelman's poor skull. That way they'd all be equally guilty and have to keep quiet. They might all have liked birds, but not each other."

"Sounds like you been watching too many old Agatha Christie movies." Or Angela Lansbury shows, he thought— but it did look like the guy had been struck with three different objects. One blunt, one jagged, and one pointed.

That's what initially tipped him off Gelman hadn't died of a fall into the marsh. Could have been just the three men— still some gentlemen in that generation. "Why would they all want to kill this guy?"

Charlie Greene shrugged, as if not that interested. Her luggage and her daughter's packed and ready next to her, she sat poised on the edge of a leather sofa, looking like a tropical flower against the room's backdrop, muted by age and earth tones. She kept twisting the strap of her shoulder bag, impatiently biting at her lower lip with small, even teeth. "It was just a thought. They're all retirees and he was a stockbroker. He might have invested some of their retirement money and lost it. That doesn't explain his wife— maybe he lost their retirement money too. Now, if that's all, Libby and I have a plane to catch."

"That's not all, and you have plenty of time to pick her up at the infirmary at Mines and get to Albuquerque for your takeoff." She'd insisted Libby stay with Mrs. Beesom, for the girl's safety. Sheriff Ransom figured the largely male campus had come to a screeching halt when the jail-bait stepped out of the ambulance.

"You want to explain how one or even all of them could have killed him and thrown his body in the drink without anybody on the levee noticing? Not even your daughter and neighbor lady?"

"Listen, Sheriff, that's your job." She stood and smoothed imaginary wrinkles in her skirt. She had nice legs. "Sheriff?"

"Humor me for just a few more minutes."

"They could have killed him here, put him in the back of the van, and sat in front of him so Mrs. Beesom and Libby in the front seat might not notice. They'd have had to cover his head, but Libby expects anyone over twenty-five to nod off at a moment's notice anyway and Betty Beesom is easily distracted."

"What are you, one of them psychics?"

She took a deep breath and made fists. "No, Sheriff. Libby overheard Ian telling Shirley Gelman he'd keep them distracted in the front seat and explaining it wasn't his fault the two were here this weekend because the contest had been staged months ago. Which suggests the rest of them had hoped to have the place to themselves. And since there was a murder, that could possibly be why. But I'm the first to admit this is just guesswork and you have better methods than that."

"Why would they schedule a murder the week the contest winner would be here?"

"Mrs. Beesom had several dates she could have come, but she has various affairs at her church to schedule around. All she had to give was a week's notice of when she'd actually claim her prize. The Gelmans and Goldfarbs were already on the road driving cross-country."

Gelman had been dead a while before he was thrown into the shallow water, according to the preliminary guess of the local mortician. But the sheriff would never tell this woman that. She was too full of herself. Pushy. That type got irritating fast. "So how did they, if what you say is possible, throw a dead body in the drink on a crowded levee with no one noticing?"

"Look, I don't know. I didn't think to ask Libby, but if they'd come early when there weren't that many people around and disposed of the body right away . . . who knows?"

As a matter of fact, that evening they'd arrived for the fly-in early. Sheriff Ransom had thought to ask. "Even if there were just a few people there it'd be hard to distract everybody."

"Libby stayed in the van as long as she could, bored with the whole scene. But as for the rest of them . . . Come into the dining room with me, Sheriff."

•   •   •

The Kertelstrups, Mayos, Goldfarbs, and Mrs. Gelman sat at the tables arranged to hold a bigger crowd, with two armed deputies, coffee mugs, donuts, and scowls.

Shirley Gelman had come as something of a surprise. She must have started her childbearing as early as Charlie. She was a stunning forty-five or so, and nobody's fool.

They were not speaking to each other and appeared to prefer that condition—but the air in the room fairly blistered with silent accusation. Charlie picked up a donut from the serving cart and sauntered over to the wall of windows, studied the birds while eating, and turned back to the room, only to swing right around and point with the donut. "Isn't that one of those pyrrhuloxias?"

She had planned to add, "that everyone got so excited about at dinner last night," but she was nearly trodden by birders with binoculars crowding together, their separating silence forgotten.

Two confused deputies, a sheriff, and the widow hadn't moved. Shirley Gelman's glower was potent enough for Charlie to understand how a daughter-in-law might cut husband and children off from grandma.

"We were watching *Murder, She Wrote,*" Betty Beesom told Charlie, and leaned back in her neighbor's breakfast nook, warm pecan rolls fragrant with caramel, cinnamon, butter, and sugar on the table between them. It was no wonder Betty knew the pastries' ingredients—she'd baked them herself. Young women these days didn't know how to cook, or eat either.

"Mrs. Gelman and me. Up in her room to take her mind off the murder. It was a rerun. Jessica was on a cruise ship. Poor Shirley started telling me about them all meeting."

Three years ago Shirley and George Gelman had met not only the Goldfarbs on that cruise, but the Mayos as well. And Ian and Sara managed one of the hotels on a cay off the coast of Belize to which a number of the guests on the cruise ship had retired for a weekend of relief from the hectic frolic at sea.

"I asked Sara to bring us up some tea to take the poor woman's mind off her flask of gin. It started Shirley talking her fool head off. I couldn't get a word in edgewise and then I thought well, maybe Jesus just wants me to listen. That can be a comfort too." Betty eyed the black cat eying her from atop the refrigerator.

When Sara brought up the tea, she'd taken one look at the inebriated widow and said, "We've got to do something."

Betty thought that message for her, that she should do something about the liquor going down the brand-new widow, bring up the subject of the true comfort offered by the Lord. But what Sara had been saying was, "You've told this woman too much. Now we'll have to do something about Betty Beesom too."

The slant-eyed devil blinked at Betty, stood to stretch from front claw to tail tip.

So Shirley Gelman started slipping a blend of prescription drugs into Betty's tea whenever she looked away. The medicinal blend had been donated by other couples and pounded into powder. It was left over from that used to stun her husband and was right at hand. When Betty remarked that the brew was bitter and set it aside, Shirley added sugar, promised to start sipping tea instead of gin if she didn't have to do so alone.

"Should have known right then, but I was feeling woozy already. Next I know I'm in that student infirmary."

The Goldfarbs, Gelmans, and Mayos were able to retire three years ago, and the Kertelstrups to buy the Posada, because they'd pooled their savings with that of yet another couple to buy a hotel and yacht-charter business on a neighboring cay. George Gelman had talked them into it.

There was no doubt Belize was the dream destination of the upscale and adventurous new breed of tourist from all over the world. You couldn't jump into the water without hitting a medical doctor from the States.

For two and a half years the investment paid handsomely. It was like drawing a paycheck without having to go to work. But about six months ago a hurricane's storm surge washed the cay clean. The couple running the enterprise and several guests were washed out to sea and lost, along with the security and lifestyles of the remaining investors.

That hotel, solidly built, newly expanded and remodeled, had stood for over thirty years, and the price was incredibly right. So right that insuring it other than minimally would have made no sense.

The disaster reduced the Mayos and Goldfarbs to pensions, social security, and small investments that paid nothing monthly. It put the Kertelstrups in danger of losing the Posada and left Shirley Gelman essentially penniless. Because of her drinking, penchant for control, and youthful looks her husband put what was left of their money in a trust for the oldest son to parcel out to family members as he saw fit.

"Bastard even tricked me into signing the papers," Shirley told Betty that fateful night. Mrs. Beesom figured he'd waited for his wife to get so liquored up she wouldn't know what she was doing.

The black cat on the refrigerator parted its lips, sniffing at the air in Betty's direction. It had white feet and chest and teeth. Betty moved the cinnamon rolls to the far end of the table.

Shirley Gelman administered the knockout medicinal blend to her husband, Molly Mayo and Pearl Goldfarb having pounded the mixture of pills into powder. The three men each administered a deadly wallop to George Gelman's head. His neck had broken after his death when Ian Kertelstrup hurled him into the Bosque while his sister, Sara, drew everyone's attention but Libby's to the other end of the levee. Sara did this by pretending to hear the "ker loo" of a whooping crane in that direction.

So they'd all killed George Gelman and hoped it would look like he'd fallen into the Bosque and struck his head.

The drugs in his body, they figured, could be mistaken for those prescribed for a man his age. They chose the location for the crime when Ian assured them the local law was underfunded, understaffed, undertrained, and not terribly bright anyway. Like most criminals they made mistakes, that last probably the biggest of all.

In a group crime, it takes only one to break and loosen the terrified tongues of the rest. Pearl Goldfarb, in relentlessly editing her husband's comments, had struck again. The others attempted to save the situation but had no time for rehearsal.

Sheriff Ransom shared the inept confessions with them by phone. Mostly because he was taken with the idea that Charlie must be psychic to know what she insisted she'd simply guessed.

"You don't think of birders as evil enough to plan a murder." Betty had always looked to the eyes to convey the presence of evil. Those people had looked straight at Betty and hadn't given away a thing. It was like they'd made a practice of murder.

"I guess stereotyping people can be as dangerous as ignoring them, huh?" Charlie slid out of the bench seat and headed for the coffeepot.

The savager of innocent bird life gurgled deep in his throat. He flew through the air like a bird with fur to land in front of the door. Charlie let him out and refilled the cups.

Betty knew "stereotyping" was Charlie Greene's way of providing her with an excuse for her inability to determine good from evil, right from wrong. She also knew herself to have been overawed by the magnificent birds at the Bosque and her sense of responsibility for the terrible teen.

Tuxedo Greene strutted majestically past the window. He turned to stare at Betty over the tiny house finch struggling uselessly between his jaws. Oh yes, when Betty Beesom had her wits about her, she did too know evil when she saw it.

While I've never really been one for parties, some people seem to thrive on them. After all, there's so much to worry about when planning them, they make writing a mystery look easy. The victim in this next story perhaps would have done better to scale back her social calendar before it was too late.

The Potluck Supper Murders

Nancy Pickard
(Based on the character created by Virginia Rich)

You're Invited!
Valentine's Day Potluck Supper at the Marshalls'
7 P.M., February 22
Bring red or white food.
Regrets Only.

P.S. Guest list enclosed so you may bring Valentines to put in our old-fashioned, decorated shoe box!

The six large, gorgeous yams which Mrs. Potter had boiled were cool enough to peel now, a little more than one hour before the party. The three cups of fresh cranberries had boiled in twelve ounces of undiluted frozen concentrate orange juice just long enough to pop open, revealing the soft red hearts beneath their fragile skins.

But Eugenia Potter, standing in the comfy old kitchen of her childhood, in Harrington, Iowa, didn't have her mind on her cooking. After peeling the yams, she absentmindedly cut them into rounds that were, ideally, supposed to be half an inch thick. Under her knife they were coming out looking more like orange coins of varying denominations, ranging from thin dimes to thick silver dollars.

"Isn't it *just* like Evelyn Marshall," she muttered, talking entirely to herself, "to tell us all what to cook and what to bring to her party. The woman's been commanding this town for more than sixty years, and everybody's always hopped to just on Evelyn's say-so. I can't imagine why we still do it, after all these years."

It was enough to make her glad she had moved away from her hometown long ago, first to college and then to marriage. Even so, and especially now in her widowhood, she loved her annual visits to check on the old homestead and to catch up with cherished friendships. She would get the chance to see several of those old friends tonight at Evelyn and Foster Marshall's party. Five of the dearest of them would be coming round to pick her up in Perry Bain's roomy Dodge van.

"It's white," Perry had told her sarcastically when he called to offer her a ride. "To fit Evelyn's color scheme, of course. No doubt that's why it's snowing, even as we speak. Even God follows Evelyn's orders, if He knows what's good for Him! I'll pick you up last tonight, Genia, if that's all right, after I fetch Marge and Jack Thurgood, Bertie Parsons, and Lorraine Forrest."

"You're an angel, Perry," she told him. "I've lived in Arizona for so many years that I hardly know how to drive in this kind of weather anymore."

"My heart," he said dryly, "bleeds for you."

"Good," she retorted, "that'll match Evelyn's color scheme, too."

They both laughed, a rueful mirth based on shared experiences that extended way back to Harrington Elementary School, which for all of them was more than a half-century ago.

Now, with the snow still falling outside and the street lamps coming on all over Harrington, Mrs. Potter stood in her late mother's big, warm kitchen and layered the yam rounds in a glass baking dish, just as her mother had taught her. She removed the cranberry/orange mixture from the stove and stirred in sugar, tablespoon by tablespoon, until she felt the mix was just sweet enough. Then she stirred in a quarter of a teaspoon each of ground nutmeg, ground cinnamon, and ground cloves, and a pinch of ground ginger.

"Evelyn," she said to herself, "goes far beyond 'tangy,' and even way past 'tart,' all the way to 'acidic.' Maybe that's why I'm making this dish more sweet, to counteract Evelyn's effect on people!"

As she poured the pulpy mash over the yam rounds, she finally recognized their resemblance to coins.

"Actually, I do know why everybody kowtows to Evelyn and to Foster," she told herself. "It's money, plain and simple. If Foster didn't own the bank which holds nearly everybody's mortgage, and if his position didn't elevate Evelyn to such social prominence, people wouldn't bite their tongues around her. They'd say *no* when she's bossy. They'd tell her to mind her own business, for once in her life. They'd tell her off, which somebody should have done years ago, about the same time that her parents should have spanked her!" Mrs. Potter thought the current fashion of placing children in "time-out," which worked so well with her own sweet-natured grandchildren, probably wouldn't have worked at all with Evelyn: She'd have used the time to think up new ways to run her little friends' lives or hurt their feelings!

When the preheated oven reached 350, Mrs. Potter slipped in her acceptably *red* potluck supper offering. Uncovered, it would heat for the half hour she needed to dress for the party. She could hardly complain about fixing this particular dish, because "YamBerry" was easy to prepare, presented beautifully, and earned heaps of Valentines for the fortunate cook.

"I even have to admit," she had told Perry Bain when he'd called to offer her the ride, "that I got a kick out of doing the Valentines." She'd gone to the drugstore and picked up a box of children's Valentines, the kind shaped like hearts, with old-fashioned rhymes and little white envelopes. "I felt ten years old again."

"And terrified that nobody will give you a Valentine, Genia?"

"Oh, of course, isn't that every child's worst fear?"

"Well, *I'm* bringing you a Valentine," Perry had assured her.

"Good," she'd laughed. "At least I know I'll get *one!*"

As she slipped into the shower upstairs, Mrs. Potter recalled one new little girl in their school who hadn't gotten even one. All because Evelyn, the social ringleader even then, had whispered into everybody else's ears that they mustn't bring any Valentines for that new little girl, because it was against the family's religion. It was a complete fabrication, though they didn't know it until later. How terrible it had been when the child's decorated shoe box sat empty on her desk, and she'd fled the schoolroom in tears, never to return. To this day, Mrs. Potter remembered how stricken and guilty she and her friends had felt, and how they'd wished they had a chance to say they were sorry. But the child's parents didn't allow their daughter to return to that school with the children who'd been so cruel. As for Evelyn, she'd feigned innocence. "I thought it was true!" she'd protested. "I was only trying to help!"

Mrs. Potter thought she would never forget the secret little smile on Evelyn's face as she counted her Valentine's Day cards that day. Evelyn had laid them out on top of her

little desk, one by one, side by side, as if they were playing
cards and she was deciding which one to discard next.

Even under the warm water, Mrs. Potter shivered.

It wasn't just that Evelyn Marshall was bossy that made
so many people in Harrington dislike her; it was that they
were afraid of her.

Wearing a pair of her late father's galumphy old rubber
boots, Mrs. Potter navigated her way through the snow to
Perry Bain's white van. She glanced once behind her, to
enjoy the sight of the shingles and cupola of the house,
glowing with a soft silvery sheen by the light of the moon
and the falling snow. She pleasurably sniffed the cold Mid-
western winter air, and thought, "Arizona never smelled
like this!"

"Get in this van, Genia, before we freeze everybody's
tootsies!" Perry teased her as he lent her a hand up into his
van. His once-red hair was thin now, she couldn't help but
see, but he still went bareheaded in the foulest weather, and
his blue eyes still twinkled like those of a little boy up to
mischief. She greeted and thanked him with a squeeze of
her hand in his.

Inside the warm van, four other familiar faces smiled affectionately back at her. Like Mrs. Potter, the passengers
held covered dishes in their gloved hands, and they'd
brought their sacks of Valentine's Day cards, too. While
Perry drove them to the party, they confided to one another
their red—or white—potluck contributions.

"Fettuccine Alfredo," announced Marge Thurgood. In
her petite red coat and black velvet stretch pants, Marge
looked too fragile to be the mother of four, much less the
grandmother of six. "I was sorely tempted to color the
white sauce green!"

They all laughed as if they well understood her impulse.

"I've told you for years," Marge's husband, Jack Thurgood, reminded them, "that we ought to put dear Evelyn
out of *our* misery. I've even volunteered to do it, but none

of you has ever had the nerve to dare me." He was a tall, muscular, and handsome man of sixty-five, with beautiful silver hair that had once been blond.

"Jack!" his wife scolded lightly.

"Is she still like that?" Mrs. Potter inquired of her friends. "Does she still run roughshod over everybody, all in the name of good works? Does she still hurt everybody's feelings, then tell them they're too sensitive?"

"That's what bullies say," murmured Lorraine Forrest. The friends were accustomed to bending their ears to her soft words, spoken with a shyness that more than six decades had never entirely conquered. Now, even in the darkened van, they could all see that Lorraine had colored as pink as the beret pulled down over her gray curls. *"I'm only telling you this for your own good!* That's what Evelyn always tells me when she makes me feel bad." Lorraine hesitated, as she always did. They waited, as they always had. "Did I ever tell you what she did to me right after my Fred passed on?"

Her friends shook their heads, even though they had heard the painful story often in the couple of years since Lorraine's husband had died. They knew, as they always did, that Lorraine needed to tell it one more time, because each time it seemed to hurt a little less.

"She invited me to dinner with her and Foster, and I was naive enough to think it was really sweet of her, what with me feeling so terrible and lonely with my Fred gone. But when I got there, I found out it was their anniversary dinner! It was just them, and me, their only guest to dinner, and they had presents for each other, and special glasses to drink out of, and a beautiful cake. Oh, I was so hurt, I burst into tears right there at the table. Foster just sat there like a lump, as if he didn't even understand how painful that might be for a new widow."

"Poor old Foster," Bertie Parsons interjected. "I hear he has early-onset Alzheimer's."

A sympathetic murmur traveled around the van, but it stopped when it got to Jack Thurgood, who laughed and said, "I guess that's one way to get away from Evelyn. Pretty soon, he'll just forget she's there."

"Jack!" his wife scolded, more strongly this time.

Lorraine Forrest, intent on retelling her painful story, appeared not even to have heard the interruptions. She just kept talking about the anniversary dinner at the Marshalls' house. "Evelyn told me she'd only meant to be kind, and to include me, and that I shouldn't take things so hard. Oh! I could have killed her!"

"I keep offering . . . ," Jack Thurgood reminded Lorraine. In the dark van, where Mrs. Potter couldn't see his face clearly, she thought Jack's tone sounded more grim than witty. After his next words, she understood why. "I wanted to kill her, too, after Marge had those two miscarriages in one year. We were so young, and we wanted babies so much, and it was devastating to us, but especially to Margie. And what did dear Evelyn do on Mother's Day that next year? She showed up with a Mother's Day gift for Marge, that's what! She claimed she didn't want Marge to feel left out on such a special day. I think it was the cruelest thing I've ever seen anybody do." He took one of his wife's gloved hands in both of his own.

"It's okay now," Marge murmured, but her face looked like a pale little moon in the darkness inside the vehicle.

"Hmmph" was Jack's reply. "After four beautiful children, I suppose it is." Then he added, in a voice that shook a little, although whether from the cold, from age, or from anger, Mrs. Potter couldn't tell: "Bloody Mary mix, that's what I'm bringing for dear Evelyn's potluck supper. Red, for the bloody queen of Harrington."

Mrs. Potter didn't ask them why they still put up with Evelyn Marshall's high-handed ways—and Foster's apparent obliviousness to them—after all those years. Foster's tragic illness wasn't any excuse, she knew, because he'd *always* looked the other way.

Mrs. Potter knew how it was in a small town, how important it was to try to get along with everybody. She knew Evelyn was hard to avoid, harder to snub. It would be easy, Mrs. Potter knew, for her to tell her friends they were foolish to indulge Evelyn. "But," she thought privately, "I'm not the one who has to live in the same town with the woman for three hundred and sixty-five days a year for the rest of my life. They are."

From the front, Perry Bain said, "You should all just ignore Evelyn! I always have, haven't I, Genia? I brought what a bachelor always brings to a potluck supper: plain ol' potato chips!"

"Brave lad!" declared Jack Thurgood.

He reached over the seat and jovially patted his friend's shoulder, and the women laughed. Inside the van, the mood was one of warmth and conviviality; outside, the streetlights wore snowy halos that hovered over empty sidewalks.

Mrs. Potter recalled, without saying so aloud, that Evelyn Marshall often made a point of remarking on Perry Bain's unmarried status, implying things about him that caused some people to avoid his company. Now she looked over at him, noticing with sympathy the paunch that his Navy pea coat couldn't camouflage. She decided that in Perry's own modest way, he was, indeed, a "brave lad." He had authentically lived his own kind of life in the—sometimes—judgmental, fishbowl existence of a small town, as if he really didn't care what other people thought of him.

"And you, Lorraine?" Mrs. Potter turned toward their shy friend in pink. "What have you brought?"

"My killer potato salad," said Lorraine Forrest with a sweet smile that belied her violent description. "With white mayonnaise and red potatoes."

"Stay put, folks," commanded their chauffeur, Perry, as they pulled into the Marshalls' circular driveway. "I'll come round and help you out."

While he was doing that, Bertie Parsons looked down at the plate of cherry crisp on her lap and said, "I think Evelyn did the meanest thing that anybody's ever done to me." But she didn't tell them what it was, and Perry was there to pull open the doors before any of them could think to ask her.

"We have to give her credit," whispered Marge Thurgood in Mrs. Potter's left ear. "None of us can match Evelyn when it comes to putting on parties."

It was true, Mrs. Potter agreed, that Evelyn Marshall had a wonderful talent for bringing together just the right mix of people to have a good time in elegantly decorated surroundings with great food. Provided, of course, that Evelyn herself didn't do anything to spoil her own effects. As Mrs. Potter looked around the spacious Marshall living room, with its sweeping staircase that ascended to the second-floor living quarters, she recognized most of the faces as belonging to folks she'd known all the way back in grade school. The other faces belonged to their spouses. The party immediately became, for her, a festive reunion with friends she didn't often get to see.

She mixed happily among them, enjoying their company and admiring Evelyn's beautiful Valentine decorations, all gold and red and white. The centerpiece on the long buffet table was a large box decorated just like a schoolchild's Valentine shoe box might be, and there was even a slot in the top of it where all the guests inserted their cards.

"Clever," admitted Lorraine Forrest grudgingly.

The food, as always at a Marshall party, was scrumptious.

"I have a new caterer," the hostess bragged to Mrs. Potter and Perry Bain. Evelyn looked regal in a long red velvet dress and with her expertly dyed black hair piled on top of her head. Beside her, Foster was elegant, and inexpressive, in black trousers and a crimson dinner jacket. He seemed to have trouble remembering names, Mrs. Potter noted sadly as Evelyn was saying, "I imported her all the way from Chicago just for this little party."

"A caterer?" Perry Bain arched his eyebrows at his hostess and grinned. "For a potluck supper? As the younger generation would say, Evelyn, aren't you a little unclear on the concept?"

But their hostess was unfazed. "Perry, dear, you know that potluck suppers never really turn out right; it's just an old wives' tale that they do. Either people bring too many salads and not enough meat, or not enough desserts and too many vegetables. Somebody's got to make it all work out, and that's why I had my caterer provide the baron of beef, and a few other little things." In Evelyn's smile there suddenly appeared an expression that caused Mrs. Potter to feel tense. The hostess's tone turned malicious as she said, "But then you know how it is, don't you, Perry? You have such a knack for these girlish concerns."

"No," he retorted as he pushed his sack of potato chips at her. "I have a *snack* for them." He winked at Mrs. Potter and then walked off, taking his own advice, which was to ignore Evelyn Marshall.

Mrs. Potter, who thought potluck suppers worked out just fine if you let them alone, and who had *never* owed a mortgage to Foster's bank, said, "Evelyn, stop that." She used exactly the firm, gentle tone of voice she might have used with her grandchildren. In their case, she would have added a "please," a hug, and a kiss, which may (she thought) have been what Evelyn had also needed all along. Maybe even more than the spanking. It had long seemed to Mrs. Potter that cruelty was but a confused and perverted way of asking for love.

Her hostess made an amused face at her. "Oh, Genia, always so sensitive. You're *such* a nice person, it's a wonder no man has snapped you up in all these years."

Mrs. Potter only shook her head and smiled, refusing to be baited.

"Lovely party, Evelyn." Turning to her host, she added, "Foster."

Then she followed Perry's wise example, and walked
away.

When time came to distribute the Valentine's Day cards,
Evelyn Marshall announced to her assembled guests, "Foster will do the honors, won't you, dear?"

"No!" whispered Bertie Parsons to Mrs. Potter. "That's
cruel! What if he can't read the names? What if he can't
match the names to the people? How can she *do* this to him!"

Jack Thurgood didn't just murmur in shocked tones, as
the other guests did; instead, he stepped forward and said,
loudly, but with a gracious smile, "Not on your life, Evelyn. Why should Foster have all the fun? I'm the oldest one
here, let me play Cupid." And, without waiting for her
reply, he boldly walked over to the big shoe box, lifted its
lid, and reached in to grab a handful of envelopes.

"Bless you, Jack," Bertie whispered, and Mrs. Potter
nodded, in heartfelt agreement. She observed that Evelyn,
her cruel plan ruined, flounced out of the living room, disappearing through the swinging door that led to the kitchen.
She also noticed that Foster appeared not to have understood the scene that had just transpired, or to realize that
Jack Thurgood had rescued him. With a blank expression
on his face, Foster watched his wife leave the room.

Then Mrs. Potter got caught up with the others in laughing and exclaiming over the cards. Some of them were
store-bought, like hers, but many were quite charmingly
handmade.

The fact that everyone was enjoying themselves so much
made it seem all the more terrible when a scream issued
from the kitchen.

While everyone else turned to stare at the kitchen door,
Mrs. Potter looked over to where Foster Marshall had been
standing. He wasn't there anymore.

Seconds later, Foster came out of the kitchen to an-
nounce . . .

"Evelyn's . . . dead." He spoke haltingly, as if he couldn't think of the right words to use, and his face looked pinched with anxiety. "Somebody . . . stabbed . . . her."

"He's confused," Mrs. Potter thought, even as she re-acted in horror, "and as lost as a child without his mother."

"But all the rest of us were here in the living room, Genia," said Perry Bain in an intense whisper. "Weren't we, Jack? You should know, you were passing out the cards. Was anybody missing?"

They had, a few of them, rushed into the kitchen to see if anything could be done to help Evelyn, and then come back out again, white-faced, to report that she'd been killed with a cooking knife stuck up to its hilt into her back in the re-gion of her heart. "Sitting at her own kitchen table," some-one said in shocked tones, "facing the window, with her back turned to the door."

Now, knowing they mustn't leave, all awaited the arrival of the Harrington police.

"Everybody was here," Jack Thurgood confirmed. "Ex-cept Foster."

The friends looked at one another, appalled at the impli-cation.

"He was here while I handed out the first bunch of cards," Jack told them, "but then I couldn't find him in the room, and I had to save his other cards for him." He pointed to a forlorn little pile of white and red envelopes stacked on the buffet table near the decorated shoe box. It only deepened their shared sense of unhappiness.

Marge Thurgood came up to them and leaned heavily into her husband's side. Jack put his arms around her and held her tight. "I guess he couldn't bear it," Marge said softly.

"Couldn't bear what, honey?" Jack asked her.

She looked up at him. "Being at her mercy. Imagine, growing ever more incapacitated, and knowing that eventu-

ally you would have to depend entirely on the kindness of
Evelyn. I'm sorry, I know it's an awful thing to say, but . . ."

"But that must be why he did it," her husband finished
for her.

"Except that he didn't," Mrs. Potter said.

They all stared at her.

"Well, of course he did, Genia," Perry Bain said in a sad,
kind voice. "I mean, we don't want it to be true, any more
than you do, but we were the only ones in the room, and he
was the only one—besides Evelyn—who was in the kitchen
at the time she was murdered. It had to have been Foster.
Who else could it have been?"

"Well, for one thing," she said crisply, "is it really true
that all of us were here in the living room all of the time?"
She looked at Jack Thurgood. "Jack, do you mean to say
that you always found every single person you were delivering a card to? It seems to me that I remember you didn't,
that sometimes you had to stick a card back in the pile. . . ."

"Yes," Jack said, sounding reluctant, "but only because they'd gone to the rest room, and they came right
back. . . ."

"And who was that?" she pressed.

"I did," Marge volunteered, "but I wasn't gone but a
minute, because Bertie was in the one on this floor and
somebody else was in the one upstairs."

"So that's three people gone, for at least a short while,"
Mrs. Potter pointed out to them. "And who else left the
room, Jack?"

"Genia, I don't know," he said, looking upset. "I can't
possibly remember that!"

"Which means," said Perry Bain grimly, "that any of us
could have been gone for the short time it would have taken
to kill Evelyn."

"Genia," exclaimed Marge, "what are you doing to us?"

"Trying to help Foster, for one thing," Mrs. Potter said
gently, "so that we don't have him accused and convicted
before the police even get here. But I'm also trying to clear

my own mind about what happened. It does seem to me that we have an entire houseful of people who had not only opportunity, but also, unfortunately, plenty of motive."

"Genia, stop this!" said Perry in shocked tones.

She placed her hand on his arm to calm him. "Don't worry, Perry, after considering everyone here, I do think there was really only one person in this house who had the opportunity *and* the motive."

Around her, everyone seemed visibly to relax.

"So it was Foster," murmured Marge Thurgood.

"No," Mrs. Potter corrected her, and then added, with considerable urgency, "Has anybody seen the caterer?"

The police stopped the caterer as she was driving away in her van, without even having stayed long enough to gather all the utensils and food she'd carried into the house.

"I was terrified," she claimed as her reason for leaving.

"And that was probably true," Mrs. Potter said to her friends when they gathered in her parents' living room the next day. "She *was* terrified—that she'd get caught."

Bertie Parsons, the Thurgoods, Perry Bain, and Lorraine Forrest were all there for coffee and conversation—and thick slices of warm walnut raisin bread they were covering with YamBerry butter that Mrs. Potter had concocted out of the little bit of berry mixture she had saved over from her potluck casserole. (Into a stick of softened butter, she had stirred about two tablespoonsful of the cooled berry mix, a tablespoon of good local honey, and enough sliced almonds to add crunch. She'd spooned it into a pretty antique butter bowl, provided her mother's little silver butter knives, and let her guests help themselves to it.)

Now, holding her own slice, half-eaten, Mrs. Potter admitted to her friends, "The only reason I know all this, of course, is that Pete Feldercamp said I earned it, by tipping him off before she got away." Of course, they all recognized Pete's name; he was that nice Feldercamp boy who'd grown up to be chief of police. "If I tell you her name was Sonia Walden, would you recognize it?"

Her friends all shook their heads no.

"What do you mean it *was* Sonia Walden?" asked Perry.

"That was her maiden name . . . when we knew her."

This time, the friends exclaimed in astonishment.

"Knew her? When?"

"What do you mean, we knew her?"

"I don't even remember her from the party!"

"Genia, what are you talking about!"

Mrs. Potter looked around at their dear faces, and knew she had some sad information to give them. Slowly, she put her piece of walnut raisin bread back down on her plate. "Do you all recall, when we were in fourth grade, there was a new little girl that year? She came into our class after Christmas, and she left on Valentine's Day. . . ."

The men still looked puzzled, but Lorraine said softly, "Oh, Genia, her name was Sonia, wasn't it? I'll never forget that terrible Valentine's Day, when we didn't give her any cards. Not a single one. Is that who Sonia Walden is? Oh, my heavens."

One by one, the recollection came to each of them.

It was Perry Bain who put it all together for the rest of them, while Mrs. Potter nodded her agreement. "It was Evelyn who caused it, wasn't it? She told us that we shouldn't give Sonia any cards, because it was against her family's religion. I remember she ran crying from the room, and we all felt terrible, but she never came back, so we could never tell her." He paused, thinking, putting his facts in order. He glanced at Mrs. Potter. "I'm guessing that all these years later, Evelyn happened to encounter Sonia, probably at some catered party in Chicago. And somehow she found out they had lived in the same town, and Evelyn put it together that *this* Sonia was *that* Sonia. . . ."

He trailed off, looking appalled.

Mrs. Potter took up the task for him. "Evelyn hired Sonia with the idea of duplicating that childhood scene. Once again, Sonia would be the outsider. Once again, we would all get Valentines, and she would not. It was Evelyn's idea of a cruel joke, just as it was the first time."

"But," objected Bertie Parsons, "to kill a person over Valentines?"

"I don't believe there's any such thing," Mrs. Potter said in a musing tone of voice, "as an isolated act of cruelty, do you? It's like kindness, don't you think, in that it produces ripples of effects that may go very far out into the future, and which we may never even see? In Sonia's case, the first effect was that her parents took her out of our school. The next ripple, as I understand it, was that they had to put her in a private school, because that was the only alternative, and it was far too expensive for them, and so they moved out of town. I'm afraid the ripples sound like melodrama after that, because I'm told that Sonia's parents never found good jobs again. There was pressure, tension. A nasty divorce. Many, many unfortunate things occurred to the child we barely knew, and it all started with that one cruel trick of Evelyn's."

The friends were intensely quiet, listening.

"Some people," Mrs. Potter said, "have that magic about them that helps them rise above adversity, but Sonia Walden is not one of those people. I gather she has always looked for other people to blame for all of her misfortunes, and last night she found Evelyn, and took it all out on her."

After a moment, Marge said in a shocked voice, "I can't even remember seeing her last night. I don't even remember what she looks like."

It was Bertie who began what happened next: She reached for the hand of Perry, who was seated next to her, and then she placed her other hand in Marge's, and then Perry and Marge grabbed the hand of the person closest to them. Suddenly, the old friends were all holding hands in a circle, affirming the ties that still bound them.

"Once upon a time, I wanted to kill her," Bertie confessed to them. "When we were in high school, I was in love with Foster. I've always suspected that Evelyn told him lies about me, to take him away from me. And now he's free again . . . and I feel so sorry for him."

"We would have let Sonia into our circle," Lorraine whispered.

Marge added, "If we'd only known."

With one accord, the six of them lowered their heads for a moment of silent prayer, for the girl who had wanted to be their friend, and for the one who had never really been anybody's friend.

Then Perry Bain leaned over and planted a kiss on Mrs. Potter's cheek. "Happy Valentine's Day, Genia. From now on, let's be sure to say that to everybody we know; let's not ever leave anybody out again."

Mrs. Potter felt tears on her eyelashes.

"I love you all," she said.

The friends squeezed hands once more while the snow fell outside, lightly covering the town of Harrington, Iowa, and all of the wide fields around it.

Author's note: Many thanks to Marilyn Beech for Yam-Berry Bake.

In Cabot Cove, as in all small towns, it's virtually impossible to keep a secret unless you forget it before you can tell anyone. Here, small-town gossip undoes the plans of a man who only wants what's best for himself, but ends up in over his head, as it were.

Anne Hathaway Slept Here

Marjorie Eccles

BY THE SIMPLE reason of being murdered on Christmas Eve, Mrs. Muriel Endicott managed to cause all concerned as much trouble in death as she had in life.

It appeared very shocking at first, indeed, scarcely possible, that such a terrible thing as murder should actually have happened in a quiet, rather dull little village like Kirby Purefoy—and on Christmas Eve, too—but the victim being Mrs. Endicott went a long way toward removing incredulity. A plastic bag pulled over her head removed any further doubt.

Her body was found at half past ten in the evening, and the police doctor, whose duty only required him to certify the fact of death, did so as expeditiously as possible. Anxious not to spoil his Christmas, he then hurried on to the Carol Service in the village church, which was followed by Midnight Mass. He did, however, out of the goodness of his heart, pray for Mrs. Endicott's soul, an act of Christian charity which would one day earn him rewards in Heaven. He was probably the only one in the village to do so.

The pathologist, meanwhile, had also arrived at the scene of the crime, having reluctantly left his Christmas Eve party to answer the summons to examine the body. Declaring that in his opinion Mrs. Endicott had been dead for about six hours and that she'd suffered a wound to the back of her head before being suffocated by the plastic bag, he pontificated further without adding anything to the already known sum of knowledge about the cause of death and refused to do the postmortem until the day after Boxing Day; his wife, he rightly concluded, would not care to eat her slice of turkey, carved by him, after he had so recently carved up Mrs. Endicott.

The thought of slicing up a turkey also caused a delicate shudder to run down the spine of Mrs. Endicott's only son, Hugo, a plump, petulant, and slightly balding person who dealt in antiques, but the shudder came only from the ghastly notion of such hackneyed Christmas fare. He had a friend staying with him, and had arranged a civilized Christmas Day *dîner à deux* in his luxury flat, with a brace of pheasant, a bottle of Margaux, and some fine ripe Stilton to follow. Since he'd already had his Christmas Eve interrupted by the arrival of the police, and by having had to identify the body, he saw no reason to postpone any further arrangements. His mother was, after all, in no position to object, and wouldn't have been eating with him, anyway. Hugo had not been fond of his mother, nor she of him.

She'd been about to enter her front door when she was attacked. A window at the back had been forced open, and it was thought she had surprised a burglar, causing him to panic. The door was unlocked and the key still clutched in her hand. Her Christmas dinner—a small chicken and a prepacked individual pudding—plus a few other groceries were scattered over the path, and the Sainsbury's plastic bag which had contained them was drawn tight over her head.

She was found by two venturesome young carol-singers, who'd been dared by the rest of the group to sing at old Ma

Endicott's cottage. They'd have been better off not bothering, Hugo considered. They must have known there'd be no invitation inside to partake of mince pies, and that they'd be lucky if they came away with a five pence piece, let alone without having the door slammed in their faces.

The cottage was near the center of the village, with only a narrow strip of garden and a picket fence at the front to separate it from the road, a space no more than three or four feet wide, which Mrs. Endicott had kept filled with old pots that spilled over with cottage garden flowers in the summer, and ivies, ornamental cabbages, and universal pansies in the winter. It was of Elizabethan vintage, low and white, with an old pantiled roof and windows with tiny square panes. Roses and clematis bloomed round the door, and it was much admired by the visitors who came to buy the plants she propagated and sold in the large garden at the back, undercutting the family-owned nursery garden on the main road by 20 percent. The back garden had been small, too, when she and Hugo had first come to the cottage, but Mrs. Endicott was always prudent, and in order to extend her acreage, she'd purchased the field behind from the farmer who owned it, getting it at a bargain price because he'd been going through a bad patch at the time.

When she discovered the interest paid to the cottage by the customers was nearly as great as that in buying the plants, Mrs. Endicott had begun to serve English Cream Teas at small tables set on the flagstones at the back of the house if the weather was clement, and indoors if not. Miss Pilgrim, who ran the Tudor Café, hadn't been pleased about this, but it proved to be a more lucrative and dependable source of income than that gained from selling plants, which tended to be unreliable in regard to damping-off, greenfly, and all manner of other annoying plant ailments. It led on to her offering bed-and-breakfast accommodations, which were very popular with visitors who preferred home comforts to the damp beds and leathery bacon and eggs which the Dusty Miller offered.

And after all, who could resist the appeal of staying in a cottage where Anne Hathaway had once slept?

Mrs. Endicott had, shortly after acquiring it, renamed her cottage. Instead of being 5, Church Road, it was now Hathaways. Gullible visitors were intrigued by this—those who believed what they wanted to believe, and who were delighted to learn that Anne Hathaway had indeed briefly stayed there, before her marriage to William Shakespeare.

"Why do you tell such lies? There's no evidence she ever came near the place!" Hugo demanded pettishly of his mother.

"She might have. It's only a bus ride from Stratford-upon-Avon."

"They didn't have buses in the sixteenth century, for God's sake!"

"They had good strong legs. Twelve miles there and twelve back; they thought nothing of it. And there were Hathaways in the next village at one time—that's a provable fact. They may have been related. Besides, there's the letter, isn't there?"

Yes, Hugo was forced to agree, there was the letter. But, not wanting to pursue this subject, he added, "You'll be telling them next that the four-poster in the back bedroom is Shakespeare's second-best bed!"

"Now there's an idea—why didn't I think of that?" Mrs. Endicott looked thoughtful. "He did will that to his wife, didn't he?"

"Leave me out of it this time!" Hugo warned. "That letter's bad enough. It'll get you into trouble one day."

"Oh, rubbish! I've never actually claimed it was genuine. People put their own interpretations on it. Now, about that bed . . ."

But, meeting his glance, she understood what he meant, and gave in. They had been blackmailing each other in this sort of way for years. It was how he'd got his antique shop started.

His mother was, if not exactly rich, worth a bob or two by now. She'd always had an eye to the main chance, which was why she'd married his father. Unfortunately, Basil Endicott, a minor civil servant of some promise, had disappointed her by inconsiderately dying before his promise could be fulfilled. And even more inconsiderately, by not leaving any money, so that the Building Society very soon foreclosed on the mortgage of their house.

In order to provide a home for herself and fifteen-year-old Hugo, she had been forced to take a position as housekeeper to a Mrs. Neasden, the bedridden old woman who owned and lived in what was to become Hathaways with her sour-faced, resentful daughter, Vera. A necessity which had, in the end, proved to be a blessing in disguise. The old lady had taken a fancy to Muriel Endicott, who knew on which side her bread was buttered and acted accordingly. Unlike Vera Neasden, she let it be seen that she didn't mind how menial or how distasteful were the tasks she had to perform. When Vera took the huff about the favoritism her mother showed to the newcomer, and to having a clumsy, disagreeable adolescent about the place, and upped and left, old Mrs. Neasden quickly came to see that her housekeeper would be a more worthy beneficiary under her will. She died soon after altering it, leaving Mrs. Endicott everything she possessed. It wasn't a fortune, just the cottage and a small sum of money, but it had marked the start of Mrs. Endicott's upward mobility.

It was almost immediately afterward that she'd seen the possibilities of the Hathaway letter.

Her only regret about her bed-and-breakfast trade was that she could offer but one set of accommodations at a time, even though the cottage, like the garden, had been extended. It was originally three small laborers' cottages, but over the years a wall or two had been knocked down here and there, a staircase removed, fireplaces opened up, doors stripped of their 1950s hardboard flushing and a damp course installed, so that now it was charmingly unexpected:

low-ceilinged, dark-beamed, with cozy alcoves and floors at different levels to trip the unwary.

The "letter" was a scrap of tattered paper which had appeared during the demolition of a wall behind which was a tiny room, formerly used as a cold store in the days before refrigerators and freezers. Opening up the room considerably enlarged the living area, but the storeroom having originally been built out into the rising ground at the back of the cottages, it was cold and dank as the grave and gave off a peculiar smell. Hugo and his mother stuck it out for a while, but the wall was eventually reinstated and the door bricked up.

The torn piece of paper was stained with mold and covered in crabbed, faded handwriting with long s's, the lines sloping upward across the pages. The barely legible signature might, by an adroit exercise of the imagination, be construed as "Anne Hathaway." How it had remained intact for four hundred years, considering the damp state of the room where it was found, was not a question visitors were encouraged to ask, but if they did, Mrs. Endicott was ready to explain its state of preservation as being due to the drafts which whistled through the cavity wall and had presumably preserved it, like a mummy. It had been framed, and now hung in the place of honor over the fireplace of the room set aside for serving tea, scones, and homemade jam at four round oak tables.

Despite other grave faults, the late Mrs. Endicott had been a woman of taste. She had a flair for reproducing the right atmosphere without allowing it to become twee. A comfortable casualness and mixing of periods was apparent in the furnishings, yet they blended happily together against cream-plastered walls and the vibrantly patterned old rugs spread over the polished, original stone floors, her collection of old English porcelain adding distinction to the decor.

The collection had begun modestly with a couple of Derby figures and a few Coalport plates, but had grown enormously over the years and was now worth a tidy sum. She had an eye for a genuine piece. It was about this that she and Hugo had quarreled violently on the morning of her death.

Much of her prosperity, he'd have been the first to admit, was due to hard work and determination. She could turn her hand to anything, and frequently did. She wasn't, however, at all fussy about how she achieved her success—and she was lucky. Only a few weeks ago, at a Sunday morning car-boot sale in the car park of the Dusty Miller, she'd picked up an old Chelsea figurine; the rumor soon spread that it was worth a sum that would have had Sotheby's swooning—much to the chagrin of the Cartwright family, from whom she'd bought it for a few pounds. But they were an ignorant and feckless lot, one of their number always in trouble of one sort or another. They'd have sold off their grandmother if she hadn't died the week before, leaving them with nothing but a load of old junk even they wouldn't give house room to. They wouldn't have recognized a Chelsea piece if it had jumped up and bitten them. Mrs. Endicott had got it for less than a song.

Hugo had no objection to that. It was fair game. But he believed that such an extremely valuable piece of porcelain would be far better off being offered for sale in his shop than being kept on a shelf in the dark recesses of the cottage, where it might, God forbid, get knocked off by that dozy Sharon Simmonds.

Young Sharon, the desperate end of Mrs. Endicott's long line of disgruntled cleaning women, was hovering in the kitchen, languidly polishing silver, when she overheard this. Bridling indignantly, she made it her business to overhear almost every word of the following heated exchange, and what she couldn't manage to catch, she interpreted. Apart from anything else, Hugo had argued, his mother's china collection was beginning to go over the top. How could one fully appreciate fine pieces amongst all this clutter?

"Clutter?" Mrs. Endicott had repeated dangerously, and they had gone on from there, Hugo to remind his mother of what he knew of her past, if unspecified, activities, and she to remind him, in her turn, of equally unspecified things he would rather forget. It had ended by Mrs. Endicott informing Hugo that she was going to make an appointment to see her solicitor after Christmas to change her will.

Well! thought Sharon, whose boyfriend was Kevin, the middle Cartwright boy. Her mind boggled at what Hugo said the Chelsea figurine would fetch.

Speculation was rife in the Dusty on Christmas morning when the news of Mrs. Endicott's untimely demise had become public.

In charge of the investigations was a young woman detective inspector named Mary Treadwell, highly ambitious and unmarried, with no responsibilities other than presents to buy at Christmas. She had been going to spend Christmas Day with her family: her parents, two sisters and their husbands, plus five rambunctious children under five. She was quite willing to forgo these pleasures in the interests of her career.

Though it would soon become apparent to everyone who she was, Mary preferred for the moment to retain her anonymity. Women drinking on their own were likely to be looked on with suspicion in the Dusty at any time, but especially on Christmas morning, when they should have been at home stuffing the turkey, cleaning the sprouts, coping with overexcited children, and putting the plum pudding on to steam. So she had with her a young police constable in plainclothes, a Scotsman who had volunteered for Christmas duty because his own holiday celebrations were centered around New Year rather than Christmas. An easygoing type who knew he'd only been roped in as cover, he was content to drink his pint and leave the detecting to her.

The season of peace and goodwill didn't extend to being charitable about the late Mrs. Endicott, Mary soon discovered, listening quietly in her corner. Though not overtly expressed, the general consensus of opinion appeared to be that she'd had it coming to her one way or another.

"It'll be that Hugo that has it coming to him now," remarked someone. "All that lovely, lovely money," he mimicked, dropping a limp wrist.

Sniggers all round accompanied this jest. In the macho ambience of the Dusty, antique dealers were apt to be thought quite likely to varnish their toenails.

"What about Vera Neasden, then? She'll be sick as a parrot to hear that. Wheresoever she may be."

"Serves her right. Should've been nicer to her old mum in the first place."

"Oh, I don't know. The old 'un led her a right old dance, I reckon."

"Two for a pair, then. Vera weren't above proof. Funny old business, that, though, her going off so sudden after sticking it out all them years."

"Who d'you think's done in the old witch, then?" asked the landlord, and the ensuing conversation became very interesting to Mary Treadwell. By the time she left, she'd added further names to Hugo's on the list of suspects: the Cartwrights, simmering under a sense of injustice about the figurine Mrs. Endicott had swindled out of them . . . the belligerent son of the outwitted nursery garden owners . . . Miss Pilgrim, who'd been forced to reduce the price of her afternoon teas, although her scones were *much* lighter than Mrs. Endicott's. Not to mention Trowbridge the farmer, who considered she'd pulled a fast one on him over the sale of the field, and swore, moreover, that she'd thrown fresh yew clippings over the hedge and poisoned his cows; if the cows were daft enough not to know what they could eat, that was nothing to do with her, Mrs. Endicott had retorted, but Trowbridge hadn't forgiven her. And she hadn't exactly been a favorite with the landlord of the Dusty, either, putting it about that his beds were damp.

Hugo met Mary Treadwell for a second time, this time at the cottage on Boxing Day at her request. He didn't care for women police, or women at all for that matter, and this one he sensed was sharp and intuitive. He repeated his previous statement to her. Sharon had exaggerated the extent of his quarrel with his mother, whom he certainly hadn't seen again after that visit to her on Christmas Eve morning. Then, unable to stand it any longer, he made a beeline for the back recesses of the cottage and the shelf where the figurine had stood. He gave a yelp. He cried in anguish, "The Chelsea piece—it's gone!"

"What Chelsea is this?" Mary asked. "Tell me about it."

He launched into a precise and loving description. According to Hugo, it had been an exceedingly fine and rare composition, a pair of rustic figures on one simple base, a shepherd and shepherdess. Tears came into his eyes at the thought of it. Perfect in every respect—of superb quality, from the much-desired Red Anchor period, with rich, bright colors that blended perfectly with the soft-paste glaze. Worth—oh, my God, Hugo couldn't bear to think about it!

There were other things missing, too, he added, looking round, bits and bobs, a few small pieces of silver . . .

"Is that so? Perhaps you'd give us a list," she said casually over her shoulder, as though the framed Hathaway letter which she was facing and reading was of more importance. She turned round, smiling slightly. "Where did you come across this?"

Hugo swung into the usual glib explanations about finding the letter when they'd had the mistaken idea of taking down the wall, while she moved interestedly round the cottage interior, coming to a halt by the rebuilt wall as the flow of words finally faltered to a stop.

"Well, I daresay that'll do for the tourists, but I don't believe a word of it," she said cheerfully.

"Oh," said Hugo.

"You don't really expect people to swallow that, do you?" she said, though plenty of people had. "Cavity walls, for one thing—in a house this age?" she went on, laying her hand against the wall in question. "Hardly likely, I'd have thought. Nice piece of fakery, though, that letter. Your own work?"

"It wasn't difficult," Hugo declaimed modestly, after a small silence. But he was beginning to sweat, even though the forgery was harmless, nothing actually illegal, as his mother had repeated often enough.

The policewoman had bright blue eyes which regarded him with interest. She removed her hand from the wall, rubbing it fastidiously. "Feels clammy. No wonder you bricked up the room behind again."

Oh God, this was it. Despite her apparent casualness, he was suddenly, absolutely, convinced that she knew. Somehow, she'd sussed it out. The police never took anything on face value—she must have been listening to gossip in the village. . . . His glance slid hopelessly away, and her eyes sharpened.

Hugo wasn't a clever man. Astute, like his mother, when there was money to be made, but not very intelligent in the long term. But it was apparent even to him, that retribution, the thing he'd dreaded for twenty-five years, was snapping at his heels. He should have told the truth in the first place, never mind his mother's advice. Well, it was too late now for those sort of regrets, and his mind began to see other ways out.

Dimly, he reasoned that if the police saw he was being honest with them over this, however belatedly, it would go better for him in the matter of his mother's murder. Better to confess than to let them find out.

Because they surely would find out. He knew with terrible certainty that this woman inspector had put two and two together and that they would dig under the flags of the room behind the wall, and that when they did, they'd find the bones of Vera Neasden.

He hadn't meant to kill her. He'd only been fifteen. She'd been sniping at him and he'd pushed past her, a big clumsy youth who didn't know his own strength. And she'd fallen and hit her head against the ironbound corner of the oak chest. . . . The words tumbled out as he explained; years of pent-up guilt fell away. "It was an accident," he said, "an accident."

Mary Treadwell had sat down abruptly on the nearest chair as he began, and thereafter listened in silence.

It had been his mother who'd said they must hide Vera in a cupboard at first, until they could think what do to with her, telling him that the police would never in a million years believe it had been an accident. Hugo would have done anything she said, he'd been so terrified. Then she'd come up with the idea of burying the body under the flagstones of the cold-store room, of pulling down the wall to give more credence to what they were doing if anyone should inquire, and at the same time gaining themselves a little more much-needed living space. When the old lady asked what all the noise was downstairs, his mother had replied, "Spring cleaning. I'm afraid Vera wasn't always as meticulous as she should have been."

"It seems there were a lot of things Vera wasn't. One of them was grateful," said the old lady sharply, fingering the note her daughter had left behind, the note which, at his mother's command, Hugo had forged in Vera's handwriting. He'd always had the knack of being able to copy anything, had carried on a brisk trade at school in forged sick notes, dodgy bus passes, pop concert tickets, anything really. It was a facility that had come in very useful later, too, when he began to deal in antiques, in faking documents of provenance and the like. But his success in fooling old Mrs. Neasden had unfortunately given his mother the idea for "finding" the Hathaway letter.

He'd always known that little piece of unnecessary deception would land them in trouble one day.

Unfairly, his mother, the instigator of it all, was beyond punishment now. Despite the fact that it was she who'd forbidden him to go to the police when Vera died, had told him what to do and helped him to bury her. Despite the pillow she'd held over the face of Mrs. Neasden as soon as decently possible after she'd changed her will.

When the policewoman had questioned Hugo carefully over every detail, she was silent for a while, then asked him to accompany her to the station to make an official statement. "Before we go, I must tell you that we're questioning Kevin Cartwright in connection with the murder of your mother. He left his fingerprints all over the place, and he's also confessed to breaking in."

Hugo reeled. What had he done? Had he delivered himself into her hands—confessed to a crime when there was no need to have done so? With no guarantee that his claim that it had been an accident would be believed, either. He felt ill. His asthma was coming back.

"The Cartwrights started celebrating Christmas early and Kevin was drunk enough to think he could get the Chelsea figurine back," the inspector was continuing. "He got in through the back window but couldn't find what he'd come for. While he was searching for it, he heard your mother's key in the lock and rushed out, knocking her over. He thought she was only stunned, but he wasn't sure. . . ."

"So he put the plastic bag over her head to make certain she wouldn't recover and name him," Hugo intervened quickly.

"Not quite. He couldn't find what he came for because it had already gone, hadn't it? You came back after your quarrel with your mother, knowing she'd be out doing her Christmas shopping, broke in at the back, and lifted the figurine, together with more bits and pieces to make it look like a genuine robbery. . . ."

Hugo's breathing became noisy.

"Then you heard Kevin getting in, kept out of sight while he began to search—until he heard your mother's key in the lock, in fact, and rushed out. You followed him but by the time you reached the door, he'd gone and you found your mother lying there, unconscious. It was you who suffocated her with the plastic bag."

He hadn't, after all, fooled her for one minute by that clever piece of playacting over the disappearance of the Chelsea piece. He didn't bother to ask her how she knew it had happened exactly as she said. Had it been anyone else, he'd have accused her of making wild and unfounded guesses, but you never knew with women. They had mysterious powers beyond his ken. Her instincts had probably told her, though he had to admit it was probable that she had some sort of proof—his prints on the plastic bag, he supposed dully; he'd been in too much of a hurry to think about that. It didn't matter. All that really mattered was that he was in for it, one way or another.

Hugo was crushed. Women had bedeviled him all his life. He'd never been able to follow the labyrinthine twists and turns of their minds, to understand in any way what they might be thinking. But now, he knew exactly how Anne Hathaway must have felt when she discovered she'd been left only her husband's second-best bed.

He'd risked everything for a piece of porcelain. Furious at his mother's threat to cut him out of her will, he'd returned to the cottage and taken the figurine, together with other trifles to add verisimilitude to the idea of a burglary, reckoning on certain outlets he knew of where he could later secretly sell the porcelain.

He should have known better. Even dead, his mother had followed him and exacted her revenge. As he'd fumbled for his door key, the piece of porcelain had slipped through his sweaty palms onto the expensive, imported Etruscan tiles in the entrance hall to his flat and smashed into a thousand pieces, utterly beyond repair.

"Shall we go?" asked Mary Treadwell.

A jigsaw puzzle and a murder have several obvious things in common. Each has many parts that must be pieced together to form a complete picture. But where one may have all the parts in a jigsaw, that isn't always the case when solving a murder. The detective in our next story does a fine job of putting the pieces together for both.

Framed

Sally Gunning

EDDIE BREWSTER SIGHED happily as he carried the puzzle box out to the sun porch. It was Sunday at two o'clock, and this is what he did on Sundays at two—he made a puzzle on the sun porch. Mondays through Fridays, for twenty-three years straight if you didn't count the two weeks off at Christmas, Eddie worked for the telephone company, handling new accounts. And on Saturdays Eddie mowed his lawn, trimmed his hedge, washed his car, and made any minor repairs that were necessary for the proper maintenance of his home. Sunday mornings Eddie read the newspaper front to back, including the classifieds. Then he clipped his toenails, trimmed any unsightly hairs, and lined up his clothes for the week ahead.

But every Sunday at two o'clock Eddie Brewster made a puzzle. He didn't always make the same puzzle, of course, but today he was making his favorite—*Visit to Grand-mother.*

Eddie set the box down on the table in the sun and checked
to make sure the glass panels on the porch were tightly
closed. It was September, and Eddie had a mild ragweed al-
lergy. It was important that the glass panels were closed
tightly in September. Next Eddie went to the refrigerator
for his glass of cranberry juice. He always had a glass of
cranberry juice Sundays at two. The cranberry juice filled
two of his body's daily requirements—it was full of vita-
min C, and it was one of the eight glasses of clear fluid a
day necessary for proper flushing of the kidneys. At first
Eddie had been unsure if cranberry juice counted as a clear
fluid, but he had checked with Dr. Snow, and Dr. Snow had
assured him that cranberry juice was clear. At four Eddie
would have a Pete's Wicked Ale, and although a case could
be made for the clarity of the ale, Dr. Snow said Eddie
shouldn't count the Pete's as one of his clear fluids because
of the alcohol. Once in a while Eddie was tempted to have
two Pete's Wicked Ales, but he never did. He knew if he
ever opened that second bottle it would only be a matter of
time before he found himself opening a third, maybe even a
fourth. No, one Pete's Wicked Ale at four o'clock on Sunday. That was Eddie's rule.

Eddie returned to the sun porch with his cranberry juice
and set it down to the left of the puzzle box. Eddie was
right-handed; that's why the cranberry juice had to go on
the left—right hand for the puzzle, left hand for the juice.
But Eddie didn't pick up the juice right away. First he
opened *Visit to Grandmother,* using two hands. *Visit to
Grandmother* was one of Eddie's oldest puzzles, and
maybe that's why it was his favorite. The pieces were
thicker than they made them today, and they had that rich,
waxy feel. Eddie never upended the *Visit to Grandmother*
box over the table the way some people did. He removed
each piece by hand, and that way the corners stayed sharp,
the cardboard unfrayed. He set the pieces on the table,
straight-edge pieces on the right, center pieces on the left.
Eddie always did the edges first; it was important to con-

struct the frame within which he could work. When he'd
emptied the box completely he put the bottom of the box
inside the top, set it on the floor under the table, and got
down to business.

Eddie had completed the edges, the dark interior of the
grandmother's room, and had just begun the little girl's
brown boots when he heard Gert's heels click across the
kitchen and stop in the sun porch doorway.

"All right, Eddie, I'm going."

Lately Eddie's wife had taken to visiting her sister every
Sunday afternoon. Eddie started to look up but checked
himself—he'd just found the corner to the basket of flowers
the little girl was bringing to her grandmother. The basket
of flowers was his favorite part.

The heels clicked closer. "Ah," said Gert. *"Visit to
Grandmother.* It must be the third Sunday of the month."

"Yes," said Eddie. He only allowed himself to do *Visit to
Grandmother* on the third Sunday of the month, in part because he didn't want the puzzle to wear out and in part because he knew if he allowed himself to do it more often he
wouldn't enjoy it as much.

"Good-bye," said Gert.

"Good-bye," said Eddie. He spied another piece of basket, slid it into place, and sighed happily.

"Oh, for God's sake," said Gert, and suddenly Eddie felt
his chin grasped in a vice and his head twisted uncomfort-
ably sideways. *What on earth?*

"Look at me," said Gert. "I want to see it register. I'm
going."

Eddie blinked. "Of course you're going, Gert. Have a
nice time. Say hello to your sister."

As quickly as Gert had grabbed his chin, she dropped it.
"Yes," she said. "Good-bye then."

Still she lingered. Eddie could feel her there, watching
him fit the first white rose into the basket. He loved the
white roses—the old-fashioned, creamy color was in perfect keeping with the mood of the picture.

Then Gert was gone.

Eddie worked on, content in the September sun, until the little girl's last golden lock was in place. Then he began on the grandmother. In the early days, Eddie had often confused the cream lace of the grandmother's shawl with the cream white of the roses, but not anymore. He was already up to the grandmother's matching lace cap when the phone rang.

Eddie considered not answering it. The lace cap was an engaging piece. But in the end he slid back his chair, careful not to jog the leg of the table and disarrange his puzzle. He went into the living room and picked up the phone. "Hello."

There was nothing on the other end but dead air.

"Hello? Hello?"

Nothing. Eddie hung up and looked at the clock. 3:08. Not yet time for his Pete's Wicked Ale. He would have liked to synchronize his trip to the phone with the trip to the refrigerator, but sometimes things just didn't work out.

Eddie returned empty-handed to the sun porch and his puzzle and worked away diligently until he heard the knock on the door. This time he didn't mind being interrupted so much—he had reached the doorway in the upper-right-hand corner of the puzzle, and the doorway was one of the least interesting parts. He pushed back his chair for the second time and went to the kitchen door. He pulled back the gauze curtain and saw a white slab of a face and thinning blond hair. It was his neighbor, Abel Coates, a sergeant on the local police force. Eddie's forehead creased in puzzlement. It was unlike Abel to stop by this way.

Eddie opened the door. "Hello, Abel. Come in?" He phrased it like a question. It was, after all, Sunday afternoon, and *Visit to Grandmother* was waiting. But Abel Coates shouldered his stocky body through the door, and as he passed Eddie he reached out and gripped his shoulder. Eddie couldn't recall Abel ever touching him before. Eddie didn't care to be touched. He drew back, and Abel's hand slid off his shoulder and fell to his side. Only then did Eddie notice the long, lumpy canvas parcel in Abel's other hand.

"Would you like—" Eddie looked at the clock. Still too early for a Pete's. He supposed he could offer his guest a Pete's while he continued with his cranberry juice, or perhaps he should offer his guest a cranberry juice. But before Eddie had finished debating the alternatives, Abel spoke for the first time.

"This isn't a social call, Eddie. I'm afraid I've got bad news."

"Bad news?"

"It's your wife, Eddie."

Eddie blinked. "Gert? Something's wrong with Gert?"

"Yes," said Abel. "I'm afraid she's dead, Eddie."

Eddie took a second step back. Dead? Gert? Dead? Eddie supposed it was somewhat curious that his very next thought was of *Visit to Grandmother*. The grandmother was old. What if the poor little girl with the roses had arrived to find her dead? But Abel wasn't talking about the grandmother, he was talking about Gert, and Gert wasn't old. Fifty-four last March. Clearly, this was all a mistake.

"No," said Eddie. "Not Gert. I'm sure you don't mean Gert."

But Abel Coates only nodded once, watching Eddie with cloudy blue eyes. "Here. Sit down." He waved Eddie toward the kitchen table, pulling out a ladder-backed chair, but it was Gert's chair he pulled out. He had no way of knowing that, of course, that the chair he pulled out was Gert's, so Eddie sat down in it. He'd never sat in Gert's chair before, and it made him uncomfortable, but still, it felt good to sit. Abel dropped into the chair around the corner to Eddie's right, the chair that belonged to no one. But Eddie felt a table never looked quite right unless it had four chairs.

"I'm real sorry, Eddie. When I got the call I came straight here as soon as I could."

"I don't understand," said Eddie. "She was visiting her sister. What could have happened at her sister's?"

Abel leaned across the table. "She was stabbed, Eddie. Stabbed to death."

Stabbed? *Stabbed?* The word had no place in this kitchen. In this house. Imagine a word like *stabbed* in *Visit to Grandmother,* Eddie thought. "I don't understand," he said again. "How could Gert possibly have been stabbed?"

"With this," said Abel. He laid the piece of canvas on the table and unwrapped it. "Recognize it, Eddie?"

Yes, Eddie recognized it. It was a fishing knife. Eddie's fishing knife, the long filleting knife he got out each spring once the stripers arrived. But no, this wasn't his knife. This knife had rust on the blade, and Eddie was very careful to clean and dry his knife each time he put it away. "It isn't my knife," said Eddie. "My knife is out there." He pointed to the alcove next to the kitchen door where he kept his fishing gear.

"Show me your knife, Eddie," said Abel.

Eddie got up and went to the shelf where he kept his fishing tackle. Everything was in neat rows, the knife always placed between the pliers and the wirecutters he occasionally used for removing hooks. "That's funny. The knife isn't here."

"No," said Abel from behind him. "Did you think it would be, really?"

Eddie returned to the kitchen and looked again at the knife lying in its bed of canvas. Now, only now, did he see that what was on the blade wasn't rust, but blood. Dried blood. Gert's blood? Eddie fell into the kitchen chair. His eyes began to smart, and he blinked rapidly. "Where . . . where . . . ?"

Abel slid into the chair to Eddie's right. "Where what, Eddie? Where was your knife? You know where it was, don't you, Eddie?"

"I don't. I don't know anything. I don't understand any of this."

Abel reached out and patted Eddie's hand. "It's okay, Eddie. *I* understand. And do you know what else? Everybody will understand. That's why I came here first, Eddie, alone. To talk to you. To help you. You just tell me exactly what happened. I promise you, they'll understand."

"I don't know what happened. I told you, I don't understand any of this. Gert is at her sister's."

"No, Eddie. Gert isn't at her sister's. Gert is lying dead in room 12 of the Merrydale Motel."

"The Merrydale?" Eddie knew the Merrydale. It was just down the road, off the highway at exit 6. Or was it exit 7? But what did that matter? Gert couldn't possibly have been in the Merrydale.

But here was Abel Coates, Eddie's neighbor, a police officer, come to tell him he'd found Gert dead in the Merrydale Motel. Abel Coates wouldn't come here to lie. So it had to be a mistake. That was it. A mistake.

"There must be some mistake," said Eddie. "We're speaking of my wife, Gertrude Brewster. She's five feet four inches tall. She's approximately twelve pounds over her ideal weight. Her hair appears blonde although in actual fact it's nearly sixty percent white. She—"

Abel leaned forward in his chair. "I know what she looks like, Eddie. I've watched her drive in and out for nearly fourteen years. And I've just come from a good close look at her at the Merrydale. Listen to what I'm telling you, Eddie. Everyone will understand. No one will blame you. You just tell me what happened. When did you find out about the other man?"

"What other man?"

"The man she'd been meeting at the Merrydale every Sunday since early August. At least that's what the manager says. Big, red-haired guy, in a pickup with New Hampshire plates. Until today, of course. He didn't show up today. But you know who showed up today."

"No," said Eddie. "I don't."

Abel leaned closer. "Come on, Eddie. They saw you. The manager saw you. He saw your gray Ford Tempo. He saw a license plate ending in STE. That's your plate, isn't it, Eddie? 620 STE? But he couldn't see the guy too well— he was wearing a black rubber raincoat with a hood. *Your* black rubber raincoat, Eddie. So tell me. When did you first find out? Was this your first trip to the motel, or had you tracked her there before, one of those other Sundays in August?"

Eddie didn't speak. He couldn't seem to think straight. Gert at the Merrydale, every Sunday since early August. Something wasn't right.

"Okay, Eddie. Let's start like this. I'll tell you what I think happened, okay? I think today was your first trip to the Merrydale. The manager says today was different than the usual Sunday. This time Gert had luggage. Three suitcases, in fact. She told you she was leaving you, didn't she, Eddie?"

Gert, leaving him? "No," said Eddie. "She was visiting. Visiting her grandmother. I mean her sister."

Abel leaned back in his chair. He leaned so far back that Eddie could see the quivering flesh of his belly where it strained against his shirt. "Oh, Eddie," said Abel. "I can't help you if you don't help me. It'll be so much better if you tell me yourself. Of course, I'll have to take you in, anyway, Eddie, you know that, don't you? And they'll find your prints all over that knife."

"Of course you'll find my prints. It's my knife."

"Ah." Abel shot up straight in his chair and smiled. "Good, Eddie. Good. Now we're getting somewhere. You admit it's your knife. Now why don't you tell me when you first found out about your wife's affair."

"I didn't," said Eddie. "She wasn't."

"When did you find out she was leaving you, Eddie? Was it today? Did she come up to you with her bags all packed and say good-bye?"

"No," said Eddie. "She had no bags. She was going to visit her sister." But suddenly Eddie remembered that uncharacteristic, vicelike grip on his chin, her insistence that he register her going. Is that what she had meant? That she was going for good? No. *No.* Eddie pushed himself unsteadily to his feet and left the room. He went first to the bedroom and threw open the doors.

The suitcases, usually neatly stacked on the top shelf, were gone.

Eddie turned slowly and opened Gert's drawers, one after the other, but one would have sufficed. The drawers were nearly empty, and what was left in them was old and worn.

So she *had* left him. In the middle of *Visit to Grandmother.*

Eddie walked slowly back to the kitchen and sat down in his chair. What could possibly have gone wrong? He'd provided for her, hadn't he? Her own house, her own car, clothes on her back, food on her table. He'd been reliable, never lied, never cheated, and except for the one Pete's Wicked Ale Sundays at four o'clock, he rarely drank. What had happened? He couldn't think.

Abel Coates sat at the kitchen table, watching Eddie, those cloudy eyes full of sorrow. Eddie's sorrow. "So tell me about it, Eddie," he said. "It will be easier once you let it all out. I'll be with you every step of the way, I promise you. I'll help you, but you have to help me. You have to tell me the truth. Did you follow her to the motel? Have it out with her? Demand to know who the other guy was?"

"I didn't go anywhere," said Eddie. "I was here, alone, making a puzzle. *Visit to Grandmother.*"

"Ah," said Abel, smiling. "Third Sunday of the month." Then he slapped his open palm on the kitchen table.

Eddie jumped.

"Listen to me, Eddie. Time is running out. The rest of the crew is just finishing up at the Merrydale as we speak. They'll be here any minute. Grandmother can't talk.

You've got no alibi. You've got one chance, and that's to tell me what happened of your own free will. Turn yourself in. Can't you see that? It served her right, Eddie. Everyone will see why you did what you did. There's nothing to be ashamed of. Tell me what you did."

"I don't know," said Eddie. "I can't think. I don't understand any of it."

"What's not to understand? It's the same old story, isn't it? A woman gets bored, she starts looking for a little romance—"

Romance? What was he talking about, romance? Didn't Eddie send Gert a half-dozen white roses every single solitary birthday? Didn't he, every week, log into his budget book twelve dollars and fifty cents for take-out fish and chips on Thursday?

But now there would be no more roses. There would be no more fish and chips. The room began to swim.

But Abel was still talking. "So she went looking for a few thrills. She ran into some regular Joe, out for a few laughs, and then what? Did she decide to play it for keeps? Packed up her bags—"

"No," said Eddie. "It makes no sense."

"Sure it does, Eddie. Sure it does. She packed up her bags and went to the Merrydale, expecting to meet her Joe. But Joe never showed up. Someone else did, though. Someone in a gray Ford Tempo with a license plate ending in STE. Someone who'd disguised himself in a raincoat on a nice sunny day like this." Abel leaned forward. "There's blood on the steering wheel of your Tempo, Eddie. And on your black rubber raincoat in the backseat. You followed her to the Merrydale and you killed her with your fishing knife. They have the knife, and they have the car, and they have the witness. They even have the motive. Not that they need it, but it always makes it nice. She cheated on you. She was scum. You wanted her dead. I don't blame you, Eddie. Neither will a jury."

Still Eddie didn't speak. He hadn't killed Gert. He'd been here making *Visit to Grandmother,* thinking about the little girl and how nice she was to bring the old woman roses. White roses. The white roses were so unusual. That was what Eddie liked best about *Visit to Grandmother*—the white roses.

But when Gert had come to say good-bye she had gripped his face and twisted it to make sure it registered. She'd never done anything like that in her life. And her bags, and clothes. Oh, Abel was right about that: Gert had planned to leave him. So maybe he was right about the rest? Was it possible? *Had* Gert told him she was leaving him for another man? Had Eddie gone into some kind of a trance, staring at his beloved puzzle? Had he followed her in his gray Ford Tempo with the 620 STE plate, had he put on his raincoat, killed her with his knife, come back here, sat down in front of *Visit to Grandmother,* and gone back into his trance?

Eddie looked at the clock. Almost four. It was possible. It was more than possible. A lot of time had gone by, a lot more time than he could reasonably account for. It was almost four, and Eddie couldn't remember anything since the phone call at 3:08. Maybe Gert had called him. Maybe that was it. She'd told him where she was, and that she was leaving him, and Eddie had gone temporarily out of his mind, blocking out the voice on the phone and everything that happened after that.

Something seemed to be squeezing at Eddie's chest, constricting his lungs, interfering with the natural rhythm of his heart. He looked at Abel. "What time was she killed?"

"Why don't you tell *me,* Eddie? But okay, we can play it like that if you want. Piecing together what the manager saw and heard and what we found at the scene, we can say with some certainty that you killed Gert sometime between three and three-thirty."

So that was it. He'd gotten the phone call, driven to the Merrydale, and killed Gert. Then he'd driven home and

gone back to work on his puzzle, erasing from his mind
every detail of the hideous event. But suddenly it seemed to
Eddie that he could remember it just as Abel described it,
or pieces of it anyway, pieces out of a dream. Or was he
dreaming *this?*

Eddie looked at the clock. It was now four. He wasn't
losing track of time now, at any rate. So he must have lost
track of time before. Before, when he killed Gert. Abel
Coates had come here to tell him this. And to help him. It
was nice of Abel. Eddie had never been as good a neighbor
to Abel as Abel was being now to him. But it wasn't too
late. Eddie could do something for Abel. He could tell him
the truth.

Abel sat back and looked at the clock. "Look at that,
Eddie. Past four o'clock. Let me get you your Pete's, and
you can sip away and tell me if I left anything out."

Abel pushed back his chair and went to the refrigerator,
removed a Pete's Wicked Ale, opened it, and handed it to
Eddie. Eddie took the beer numbly. He couldn't think. If
only he could get his mind clear and think. He took a tenta-
tive pull at the ale. It tasted good. It was nice of Abel to remember about the Pete's at four o'clock. Eddie should tell
Abel the truth. It was the least he could do. He'd tell him
the truth about how he killed Gert.

But still Eddie didn't speak. There was one thing that he
couldn't seem to make fit. Even now, now that he remembered what Gert had done, how she'd said good-bye, how
she'd planned to leave him, he could identify none of the
emotions Abel had assigned him. Gert *didn't* deserve this.
No one did. She had hurt him, she had planned to leave
him, but that was a decision she was entitled to make. She
shouldn't have been killed because of it. But someone had
killed her. And if Eddie didn't do it, who did?

Eddie took another sip of Pete's Wicked Ale and looked
up at Abel. Where to begin? With Gert's good-bye, with
her grabbing his chin, with the sound of her tires in the
drive as she snuck away with her bags in the backseat? He

raised the bottle of ale, but stopped with it in front of his eyes, still six inches from his lips. If Eddie confessed, if he went to jail, this could be the very last time he had a Pete's Wicked Ale on Sunday at four o'clock.

Pete's.

Four o'clock.

And suddenly Eddie Brewster was thinking straight.

"Okay, Eddie," said Abel. "I can't hang around here all day. As a matter of fact, I'm surprised they haven't arrived already to read you your rights and slap on the cuffs. Let's beat 'em to it, shall we? Come on. Drink up."

But Eddie set the bottle down, his mind a jumble of sharp-edged pieces. *Think.* What to do? Where to start? Then it came to him. Start with the edges. Turn them over one at a time. Construct the frame within which to work.

When Eddie turned to face Abel he found him still watching him, waiting for him to speak. "All right," said Eddie, laying out his first corner piece, "I'll tell you what happened. Everything. Right from the start."

Abel Coates exhaled softly.

"Of course," said Eddie, "you appear to have figured out most of it already. Except for one small part. Gert. She was quite a woman. If you'd known her better you'd have understood what it would mean to me to lose her. You'd have understood why I'd have to do something about it. But you didn't know her very well, did you?"

"No," said Abel.

Or me, thought Eddie, *if it comes to that.* He set down his second corner. "Everything seemed fine until today. Right up until *Visit to Grandmother.* It's my favorite puzzle. Would you like to see it?"

Abel held up a thick hand. "That's okay."

"It's a picture of a little girl just coming through an open door, being greeted by an old woman in a rocker in a lace cap and shawl."

"Don't tell me," said Abel, smiling. "The grandmother."

Eddie nodded, concentrating, thinking about the puzzle, searching for his third corner. "Yes, the grandmother. The room is very dark, full of old mahogany furniture. The only light is from the open door, and it illuminates the scene so brilliantly, you see, the grandmother, the little girl. . . ."

Eddie could sense Abel's growing impatience. He jerked his head up and down, egging Eddie onward. But Eddie plodded on, completing his frame.

"The little girl has a basketful of flowers. She's a nice little girl. You can tell right away from the picture, by the fact that she's visiting the old woman. Nowadays young people don't visit their older relations much. But you can tell right away from the little girl's face that she's just as happy to see the grandmother as the grandmother is to see her. But the important thing, or perhaps I should say my favorite thing, is the roses."

"I know, I know," said Abel. "The white roses. So you were doing the puzzle. Then what happened? Gert came in. . . ."

"Yes," said Eddie, connecting his corners with neat, straight lines. "But as I was saying, it was the business of the puzzle that gave me the first clue there was something wrong. *Visit to Grandmother.* Gert laughing behind my back about *Visit to Grandmother.* Laughing at my doing *Visit to Grandmother* the third Sunday of the month while she was fornicating with a virtual stranger."

Abel Coates shifted in his chair and looked at the clock. "Right, Eddie. As I've told you before: Me, the jury, the whole world, everybody will think what you did was right. So let's cut to the chase here. You went to the Merrydale Motel. . . ."

But Eddie refused to be rushed. It took time to complete a picture, but it took less time if you did it in the right order. Right now, he was filling in the stranger. "I said the man was a virtual stranger, and that is, indeed, what I would have to consider him. Someone I might pass on the street, wave to over the hedge, but not someone I'd invite over. Certainly not someone I'd talk to about something like *Visit to Grandmother,* about the third Sunday of the month, or the white roses. No one knew about those things. No one but Gert."

Eddie paused. Was it time for the key piece? Yes. He reached for the Pete's Wicked Ale and held it up. "And no one but Gert knew about this."

For the first time, a small, vertical line appeared in the smooth slab of Abel Coates's forehead.

"I'd be curious to know," said Eddie, "If these little habits of mine provide amusing pillow talk for the two of you, Abel."

Abel Coates said nothing.

"Of course, when you first said it, I hardly heard you. It wasn't until you looked at the clock and fetched me my Pete's that it came to me. How did you know about the Pete's Wicked Ale at four o'clock? How did you know about the third Sunday? I suddenly realized I'd never spoken to you of these things. And if I hadn't, who had? It could have been only one other person. And she could have done it for only one reason. To laugh about it. To laugh about it with you. And suddenly I realized that you knew Gert better than you let on. You knew her intimately. Intimately enough to have shared a laugh at my expense. You were the regular Joe who met her at the Merrydale Motel, weren't you, Abel?"

And there it was. The main figures completed.

Still Abel Coates said nothing, the line on his forehead deepening.

Eddie kept going, working on the background now. Turning over one more piece. Finding its proper place. With each piece the scene became clearer. "Now it seems odd to me that I didn't catch on sooner. After all, you told me what happened yourself. How did you phrase it? You were looking for laughs. But poor Gert decided to treat the affair more seriously. You didn't know her very well after all, did you, Abel? So when she told you she was leaving

me, what did you do? Did you try to break it off? I suppose
I can imagine what happened then. You see, I do know
Gert. I imagine she became alarmed. She had made a difficult decision, one from which she felt there was no graceful
turning back. So what did she do that alarmed *you*? Did she
threaten to expose the whole affair, ruin your public image,
even your career? Was that it? And you responded by doing
what? I suppose you must have pretended to reconsider. I
suppose you told her to pack her bags and meet you on
Sunday as usual."

It was a painful image, so painful that for a second it
stopped Eddie in his tracks. Gert, *his* Gert, waiting at the
Merrydale for a fate that would change her life, only to be
met by a fate that would end it forever. But right now Eddie
couldn't afford to dwell in black grief over Gert. Gert was
no longer in the picture. Abel Coates was.

Eddie kept on. "I'm sure the rest was easy for someone
like you, someone with your experience with the criminal
mind. You stole my knife, and my raincoat, and my car.
You knew I was on the other side of the house, absorbed in
Visit to Grandmother. You drove to the Merrydale Motel,
where you knew Gert was waiting patiently. It would have
been a simple matter to make sure you were seen by the
manager, just the way you were seen in your other disguise
all those other Sundays—the dyed red hair, the borrowed
truck with the New Hampshire plates. Or was that stolen,
too? But those are pieces to a different puzzle. Right now
we must work on today's picture—you meeting Gert at the
Merrydale Motel, killing her, and attempting to frame me
for her murder."

And suddenly there was the final piece, staring Eddie in
the face. *"You* made the mysterious phone call to me at
3:08, didn't you? You called to make sure I was still here,
alone, without an alibi." Eddie looked down at his hands,
clamped tightly around the Pete's Wicked Ale. His throat
was bone dry, but he knew if he lifted the ale in his shaking
hands it would clatter against his teeth. Better to go thirsty.

Beside him, Abel Coates stretched his pasty face into a humorless grin. "Good thinking, Eddie. And all because of *Visit to Grandmother*. It's some story, but who do you think will believe you? I've got all the evidence, and it's all against you."

Oh, not quite, thought Eddie. The Merrydale Motel was close by. So close by, in fact, that most local residents neglected to dial the long-distance code before they called it. But a call to, or from, the Merrydale Motel was indeed a long-distance call, and Eddie, who worked at the telephone company, was well aware of that fact. He was also well aware that the telephone company would have a permanent record of any completed long-distance call. And Abel Coates's call from the Merrydale to Eddie's house had been completed, because Eddie had answered it. Eddie had been here, at home, when Gert was killed. He had an alibi, of sorts. But was the phone company's proof going to be proof enough? Eddie doubted it. So what else did Abel have? A car he could have easily stolen. A raincoat that was readily available in the backseat. A fishing knife stored close to an open back door, also easily stolen.

But there still remained the small matter of Eddie's prints on the knife. Abel most certainly had taken some care to preserve Eddie's prints, and to camouflage his own. Perhaps he had even used a different knife for the crime, and applied Gert's blood to Eddie's after the fact. Sadly, Eddie had to admit Abel just might be right: His case against Abel would be hard to prove. But he knew two things for certain—that his wife Gert had gotten something she didn't deserve, and that Abel Coates had *not* gotten something he did.

And then Eddie's eyes fell on the knife.

Abel leaned back in his chair, still grinning. "Let's face it, Eddie. You're better off doing what I first suggested. Confess to the crime, plead temporary insanity. Throw yourself on the mercy of the court. It's jungle justice,

Eddie. Trust me—you'll get off with a couple of years, max."

"You're forgetting one thing," said Eddie.

"Yeah?" said Abel. "What's that?"

"This." Eddie lunged for the knife, but Abel beat him to it, grabbing it firmly by the part nearest him, the handle.

"Nice try, Eddie." It seemed to take less than a second. Abel drew his revolver, whipped out his cuffs, and secured Eddie's hands behind his back. "I tried to help you, Eddie," said Abel. "I would have worked it all out for you, a couple of years, max. But you had to do it your way, didn't you? Now you're done for. Now I press ahead with my case. Come on, Eddie, you're under arrest."

Abel Coates bundled up the knife in the canvas, the knife that now held his own prints superimposed over Eddie's, and pushed Eddie roughly out the door toward the cruiser.

But Eddie didn't despair. He'd almost completed the frame to an entirely new puzzle, and with the help of a good lawyer, Eddie knew, the rest of the pieces would fall in place. In no time he'd be back home on the sun porch, finishing *Visit to Grandmother*.

And next time, decided Eddie, he'd throw caution to the winds and have that second Pete's.

*It never ceases to amaze me how clever murderers are at concealing
how they've executed their crime. Luckily, with the application of
a little logic, common sense, and, occasionally, a bit of science, even
the most confounding plots are eventually unraveled. Such is the
case with this story.*

A Deadly Attraction

Jean Hager

AS THE FIRST female deputy in the Plum County Sheriff's
Department, I was not welcomed with open arms by all of
my cohorts. Therefore, I felt I had to work harder and complain less than the other deputies. So I bit my tongue a lot,
particularly when I was around Deputy Jed Roy Corn, who
seemed to be Sheriff Fortner's golden-haired boy. That
might be due to the fact that Jed is the Sheriff's nephew.

How should I describe Jed? Well, he drives a three-quarter-
ton four-wheel-drive Ford pickup with oversized tires and
fuzzy dice hanging from the rearview mirror. A 30.06 rifle
and a rod and reel hang on a rack in the back window.
There's a dragon tattooed on Jed's right bicep, and the
Sheriff lets him get away with shaggier hair than he'd toler-
ate in another deputy, though he drew the line at Jed's
beard and made him shave it off. That pleased me no end—
I was tired of seeing specks of Levi Garrett chewing tobacco in that beard. When not in uniform, Jed wears a
black cap with a yellow Cat Diesel patch and hangs out at

gas stations and pool halls. He refers to all women, except his mother, as gals or ol' gals. His mother is Mama and always addressed as ma'am.

In all fairness, Jed isn't mean-spirited. The most exasperating thing about him is that when it comes to dealing with a woman as an equal, he is clueless. In short, Jed could be the poster boy for the Bubba Society of America.

For reasons which I've yet to comprehend, the Sheriff partners me with Jed when a call requires two deputies. The first time we went on a call together, Jed told me he didn't hold with female law officers. When I asked why, he said, "It just ain't natural." But dragon tattoos are?

Maybe Fort, as the Sheriff is called by his friends, hopes Jed's redneck consciousness will be raised by associating with me. Yeah, right.

Or maybe he hopes I'll get so tired of putting up with Jed that I'll quit. (My hiring was a political move; I don't kid myself about that. It was no coincidence that I was put on the payroll shortly after several women's organizations wrote letters to the editor labeling the Sheriff's Department an old boys' club which barred women.) If I quit, the Sheriff can say, "Hey, I hired a woman but she couldn't take it."

Whatever motivates the Sheriff, he won't hear me whining. I'm determined to stick it out. Actually, Jed's starting to get used to me. I think he's decided to take me under his big, manly wing.

Anyway, I like the work and the other deputies, except for two or three oblivious buttheads like Jed. The fringes are good, the pay is decent, and I have a ten-year-old son to support. (My ex hasn't sent a support payment in over a year. Hey, the money for the Jag payments has to come from somewhere.)

I'd been with the department a couple of months when the call came in from Maggie Gillespy. Maggie's husband, Earl, was a well-known wood-carver. He'd made a fortune at it, folks said—and appearances seemed to back them up. The Gillespys had built a big house and workshop for Earl in the middle of twenty acres a few miles out of Berryville, the county seat.

The gist of Maggie Gillespy's phone call was that she'd been working in the yard when she heard what sounded like two gunshots. They'd been having trouble with trespassing hunters recently, and she went into the house to tell her husband, who was in his office, that she thought the hunters were back. She found the office door locked. She tried the key but the door still wouldn't open, and Earl didn't respond to her knocks or yells. In addition, the drapes were closed, so she couldn't see into the office from outside.

Since the Sheriff was due at a meeting with the County Commissioners, he sent Jed and me out to the Gillespy place. The house was a two-story brick with white columns across the front. It would have looked more at home in Georgia than in east Texas. They probably called it Tara.

The workshop behind and to one side of the house was bigger than my two-bedroom rental and made of redbrick to match Tara. My dad's hobby was woodworking, but his shop was a shed in the backyard. He'd drool all over the place if he could see Earl Gillespy's shop.

Maggie Gillespy was waiting for us on the front porch or verandah or whatever you call it. She was a slim, still-attractive woman in her forties (in spite of the fine lines fanning out from the corners of her eyes), with dark red hair tied back in a ponytail. Her mouth had a hardness about it, though, as if she'd seen some tough times. I've been told she and Earl barely scraped together a living for years before he made it big in the wood-carving biz.

Evidently, Maggie wore mascara for gardening—there were dark streaks on her cheeks where she'd been wiping away sweat or tears. She still wore her gardening clothes—loose slacks with dirt ground into the knees, a plaid shirt with the sleeves rolled up, and once-white tennis shoes.

Hands clasped tightly to her breasts, she frowned anxiously as Jed and I got out of the patrol car—Jed from the driver's seat, of course. In Jed's world, if there's a man in the party, he always drives. It had never occurred to him to ask if I'd like to take the wheel now and then. One of these days, I was going to get to the driver's seat first and refuse to budge.

"Mornin', Miz Gillespy," Jed greeted her. She nodded, then looked at me curiously. "This here's Sally Morrison, our brand-new depadee. I'm showin' her the ropes." Jed beamed at me as though I were a particularly cute speckled pup. It wouldn't have surprised me if he'd patted me on the head. I swear I'll slug him if he ever tries.

I got right down to business. "Your husband still locked in the office, Mrs. Gillespy?" She nodded anxiously.

"And you still haven't gotten any response from him?"

She shook her head. "No, and I'm beside myself. I'd started out back to break a window when I saw your car coming up the road." We followed her inside, where we walked across gleaming oak floors and waded through what seemed like miles of thick hunter green carpet to reach the office door. She looked up at Jed helplessly. "What if he's had a heart attack or—" She let the thought hang there, unfinished.

"Does your husband have a history of heart trouble?" I asked.

"No. His cholesterol's too high is all." She hesitated. "But, lately, he's not really been himself. It would be just like him to have heart symptoms and ignore them."

"How long ago was it you heard those shots?"

She thought about it. "An hour, maybe a little more." I glanced at my watch. She'd called the station less than forty-five minutes ago. I guessed she'd spent fifteen minutes or more trying to get a response out of Earl. Jed banged loudly on the door with his big, hammy fist. "Mr. Gillespy? It's Depadee Corn. Can ya hear me?"

No sound came from beyond the office door. "You say your key won't open it?" I asked Maggie Gillespy.

She shook her head. "I tried shaking the door, but I think he's bolted it. It's one of those slide-bolt locks that you can only open from inside."

"Why does he need that kind of lock on his office door?"

She looked at me sharply, then shook her head. "Earl's a fanatic about privacy. He installed the bolt a few months ago. I told you he's been acting strange."

Jed stepped away from the door. "Hate to spoil yer purty door, Miz Gillespy, but it's the only way. You gals stand back now. Wouldn't want nobody gettin' hurt." He raised his leg and rammed the door with his cowboy boot. It splintered. Jed gave it another mighty kick which left a hole big enough to reach in and release the slide bolt. I opened my mouth to tell him to use his handkerchief to touch the bolt, but I was too late. The door swung open.

Earl Gillespy sat behind a massive mahogany desk which faced the door. His head, what was left of it, was slumped forward, his chin on his chest. The right side of his head was nothing but bloody pulp. One arm hung over the side of the chair. A semiautomatic Smith & Wesson lay on the floor near his hand.

After a moment of stunned silence, Maggie Gillespy cried, "Oh, my God! Earl! No, no . . ." She fainted then, sliding down the wall of the hall opposite the office door until she was sitting on the floor. I grabbed hold of her shoulders to keep her from banging her head. She was only out a couple of seconds before her eyelids fluttered and she came around. She blinked up at me. Her eyes were dazed, and then I saw the awareness come back. "Earl . . . is he still alive?"

Not with a big chunk of his brain gone, I thought. "I don't know, ma'am. Are you up to phoning for an ambulance?" I wanted to get her away from the office while Jed and I checked out the scene.

"I—I think so."

I helped her to her feet and she wobbled down the hall toward the kitchen, sobbing quietly.

"After the call, why don't you wait for us in the kitchen."
She didn't answer, but I thought she'd heard.

When I turned around to go into the office, Jed was
reaching for the gun.

"Don't touch that!" I snapped. "Don't touch anything!"

He jerked upright. "Dayum, Sal. You skeered me. Whatcha
got yer bowels in a uproar about?"

"You can't compromise the scene of a suspicious death."

"Ain't nothin' spishuss 'bout it. The man done gone and
shot hisself in the head."

I stepped around Jed for a better look at the room.
"That's sure what it looks like."

"Looks like! That's what it *is.*"

"Still, I'm sure you're familiar with the procedures to be
followed at the scene of any unnatural death." He puffed
out his chest, looking insulted that I would even doubt it,
but I suspected he didn't know what procedures I was talking about. "You walk in my footsteps going in," I clarified,
"and we take the same trail out. We can look but not
touch."

I took five cautious steps around the body and the desk,
stopping beside one of the two draped windows. I took a
ballpoint pen out of my uniform pocket and used the blunt
end to pull back one side of the drape a few inches, far
enough to see that the window was locked. I let the drape
fall back into place and moved to check the second window. It was locked, too.

Jed hadn't moved from just inside the door. He stood
with his arms crossed over his chest, watching me, stu-
diously avoiding looking directly at the body. "Both of 'em
locked, huh?" I nodded. "You satisfied now?"

It wasn't a question of being satisfied at that point. It was
a question of following procedures. But I didn't bother explaining that again. Jed turned to stare at the blood that had
splattered on the white wall. "He flat made a mess in here,
didn't he? I bleeve this rug's ruint, too."

I nodded absently and scanned the room from my position by the window. There was what looked like a bullet hole in the wall where the windows were, down near the floor, and I remembered that Maggie Gillespy had said she'd heard two shots.

"I think we'd better call the Sheriff out of his meeting," I said.

Jed nodded. "Yeah, he'll prolly wanta come out." He looked at the phone on the desk and then at me. "I'll find 'nother phone."

"Ask him to bring the camera and fingerprint kit with him." The only camera and kit we had were kept in the Sheriff's office. I was kicking myself for not having thought to bring them along. Spending so much time with Jed was making me sloppy. I told myself I'd have to watch that.

"How come? Oh, procedures," he said, nodding sagely as he left.

I spent another few minutes looking around the office, then went to the kitchen, where Maggie Gillespy sat at a round maple table with a half-full whiskey bottle and a shot glass in front of her. Evidently, she'd just had a drink. Good idea. She'd needed it.

She looked up at me. Her eyes were red, but she'd washed her face; the mascara streaks were gone. "He's dead, isn't he?"

I put my hand on her shoulder and squeezed lightly. "I'm sorry." She merely nodded, as if she'd known it all along and had accepted it.

After a moment, she said, "I should've hid that gun. It just never occurred to me . . ." She gestured helplessly.

"So the gun belonged to your husband?"

"Yes. He bought it after we had a burglary about three years ago. He always kept it in his desk."

Jed, who'd been talking low-voiced into the kitchen phone, his back to the table, hung up and turned around. "The Shurf's on his way," he said, glancing at the whiskey bottle. I wondered if he'd have joined Maggie

Gillespy in a drink if I hadn't been there. I wanted to ask if he'd mentioned the camera and fingerprint kit, but I didn't want to do it in front of Earl Gillespy's widow.

I pulled out a chair. "Mrs. Gillespy, you said your husband hasn't been himself lately. He installed that bolt in the office, you said. What else did you notice?"

She fingered the shot glass but didn't pour herself another drink. "He acted depressed. Some days he'd barely say two words to me. I kept asking him what was wrong, but he'd just say he was tired. I tried to get him to see a doctor, but he wouldn't."

"Do the two of you live here alone?"

She nodded. "We never had any children."

"I was thinking about servants."

"Oh." She hesitated. "We used to have a live-in maid, but that didn't work out. Now we have a woman who comes in a couple times a week to clean. Cora Sellers. She lives just down the road. I do everything else, even mow the lawn. Earl hates—" She paused and swallowed hard. "—hated yard work. He—" She halted as a siren sounded in the distance.

I went into the foyer to open the front door. The Sheriff's car pulled in behind the patrol car and beside the ambulance. The Sheriff and the medical examiner, Dr. Hurt, got out and followed the ambulance attendants into the house. The Sheriff handed me the camera and fingerprint kit. "Where's Maggie?" he asked.

"In the kitchen."

He went to the kitchen and I followed Dr. Hurt and the medics to the office. Hurt pronounced Earl Gillespy dead, a formality, and I snapped a couple of shots of the body before the medics moved it to the ambulance. Doc Hurt acknowledged me with a nod and went in search of the Sheriff, leaving me alone in the office. Which was fine with me.

I dusted and photographed the doorknob, slide bolt, gun, and desk telephone. There were no discernible prints on the windowsills or locks. They'd been wiped recently, probably by the housekeeper.

When the ambulance attendants had moved the body, I'd half-expected to find a suicide note under it. But there hadn't been one. There was no note in any of the desk drawers, either.

Just as I finished riffling through the last drawer, the Sheriff came in, looked around the office, and dug a cartridge out of the hole in the wall I'd noticed earlier. "Hell of a note," he muttered angrily. "That woman out there didn't deserve this, with everything else she's been through." He didn't elaborate, and I knew by his look that I shouldn't ask. He pulled an evidence bag out of his pants pocket and dropped the gun in it.

"When can the ME do the autopsy?" I asked.

He looked at me closely for a long moment. "Tomorrow, I reckon."

"What about the forensic tests? Tomorrow, too?"

"Probably. You worried about something?"

"There's no suicide note, for one thing."

"Not every suicide leaves a note."

"The two shots bother me, too."

He nodded. "Yeah, it's kind of unusual, but I figure he was just trying to get up his nerve with the first one. The main thing is, he was alone in a locked room."

True. That pretty much made a suicide verdict inevitable.

The Sheriff and ME left shortly. I asked Maggie Gillespy if she wanted me to call somebody to come and stay with her. She said no, she'd be all right.

Jed and I left.

"That ol' gal's handling it purty good, ain't she?"

"Seems to be," I agreed, "but the full impact of what's happened might not hit her until later."

We were coming up on a rural mailbox with "Sellers" printed on the side. I yelled "Stop!" as Jed passed it.

I guess I scared him. He screeched to a halt. "What in tarnation's wrong with you?"

"This must be where Cora Sellers lives."

"Who?"

"The Gillespys' maid."

"So?"

"Back up and turn in. We need to talk to her."

He stuck out his lower lip. "You ain't my boss, ya know. I don't like a female tellin' me what to do."

"There's a shocker." He looked blank. "It's procedure," I added.

Without further argument, he turned in to the graveled drive and parked near a double-wide mobile home. Cora Sellers was a plump, fiftyish woman with freckles and dimples, which must have been a cute combination when she was five. I told her what had happened at the Gillespys. Her eyes went wide and she said, "I thought I heard gunshots earlier. But that's not too unusual around here. Hunters, you know. Oh, mercy, what a shame."

"Could we come in and talk to you?" I asked.

She held the storm door open. "Come on back to the kitchen."

When we were seated at Cora Sellers's kitchen table with three big mugs of strong coffee, I asked, "When did you hear those gunshots, Mrs. Sellers?"

She frowned thoughtfully. "Must've been a couple hours ago." That fit with what Maggie Gillespy had told us.

"Was Earl Gillespy acting different lately that you could tell?"

She chewed on her bottom lip for a moment. "I've only worked there a couple of months, so I can't really say."

"Did he seem worried or depressed?"

She hesitated, then nodded slowly. "Worried, I'd say. 'Course he stayed out in his workshop mostly while I was there, but the times I did see him, he looked like a man with something heavy on his mind."

Jed had been blowing and sipping his coffee. Now, before I could ask another question, he jumped in. "Any notion what that mighta been?"

She looked at Jed and then at me and frowned. "I don't like to gossip, and I don't know much for sure—it's all just rumors." Jed started to say something, and I gave a quick shake of my head. I didn't want Cora Sellers diverted. Whenever anybody says they don't like to gossip, they're about to do just that.

"I don't even know if the affair's still going on. I *heard* she caught 'em having sex late one night on that couch in Earl's office."

Earl must have put the bolt on the door after that, I thought.

"All I know for sure," Cora Sellers went on, "is that Mrs. Gillespy sent that little tart packing and the next day she called me and asked if I'd be interested in cleaning for her a couple of days a week."

All of a sudden, Jed was looking a lot more interested. He set down his coffee mug and leaned forward. "You sayin' Earl was gettin' it on with the maid?"

Her mouth made a disapproving moue at Jed's choice of words. "That's the rumor. Naturally, I never saw it with my own eyes." She shook her head. "She was at least twenty years younger than him. No fool like an old fool, as they say."

I got out the small Spiral tablet and pen I carried in my shirt pocket.

"What's her name?"

"Morgan Burke."

"Do you know where she lives?"

"I heard she moved back in with her dad, Dave Burke, in Berryville."

I asked a few more questions and we finished our coffee, but Cora Sellers had nothing else useful to tell us. On the way back to the courthouse, Jed said, "I reckon you wanta stop at Dave Burke's house now."

"Maybe we better wait till we get the results of the autopsy."

He looked disappointed, as though he'd been looking forward to a stop at the Burkes. His next words told me why. "That Morgan Burke is one flat purty ol' gal."

"Oh?"

"What'd she see in ol' Earl?" Jed went on.

Earl Gillespy had been balding and twenty pounds overweight. "Money?"

"Had to be," Jed agreed.

As soon as we reached the Sheriff's Department in the basement of the courthouse, I found a private phone and called Dave Burke's number. When he answered, I asked for Morgan.

"She moved to Dallas last week."

"Do you have her phone number?"

"Who wants to know?" he asked rudely.

I told him who I was and what had happened at the Gillespy place.

"That's too bad," he muttered, though he didn't sound sorry, "but it's got nothing to do with Morgan. She told Earl last week, the day before she moved, that she didn't want to see or hear from him again as long as he was married." He hung up before I could ask for Morgan's telephone number again. But I didn't really need it anymore.

It appeared that Morgan had given Earl Gillespy an ultimatum. Divorce Maggie or get lost. In spite of my reservations, he'd evidently chosen a third option, suicide.

We got the autopsy and forensic reports the next afternoon. Earl Gillespy had died from a nine-millimeter gunshot wound to the brain. The cartridge, which had lodged against bone, was retrieved by the medical examiner. According to Forensics, the cartridge in Earl's head and the one in the wall of his office had come from the gun found beside the body. It was registered to Earl Gillespy. The only fingerprints found on the gun were Earl's. The gunshot residue found on his hand proved he'd shot the gun himself. All the other identifiable prints I'd lifted from the office belonged to Earl, too, except for those on the slide bolt. Those were Jed's, and they'd obscured any other prints that might have been there before.

The evidence certainly pointed to suicide, although I did find one mildly surprising thing in the reports. Forensics estimated the gun had been ten to twelve inches from Earl's head when the fatal shot was fired.

I pointed this out to the Sheriff. "He held the gun a foot from his head. Does that make sense to you?"

He shrugged. "Nothing about suicide makes sense to me, Sal. You still trying to turn this into something else?"

"He was having an affair with Morgan Burke."

"Yeah, I heard. I also heard she left town, which must mean it was over."

"According to her father, she told Earl only last week that she didn't want him contacting her again as long as he was married."

"You talked to Dave Burke?"

Oops, I'd put my foot in it. "I thought somebody ought to let the Burkes know what happened."

He looked at me hard for a minute. "What if," I rushed on, "Earl asked Maggie for a divorce and she wasn't about to give up her nice, cushy lifestyle, so she killed him?"

He was shaking his head before I finished speaking. "How'd she get out of that room after she did it?"

"I don't know," I admitted.

"And why didn't we find her fingerprints on the gun?"

"I've been thinking about that. She could have shot him, wiped her prints off the gun, and put the gun in his hand with his finger on the trigger so we'd find his prints. That second shot still bothers me. She could've put her finger on top of his and fired into the wall."

The Sheriff looked a little startled. "The things you come up with, Sal. Why would Maggie shoot the wall if he was already dead?"

"So he'd have gunshot residue on his hand. People learn about that kind of stuff on television."

"Sal, Sal. You're itching to play detective, aren't you?"

"It just doesn't feel right to me," I said stubbornly.

He reached out and patted my head. I stood there and took it. Jed I would have slugged, but I didn't think I could get away with hitting the Sheriff. "Tell you what," he said, "you figure out how Maggie got out of that locked room after she killed him, and we'll look into it a little more. Till then, we got other work to do."

I hadn't really expected any other reaction, but it had been worth a try.

I spent the rest of the day on a call twenty miles out of town. A rancher was missing a couple of calves and was convinced they'd been stolen. I trudged all over his 320 acres and finally found their carcasses. The vet would have to determine cause of death, but I suspected it was the same virus that had afflicted other cattle in the eastern part of the state.

After all that walking, I was pooped by the time I got home from work. Sam, my ten-year-old son, was at the kitchen table doing his homework. Sam loves school and never had to be told to do his homework. In fact, he sometimes does more than is required. I figured after he'd been in school a few years, he'd get some of that curiosity and hunger for knowledge he'd been born with knocked out of him, but so far it hadn't happened. My son is so bright it scares me sometimes. His teacher told me that Sam made the highest score in his class on the IQ test they give fifth graders. I'm so proud of him that sometimes I want to run all over town telling people what a great kid he is.

"Hi, Mom," Sam greeted me as I sank into a kitchen chair with a big sigh.

"Hey, cowboy. What're you working on?"

He grinned and his brown eyes sparkled. "Science. We're studying magnetism. It's fascinating."

"Really?" Frankly, I'd never thought much about it.

"Yeah. Did you know that there are still a lot of mysteries about magnetism that scientists haven't solved?"

"Nope, can't say that I did."

He nodded eagerly. "The earth is surrounded by this huge magnetic field, and they don't know exactly what causes it. Well, obviously there are enormous electric currents deep within the earth. . . ."

It wasn't obvious to me, but I nodded anyway.

"But they don't know what produces those currents."

"You're right. It is fascinating." I got up to put on a pot of coffee so I could have a cup after dinner. Then I got the chili I'd made that morning out of the refrigerator. "I'm starving, Sam. Are you ready for some chili?"

"You bet." He moved his books and notebook to the sideboard. "I'll finish this after we eat."

"You want to set the table and pour us some milk?"

"Sure." He got out bowls, napkins, and silverware and laid them neatly on the table. "Mom, did you know that no one has ever found a single magnetic pole? By itself, I mean."

"Uh, no." I wasn't sure what he was getting at.

"It's true. There's always two, a north pole and a south pole. We did some experiments in class today. If you hold a bar magnet by a string tied around its middle, one end will point toward the north and the other toward the south. Every time."

"That's truly amazing, Sam."

"The magnetism is always strongest at the ends of the magnet—the poles, I mean. And if you break a bar magnet in the middle, the ends of both pieces become new poles, one north and the other south."

"Hmm," I murmured. Sam went on talking about the experiments he'd done in science class, but my mind had wandered to Earl Gillespy's death. I was still bothered by some of the evidence, but I'd thought about it all day and I simply couldn't get around that locked room.

Later that night, when I was in bed and unable to fall asleep, I pondered on it some more. To no avail. I kept thinking I was missing something. There was an idea niggling at the back of my mind, but I couldn't get hold of it. It was like an itch I couldn't scratch.

The itch was still there the next morning. Finally, it occurred to me that if I went back out to the Gillespy place and looked around again, maybe I could figure out what was bugging me.

I sent Sam off to school and phoned the Sheriff's office. The Sheriff wasn't in yet—I'd known he wouldn't be—so I left a message with the dispatcher that something had come up and I might be a little late. Then I drove out to the Gillespy house.

Maggie Gillespie was still there alone. There were dark smudges beneath her eyes, as though she hadn't slept much. "Just thought I'd stop in and see how you're doing," I said.

She looked surprised and invited me in. "I have to finish making the funeral arrangements today," she said. "The funeral will be tomorrow. Just a private service for a few close acquaintances."

I wanted to ask if Morgan Burke was among those "close acquaintances," but I didn't want to put Maggie on the defensive. "Will you stay on here?"

"I don't know yet. I might move to Tulsa. That's where my brother lives." She expelled a deep breath. "I'll just have to wait and see." She looked at me questioningly.

We were still standing in the foyer and she was obviously asking herself why I didn't leave, now that I'd seen she was okay. "I was wondering if I might look around the office again," I said.

She frowned. "What for? I've already cleaned up all that messy powder you left in there. Was that for fingerprints?" I nodded and she said, "I can't understand why you'd need fingerprints with a suicide."

"It's routine in all cases of unnatural death," I said glibly. "I just need to check out a couple more routine things and I'll be out of your hair."

She hesitated, then shrugged. "Why not. Go ahead. I'll be in the kitchen."

I was glad she didn't follow me into the office because I didn't really know what I was looking for. I searched the desk more thoroughly than I had before. That's when I discovered that the partition at the back of one of the drawers could be removed, exposing a small secret compartment. My heart leaped with anticipation at the discovery, but the only thing in the compartment was a small notebook calendar with a page for each day of the year and a space in back for names and addresses. I checked the names first, but Morgan Burke wasn't listed. Then I flipped back through the weeks prior to Earl Gillespy's death. Nothing unusual there. On the day of his death, a cryptic note appeared: *I can't go on like this. I'm going to do it.* Which could have been taken as a suicide note except that on the current day's page, two days following Earl's death, was written *Greg Schwartz, 10 A.M.* Greg Schwartz was a Berryville attorney.

I put the notebook back where I'd found it and replaced the false partition. Then I stared at the splintered door, but no brilliant insights came to me. It was certain that nobody could have killed him and left by the door. There was no way to bolt it from the other side.

I walked over to one of the windows. The drapes were open, and I looked out at Earl Gillespy's workshop for a few minutes. If Earl was murdered and the killer didn't exit through the door, that left only the windows. I examined one of the locks, which consisted of a little slide bar similar to the one on the door and which was attached to the bottom half of the window. To lock the window, you pushed the bat into a metal receptacle embedded in the top half. I tugged on the bolt. It was tight and resisted at first, but after a few tugs, it came out of its receptacle. I pulled the lower pane up a few inches, then lowered it again and relocked the window.

I tried the second window, expecting the bolt to resist as the first one had, but it slid toward me easily. I pushed it back and forth a few times. It moved as smoothly as if it had been oiled. Curious, but there was still no way I could think of that somebody could have locked it from outside.

I left the window unlocked and looked out at the workshop again. That niggle at the back of my mind got a little stronger.

I went into the kitchen, where Maggie was putting together a casserole. "Looks good," I said.

"I haven't felt like eating since—well, you know. But it helps to keep busy."

I nodded. "Before I leave, I wonder if I could take a look at the workshop." She was about to say no; I could see it on her face. I forced a smile. "My reason is purely personal." I put a little wheedle into my voice. "My dad's a woodworker and I'd love to be able to describe the shop to him."

She sighed. "All right. Earl was so particular about his workshop that he didn't want anybody else in it. Not even me. I haven't been inside since it was built, before he got all his equipment in and unpacked his tools. But I guess it doesn't matter who goes in there now." She opened a cabinet door and took down a key ring. "This is the workshop key. Be sure to lock it when you leave. You can put the key under the mat by the back door and I'll get it later." A nice way of telling me she didn't want to talk to me anymore.

I left by the back door because I wanted to get a look at the screens on Earl's office windows. As I'd thought, they could easily be lifted up and off by somebody wanting to enter or leave the office through a window.

The workshop was every woodworker's dream. There were three lathes of various sizes, electric sanders and saws, a central vacuum system, and some other pieces of equipment I couldn't even identify. On one wall were dozens of sizes of sandpaper, each size in a separate cubicle.

"Oh, Dad, I wish it was yours," I said aloud.

I walked around, taking it all in so that I could describe every detail to him the next time we talked. But that wasn't the only reason I'd come, and I wasn't sure what the other reason was. I only knew that yesterday at supper, while I listened to Sam go on about his experiments with magnets, I'd thought about Earl Gillespy's shop, comparing it to Dad's little shed, and something had clicked in my mind.

Now as I gazed around Earl's shop, my eyes fell on a row of wood-carving tools on one wall. They hung there without any visible means of support, reminding me of some small tools hanging on the wall above Dad's workbench. I walked over to the tools, took hold of one of them, and pulled it away from the heavy rectangle of metal behind it. The rectangle was a magnet like the one that held my dad's tools on the wall, except this one was much bigger.

It all fell into place then. Almost. First I had to prove to myself that what I thought had happened *could* have. I removed all the tools from the magnet, being careful not to touch it. The magnet had a hole at each end and hung on two big nails. I tore off a piece of paper toweling from a roll I found in a cabinet and carefully lifted the magnet off the wall. With the paper towel over my fingers, I carried the magnet by one corner to a window of Earl Gillespy's office. It was the window with the lock that slid in and out so easily, the one I'd left unlocked.

I pressed one end of the magnet against the glass pane, right where the lock was. Almost like magic, the bolt slid toward the magnet and into the metal receptacle, locking the window. Now I was sure. Maggie Gillespy had oiled that lock so it would slide easily. Then she'd gotten Earl's gun and called him into the office. Somehow she got him to sit down in the chair at his desk—she probably had the gun behind her. She'd shot him, wiped the gun, put his hand on it, and shot the wall. Then she'd bolted the door, left by the window with the oiled lock, used the magnet from Earl's workshop to lock it, and returned the magnet to its place in the shop before calling the Sheriff's office.

I hurried back to the shop, replaced the magnet, still without letting my fingers touch it, and put all the tools back where they'd been. If I was right, Maggie Gillespy's fingerprints were on that magnet, but the workshop, unlike the office, hadn't been the scene of a death, natural or otherwise, so I didn't dare take the magnet without Maggie's permission, and I wasn't about to ask for that. I had to persuade the Sheriff to get a search warrant so we could legally confiscate the magnet.

It took some doing, but after I described my experiment with the magnet, the Sheriff got the warrant. Maggie Gillespy's fingerprints were all over that magnet. Evidently she'd been so sure nobody would ever figure out how she'd done it that she hadn't bothered wiping the magnet after she'd used it.

When confronted with the fingerprint findings and her statement that she hadn't been in the workshop since the tools were unpacked, she broke down and confessed. It was almost as if she'd been waiting for a chance to get it off her chest.

When she'd kicked Morgan Burke out of the house, Earl had demanded a divorce. Maggie had refused to discuss it, on the theory that if she ignored it, it would go away. He'd continued to see Morgan, who had pressured him into filing for the divorce himself, and he had made an appointment with an attorney. Until then, Maggie hadn't really believed he'd go through with it.

"The old fool wanted to marry that cheap little whore," Maggie sobbed.

After giving Earl the best years of her life, she explained, she wasn't going to stand by and let Morgan Burke take over her home, her husband, and her husband's income, which hadn't been all that great until the last few years. Oh, she could probably have gotten the house in the divorce, but she wouldn't have had the income to keep it up. It was obvious that Earl was going to be out of her life, one way or another. All in all, killing him before he saw the attorney had seemed the best solution at the time.

Later that day, I was congratulated and got my back slapped a lot by the other deputies. Even Jed Roy Corn surprised me by saying loud enough for the others to hear him, "I gotta hand it to ya, gal. You're like a pit bull with his jaws clamped on a bone, when you get a bee in your bonnet."

I didn't particularly care for the pit bull simile, but I decided to take it as a compliment.

After work, I took Sam out for dinner. I even let him choose the place. I was imagining a tender fillet at the best steak house in Berryville with Key lime pie for dessert, but Sam wanted a Big Mac, curly fries, and a chocolate shake. I didn't argue with him. After all, if he hadn't been talking about magnets that night at dinner, I might never have thought of the one in Dad's workshop. And Maggie Gillespy would have gotten away with murder.

If there's one thing I love on a rainy afternoon when I'm stuck in the middle of writing a particularly difficult chapter in my latest book, it's a nice hot cup of tea. I'm not sure if I'd care to sample the blend poured out in this particular story, however.

A Nice Cup of Tea
Kate Kingsbury

SAM WILSON WAS as regular as high tide. I reckon there wasn't a man in Rainbow Bay who couldn't set his watch by him. Every morning, just five minutes after Maisie put the kettle on the stove, we would see Sam come whistling up the path with the mail. That's why, when he didn't appear at the usual time last Wednesday, Maisie just about had kittens.

Maisie is my older sister. We don't look much alike. She is thinner than I am, and taller. Her hair is iron gray while mine is milk white. We both wear glasses, but I still have all my teeth and I smile more than Maisie does.

We don't get out much anymore. Maisie doesn't see too well, and the damp gets into our bones and triggers our arthritis. That's the trouble with living close to the ocean. Not that I mind all that much. I never was one for socializing, even when my Harry was alive.

Maisie's looked out for me ever since our parents died in an avalanche when I was only eleven. Maisie used to be a schoolteacher until she retired several years ago. She taught biology to fifth graders—a waste of time, if you ask me.

The only thing those kids are interested in nowadays is how to attract the opposite sex, and what to do with them when they succeed. They don't need biology lessons to find that out.

Maisie never married. She used to say there wasn't a man on earth good enough to make her give up her freedom. Personally, I think she frightened the men off. Those who were brave enough to get close to her, that is.

Maisie made a great teacher, but she doesn't know much about being a woman. She liked to take charge, and you either do things her way or not at all. Most men don't like that. At least, my Harry didn't. He always said that marriage should be a partnership. Though I always let him think he was the boss.

Maisie made a big fuss when I told her I was getting married. She was afraid that Harry wouldn't take care of me as well as she had. But then she didn't know my Harry the way I knew him.

When he died a year ago last November, Maisie came to live with me. I think she'd been waiting forty-eight years for that moment. That's how long Harry and I were together. I miss him a lot.

Maisie's highlight of the day is when the mail arrives. I don't know what she expects to find in there. More often than not we get nothing more than some fool advertising circular trying to sell us magazines we don't want, insurance we don't need, or storm windows we can't afford.

It doesn't matter to Maisie. She treats every piece as if it's a letter from the President himself. At least, she did so until last Wednesday.

Life in our little town can be pretty dull, especially in the winter. There's only one main street, and no big stores like the ones in Deerport a couple of miles up the road.

Visitors tend to stay away from the beach when the cold, wet wind comes roaring in from the Pacific Ocean. They call it Rainbow Bay because if you stand on Satan's Point between the twisted pines and look west, straight out to sea, you can nearly always see a rainbow. I always wish on a rainbow. At least, I used to. I don't go up there anymore. It's not much fun without Harry.

Maisie isn't impressed by rainbows.

In fact, there isn't much that excites Maisie. She spends most of her time in the backyard when the weather's good. I must admit, the garden has never looked better. Except for the yew.

Maisie has always wanted to live in England. She visited there once. Now she drinks tea out of English bone china cups and keeps a curio crammed full of English figurines. She even has a picture of Queen Elizabeth over her bed.

One day she decided we needed English topiaries in the backyard. She took a pair of shears to the yew and hacked at it for hours. She said she was forming peacocks, but by the time she was done, the hedge looked as if it had been attacked by a giraffe with hiccups.

Sam said he liked it, though. I think that was when Maisie decided she liked him. Sam was one of the few mailmen I've met who truly believed in the carrier's code. You know . . . through wind and rain, and whatever else the Good Lord chose to put in his path.

Mind you, Sam was no youngster. His face was as wrinkled as a boiled handkerchief, he had no hair to speak of, and sometimes I wondered how he had the strength to ride that bike of his in the teeth of a nor'easter.

But his smile could warm your heart on a cold day, and the twinkle in his eye could make a woman feel like Miss America. He was quite a ladies' man, our Sam.

Maisie always had a cup of tea ready for him, every morning except for Sunday. Sam loved Maisie's tea. "A cup of your tea can keep me going for the rest of the day," he told her. "Never tasted tea like it. You should sell it. You'd be a wealthy woman in no time."

But Maisie isn't much of a businesswoman. She prefers to give the stuff away. She packages it in hand-sewn pink silk bags and gives them to people for birthdays and Christmas. I reckon just about everyone in Rainbow Bay has tasted Maisie's tea at one time or another.

It was raining last Wednesday, and blowing up for a winter storm. I could see the cedars at the edge of our yard fanning the rhododendrons. Sam would need a hot cup of tea, I thought as I watched the big, sooty clouds roll across the sky.

But the tea grew cold and bitter while we waited for him.

"He must be ill, Annie," Maisie said. "He's never this late." She kept getting up and going to the window, until she made me feel dizzy. "The tea will be too strong," she said. "I'll have to take it off the stove."

"Well, pour it out," I told her. "We don't have to wait for him."

She looked at me as if I'd suggested she walk down Main Street naked. "We always wait for him," she said, "and we'll wait for him today."

Maisie makes the best tea in the world. She dries and blends her own, from the leaves of herbs and flowers, and every one of them tastes different. I look forward to my tea and muffins in the mornings. I didn't want to miss out on them just because the mailman happened to be late.

"But if he doesn't come, we won't get to drink the tea ourselves," I said. I was getting a little annoyed at her. Not that it did any good. Once Maisie has made up her mind, the Good Lord Himself wouldn't be able to budge her. I resigned myself to waiting for Sam.

He was getting ready to retire from the post office. He was due for a nice pension, and the mortgage on his house was all paid up. He told us about it, the last time we saw him.

"All I need now is to find a woman willing to cook and clean for me," he said, with a sly wink at Maisie, "and I'll be all set. I reckon it's time. It's been lonely since Ellen died last year, and it'll be lonelier still when I don't get to bring the mail to all my charming ladies."

He'd been talking about "finding a new woman" for weeks, but when he said it that last morning, Maisie got more fidgety than I ever saw her before.

I wondered if she was thinking about Louise Daniels. Louise is a member of our gardening club, and quite the chatterbox. She used to be pretty at one time, until the years caught up with her. She wears a lot of makeup, and stinks the room out with her perfume. She dyes her hair a horrible red. It's been permed so much you can see patches of scalp in the frizzy mess.

Louise lives by herself in a room over the beauty shop on Main Street, and I think she's pretty lonely. She's always talking to the members of the garden club about Sam, telling us what he said to her and what she said to him. It's mostly the same things Sam said to the rest of us, but we let her go on thinking she's the only one he paid attention to. I guess, deep down, we all feel sorry for her.

Maisie doesn't like Louise. But then Maisie doesn't like a lot of people.

I have to admit, I looked forward to Sam's visits, too. Sam knew everything there was to know about everybody. He was the first one in town to know that Eleanor Madison was expecting a baby in the spring (except Eleanor and the doctor, of course), when we'd all gone to her wedding just before Thanksgiving.

I remember when he told us about that. I thought Maisie was going to swallow her dentures. She was almost as shocked as she was the time Sam told us that the mayor was in trouble with the IRS for evasion of taxes. Or that Beatrice Harrington's son had been expelled from college. I think Sam knew about that before Beatrice did.

Anyway, when Sam didn't come last Wednesday, Maisie kept insisting that he must be ill. She wanted me to make him some chicken soup.

"Call the post office, Annie," she said. "Ask if he came in this morning. Perhaps the mail is late arriving and he's waiting for it." Maisie doesn't like talking on the phone. She says she likes to see people's faces when she talks to them. That's the only way she can tell what they're really thinking.

Well, I called Pauline, the head clerk at the post office. What she told me shocked me speechless. Poor Sam had died.

She'd heard that it was a heart attack, Pauline said. He was alone in the house and died sometime during the night.

I hung up the phone and stood there for a minute, trying to get my heart to believe what my ears had heard. Sam . . . dead. We'd never see him again. Never hear his cheerful whistle or feel warmed by his compliments again. It was a great loss, and I don't think I fully realized just how devastating a loss until that moment.

"What's the matter?" Maisie demanded, in the kind of voice she must have used on her more unruly students.

It was then I realized I was crying. "It's Sam," I said, hunting for a tissue in the pocket of my sweater. "He died of a heart attack last night."

Well, I thought Maisie was going to drop dead herself. Her face went this dreadful gray and she grabbed ahold of the table to steady herself. "Sam? Heart attack?"

She said it so faintly, I barely heard her. Seeing her look so awful like that made me forget my own misery for the moment. I hurried over to her and made her sit down in her chair. Her hands were as cold as an Arctic wind, and her expression reminded me of the time we'd seen Father Jamison's pet poodle run over by a tractor.

I'd never seen such a terrible look on a man's face as I saw that day when the priest carried that pitiful, broken body to his car. The memory of it haunted me for weeks. It was that kind of look I saw on Maisie's face when I told her about Sam.

"We'd better have that tea now," I said, rubbing her hands. "It will make you feel better."

Maisie jumped out of that chair as if she'd been stung by a yellow jacket. "I don't want any tea," she said, and her voice sounded as if she were choking. "I'll never touch another cup of tea as long as I live!"

She rushed out of the living room and I heard her bedroom door slam. It got awful quiet after that. I thought I heard her crying, but when I crept down the hallway to listen, she must have heard the floorboards creak. I couldn't hear any sound at all from that room.

It was two days later that I heard the news. Sam hadn't died of a heart attack, after all. He'd died of food poisoning. Betsy Mae told me, when I went into the bank to deposit the pension checks.

Betsy Mae loves to gossip. She has sharp eyes that never miss a thing. Her hair is blonde, except for the roots, and she wears teenager clothes. She hasn't been a teenager for at least twenty-five years.

"Poor old devil," Betsy Mae said that day. "He must have kept something too long in the fridge. Chicken, I shouldn't wonder. They say it's the worst thing to hang on to. That's the trouble with men living all alone. Don't know how to take care of themselves. Not like us women, that's for sure."

I didn't really want to talk about Sam. My voice didn't hold up too well whenever someone mentioned his name. And it seemed as if everywhere I went, people were talking about him.

"Mind you," Betsy Mae said, looking at the pension checks as if she'd never seen one before, "I don't reckon he would have been alone that long. I heard that he and Louise Daniels were getting very friendly, if you catch my drift. Too bad he waited so long to make up his mind about her. He might have been alive today."

She scribbled something on the deposit slips and held them out to me. "Just goes to show, you have to live for the moment. That's what I always say."

I took the deposit slips from her and tucked them inside my purse. I said good-bye and started to leave, but Betsy Mae was in a talkative mood, as usual.

"How's Maisie doing?" she asked. "I saw her in the post office the other day and she said her arthritis was playing her up."

I looked at Betsy Mae, wondering if I'd heard her right. "You saw Maisie?"

"Yes, and she told me she was mailing a package of tea to Louise Daniels for her birthday." Betsy Mae leaned over the counter as if she didn't want anyone else to hear what she said. I thought that a bit strange, because I was the only customer in there at the time.

"To tell you the truth," she said quietly, "I remember thinking she hadn't done a very good job of wrapping the gift up. It was in a paper bag tied around with string. No tape on it or anything."

That didn't surprise me. Maisie never could wrap up a package. Her Christmas gifts always looked as if Santa's reindeer had used them to play football. Since she'd lived with me I'd done all her packaging for her.

"I did wonder if Louise would ever get the tea," Betsy Mae was saying. "But I asked her yesterday when she was in here and she told me she'd almost finished it. She seemed surprised that Maisie would send her a birthday present. Specially since it wasn't her birthday."

Not nearly as surprised as I was, I thought. In the first place, Maisie hardly ever went out without me. She didn't like to drive because her eyes are not what they used to be. I didn't even know she'd left the house. And what was she doing sending Louise Daniels a birthday present when she'd made it plain to me that she didn't like the woman?

"I bet Louise is going to miss Sam," Betsy Mae said, studying her fingernails. They were long and pointed, painted bright red. One of them was cut right down to the quick. She's always cussing about breaking them. I don't know why she doesn't just cut them all short. That way they'd all be the same length.

"I'm sure we'll all miss him," I said, edging away from the counter. "I have to go now, Betsy Mae."

She went on talking as if I hadn't spoken. "I don't mind telling you, I'll miss him. He was like a breath of fresh air coming into this stuffy place. Brightened my day. Always had some juicy bit of gossip to tell me. I don't know how he found out so much about everyone. My Joe reckons he read everyone's mail, and that's how come he knew so much."

I could feel the tears starting to sting my eyes, so I just nodded and hurried out of there. I didn't want Betsy Mae to see me cry. She'd pester me to find out what was wrong. I could just imagine what she'd say if she knew a foolish old woman like me was breaking her heart over a man who preferred someone like Louise Daniels.

All the way home I kept thinking about what Betsy Mae had said. Maisie must have slipped out while I was taking my afternoon nap that day. Why hadn't she told me she'd been out? Obviously because she didn't want me to know that she'd mailed a package of tea to Louise.

That was not at all like Maisie.

The more I thought about it, the more uneasy I got. We had never kept secrets from each other before, and I didn't like the idea of her doing it now.

As far as I knew, Maisie hadn't been out of her room since she'd heard about Sam dying. I'd taken her meals in to her, but most of the time they came back untouched. She wouldn't even drink her tea. Maisie was taking Sam's death very hard, indeed. Harder than I was, in fact.

I thought about that for a long time, too. And I didn't like what I was thinking. It was time, I decided, for some straight talk between my sister and me.

Maisie wouldn't open the door when I knocked at first. I was just about to give up when I heard the bedsprings creak. The door opened a crack and Maisie peered at me through the opening. "Annie?" she said, as if she were expecting someone else. Her voice was quavery and I could tell she'd been crying a lot.

"Of course it is," I said, trying not to sound annoyed. After all, I was heartbroken about Sam, too, but I managed to go on living. "Who else would it be?"

"I thought—" She shook her head, as if she didn't know what she thought.

"I want to talk to you," I said.

"I don't feel like talking right now."

She started to close the door, but I held it open. "Why did you send Louise a package of tea?" I asked, watching her face very closely.

I could tell, by the way her eyes slid away from mine, that she knew that I knew. "It was her birthday," she said. "I thought it would be a nice gesture."

"It wasn't her birthday, Maisie. You don't know when her birthday is."

She looked at me then, and her face wore that stubborn look I knew so well. "I thought it was last week," she said.

I knew I would have to come right to the point. "Sam was poisoned," I said. "I think he opened the package meant for Louise."

I couldn't believe I was actually saying those words to her. I couldn't believe she would really do what I knew she had done. But after a moment or two, her face kind of crumpled up, and she nodded. My stomach felt as if somebody had kicked it.

"What did you put in the tea, Maisie? What kind of poison?"

"Clippings."

I barely heard her, but I could read her lips. I pushed the door open wider, and this time she didn't try to stop me. "Clippings from what?" I demanded.

"The yew."

Then I remembered. Of course. The English yew, one of the deadliest of poisonous plants. I could feel the shudder go all the way down my back to my feet. "Oh, Maisie," I said. "Why? How could you? Everybody loved Sam. I loved him."

"I loved him, too." Her eyes were bright with tears when she looked at me. "I loved him more than anybody. I didn't know he would open the package."

"Sam opened a lot of people's mail," I said. "Everybody knew that. How do you think he knew so much about what was going on in town?"

"He shouldn't have stolen the tea," Maisie said. She walked over to the bed and sat down, making the springs creak again. "I didn't know he would steal the tea."

"He must have replaced it with some of his store-bought tea," I said, trying to work out in my mind what had happened. "You know how much he loved your tea. Betsy Mae told me that Louise got the tea you sent to her, and she's perfectly all right."

"Betsy Mae knows?" Maisie said, her voice going up a notch or two.

"Not about the tea being poisoned. At least, not yet." I tried to think what was best to do. "I suppose everyone will know sooner or later," I said. "The police will want to know why you did it."

Her face went chalk white when I said that, but her chin went up. "I won't tell them," she said, and I could tell by her tone she meant it. "I won't have everyone laughing at me."

"I don't think they'll be laughing," I said, trying not to let her see how much I was hurting inside. "Why did you want to kill Louise?" I asked her, although I thought I already knew the answer to that.

"Sam was going to ask her to marry him. I thought if something happened to her, he might eventually get around to asking me."

Even though I'd half-expected it, hearing her say the words so matter-of-factly shocked me. "You wanted to marry Sam?"

"You've had a husband," she said, making it sound like an accusation. "You were so wrapped up in Harry you didn't need anyone else. All I ever had was loneliness. I wanted to know what it was like to be married, to be loved by a man, at least for a little while before I died."

"I always thought you were happier living alone," I said. "You never told me . . ."

I didn't know how to finish the sentence, but she finished it for me. "That I envied you? No, I never told you. But there wasn't a night went by when I didn't long for someone to love me, the way Harry loved you."

There was such a look of sorrow in her eyes, I almost cried. "So what are we going to do now?"

"We don't have to do anything," Maisie said, sounding more like herself. "No one has to know Sam was poisoned. No one will suspect me. We can just pretend it never happened."

"I don't think I can do that," I said. "I need to think about it."

"There's nothing to think about." She narrowed her eyes, and for a moment she looked like someone I didn't know at all. "You are not going to tell everyone your sister is a murderer. What would people say?"

I could tell she didn't really believe that I would tell anyone what she'd done. I left her alone and went for a walk in the garden to get my thoughts together. When I came back inside, Maisie was looking like her old self again. She'd even made me a nice cup of tea.

I told her that something had been eating the rhododendrons, and when she went to take a look at them, I called the police. Deputy Reynolds took her away a little while ago, after I'd told him everything.

Maisie didn't say a word the whole time I was talking. She looked at me, though, just as she was being led out of the door. I knew what she was thinking.

I might have forgiven her for Sam. After all, she is my sister, and Sam's death was an accident . . . in a way. No one need have known what really happened. But I knew. And I couldn't forgive her for Harry.

You see, my Harry died of food poisoning, too. It was the same day that Maisie had paid us a visit. I didn't think anything of it at the time, because we all ate the same thing for lunch and Maisie and I were just fine.

The doctor put it down to the crab Harry had caught himself. He'd eaten it the day before he died. I don't like crab so I hadn't touched any of it.

Now I know that it wasn't the crab. Maisie had made the tea that afternoon. I remember distinctly. She must have given Harry her special brew.

She was so lonely after she retired. She was always telling me that when Harry died she'd come and live with me and keep me company. I guess she decided to hurry that along a little bit.

Harry suffered terribly before he died. Sam must have suffered, too. Maisie had to pay for that. I'd loved only two men in my life, and she'd sent them both to the grave. She might have sent me there, too, if I hadn't poured that last cup of tea down the drain.

Directing a play is a lot like writing a novel. One has to keep track of the comings and goings of a cast of characters, make sure they are holding the audience's or reader's interest, and above all, keep everything running smoothly and believably. Both jobs require attention to detail and a knack for understanding people, whether they be characters, actors, or any combination of the two.

Sight Gag

Ellen Hart

CORDELIA THORN WASN'T an early riser. As far as she was concerned, anything before noon was the middle of the night. Even so, on this fine September morning, she had an important meeting at the Allen Grimby Repertory Theater in St. Paul that necessitated her presence.

She'd been the creative director at the theater for the past two brilliant—if she did say so herself—seasons. This season, six productions were scheduled. The first on the agenda, three experimental one-acts by new women playwrights, was just about to open. The meeting she'd scheduled this morning was with the Golden Twelve. A dozen local media folks—journalists, radio and TV people, and a few highly placed reviewers, all of whom were crucial to launching the production with proper fanfare.

Cordelia believed strongly in allotting space on the Allen Grimby's prestigious schedule for new work. Not that her efforts were universally appreciated or approved.

Stanley Walcott, the executive director and resident curmudgeon, had also been at the Allen Grimby only a short time. No matter how hard Cordelia tried to be pleasant to him and communicate her thoughts clearly, they simply didn't connect. Sometimes she felt as if they didn't even share a common language. Stanley's tastes were planted firmly in the past. When they got together, it was sort of like Madonna meets Queen Victoria. Fancy bloomers were about all they had in common.

Stanley didn't like one-act plays. He also didn't much care for Cordelia's desire to produce and promote new women playwrights. As one might expect, he admired the tried and the true, the bedrock classics upon which the Allen Grimby had forged its national reputation. Classics such as Shakespeare, Eugene O'Neill, Tennessee Williams, even an occasional Pinter, which was about as avant-garde as he ever got. A war had been raging at the theater for almost two years. The present skirmish was over these three experimental one-acts. Stanley maintained that the production would be a financial flop, which would bode badly for the rest of the season. Cordelia crossed her fingers tightly behind her back and declared it would be a rousing success.

As she marched resolutely into the main lobby, tugging on her mauve silk turban, she breezed past Paula Jensen, the young woman who, when she wasn't at the university destroying various professors' peace and tranquillity, took ticket orders for the new fall season. Cordelia gave a brief wave.

Paula waved back, the phone propped between her double chin and her ear. She also winked.

Cordelia could feel herself cringe. She recognized flirting when she saw it. Paula had been flirting with her for months. It wasn't that Cordelia had anything against large women. She'd dated many. At just under six feet tall and well over two hundred pounds herself, she understood intimately what the more Rubenesque women of the world could bring to the human table. And she certainly understood why Paula, enamored with the theater as she was, would develop a crush on one of the future icons of the American stage. It was just that . . . Paula was a putz. Plain and simple. All these winks and meaningful glances were getting on Cordelia's nerves.

Noticing a group gathered around the cast photo wall, Cordelia flitted quickly past the ticket counter, glad to be able to turn her back on all of Paula's facial machinations.

The theater had recently dedicated part of the main lobby to publicity shots of the various cast members, both past and present. Old Allen Grimby was well represented by an oversized photo portrait which dominated the center of the arrangement. Stanley Walcott was there as well, appearing prim and precise in his three-piece Brooks Brothers suit. The Queen would have approved. A particularly lovely publicity shot of Cordelia looking for all the world like Norma Desmond in *Sunset Boulevard* rested right next to Stanley's more restrained photo. Except that today, as she approached, the crowd parting like the Red Sea, she could tell that something was wrong with her likeness.

As she swept up to it, her mouth dropped open and her eyes bulged in surprise. Someone, a lunatic no doubt, had pasted a thick black construction-paper mustache right across her upper lip. She was aghast. With one cut of the paper she'd gone from the lovely, middle-aged Gloria Swanson to Snidely Whiplash!

"Makeup!" she screamed, realizing the moment she said the words that it was a mistake.

The assembled crowd, the Golden Twelve plus a few other amused onlookers, all seemed to be enjoying Cordelia's bewilderment immensely.

As Cordelia tugged at the mustache, realizing it was stuck quite firmly to the glass, she noticed the head janitor emerge from the elevator.

Ferris Keegan was a short, reedy man, with gray hair that was thick around the sides and back of his head but tended toward wispy indecision on the top. During the winter

months, when the air became dry and people created sparks
by touching just about anything, Ferris's hair often stood up
straight, as if his sparks were more on the order of an elec-
trocution. He sauntered over to the portrait wall carrying a
broom and a dustpan. "Morning," he grunted, slinging the
broom over one shoulder.

"Do you know anything about this?" demanded Cordelia,
pointing to the offending mustache.

"Not bad," he muttered, eyeing it curiously.

Cordelia knew that Ferris considered himself an artist.
Early in his life he'd wanted to be a professional painter.
He often brought in his sketches for Cordelia to look at—
and admire. Just the other day she'd told him that his portraits tended to make everyone look like Beethoven. It was
just a bit of helpful criticism.

"Does this sort of thing happen around here a lot?" asked
the theater reviewer from the *Minneapolis Times Register*,
a smarmy woman in her mid-fifties.

"At least once a day," quipped Cordelia, attempting to
put a comic spin on what was essentially a hideous desecra-
tion. She turned to the janitor. "Ferris, why don't you see
what you can do to remove the, ah . . . upper lip . . . problem."

"Sure thing, Ms. Thorn."

"See that it's done right away."

He snapped to attention and saluted.

She hated it when he did that, but let it pass.

Ushering the crowd into the main auditorium, Cordelia
waved to Rowena Todd, the lead actress in two of the one-
act plays, who had already assumed her place on stage,
ready to give the performance of a lifetime.

Cordelia scuttled around the orchestra pit and up the side
stairs. She had to do the introductions, and set the stage, as
it were, for this morning's special preview.

After introducing Rowena and the three new women
playwrights, Cordelia moved into the wings. As the house
lights dimmed and the stage lights came up, Rowena started

her soliloquy. She was an incredibly funny woman, with a
commanding voice and the kind of dead-on comic timing
other actors would have killed for. She and Cordelia had
met in college. They'd been friends for almost twenty
years. Last season, Rowena had starred in the only flop of
the season. She'd confided some misgivings about her present work as well. The one-act play about to be previewed
was nothing short of comic genius, and when Rowena was
on, she could bring the house down with laughter. Yet, it
was a difficult task to be *on* at any given moment. Lately,
Cordelia had begun to wonder if Rowena wasn't experienc-
ing a rather chilling blast of cold feet.

Leaning against a large wooden pillar, Cordelia saw that
the audience was already caught up in the intelligently
talky humor of the story. Rowena, clutching a pillow to her
stomach, moved her catlike frame over to a coffee canister
sitting on the set's kitchen counter. Slowly, explaining that
her boyfriend had just left her for a much younger woman,
she removed the cover. In an instant, the ironic mood she'd
worked for the last ten minutes to create exploded with the
audience's laughter as a half-dozen large, brightly colored
cloth worms erupted from the canister. Reflexively, she
screamed and jumped back, inadvertently knocking over a
small table and sending a vase of fresh-cut flowers crashing
to the floor.

The audience, thinking it was part of the play, continued
to roar.

As Rowena stood in shocked amazement, her gaze dropping to the worms and then returning to the blackness in
front of her, she seemed to be listening to the crowd's hilar-
ity grow to a feverish pitch. Finally, standing up straight
and squaring her shoulders, she turned to Cordelia, her eyes
flashing with anger.

Cordelia moved immediately away from the pillar. As
she inched onto the stage, shrugging her shoulders to let
Rowena know she didn't have a clue what was happening,
the crowd grew ill at ease. Watching the scene unfold, they

were no longer certain what was going on. A few people began to murmur, then snicker. Then . . . total silence.

Kicking the booby-trapped canister across the floor, Rowena shouted, "I refuse to work under these conditions any longer!"

Cordelia gave her head a tiny shake. If Rowena had any sense of body language, she knew Cordelia was pleading with her to keep quiet.

"Unless you can promise that these ridiculous jokes are going to stop," she continued, her back to the audience, "you'll have to get yourself another actress for opening night."

"Just calm—"

"And don't tell me to calm down!"

Rowena could be a real prima donna when she was in the mood. Cordelia moved closer, whispering, "Just zip it, will you! We'll talk about this later."

"Be more specific," called one of the members of the press, a young man in the first row. "What were the other jokes?"

Cordelia turned to the assemblage and smiled a less-than-confident smile. "I'm afraid Ms. Todd's concentration has been adversely affected by this—"

"You're damn right it has," said Rowena. In utter frustration, she picked up one of the worms and hit Cordelia over the head.

Again, the audience began to roar. Unfortunately, this time it sounded more like jeers.

"Stop it," snarled Cordelia, yanking the worm away from Rowena. "You're acting like a two-year-old."

"Why don't you tell them?" demanded Rowena. "Tell them what it's been like around here the past couple of weeks! I've never worked on a set like this before in my life. You'd think the ghosts of Laurel and Hardy were bored with paradise and wanted to run a few sight gags down here just to keep in practice. It's . . . bizarre! Nobody can work under these conditions. I nearly killed myself on that banana peel last week. And the week before that—"

Cordelia grabbed her arm, turned to the audience with a sweet smile, and then tightened her grip.

"Ouch! You're hurting me."

Cordelia glanced longingly at one of the cloth worms, wishing she could stuff it down Rowena's throat.

"At this rate, opening night's going to be a freaking disaster!"

"Shut up," whispered Cordelia out of the corner of her mouth. She was still maintaining her smile, though the sweetness had turned to pain. She could feel the audience glaring at her, demanding an explanation. She had none to offer. The preview had, for all intents and purposes, ended.

Rowena yanked on her black sweater. "I'm outta here," she announced dramatically, exiting stage left.

As Cordelia's eyes rose to the intense, amber spotlight shining down on her, she wondered idly if she'd made a big mistake becoming a director. Instead of the theater, perhaps she should have picked a less stressful, more lucrative profession. Something like, oh . . . cleaning furnace ducts.

Two days later, as Cordelia emerged from the elevator nearest her office door, once again annoyed that she had to be up and functioning so early, she saw Stanley Walcott gliding down the hall toward her, humming the opening strains to Beethoven's Fifth Symphony. For him, this was Easy Listening music. Normally, he leaned more toward Stravinsky. He was wearing a dark blue suit with a yellow silk tie and matching handkerchief stuffed rakishly—for Stanley—in his breast pocket. Until he'd spotted Cordelia, he'd seemed to be in a good mood. Then, his face puckering into a frown, he came to a dead stop.

"I've been wanting to talk to you," he said, sotto voce.

"So talk." Hers wasn't a friendly response. So sue her, she thought; it had been a bad week. She'd heard from Paula on her way past the ticket counter that ticket sales for the one-acts were still extremely low for the opening performance—not a good sign.

"Come into my office," he said officiously. He led the way.

Cordelia made herself comfortable on the rose brocade couch. She knew he would have preferred her to sit in one of the chairs on the other side of the desk, but she wasn't going to play his power games today. Besides, her back hurt, and the couch was softer. She draped herself dramatically over the cushions and gave him a bit of innocent eye flutter. "What's up?"

He sat down in his leather chair. "Have you seen the morning paper?"

"I try not to read anything before noon. It upsets my metabolism."

"Well," he said, flipping through the pages quickly, "I think you might make an exception for this." He folded the newspaper to the right spot, got up, and dumped it in her lap.

She read through the article quickly. It seemed that the smarmy, fiftyish theater critic had made a small mention of the preview she'd attended at the Allen Grimby two days before. She'd hinted that the theater was being plagued by an unbalanced weirdo intent on ruining the new production with a series of badly timed sight gags. She'd even quoted Rowena Todd about the spirit of Laurel and Hardy creating havoc on the set.

"Great," said Cordelia, allowing the paper to drop to her lap.

"Why didn't you tell me the preview performance was such a disaster?"

"We . . . just got off to a bad start."

"An exploding canister of worms! That's an understatement, wouldn't you say? I had to call Rowena to find out what really happened. I should have heard it from you!" His face flushed, but not as red as Cordelia might have imagined, given the set of circumstances. She wondered why. Perhaps, in some part of his heart, he was pleased that his prediction about these experimental one-acts would be proven right.

"Stanley, just chill, will you? Nothing else is going to happen, I'll see to it. The production will go on as planned."

"Not according to Rowena! She's ready to bail . . . I mean, back out." He cleared his throat. Cordelia knew he hated it when even the least little bit of contemporary slang crept into his classic Oxford vocabulary.

"She told you that?"

"In no uncertain terms."

Cordelia gave a deep sigh. "She's just being dramatic, Stanley. It goes with the territory."

"Maybe." He plopped back down behind his desk. "All I can say to you is, you'd better be right. Put a lid on this publicity, is that clear? The reputation of the theater is at stake."

She couldn't have agreed more, even though she found his melodrama both tedious and amusing. He'd uttered that last line with complete sincerity. Cecil B. DeMille would have been proud. "Try the decaf this afternoon, Stan. Might help with some of your tension."

As his chin sank against his chest and his eyes rose disapprovingly over his bifocals, Cordelia made a swift but graceful exit.

Walking quickly down the hall to her office, she was about to duck inside when she spotted one of the staff secretaries steaming toward her.

"Sorry, Ms. Thorn. I hope you're not upset." The young woman seemed uncomfortable, fidgeting with the button on her Peter Pan collar. She was new on the staff. Another university student. Unlike Paula Jensen, however, she had no particular interest in the theater.

"First, call me Cordelia, not Ms. Thorn."

"Right . . . Cor . . ."

"Delia." Even though Cordelia thought of herself as a basically good person, she had no patience for people who talked slowly. She always ended up finishing their sentences for them. Irritating, of course, but there it was.

"Two gentlemen are here to see you. One arrived a few minutes before the other. They're from *Entertainment Lines Daily* and *Twin Cities Arts Weekly*."

"No kidding." Cordelia was surprised . . . and delighted. These were two reporters she'd invited to the preview who hadn't been able to come.

"I showed them into your office. Was that all right?"

"Just dandy, dear heart. Now you trundle on down to Stella's desk and tell her to bring the three of us some coffee. Chop-chop. She'll know just what to do."

"Absolutely," said the young woman. She bounced off.

Cordelia rubbed her hands together in anticipation. This was an incredible stroke of luck. She'd planned to call these guys later in the day and see if she could set something up. Having them arrive uninvited, ready and waiting for her to turn the full force of her sparkling personality on them . . . well, they were like two sitting ducks. Set 'em up and mow 'em down. Cordelia had never had a problem with confidence. She attempted to wipe the smirk off her face as she entered her office.

"Gentlemen, what a pleasant surprise." She floated over to her desk, keeping her expression mild. "What can I do for you?" Before they could answer, she continued. "Oh, I suppose you're here about our opening production next week. The Allen Grimby is pleased to offer three dazzling new one-acts. Were you able to read the publicity I sent you?"

The men exchanged glances.

"I see perhaps you haven't. Well, never mind. I can paint the picture for you without too much trouble." She sat on the corner of the desk and moved her arms apart expansively. "This production is going to be our signature piece for the entire season. Three new women playwrights, and I highlight the word *women*. Women with style, and a ribald and wry sense of humor. I'll spell their names for you. We wouldn't want to get that wrong." She hesitated. When they didn't move, she asked, "Can I assume you fellows know how to write?"

"Actually," said the man from the daily, "we came to talk to you about what happened at the preview the other day."

Cordelia swallowed hard, but kept on smiling. "The . . . ah, preview?" Her voice squeaked. "Why ever would you want to know about that?"

The man from the weekly responded, "We read the piece in the *Times Register* this morning. Sounds like you might be having some troubles over here. Trouble at the largest repertory theater in the Midwest is news."

"Now now, gentlemen—and I use that term . . . carefully—you must understand. There is *so* much more interesting material we could talk about today. I don't know what you've heard, but—"

A knock on the door interrupted her.

Stella entered the room carrying a thermal carafe of coffee and three cups. She set everything down on the desk in front of Cordelia and then asked if anyone took cream or sugar.

The man from the daily said he'd like some skim milk, if possible.

Cordelia eyed him suspiciously. He was obviously fatphobic. They wouldn't get along. "Thanks, Stella."

"Right," said the red-haired woman. "Oh, before I forget: A courier service dropped this off for you a few minutes ago." She pulled an envelope out of her pocket and handed it over.

Cordelia examined it briefly, looking for a return address. There wasn't one.

"The courier said it was important. You might want to read it right away."

As Stella left the room—in search of a fat-free cow—
Cordelia excused herself for a moment and took out her letter opener, slicing open the envelope. Inside was a sheet
torn from a yellow legal pad. She studied it for a moment,
then said, under her breath, "Everybody's a comedian."

"Excuse me?" said the fat-phobic reporter.

Cordelia stuffed the note back into the envelope and then
pushed it under her monthly planner. "Will you boys excuse me for a minute? There's something I need to do. Help
yourself to some coffee while I'm gone."

"No problem," they both said eagerly, almost in unison.

She did a double take, but continued on out the door,
shutting it softly behind her.

Both men waited for several seconds and then leapt to their
feet and attacked the monthly planner, slipping the letter
out from under it.

"Get your sticky fingers off that," growled the reporter
from the *Twin Cities Arts Weekly*. He grabbed the letter out
of the other man's hand.

"Hey, who do you think you are?"

"A card-carrying member of the Fourth Estate."

"The what?"

"Just shut up and listen." He unfolded the paper and read
out loud,

"DEAR MS. THORN,
IF YOU THOUGHT THE PREVIEW WAS FUN,
JUST WAIT UNTIL OPENING NIGHT.
YOU'LL LAUGH YOURSELF SICK!!!"

"Is it signed?"

"Yeah."

"By who?"

"By *whom*, asshole."

"Just cut to the chase."

The weekly reporter looked up, a triumphant sneer on his face. "The Unbalanced Weirdo."

"Creepy!"

"No lie."

"I wonder where he came up with it." He pried the letter out of the other man's hand and scanned down the page.

"It's what the *Times Register* called him this morning."

They stared at each other for a long moment, then broke into wide grins.

"I think we got what we came for," said the arts weekly man.

"Yup," agreed the fat-phobic daily reporter, sucking in his stomach and giving it a pat.

"Hey!" The arts guy put a finger to his lips. "Get rid of it! I think she's coming back."

The daily reporter jammed it back under the monthly planner, then both men resumed their seats, plastering on bored expressions as they waited for Cordelia's return.

A few moments later, Cordelia entered the room and once again stepped over to the desk, this time standing behind it. "Sorry that took me so long, boys. Everything's under control now. So, where were we?"

"Is it?" said the weekly reporter.

"Is it what?" said Cordelia, glancing down at her desktop. She touched the edge of her planner, narrowing her eyes in thought.

"Under control."

"I don't know what you mean."

"Sure you do," said the arts weekly fellow. "You know exactly what I mean. The Unbalanced Weirdo? You remember him, don't you?" His voice dripped sarcasm. "What do you suppose he'll be up to next?"

Cordelia stiffened. "That is absolutely no concern of yours." She punctuated her statement by sitting down. As she did so, a loud fart ripped through the room.

The men were startled. Then, slowly, they began to laugh.

Cordelia's face flushed with embarrassment. She erupted out of her chair and whisked a whoopee cushion from the seat, holding it by the edge as if it might bite her.

"The Unbalanced Weirdo strikes again," snickered the arts weekly guy.

Cordelia gave him a sickly smile, then said, "All right. You win. I can see this is hopeless. Continuing to stonewall isn't getting us anywhere. Besides, unless I'm badly mistaken, you two have already looked at that note I just received."

The giggles and snickers dissolved into indignation.

"I beg your pardon," said the daily reporter.

"Come on. If I can cut the act, you can too. And anyway, it's my fault. I should know better than to leave two piranhas in here alone." She sat back down tapping her fingers impatiently on the desktop. "And since I can't exactly ignore this mess, I'm going to give you lads a statement. That is, if you promise to quote me accurately."

Both men whipped out their pad and pen.

"All right. I'll speak slowly and to the point. We wouldn't want you to get writer's cramp, now would we." She paused, allowing the tension of the moment to build. Finally, she began, "I, Cordelia M. Thorn, being of sound mind and under no duress or outside pressure, do hereby promise that before opening night, I shall find out who is responsible for these malicious tricks, and will put a stop to it. Nothing, and I emphasize the word *nothing*, other than great theater will happen here next Friday evening."

The men wrote quickly.

"Now, I'd be delighted to answer any questions." She sat back and made a bridge of her fingers.

"Who do you think's behind it?" asked the daily reporter.

"No comment."

"But you have a theory?"

"No comment."

"What about Rowena Todd? Our sources tell us she's about to back out of the production."

"No comment."

"We understand the executive director never wanted to see these one-acts produced in the first place."

"No comment." Cordelia stood. "Now, I really *am* enjoying this little professional give-and-take, but I'm afraid I'm going to have to ask you guys to shove off. I've got several other important matters that require my immediate attention."

"*Some* question-and-answer session," grumped the arts weekly man as he rose, returning the pad and pencil to his backpack.

"Oh . . . and one other thing," added Cordelia pleasantly.

"Yes?" said the daily reporter, looking hopeful.

"Spell my name right this time, guys—as a professional courtesy?" She winked, then pointed to the door.

The following Tuesday afternoon, Cordelia was on the phone talking to Rowena Todd when Stanley Walcott burst into her office.

"Did you see this!" he demanded, holding the morning paper in his clenched fist and waving it around as if he were swatting deerflies.

"Rowena, I've got . . . a situation here. Can I call you back?" She held her hand over the receiver. She didn't want Rowena to hear any of Stanley's muttered comments.

"What's going on now?" asked Rowena. "Who came in?"

"Oh . . . just one of the Seven Dwarfs."

"Really. Which once? Sneezy? Happy? Dopey?"

"Grumpy."

"Ah. Stanley." She paused. "Well, get rid of him. We're not done talking."

"I, ah . . . can't. I'll call you right back."

"You better," she huffed. "We've got some serious discussing to do."

"Later," said Cordelia, returning the receiver to its cradle. She turned her full attention on Stanley, who had finally gotten tired of flouncing around the room and had lowered his elegant frame into a chair. "What's up?"

"Have you found out who's behind these ghastly vaudeville pranks yet?"

"I've been too busy putting out small fires." She nodded to the phone. "Besides, I was hoping they'd just stop."

"Well, they haven't."

"Meaning what?"

"*This,*" he said angrily, tossing the paper across the desk.

She spread it out in front of her, immediately spotting her photo next to the caption, "Cordelia Thorn, creative director of the Allen Grimby Repertory Company, sporting a new mustache. Is it the new gay chic? Or is this prestigious theater really being plagued by the spirit of Laurel & Hardy?"

"I thought I told you to put a stop to this!" he barked.

"Well, I . . ." She studied the photo a moment more. "You know, I sort of like myself with a—"

"This has got to stop! I thought you were trying to find out who's behind it!"

"I was. I mean, I *am.*"

"Not that I can tell." He glared at her.

She glared back.

After a long moment he said, "You know, if I didn't know better, I'd say you sent that photo to the paper yourself."

Cordelia was aghast. "I did not!"

"No?"

"Absolutely not! This is ridiculous, Stanley. Why would I do something like that?"

"Publicity," he said without missing a beat. "You know the old adage: *Any* publicity is better than *no* publicity."

"That's a matter of opinion."

"Is it?"

"Yes! I had nothing to do with that picture appearing in the morning paper. I swear it!"

He looked her up and down and then said, after a meaningful pause, "Well, whatever." Folding one leg over the other, he continued, "We still have a situation that needs our immediate attention. Say, what about that friend of yours? The one who goes around solving murders."

"You mean Jane Lawless?"

"Right."

"I don't need her help. Or anyone else's, for that matter. Besides, there hasn't been a murder here."

"Not *yet* there hasn't," he said, wiggling a menacing eyebrow at her. "But there *may* be one if you don't put a stop to this. I suggest you start by finding out who slipped this picture to the *Times Register*."

"And how, pray tell, am I supposed to do that?" She folded her arms in front of her.

"How should I know. *You're* the part-time sleuth. At least that's what you're always telling me. This Jane Lawless person never solves a *thing* without your help. If I'm to believe you, she does nothing but follow your lead."

"Well . . ."

"So lead!"

Cordelia cleared her throat. "All right. I think I might have an idea or two."

"Good. I'm waiting."

"For what?"

"I'm coming with you."

"But—"

He stood. "Let's go."

Wondering what had changed Mr. Delegate-the-Dirty-Details-Whenever-Possible into Mr. Take-Charge, Cordelia sat back and considered the issue. "All right," she said finally. "But first I have to make a phone call."

He plunked back down.

"A *private* phone call."

Rolling his eyes, Stanley got up and walked to the door. "I shall be waiting right outside."

The more Cordelia thought about it, the more irate she became. Who would have the gall to take a snapshot of her defiled publicity photo and then send it to the Minneapolis paper? Even though she didn't have the answer, she thought she knew a good place to start her search.

Breezing down the subterranean hallway that led to the janitor's office, she stormed into the small room, ready to confront Ferris Keegan in his lair. Stanley inched in behind her, emboldened by his newfound potency.

Ferris sat in a beat-up old chair, feet on his desk, eating a ham sandwich. "Afternoon," he said pleasantly enough, though Cordelia was certain she heard a whiff of snideness in the greeting.

"Where's your camera?" she said, not wanting to waste time on niceties.

"What camera?"

"The one you just got for your birthday."

"Oh. *That* camera." He continued to chew. "In the file cabinet over there." He pointed.

"You admit it!" said Stanley, his eyes popping.

"Admit what? That I have a camera? Lots of people own cameras, Stanley. Last I heard, it's not against the law."

Cordelia leveled her gaze. "Before you cleaned up that publicity photo of me last week—"

"You mean the one with the mustache?" A smirk formed.

"Yes. Did you take a picture of it first?"

"Why would I want to do that?"

"To sell to one of the local papers!" barked Stanley. "It's you, isn't it? You're the one behind all these pranks. I've seen it coming for months. You're not happy here any longer."

"What was your first clue?"

"Is it really you?" said Cordelia. She shot him a perplexed glance. "I don't understand. Why would you do it? You're giving my actors a nervous breakdown!"

"You feel you've . . . outgrown us, isn't that right?" declared Stanley, his lower lip inching ever so slightly outward in what appeared to be a pout.

"What makes you think that, Stan?" said Ferris. His smile was slow and pregnant with meaning. "Just because I was recently offered a show at an art gallery in Manhattan? What difference could that make?" He waited, giving the information a moment to sink in. "I've been discovered, folks. Soon to be a household name. Aren't you happy for me?" He eyed Cordelia evilly. "It seems some people don't share your opinion that all my portraits look like Beethoven."

She returned his evil glance. "Maybe this gallery is into depressed German composers," she huffed. "By the way . . . congratulations."

"Thanks." He downed several gulps of Coke. "But getting back to your question—or I should say, your accusation. No, I didn't take a snapshot of your publicity photo. I can't prove it, but I'm not lying. I saw it in the morning paper. Got quite a chuckle. What about you, Stan? You done any photography lately?"

Cordelia found the question obnoxious and at the same time startling. Why would Ferris accuse Stanley?

Stanley sputtered and then harrumphed. "Don't be ridiculous. And don't change the subject. Unless these small acts of terrorism stop, I'm going to call in the police."

"The what!" said Cordelia.

"I may even postpone the opening this Friday night. I won't have this theater become a target for . . . for unbalanced weirdos."

Ferris burped, wiped his mouth with his sleeve, and then burped again.

Stanley was appalled by crudeness. Shuddering visibly, he returned his attention to Cordelia. "I expect you to find out what's going on around here. Otherwise, I promise you, the police will be summoned."

"Stanley, let's get this straight: You're not my superior," she countered. "You have no right to make unilateral decisions. I won't stand for it. We're supposed to work together—as a team." She added, under her breath, "Not that we ever have."

"Find this lunatic!" he insisted, not hiding the acid in his voice. Without so much as a backward glance, he spun around and stomped toward the door. As he swung into the hallway, Cordelia watched in stunned silence as a gloved hand slammed a whipped cream pie right into his unsuspecting face. Footsteps echoed on the cement floor as the perpetrator rushed away.

Stanley turned and felt blindly for the doorjamb, allowing the pie to fall to the ground. In perfect vaudeville fashion, he scraped the whipped cream away from his eyes, creating an even more hilarious image. "Somebody is going to pay for this," he snarled through the cream, bits of it dripping onto his perfect Brooks Brothers suit.

Ferris took one look at him and began to laugh so hysterically, Cordelia was sure the sound would carry right out of the tiny office and up to the very rafters of the building.

"Stan . . . ah, can I get you a towel?" she said somewhat lamely.

"This suit is ruined!"

"Sorry. But—" She raced to the door and looked down the hall. "Did you see who it was? Maybe we should go after him."

Stanley shook his head. "If you want to, that's up to you. The guy was wearing a Daffy Duck mask—and a heavy black coat." He licked his lips, then his fingers.

Ferris continued to giggle as he got up and walked over to his filing cabinet, removing his new camera. "Say, why don't you two stand together and I'll get a couple of snapshots. You know—something for my scrapbook to remember you by when I'm gone. Generally I don't like posed photos, but in this case, I'll make an exception."

"I want some *action* on this!" declared Stanley, ignoring Ferris and instead staring straight at Cordelia. "Is that understood?"

She swallowed hard. "I'll do my best."

Scraping the cream off his face, he marched off toward the elevators.

After he'd gone, Ferris waited a moment and then said, "Say, Cordelia. I might just have a hot tip for you."

She was in no mood for his humor. "What kind of tip?"

"I think I may know who sent your publicity shot to the paper."

She narrowed her eyes. "Is this a joke?"

He walked over and whispered a name in her ear. "Check it out," he urged. "See if I'm not right." Then, settling back down at his desk, he picked up the uneaten half of his ham sandwich and took a bite. "Bon appétit," he said, giving her a dismissive flick of his hand.

Ten minutes later, Cordelia knocked on the ticket counter's glass window, waved at Paula, who was inside talking on the phone, and then walked around and entered the room through the rear.

As she scanned Paula's desk, her eyes darted to a large sack purse and the folder of snapshots poking seductively out of it. Sidling nonchalantly up to the purse, she moved her hand lazily along the strap. So close and yet so far, she thought, deciding that if she attempted to peruse the pictures uninvited, it would lack a certain taste. She could tell Paula's conversation was just about over, so she leaned against the desk and waited.

After hanging up, Paula gave Cordelia her most dazzling smile and said, "Howdy." She infused the word with great meaning.

Cordelia tried hard not to roll her eyes. It was a struggle.

"What can I do for you?" asked Paula, scooting her chair closer to Cordelia.

Cordelia's gaze moved instantly to the photos. "I see you like to take pictures."

The smile remained at high beam, though the eyes grew less certain. "Why . . . yes, I do."

"Can I see them?" Why stand on ceremony? If these really *were* the photos Ferris Keegan said she'd find, why pussyfoot around? Cordelia never pussyfooted.

"See them?" repeated Paula. Her smile was crumbling around the edges.

"That's what I said." Before Paula could stop her, Cordelia had whipped the photos out of the folder. Sure enough, as she flipped through the stack, she found just what she was looking for. She held one up. It was a badly cropped shot of her publicity wall portrait, complete with hideous black mustache. "Fascinating," she said, slapping it down on the tabletop.

"I . . . I can explain," Paula's face had turned ashen.

"I wish you would. And while you're at it, maybe you'd also explain why the *Minneapolis Times Register* printed one just like it this morning."

"They did?" Her eyes grew wide.

Cordelia gave a grave nod.

"Well . . . I, ah . . . you see . . . actually . . . to be honest . . ."

"Yes, be honest, dear. It's always the best policy." Cordelia hated clichés—especially moral clichés, but if the shoe fit . . .

Paula gave a tiny swallow. Then, "Yes, I took it." Her eyes dropped to her hands. "I couldn't resist. I thought you looked kind of . . . rakish with that mustache. I wanted to blow up the photo into a poster."

"A what?"

"I have several of you at home. I have my own publicity photo wall."

Cordelia was aghast—and just a tiny bit flattered.

"But . . . I'm just a poor grad student. You know that. The poster would have cost me tons of money—money I didn't have. So, when that guy came by yesterday and asked if anyone had gotten a picture of the mustache portrait—"

"Guy?" repeated Cordelia.

"Yeah. A man from the *Times Register*. He offered me a hundred bucks for it."

"And you gave it to him? Just like that?"

"Well," she said, her voice growing coy, "cash *is* cash. Besides, I thought it was great publicity for the theater. And maybe I was right. We've picked up a lot of ticket orders since last Friday—and a whole bunch this morning."

This was news to Cordelia. "Define *a lot*."

"Twenty more seats and we'll be sold out for opening night!"

Cordelia closed her eyes and heaved a sigh of relief. "That's fabulous!"

"It's just . . . ," continued Paula, "I would have told you, but I was afraid you'd think I was behind all the pranks going on at the Allen Grimby. Mr. Walcott even accused me of it yesterday."

"He did?" Interesting. Stanley was doing a pretty good imitation lately of the Spanish Inquisition. It was so out of character. "And would that be a false assumption?" she asked.

"Absolutely! I can't believe you'd think I'd do something so crazy. What would be my motivation?"

"What indeed," said Cordelia under her breath.

"So . . . do you forgive me?" said Paula, her eyes batting innocently as her hand inched ever so slowly toward Cordelia's knee.

"I'll think about it." She pushed away from the desk. At least she'd have something to report to Stanley. No matter what he said, she wasn't going to allow him to postpone the opening night. "Keep me posted on ticket sales. Let me know when we're SRO."

"Sure."

"And one more thing."

"Anything, Cordelia. I'll do anything to make this up to you."

"Give me the negatives."

"What? But—"

She gave Paula an indulgent smile as she slipped them out of the folder. "We wouldn't want that awful picture to end up on the cover of *Cosmo*, now would we?"

The moment of truth had come. It was opening night.

As Cordelia stood in the wings, peeking out at the assembled crowd, she felt the same thrill she always felt at the start of the fall season. Yet tonight, the sense of triumph was even greater. Stanley Walcott had been a thorn in her side right up to the very last minute. She could see him standing in the back of the auditorium, looking sour and defeated as people filed in. The theater would be packed tonight—not a single seat remained to be sold. Now, if her actors could just get through the opening performance with the style and wit she knew they possessed, the rest of the performances would be SRO too. This was the beginning of a long and successful run; Cordelia could feel it in her bones.

The house lights dimmed and the stage lights came up. Cordelia squeezed Rowena Todd's hand and then gave her an encouraging pat as the actress passed by and entered stage right. The rest, as they say, would be history.

Not waiting for the play to begin, Cordelia ducked out through the back and took the freight elevator up to the third floor. She had something she needed to do before she returned to the theater to watch the performance.

Entering her office, she sat down behind her desk and flipped on her reading light. Then, swiveling around, she unlocked the small refrigerator which sat right behind her chair. She carefully removed several sheets of black construction paper, an aerosol can of whipped cream, one slightly used whoopee cushion, and finally, the canister of exploding cloth worms.

Taking a moment to luxuriate in victory, she sat back and folded her arms contentedly over her chest, gazing at the props she'd used in her small but artfully crafted bit of *pre*-opening night theater.

Not that it was her victory alone. She couldn't have done it without Rowena. It had been a long shot, something that could have easily backfired. But Cordelia had been willing to take the chance. And that chance had worked! It had provided her with the audience she so desperately needed—the audience that would spread the word about these three wonderful plays. Paula had played a part too. Even though her actions weren't part of Cordelia's well-orchestrated plot, any publicity was good publicity, as Stanley so aptly pointed out.

Removing a bowl from the bottom drawer, Cordelia picked up the can of whipped cream and squirted out what was left. Of course, the ice cream, the hot fudge, the nuts, and the cherry were missing, but not to worry; she'd treat herself to all of that later. Right now, a simple bowl of whipped cream seemed appropriate. She lifted a hefty fingerful to her lips and whispered a toast: "To the Allen Grimby—long may it prosper. To our three marvelous one-act plays. And, as always"—she made a slight bow—"to me."

Sometimes a creative director had to get *really* creative.

And Cordelia, as usual, was up to the challenge.

It seems that Christmas doesn't bring out the holiday spirit in everyone after all. Although I love seeing Cabot Cove wreathed in snow come December, sometimes I'm even happier to see it leave come April. Be that as it may, however, the holiday season does give rise to its own brand of crime, as evidenced by this tale of larceny in England.

Safe Deposit

Sarah J. Mason

DETECTIVE SUPERINTENDENT TREWLEY had been sent to Coventry: but not in a literal sense.

And by no means for the first time. The burly middle-aged man with the lugubrious brown eyes and distinctive corrugated features—those who saw him could never decide whether he more closely resembled a bloodhound or a bulldog—was nowhere near Britain's Midlands force in this week before Christmas. He was in his native Allshire, in the corridor leading to his office in the Allingham police station . . . and he was, as he'd so often been before, in disgrace.

"Cold-shouldered again, sir?" His sidekick, the petite and dark-haired Detective Sergeant Stone, looked up from her desk as the door, flung open, juddered wildly on its hinges and Trewley strode in. "Same here." She smiled. "Guilty by association, that's me. As if I can help the company I keep! Good heavens, I'm only obeying orders. I don't think it's fair."

Her cheerful nonsense defused the mood. "It's victimization," agreed the bulldog with a slow, rumbling chuckle, dropping heavily on his chair. "Want to put in an official complaint to your station superior?"

Stone's look was tinged with mischief. She considered for a moment. "Now, there's a tricky problem of etiquette. Would my superior be you, sir—or Desk Sergeant Pleate? In the circumstances . . ."

"Pleate be damned," came the automatic snarl, and it was Stone's turn to chuckle at this textbook illustration of the conditioned reflex. Before entering the police the young woman had hoped to ease her social conscience by becoming a doctor. A belated realization that the sight of blood gave her nightmares had led to her serving the community in plain clothes rather than a crisp white coat, but she did not forget her original calling.

The rapid approach of the season of universal goodwill did not stop Trewley from consigning Pleate to the vocal perdition he always invoked when the two men were at loggerheads, as they frequently were. While the superintendent might be the nominal head of Allingham's police station, the good sergeant had for years regarded it as his own particular domain. He ruled it with a truncheon of iron, and brooked no insurrection. From time immemorial he had been engaged with Trewley in a boundary dispute that would, he hoped (and that Trewley was determined would not), increase his sphere of influence in the matter of Lost Property. Trewley held firmly to the notion of a one-calendar-month period before unclaimed items should be discarded; Pleate persisted in operating a three-month-minimum plan.

Many were the midnight raids to secure extra territory in some out-of-the-way interview room, or additional shelving in an obscure part of the building. Loud and furious were the arguments when such encroachments were discovered. Stone, hoping to resolve the dispute for good and all, had once innocently proposed a compromise of two months. To her surprise, *both* parties had sent her to Coventry for a week—a week during which their relations were almost amicable—and she came at last to the conclusion that some men just never grew up.

The current skirmish had arisen the previous Friday, when a law-abiding citizen brought into the station his street-corner *trouvaille* of an oven-ready goose and a black felt hat. The billycock, being less perishable than the bird, had gone immediately into the Lost Property cupboard. The bird had been more of a problem. Pleate had pondered long before finally making reluctant appeal to Trewley, who told him to dispatch it to the canteen, where it would roost in cold storage until it should be claimed either by its owner, or by fate. "Come Christmas Eve and we cook it," the superintendent had decreed, riding roughshod over Pleate's demand for a section of the station canteen's deep freeze to be designated Lost Property for the foreseeable future or, better still, for a small deep-freeze unit to be purchased for the especial use of the Lost Property Department, bearing in mind the tendency of Allingham's citizenry to misplace its groceries on buses, in taxis, and around the town in general.

Stone ventured now to giggle. "The cold shoulder," she mused aloud. "Rather apposite, sir, wouldn't you say?"

"No," growled the bulldog, who had just noticed how much more paperwork there was in his in-tray than there had been, he'd take his oath, the night before. "I said it was victimization, didn't I? Peace on earth! Goodwill to all men! He's been saving this lot up just to annoy me, damn him. I wondered why he was smirking as I came in."

"He smirked at me, too." Stone indicated her own overflowing in-tray. "We'll be lucky to finish before midnight if he digs out much more." She was wise enough now in the ways of her colleagues to abandon any hope of smoothing the matter over. Everyone, after all, needed a hobby. . . .

The telephone rang. Trewley cursed as he recognized the ring of an internal call. "And before my first cup of tea, dammit," he groaned. "Answer it, there's a good girl." He closed his eyes and shuddered. "I'm not here, all right? Just use your discretion."

"Stone," that young person announced to the receiver, which buzzed back at her for some moments in an electronic baritone identifiable, even from the other side of the room, as the voice of Desk Sergeant Pleate. "Pickpockets?" said Stone, as the buzzing died away. "Well, perhaps I'd better speak to him. . . ."

The buzz responded with a note of what was all too obviously triumph before Stone, stifling a sigh, introduced herself again. "Good morning, Mr. Windigate."

Recognizing the name of the manager of Allingham's most prestigious hotel, Trewley stifled another groan. Pleate was taking mean revenge indeed to inflict that little fusspot on them so early in the morning. And was it fair that Stone should be the only one to suffer?

On the other hand, did he want to give Pleate (who was sure to be eavesdropping) the satisfaction of surrender?

But it *was* the season of goodwill towards all men—and women. Stone was doing him proud.

Trewley made up his mind. Waving a warning finger that his own eavesdropping was entirely unofficial, he picked up his phone and began to listen.

"I understand," Stone said in a voice just loud enough to cover the click on the line, "that you'd like to report pickpockets at the Cosmopolitan, Mr. Windigate."

"Or sneak thieves," amended the prim tones of the manager quickly. "And I certainly don't *like* it—I don't like it at all! Such a thing has never happened in the twenty-three years I have been at the Hotel Cosmopolitan—twenty-three years, Sergeant Stone!"

Stone uttered appropriate words of sympathy and shock that contrived to soothe Mr. Windigate while at the same time urging him to enlarge on recent events for her professional enlightenment.

Mr. Windigate, in quavering accents, did so. "It was . . .
the plumber," he began, with a gulp. "We pride ourselves
on quality of service at the Hotel Cosmopolitan, Miss
Stone. Our guests demand luxury—gracious living—and
we do our utmost to iron out all of life's little problems for
them. When people stay at the Hotel Cosmopolitan they are
cosseted and cared for by a devoted team, I assure you. We
do our best for them—our absolute best!"

"But sometimes things can go wrong," Stone deduced
from the agonized wail in those final syllables. "The best-
laid plans, you know . . ."

"Oh," moaned Mr. Windigate, "I know, I know—only
too well! Who could have dreamed how difficult it would
be to find a plumber at the weekend? When the radiator
burst in the Countess's room . . ."

He broke off to gulp again. Stone made more soothing
noises. Mr. Windigate listened. After a moment, he made
another attempt. "The—the Countess of Morcar is staying
at the Hotel Cosmopolitan—for the entire holiday period,"
he brought out with just the right combination of hushed
awe and haughty acceptance that, with a choice of all the
hotels in Allingham, where else should a member of the
aristocracy stay?

"The Countess of Morcar," murmured Stone, in whose
memory a faint bell chimed; but Mr. Windigate, hurrying
on with his story, gave her no time to think.

"A charming young woman—and, fortunately for us,
with a . . . a sense of humor." He sighed. "Not a word of re-
proach for the—the upheaval when we had to move them to
another suite two floors down . . ." He gulped once more.

"Them?" inquired Stone. That memorial bell had chimed
again, rather more loudly.

"Lady Morcar," explained Mr. Windigate primly, "and
Miss Cusack, her personal maid."

"The Earl isn't with them," said Stone, reading between
the lines. Mr. Windigate drew in his breath with a hiss.

"It is not the policy of the Cosmopolitan to discuss the private affairs of our guests, Sergeant. The details in our hotel register are regarded as—as sacrosanct!"

"In normal circumstances, yes," said Stone. "But surely—when you are cooperating with the police—"

A hollow groan burst from Mr. Windigate even as he waxed indignant. "If you are suggesting that the Countess of Morcar or Miss Catherine Cusack could be responsible for the theft of Mr. Horner's wallet—"

"Whose wallet?" cried Stone, before Mr. Windigate should expostulate himself into silence and the tale be lost.

"John Horner: the plumber," explained the hotel manager. "He was on the premises for several hours, not only to fix the radiator in her ladyship's suite but also to overhaul the complete central heating system as a—a precautionary measure. With the approach of Christmas and colder weather one simply cannot be too careful."

"I gather Mr. Horner wasn't, um, sufficiently careful with his wallet," said Stone.

"He returned to the hotel this morning," lamented Mr. Windigate. "He asked for—demanded—a private interview! He asked me to have the various rooms in which he had worked searched by my most trusted member of staff, since he himself had no further official cause to enter them."

Mr. Windigate's voice trembled. Stone's voice was brisk. "His wallet was nowhere to be found, so he started dropping hints that some of your hotel guests might not be the honest citizens they're cracked up to be. Yes?"

"Oh, dear," moaned Mr. Windigate. Stone took this for an affirmative. She glanced at Trewley, listening on the other extension. "And naturally," she said, "you're worried. Has anyone else reported anything stolen? Mislaid," she amended hastily, as Mr. Windigate moaned again.

"No," came the answer, in a whisper. "Not yet, that is—but . . ."

"But when—if—they do," Stone told him, "you'll let us know at once, won't you?"

"At once," whimpered Mr. Windigate; and allowed himself to be dismissed with the promise that the police had the matter in hand.

"But we haven't," said Trewley. "We've more important business than a lost wallet. Damn Pleate. Plumbers and builders lose 'em all over the place—comes from sticking 'em in their back pockets instead of inside their jackets like sensible folk. And don't tell me no workman in his right mind wears a suit, because I know. Inside his overalls, if you prefer. A back pocket's just asking for trouble—I'm not surprised he had it pinched, especially when the town's so busy. No, what does surprise me—"

"Yes," said Stone, as he fixed her with a bulldog glare. "I wonder why Mr. Horner hasn't reported his loss to us himself, instead of leaving it to Mr. Windigate."

"Even money says they call him Jack," muttered Trewley, scowling at his in-tray. "What else would you expect at this time of year? *Little Jack Horner sat in his corner eating his Christmas pie. . . .*"

"*He put in his thumb, and pulled out a plum,*" continued Stone. "I wonder, though, if our friend Jack is such a very *good boy,* after all."

"Pleate only did it," said Trewley, "to annoy me." With which remark the subject was, for the moment, closed.

Desk Sergeant Pleate greeted his superior the next morning with the most correct of professional nods. There was no smirk, no sideways look, no meaningful grin—a greeting very different from that of those subordinates whose paths crossed the superintendent's on his way to the office.

Stone was already at her desk chatting with Constable Benson, who as Trewley entered jumped to his feet and snapped off a ferocious salute. "Sir!"

Trewley looked at the young man for a moment. In his eyes, too, was that strange, almost unholy gleam he had no-

ticed in the eyes of everyone else except the rigidly correct
Pleate . . . even in the eyes of Stone, though the girl was
doing her best to look serious.

But her best wasn't quite good enough. Trewley could
tell that she, too, was trying not to smile. What was wrong
with his officers this morning that the very sight of him
should set them sniggering?

"Carry on, Stone," he growled. "Benson. Don't let me
interrupt you. Why not share the joke?"

"It's no joke, sir," Stone reassured him loudly, as Benson—damn the boy!—choked back what was all too obviously a laugh. "Benson was just . . . making his report." In
her voice was an element of control Trewley hadn't heard
before. "Making his report as he goes off-duty," she said,
and gave Benson a long, hard look of warning.

Stern brown eyes turned their full force upon poor Benson, standing to attention. "Well?" demanded the belligerent bloodhound. "At ease, lad, and out with it!"

Benson opened his mouth. "Uh," he said. Trewley
waited. Stone shook her head. Benson tried again. "Uh—
sir. Sorry, but—well, I'm on nights this week. . . ."

Trewley grunted. He left the uniformed rota to Sergeant
Pleate, and for all their other disagreements seldom found
fault with the way the man assigned the more unsocial
hours. "It's no use asking me for a change," he said.
"Everyone takes turns on nights this near to Christmas, lad.
You know that."

"Uh—yes, sir, but it's not—I mean . . . It was last night,
sir. I got called to a punch-up where some bloke and his
landlord were arguing about one of them's wallet that's
gone missing—"

"What?" bayed the bloodhound, on the sudden trail of
coincidence.

Benson rocked back on his heels as Stone hid a smile.
"Uh—his wallet, sir. Name of Horner, the owner—he's a
plumber. Lodges with a James Ryder the other side of
town. Ryder's wife walked out a few months back to live

with some bloke and left him with the mortgage, so he took in a paying guest to make ends meet."

"Jack Horner," rumbled Trewley, as Benson paused and Stone gave an encouraging nod.

"Uh—yes, sir. Seems he'd looked everywhere over town yesterday for his wallet, then after a few drinks in a few pubs he remembered coming home halfway through a big job for some tools he'd forgotten, and something falling out of his back pocket, only he was in too much of a rush to get back to the Cosmopolitan to check, and when he asked Jim Ryder he said he'd never seen it, and the drink got him—Horner—going and he called Ryder a liar, and—and well, sir, you can imagine what happened next."

There was that same note of self-control Trewley had recognized in his sergeant's voice. "No," he growled. "I can't. Suppose you tell me."

Benson shot an agonized look at Stone, who frowned, then decided to come to his rescue. "Ryder and Horner slugged it out until Benson arrived," she said. "And—and Ryder's dog didn't like the way Horner was treating his master." She took a deep breath. "So he bit him. And Horner was making such threats against the poor creature . . ." She coughed. "Benson thought you and Sergeant Pleate wouldn't want the cells cluttered up with a pair of Christmas hotheads like John Horner and James Ryder, sir. But he thought the dog—he's called Breckinridge—ought to be taken into protective custody until things had calmed down again. . . ."

"And?" The crumpled bloodhound brow expressed extreme surprise. "So you invited this Breckinridge to be a guest of Her Majesty's for a few days. Is that all?"

"Yes, sir," said Stone, firmly. She looked at Benson. Her eyelid flickered in a swift wink. "Isn't it?"

"Yes, Sarge," gasped Benson. "Thanks." He turned to Trewley. "Sir!" And with another salute, he was gone.

He started chortling just two seconds before the door closed behind him. Trewley turned to glare at Stone, who was hiding another smile. "Well?"

"Well, sir?"

"Injured innocence doesn't suit you, my girl. And it doesn't fool me, either. I want to know what's going on."

"Going on? Why, nothing more than a—a kindly demonstration on Benson's part of the spirit of goodwill to all men. And dogs," she found herself adding, then added further: "Landlords and lodgers alike. Sir."

"Umph," said Trewley. He rubbed his chin in thought. "This dog, now—"

The telephone rang with its internal ring. The superintendent shuddered. "Pleate, I'll be bound. You answer it."

"Stone," she said. She listened. "Well, I'm not really trained to deal with animals, Sergeant. . . . Yes, of course, but if you're worried wouldn't you rather ask a vet?" Her voice changed. "Yes, of course. I didn't think. I'll come at once."

She pushed back her chair. "It seems," she told Trewley, "that Benson's new friend is slightly off-color, and Sergeant Pleate doesn't want to risk calling in anyone official unless he has to."

"The Dangerous Dogs Act," agreed Trewley, as she headed for the door. "One more bite, and good-bye Breckinridge."

"I expect he's just pining for his master. I doubt if there's much to worry about. . . ." And Stone hurried away to where Breckinridge, faithful companion of landlord James Ryder, lay in durance vile.

Yet not so very vile. The floor was covered in several layers of newspaper, and Sergeant Pleate had clearly raided his precious Lost Property cupboard to produce for the loyal creature's comfort an overcoat and two woolen cardigans Stone could have sworn had been on the premises for a month at most. Beside this makeshift bed was a large bowl of water, an empty plate (evidence of another raid, on the station canteen), and, cuddled sadly about an earless teddy bear, a dog.

A dog with a bloated stomach whose rumbles had aroused the concern of Desk Sergeant Pleate, now leaning anxiously over him and patting him with a tenderness Trewley, even if he'd seen it, would never have believed.

A dog with lugubrious brown eyes and a corrugated face.

A face that must have reminded all who saw it of some-one not a million miles from that lonely cell . . .

Not a bloodhound: a bulldog.

Stone thanked her stars that Trewley had not elected to accompany her on her errand of mercy. She gave what advice she could for the greater comfort of the hapless hound, then returned thoughtfully to the office.

It was as much as she could do to keep a straight face as Trewley glanced up from his paperwork with the identical look of bewilderment displayed by the wretched Breckin-ridge.

"Done your good deed for the day?"

"I . . . think so." She knew she had to tread warily here. "Sergeant Pleate . . ." Trewley snarled. Stone faced her superior boldly. "He, um, seems to have suffered an excess of Christmas spirit, sir. Only in the metaphorical sense," she added, as the brown eyes blazed. "He, um, asked the canteen to cook the wings and legs of that Lost Property goose for the dog's dinner"—Trewley's interjection would have blistered paint—"and in my opinion it was far too rich for him," she went on, doing her best to ignore the outburst. "I prescribed a gentle turn or two round the yard and nothing but water for the rest of the day."

Trewley, who had diets inflicted on him by his wife more often than he liked, growled in sympathy. Stone smiled. "It ought to do the trick for poor old Breckinridge . . . but then I wondered. That missing wallet: was it leather?"

"Ah," said Trewley. "Yes." He rubbed his chin, and frowned. "The wallet. We've no idea, of course, as Horner hasn't reported the loss officially—not even to Benson. Odd, that. But you could be right about the dog eating it. They've got strong teeth and jaws, and insides to match."

Stone marveled that anyone had been brave enough to tell the superintendent the breed to which Breckinridge belonged, but kept a straight face as she listened. "We can't," continued Trewley, "have folk bashing each other about just because there's . . . a delay in collecting the evidence. We'll keep that animal here until it . . ."

"Pays its deposit," supplied Stone with a wry chuckle. "I imagine the leather and paper will be more or less completely gone, but surely even a bulldog"—her eyes could not meet those of her superior—"can't digest metal." She grimaced. "I'm glad I don't work in a bank. We'll have to ask them to count the number of strips that, um, eventually arrive, and give us an estimate of how many notes were in the wallet to begin with. Yuck."

"Charming," agreed Trewley.

Stone frowned. "If the strips aren't too damaged they might be able to measure them, too. With banknotes being different sizes for different denominations . . ." Once more she grimaced. Trewley grinned.

"Glad you gave up the doctoring?"

"What do you think, sir?"

Trewley was still grinning at her when the internal telephone rang again. In an abstracted moment he answered it. "Trewley . . . Yes, Pleate." The superintendent stifled a sigh. Stone sighed in sympathy as at his signal she picked up her extension. "Jack Horner's there now?" Trewley brightened. "Come to report his wallet missing, I daresay . . . What's that?"

"No, sir," said Sergeant Pleate again. "Not a mention of any wallet: it's the dog he's come about. Wants to withdraw his claim that it's vicious, he says. Wouldn't like to think of it coming to any harm with it being so near Christmas, he says."

"He says," echoed Trewley. "You think there's more to it than that?"

"He wants to take it home with him now," said Pleate. "Most insistent we should sign it out to him, he is."

"Oh, is he? Well, he can insist all he likes—it's not his dog, is it? We can't go handing over valuable animals to any Tom, Dick, or Harry that comes along. Has he brought anything from what's-he-called—the real owner—to say he can have it?"

"James Ryder," supplied Stone and Pleate in chorus, the desk sergeant going on to say that as far as he could ascertain, Horner had brought no written authorization from landlord Ryder that his tenant might collect his dog.

"Then he can't have it," decreed Trewley, and issued his instructions. "Fishy," he remarked as he hung up. "Horner still hasn't reported that wallet missing, except to Windigate. If there's any chance the dog's eaten it, you'd think he'd want to stake his claim on the . . ."

"By-products of canine digestion," offered Stone.

"Yes," said Trewley, slowly. "A disgusting job, working out the value of the notes—metal strips or not. That'll be why he wants the dog, of course. He's planning to mangle—uh—everything so much that the bank'll prefer to believe him when he says it was a walletful of fifties the poor brute swallowed, not fives and tens the way it probably was. The chap'll be worried we'll spot the—uh—important bits and work things out and stop his little game."

"Which we—you—have," said Stone. "And the proof will be with us before too long, I should think."

"I can't wait," said Trewley, and chuckled.

He did not chuckle when, as he was checking his watch at the end of the afternoon, the telephone rang and the voice of Sergeant Pleate announced Mr. Windigate of the Hotel Cosmopolitan back on the line, in more of a state than ever. "If it's imaginary pickpockets again—," began Trewley, but was interrupted.

"It's robbery, no doubt about it," Pleate informed him. "A valuable diamond's been taken from one of the luxury suites—the Countess of Morcar's blue carbuncle. . . ."

Trewley looked at Stone. Stone, listening on the other line as well as to the invisible chime of memory, looked back at him. For a moment, neither of them spoke as both brains whirred and whirled with a wild surmise. Pleate, likewise, was silent.

"Ah," said Trewley at last. "Put Mr. Windigate through, Pleate—and . . ." It would be in a good cause, he reminded himself. "And meet us by the dog kennel five minutes after he's rung off, will you?"

Mr. Windigate was almost tearful as he told his story. "Such a thing has never happened in twenty-three years," he wailed. "Twenty-three years! Our reputation is ruined! Of course, her ladyship is . . . rather preoccupied at present—perhaps inclined to be a little careless—but we cannot abjure our responsibilities to a guest by claiming her personal circumstances as an excuse."

"In the middle of a divorce," said Trewley, as Mr. Windigate gulped with horror at having inadvertently betrayed the confidence of a hotel guest. Stone nodded as she at last recognized the source of all those memorial chimes. There had been tantalizing snippets in the gossip columns; rumors of threats with carving knives . . .

"I cannot," said Mr. Windigate, recovering himself, "discuss the private affairs of our guests, Superintendent. But—oh, if only you had listened when I told you of Horner's warning that there was a gang of sneak thieves in town. . . ."

"One lost wallet," retorted the superintendent, "hardly constitutes a—an epidemic of thievery, Mr. Windigate." He paused to allow Mr. Windigate to gibber for a moment before adding: "I'm not even sure one missing diamond does, come to that."

"But this is no ordinary diamond, Mr. Trewley! This is the Countess of Morcar's blue carbuncle! She is—is desperate for its return—desperate!"

"Then the sooner we get all the facts," said Trewley, "the better. So let's have them, Mr. Windigate."

Thus prompted, Mr. Windigate explained how the Countess and her maid, a native of Allshire, had spent the past few days sightseeing and visiting friends of Miss Cusack, whose social status—Mr. Windigate coughed—was such that there had been . . . no particular requirement for her ladyship to *dress*. This final word was invested with a wealth of meaning lost neither on Stone nor on Trewley, father of three teenage daughters.

"Came the day she decided to go posh again and eat at the hotel," Trewley deduced, "and she finds her jewel box has been emptied by one of these mysterious sneak thieves of yours. Yes?"

"I fear so, Superintendent. A small morocco casket beside the bed—oh, dear! The staff, who have been with the hotel for years, are above suspicion, of course, as indeed the guests should be, but—oh, if only," wailed Mr. Windigate, "her ladyship had seen fit to deposit her jewels in the safe, this would never have happened!"

"Yes," said Trewley. "Talking of deposits . . ." Stone smothered a giggle. He frowned at her. He made up his mind. "We won't be along to take statements just yet, Mr. Windigate. But you needn't worry," as the man began gibbering again. "We've got the matter well in hand." He caught Stone's eyes, and realized what he'd said. "Under control," he amended. "You might even say we already have a suspect in the case. Tell the Countess," he went on above Mr. Windigate's astonished babble, "we hope to have some good news for her within, uh, the next few hours."

The two detectives made good use of the five minutes before their rendezvous with Sergeant Pleate. Trewley detoured via the canteen, where he begged a large bucket of hot soapy water and defied anyone to ask him why he wanted it. Stone, picking its lock with her penknife, raided the cleaning cupboard for rubber gloves and disinfectant. Thus equipped, the pair made their separate ways to where Breckinridge the bulldog slept on his newspaper carpet.

His head went up at the sound of footsteps. Soft brown eyes in a crumpled countenance met thoughtful brown eyes in a countenance quite as crumpled. "Handsome animal," said Trewley, after a pause.

"He looks a lot happier than he did this morning," said Stone. "Wouldn't you say so, Sergeant?"

Sergeant Pleate agreed, with a very pointed sniff, that he did. There was another pause.

Stone reflected philosophically that she, after all, was the one with the medical training. . . .

"It's a bonny thing," said Trewley, holding up the shining gem against the light. "Some folk should keep better care of their property. Divorce or not, that woman has no business leaving valuable jewelry lying around for passing plumbers to pinch."

"We don't know for sure that he did," objected Stone.

Trewley snorted. "It's a damned funny business if he didn't. Just because this came out of Ryder's dog doesn't make Ryder guilty. Why else was Horner so keen to get the animal back when only the night before he was trying to have it destroyed? Who had better access to the diamond than Horner, when he went to fix the Countess's radiator? He popped home halfway through the job to hide the jewel, of course. Said he'd forgotten his tools—a likely tale!"

"People do forget things," said Stone slowly. For a while now the uneasy feeling had grown that this case was working out the wrong way, although in what other way it should go she couldn't think. "Suppose . . ."

Trewley ignored her. "That's when he dropped his wallet. He scrabbles about looking for a safe place under the furniture . . . something catches . . . he's too nervy to notice . . .

he trots off back to the hotel and leaves the dog wondering what he was doing. Dog finds a nice tasty lump of leather with the chap's scent on it, fancies a snack, and roots out the diamond for afters. Jack Horner pulled out a plum this Christmas, all right!"

Stone couldn't fault his logic. She put the feeling of unease to the back of her mind, and paid tribute. "When he found the wallet was missing he took the chance to set up that pickpocket story as a bluff. When the Countess eventually returned to her room and discovered the blue carbuncle had disappeared, it would be so much better to have a mysterious gang to blame than anyone local."

Trewley muttered darkly, then went on: "He had a few drinks, overdid the self-congratulation, came home and pitched into Ryder because he'd decided the bloke must've taken the wallet, and only found out his mistake when he went to check his hiding place for this chunk of crystallized carbon and found . . . oh, scratches, marks from the dog's teeth—whatever. Then he comes rushing down here with some tale about a Christmas reprieve, and . . ."

"And Benson brings him back for questioning," concluded Stone. "They'll be here any minute, I imagine."

"He'll try to bluff it out," said Trewley. "If he does, I'm going to throw the book at him. I don't care for being made to look a fool. That dog," he enlarged.

Stone blinked. Surely . . .

"Buckets of water," he went on. Stone relaxed. "They think I don't hear 'em," said Trewley, "but I know when folk are muttering about charladies, Stone. Christmas or not, a superintendent of police has his dignity." The bloodhound jowls quivered in a slow chuckle. "My own fault, mind you. If I'd learned to pick locks the way you can, it would've been you carrying that blasted bucket, not me."

"This is the age of sexual equality," she reminded him. "But I'll give you lessons, if you like, as it's Christmas. Save buying you a present. With both of us at it, Sergeant Pleate and his Lost Property won't stand a chance."

"Pleate be damned," retorted Trewley.

And on cue the telephone rang.

Stone, catching her superior's eye, picked it up. For a moment or two she listened to the electronic baritone buzz of Sergeant Pleate, then she turned to Trewley with her hand over the mouthpiece and a puzzled look on her face.

"A member of the public has just come in to make a complaint," she informed him. "He insists there's something wrong that only we can put right, apparently. A gentleman by the name of Doyle . . ."

I can't recall the number of times I've stopped by the local library just to do a bit of research and ended up staying for hours on end. If I had a nickel for every hour . . . well, I'd be very well-off, thank you. Although the library is a place for learning, some people find it useful for more criminal pursuits, as I had the opportunity to discover recently.

Deeply Dead

Charlaine Harris

THIS WAS THE second Lunch With Books we'd had at the Spalding County Library. The first had featured Marilee Du Pond, a local romance writer. I'd barely been able to stay awake, though some attendees had obviously been delighted with Ms. Du Pond's speech, "Deeply Romantic."

I was much more excited about hearing mystery writer Jessica Fletcher. I'd been at the library since ten that morning preparing the large Media Room. The coffee was perking, the Cokes were chilling, and the cookies were out on their tray.

Now the great woman herself was ushered in by Emily Scott, my minister's new wife. At the Library Friends meeting, Emily had all but fallen off her chair in her bid to be chosen to collect our visitor at the Atlanta airport. Jessica and Emily were tied for most tastefully dressed, though I decided Ms. Fletcher had the edge in her deep red suit.

"And here's our little librarian mystery buff, Aurora Tea-garden," Emily said as if she were presenting a trained monkey. I was charmed when the noted writer didn't even snigger at my name, but looked down at me with a gracious smile and shook my hand firmly.

"What striking glasses," Ms. Fletcher said, and I liked her even more. I was wearing my newest pair, the black-and-white checkered ones I'd found in a thrift store—of course, I'd had my prescription lenses inserted. We chatted for a few polite minutes about Ms. Fletcher's flight and her plans for the rest of her book tour.

"Now let me see," Ms. Fletcher said. "I'm to speak and answer questions for forty-five minutes, while the audience eats bag lunches?"

"That's right. Emily and I will take you out to lunch afterward."

"Fine. Where should I stow my luggage?" Emily had brought in Ms. Fletcher's "weekend" bag, since a different volunteer would be transporting her to her next engagement, a signing in De Kalb County.

I shouldered the black leather bag and staggered to the closet where we kept the overhead projector, TV/VCR, and other media items. Trying to smile as though my arm weren't about to fall off, I wrenched the door open. Just as I was about to swing Ms. Fletcher's weekender inside, I saw there was something on the floor, something lumpy and limp.

It was Marilee Du Pond's body, all 185 pounds of it, swathed in yards of mauve rayon. The matching scarf was embedded in Marilee's neck. I made a gagging noise as I registered the unusual color of the romance writer's face and her bulging eyes. Marilee was deeply dead.

"Oh, dear," said Jessica Fletcher from behind me. Emily shrieked and ran for the phone as fast as her suburban pumps would carry her.

While we waited in the staff lounge until the police finished with the body, Ms. Fletcher, who was quite composed, asked me about the dead woman. I was relieved; it was hard keeping up small talk when we were all three visualizing Marilee in the closet.

"Marilee was a local gal. Before she became a romance writer she was a widowed housewife who spent hours in this very library researching the genealogy of the county's founding families. She was an offshoot of the oldest, the last remaining Du Pond. She used the family name professionally, since her married name was Snert." Some said it was high time the family died out, since the Du Ponds were not contributors, but users. Now it had.

"What sort of books did she write?" Jessica (we'd abandoned last names) was looking at us with her head cocked, apparently quite willing to talk about the horribly deceased Marilee. I sensed a kindred soul.

Emily couldn't answer this one, since all Emily read were inspirational biographies.

"She wrote historical bodice rippers."

"I see. Hmmm. Did she come to the library often?"

"Oh, yes, she did a lot of research on each book." I had to admit that, though I'd only been able to choke down one of Marilee's books, and even then my husband, Martin, had commented on the wry expression I'd had while reading.

"Did she . . . get along with the staff?"

"Whatever you talked about, she topped it. If you had gone mountain climbing, she had scaled Everest. If you had a bad cold, she had double pneumonia."

Jessica shuddered. "Yes, I've met a few of those. What would she have been doing in this room?"

"My guess, from the way she was dressed, is that she planned to beat the crowd and play one-queen-visiting-another. You know, come in early to meet you as if she weren't just another member of the audience. Maybe she thought we'd invite her to eat lunch with you."

"Were you in here most of the morning, Aurora?"

I thought back. "Yes, I came in at ten o'clock and began arranging the chairs. I left twice, once to go to the ladies' room, and once to get the Cokes out of the refrigerator in here. That took a little while, since I put the drinks, the coffeepot, and the tray of cookies on a cart and wheeled it into the media room."

"Did anyone come in while you were working?"

"Yes . . . Lillian Schmidt, who works here, came in to ask me when the lecture started. She left her notebook; I guess she came back to get it later. It was gone before you came in the room. Poor Baby Kilmer came in with a book she wanted you to sign; she was too shy to ask you yourself. But she forgot and walked out with it. And Roger Packard asked if there were going to be refreshments. He comes to anything that includes refreshments," I said apologetically.

Jessica laughed. "Tell me something about each of them," she said.

Emily was frowning and smoothing her already-sleek honey-colored pageboy. To her, this was gossip. To me, it was a way to pass the time until the police got around to us. I wished Emily would priss her face at someone else.

"Well. Lillian goes to the Flaming Sword of God Bible Church, and she has two children and a husband, and she knows everyone in town. She was a Leighton. They used to be the town's first family, emphasis on 'used to be.' The Leightons lost all their money in the last generation. Lillian's husband told me that Josh Leighton, Lillian's granddad, had to pay off a black man over some tragedy. No one knows exactly what." I had been able to tell from the longing on Chad Schmidt's face that Chad would have loved to know. Lillian had honked the Leighton horn once too often.

"Poor Baby Kilmer . . . well, *there's* Baby Kilmer."

Through the open door we watched a thin, bent, middle-aged woman aimlessly wandering around the library. She'd straighten a book, read a title, push a chair farther under the table. Wearing thrift-store polyester, without a touch of makeup on her face, Baby was a sorry sight.

"Baby is her christened name?"

Emily and I exchanged uncertain glances. "I don't know. . . ." Emily said hesitantly. "Everyone's always called her Baby. And since her husband died, most everyone says Poor Baby."

"The poor woman!" said Jessica in her warm voice. "What happened to Mr. Kilmer?"

Emily made a face of distaste. Over to me.

"Dodd Kilmer was reroofing his house. Baby was in the garden, using a pitchfork to clean off the straw they'd covered it with for the winter. Dodd fell, just as Baby stood and rested the handle of the pitchfork against the ground. Dodd landed on the pitchfork."

"How absolutely horrible!"

Emily and I nodded simultaneously. "She hasn't been quite right since," Emily murmured.

"And Roger—Packard, you said?"

"Yes. Well, Roger is our town eccentric. *One* of our eccentrics. He's very—um, very—"

"Cheap," said Emily succinctly. I remembered Emily's account of Roger running her off when she was collecting for the Flower Fund.

"He reads constantly, and is always after the library to buy more books in his field, which is a pretty esoteric one. Eighteenth-century military history, I think. No one reads those books but him, and our budget is always so tight; it's really been a problem. Roger lives in a terrible old house—"

"Used to be a mansion," Emily interjected.

"Right, out by where Marilee built her place three years ago. They had a big set-to last fall about who was going to take down a tree hit by lightning. It straddled both their property lines. It was two inches more on Roger's side, so Marilee wouldn't split the cost fifty-fifty."

"That doesn't seem rational," Jessica observed.

Emily and I looked at each other and shrugged simultaneously. "Rational" was not the word that sprang to mind when one thought of Roger or Marilee.

Just then, Lynn Liggett strode into the room. Lynn, formerly on the nearby Atlanta police force, had been for five years the only detective labeled "Homicide" on the Lawrenceton police force. Tailored and brisk, she gave me a friendly pat on the shoulder before asking me the same questions Jessica had asked. When I told her whom I'd seen in the Media Room that morning, Lynn asked me to estimate the amount of time I'd been out of the room.

"The bathroom trip was, umm, brief," I said. "Maybe . . . two or three minutes. That was around eleven-fifteen. Before that, when I went to the employee lounge to collect the refreshments, I was out of the room about . . ." The coffeepot and the liters of Coke had been ready to set on the cart. . . . I'd added foam cups, the sugar and creamer bowls, and some spoons. . . . I'd slipped the cookie boxes and the tray on the bottom shelf of the cart. ". . . six minutes," I said. Lynn nodded thoughtfully. She went out and scoured the library. Roger, Baby, and Lillian were all out on the main floor. They'd had to stay put, Lillian because she was still working, and Roger and Baby because the police were preventing anyone from leaving the building.

"The detective seems to know you," Jessica commented.

Emily said, "Roe is usually on the scene if the murder is in Lawrenceton. She and Lynn ought to be old friends by now, especially since they practically shared a man." I could feel my cheeks redden, and looked off into the distance to avoid Jessica's inquiring glance. I was not about to reopen the book on my former love life.

Short, squat, coarse-faced Lillian plopped down at the round table where we were sitting. "I want to go home," she said furiously, and treated us to a five-minute lecture on why the police should let her. Baby, on the other hand, sidled in and pulled her chair out at a slight angle to ours, making her among but not of. She folded her hands and inserted them between her crossed legs, as if she were cold. Roger, who wore the ugliest black-framed glasses I'd ever seen, sat his skinny bottom down on the empty chair, put his hands on the table before him, and stared at us angrily.

"What I want to know," he said during a brief pause in Lillian's diatribe, "is why just going in that room makes us suspects."

"Because someone had to walk in that room to kill Marilee," I said. "I was in that room all morning, with a couple of exceptions, and you three were the only people I saw there."

They all focused on me, and I wished I'd kept my mouth shut.

"You didn't see Marilee come in," Lillian said accusingly.

"No."

"So. Someone else just walked in with her and killed her."

"Well, you came back in while I was in the staff lounge, because your notebook was gone," I observed. "That shaves the window of opportunity"—I'd never gotten to use that phrase before—"even tighter." I'd mixed my metaphors, but my point had been made.

While Lillian was still spluttering, Jessica said, "Mrs. Kilmer, what happened to the book you wanted me to sign? I'll do it right now." Much more subtle than me, if you'll notice. Baby Kilmer groped around in her huge bag, and then looked at Jessica with a stricken face.

"Did you realize you'd left the room with it, then go back in to leave it with Aurora?" Jessica asked gently.

"Yes," Baby said shyly. I had rarely heard Baby's voice. It was soft and deep, like a boy's.

So both Lillian and Baby had been in the room while I was gone. That six minutes was getting whittled away at quite a rate.

Roger glared at us. "You can't prove I went back in there!" he said. "Stuck my head in to ask if the cookies were out yet, didn't see them, and began to browse through the stacks."

"But I'll bet you were so hungry you checked again," Jessica suggested, while I tried to look intelligent. "I know *I* always like a snack in the morning. And if there are supposed to be refreshments out, I think they should be ready for people who arrive early." I looked down at my hands to hide my expression. This woman was *good*.

"Of course they should!" Roger exclaimed, delighted to meet a kindred soul. "People come expecting something, you should give it to them when they get there!" He gave Jessica a sharp, approving nod.

I leaned forward, eying his ancient suit. "Oreo crumbs," I said quietly.

"What? What's that?" Roger looked down at his lapels. His face flushed a hectic red. "So? I ate some at home before I came and forgot to clean up. So?"

But he looked so indignant it was easy to figure he'd dodged back into the Media Room to grab a handful of cookies before the expected crowd arrived.

Emily Scott had cottoned on to the fact that most likely one of the people in the room with us had killed Marilee Du Pond. She was gaping at me as though I'd gone mad.

"You hush up right now, Roe!" she said. "I don't want to hear this."

"But Emily, a real person, someone we knew, really killed poor Marilee."

"We don't have to find out who; it's not our job."

"It's everyone's job to help the police as much as is in their power," Jessica said with such authority that no one had the nerve to actually dissect that sentence for practical application to the present situation.

"Well, I didn't do it," Lillian said coldly. "That woman was ruining my good family name, and I'm glad she's gone. But I didn't kill her."

"Did she ever succeed in digging up the dirt on your family?" I asked.

"Like all ancient families, we have secrets," Lillian said grandly, as if she had a vampire in her lineage. "But Marilee never learned them."

"In all that digging she did, in all that research for her next book, she never hinted she'd come upon the reason your family lost all its money?"

Lillian snorted and tossed her head, an unimpressive gesture. Baby Kilmer patted her on the shoulder. "No one cares about that old scandal anymore," she said soothingly. That seemed to make Lillian feel even worse.

"Roger, had you and Marilee come to an agreement about the tree?" I asked.

"I had my half cut down."

"You what?"

"I had my half cut down, I said."

"That's possible? To cut down half a tree?"

He smiled, and it wasn't a pleasant sight. "Yes, little lady, it was. Cost me more than I'd planned, but it was worth it, to see her face."

"Sounds like you and Ms. Du Pond had quite an argument," Jessica observed, and Emily rolled her eyes in despair and crossed her arms across her chest protectively.

"Well, I settled it," Roger said smugly. His eyes blinked in satisfaction behind the disgusting glasses. He didn't seem to realize that his words might be taken to mean several things.

"Mrs. Kilmer, when you went back to leave the book for me to sign," Jessica said gently, "did you see anything?"

"I saw Marilee," Baby Kilmer said. "I came back to leave the book with Aurora, but she'd gone to get the cart, so I waited, and Marilee came in, looking for Miss Fletcher, I think."

We all stared at her. Baby seemed oblivious. She just sat there, staring at her favorite writer, basking in Jessica's attention. No one had much time for Baby Kilmer since her husband had died.

"What did Marilee do?" I asked, keeping my voice quiet and calm. Jessica nodded at Baby encouragingly.

"She was talking about herself, as always," Baby said with unexpected acumen. "She asked me how I was. I said I was fine, but for some arthritis in my hands. Well, she had bursitis in her shoulder so bad she'd had to have a shot. She asked me what I'd read lately. I showed her Jessica's book. She said her sales figures were better than Jessica's. She told me her heating bill was higher than mine, and her days were busier. I couldn't argue with that," Baby said with a little smile.

I felt a stab of guilt, that I hadn't been friendlier to the obviously solitary Baby.

"Then," Baby said, "Roger came in and grabbed some cookies from the tray."

"So, Roger?" Jessica said.

Roger didn't even look embarrassed. "So? I got my refreshments. Library promises refreshments, library should have 'em out when people get there."

"Did you leave then, Mrs. Kilmer?" I asked.

"No, I stayed."

"Did you see Lillian?"

"No."

"Did someone else come in?"

We all leaned forward, the possibility occurring to all of us simultaneously that the gentle, dim Baby might not have realized the significance of someone else's presence in the room.

Baby didn't speak. She seemed reluctant to continue.

"I'll bet she started talking about herself again," Jessica said quietly. By golly, that woman knew how to press buttons.

"She did," Baby said, marveling at Jessica's figuring that out. "About Roger, how she'd had a fling with him but he was too cheap to marry."

Our fascinated gaze swung to Roger, who definitely was embarrassed this time. I tried to picture Marilee in the sack with Roger, and my mind boggled.

Jessica and I exchanged glances. I certainly would have killed Marilee if she'd been saying I'd had a clandestine relationship with her.

"She said the tree thing wasn't about trees at all," Baby went on.

"Did you go back in that room, Roger?" I asked, naively shocked at the thought of such deep passions where I'd suspected none could be.

Roger snorted. "Just prove I did," he challenged.

"So what happened next?" I asked Baby, who'd been gazing down at her hands.

"Next? Oh. She said she sure missed her husband. I said I missed mine, too."

We nodded sympathetically.

"She said her husband dying of that heart attack was horrible."

"Must have been," Jessica agreed.

"He died right there in their living room. Watching TV. She didn't know it till she asked him to pass her the remote." Baby shook her head sadly. "She said that was the worst thing. I said, no, my husband died real bad. I had her there! But she tried to wiggle out of it."

I began to have a very uneasy feeling. I opened my mouth to ask Baby to shut up, but Jessica laid her hand on my arm.

"She said, well, it was awful to think that your loved one was sitting there dead and you were blabbing away. And I said, it was worse to have your husband fall off your roof and impale himself on the pitchfork you were holding. I thought I'd stopped her. But she kept trying to top me." Baby's voice was beginning to go up. "She said, well, his heart stopped, and his head fell forward, and here she was, mad at him because she wanted to watch *Jeopardy*. And she slapped him on the arm, she said. But you know, I watched my husband die for a whole minute, and I couldn't do a thing to help him, and it was my fault. I couldn't even get the pitchfork out. And I tried. Isn't that the worst? That has to be the worst," Baby said pleadingly.

We were staring at Baby, our eyes wide; even Jessica was disconcerted.

"And she kept trying to think about ways her husband's dying could have been worse than my husband's, but you know what? My husband died worst! He gurgled! One of the pitchfork things went through his chest, and another one went through his arm, and there was blood everywhere, and he was alive for a minute! It was the worst!" Baby looked at all of us in turn, and we all more or less nodded agreement.

"It made her so mad that she couldn't top me! So she tried another way! She loved her husband more, she said! But I wasn't putting up with that; I wasn't. I said I loved my husband most, and nothing she said could take that away or make her life any more tragic! And I took that stupid scarf and I wrapped it around her throat, and I pulled both ends. Until she couldn't top another story! Ever."

It was lucky Lynn came in after a moment. We were all still sitting, frozen in place, watching Baby Kilmer page through one of Jessica's books. We were afraid to move.

Supposedly family ties run deep, but not always, especially when money is at stake. It's sad to see how sense sometimes takes a backseat to other, less noble emotions, especially when relatives are involved.

Patience at Griffith Gulch

Janet LaPierre

"POOR OLD BASTARD not only loses the juicy babe been keeping him warm the past ten years, he's suspected of pushing her off the cliff himself! At age eighty, for chrissake, getting around with just one cane on his *good* days! Dumb cops must have been out of their tiny minds."

"Daph, I don't believe they suspected him for long," Patience said. After three months, the picture from the local newspaper was still in her mind: woebegone black Labrador peering up from the rocky outcropping that had saved him, hawk-faced old man on the bluff above, leaning on a policeman's arm and staring bleakly out at the wind-whipped sea. The body of Angie Griffith was never recovered.

"But it's a police axiom that in a suspicious death, you look hard at the surviving spouse," she added. "And David and Angie Griffith were known around town for yelling at each other." Patience Smith Mackellar, good friend of several members of the local police force, leaned back in the desk chair and looked over her half-glasses at Port Silva's best veterinarian, another good friend. Daphne Griffith was

endlessly gentle and patient with four-legged animals, but
her tolerance for the two-legged variety was limited.

"Shit!" Daphne ran a hand through short auburn-with-
gray hair already wildly disordered. "My father yells at
everybody; it's his idea of communicating. I guess Angie
yelled back. I guess that's how they lasted so long, even
though she was young enough to be his granddaughter.

"What Davey said, she loved storms, apparently got up
that night and went out even though there were gale warn-
ings from Point Arena to Point St. George and the bluffs
were soaked and shifty from earlier rains. Then that ten-
month-old pup of hers chased something over the edge, she
tried to rescue him and fell. Angie was big and strong, but
not a whole lot smarter than the Lab."

"That sounds reasonable." Patience laced her fingers together to keep them from tapping as she waited for Daphne
to get around to whatever it was she had in mind. The two
women had met after Patience rescued an injured dog, and
behind different demeanors—Patience in her mid-fifties,
soft-spoken, unabashedly plump and gray-haired, Daphne
some years younger, lean and abrupt—they'd discerned a
mutual no-nonsense view of life. But Daphne's edgy presence in the client's chair at Patience Smith, Investigations,
suggested a purpose beyond an invitation to go for coffee.

Daphne shifted uneasily in the chair. "I don't suppose
you have an ashtray here, either? No, never mind. You
probably know about my father and me? It all came up
again when he decided to live year-round at the Gulch."

Patience had moved to this California north coast town
only a few years earlier, following her husband's death; but
she'd been an investigator, a listener and watcher, for
twenty-five years. David Griffith was a Port Silva legend, a
local boy who'd gone into the woods with his logger father
and wound up buying and selling big chunks of the county.
Griffith had divorced an early wife, lost a later one, Daphne's mother, to cancer, and chased women around Port

Silva and elsewhere for years before marrying his Angie. He was loud, autocratic, and bad-tempered. And . . .

"I'd heard you two were estranged," Patience admitted.

Daph rolled her eyes. " 'Estranged' is a classy way of putting it. For the first sixteen years of my life I was Davey's best buddy. We hunted, fished, hiked, sailed. Then I told him I was gay, and that was it, might as well have been dead. He wouldn't even have paid for my education if poor Mom hadn't threatened to divorce him and break up his empire."

Daphne got to her feet, opened the office door, and propped a shoulder against the jamb while she lit a cigarette. "I'll blow the smoke outside, okay?"

"Oh, for heaven's sake. Come in and sit down." Reformed smoker Patience fished an ashtray from a drawer and pushed it across the desk. "I'll enjoy it. Just don't tell my daughter."

Daphne grinned and came back to her seat. "Thing is, I believe the poor guy thought it was his fault—he'd treated me like a boy and now here I was, sexually confused. Anyhow, he disowned me and focused all his energy on my little sister, who was about twelve and up to then had been pretty much left to Mom. Davey turned her into his teenqueen daughter. Which is what she still is at age fortyfive."

"Daphne . . ."

"Right." Daphne stubbed out the half-smoked cigarette, carried the ashtray to the door, and set it outside. "Sorry. He's been calling me, in the middle of the night."

"Why?"

"He's scared. Mostly, I think, he's suddenly realized he's old. But in the middle of the night he convinces himself that somebody killed Angie and he's next."

"What somebody?"

The other woman leaned back in her chair and shook her head. "My sister Penelope, her husband, or one of her kids—for his money. Or me, to get even. Or all of the above."

"Daph, what does he want of you?"

"God, Patience, I don't know. Just an ear, maybe. If I call him back, he won't talk to me. And he won't have me out there—that would be admitting he might have been wrong thirty-plus years ago."

"Does he live by himself?"

"Not quite," said Daphne with a grimace. "Last year Penny finally ran out of divorce-settlement money and child support about the time her third and current husband lost his job. So the whole crew moved in on Davey and Angie."

"Surely not without his permission."

"Shit, Davey wouldn't deny refuge to his blue-eyed baby doll." Daphne pressed her lips tight, shook her head. "Sorry. Penny's just this pretty little woman used to being taken care of by some big strong man. Not her fault; way she was raised. She's silly and helpless, not mean."

"I see." Patience had known such women to discover a vein of meanness once the young-and-pretty had run out.

"Besides," Daph added, "except at three in the morning when he's crying in my ear, I think all this suspicion is just an old man's sorrow."

"Is anybody there with him besides Penny and her family? Any household staff?"

"Nope. There was a cook, but Davey got the idea he was being poisoned, and fired her. My sister called in a panic— woman hasn't set foot in a kitchen in years, asked me to have Jayjay find a cook."

Jayjay, Daphne's partner of many years, ran the Joyce Jerome Employment Agency. The silence lengthened; Patience looked over her glasses again to find her friend sitting forward tensely, ice-blue eyes narrowed.

"Oh. Oh, no. Absolutely not."

"Patience, it would be perfect. You're so low-key, and these people hardly ever come into town or notice anybody here when they do."

"Absolutely not. I gave up cooking when Mike died. Cans, and deli, and fish and chips. Or plain grilled meat, and vegetables from my garden. No."

"So okay, what about that big beautiful daughter of yours? Isn't she part-time sous-chef at Purely Fresh downtown? See, what they had before this last cook was a couple, cook and gardener; and Penny says the grounds need attention. You could be gardener, and Verity could be cook, and between the two of you find out what's going on."

Patience took a deep breath, absently savoring the tobacco-tinged air of her small office. She had plenty of work waiting: background and financial checks on a couple of suitors of local women, a search for a soon-to-be heir, even a missing Arabian broodmare probably stolen by the owner's ex-husband. "You aren't even sure there's anything amiss. Probably your father should see a good therapist."

"Never happen, not unless I have demonstrable reason to apply to the authorities for some kind of intervention. Which is why I want you out there having a look, for either malice or dementia."

"The two of us would be expensive." Patience could feel her resolve weakening, her curiosity beginning to twitch. She had a feeling that Davey Griffith would be—interesting.

"Patience. Please?"

"I'll promise only to think about it. But for the moment, give me the particulars."

"I don't know, Mom. Tourists are out and about early this year; Nina thinks she could use me in the kitchen on Thursdays as well as the weekends."

Patience, seated at the round pine table a safe distance from the stove and the dinner preparations, watched her daughter—her "big, beautiful daughter," in Daph's accurate description—stir the pan, then cover it and turn to the counter, where she had earlier broken eggs into a bowl. Now she added milk and seasonings. And . . . Parmesan cheese, looked like. "Verity, what are you making? An omelet?"

Verity took the lid off the skillet, poured the egg mixture in, shoved the result around with a wooden spoon. "Broccoli frittata, with onions and mushrooms." She put the skillet in the oven and set the timer.

"Sounds wonderful. I bet they'd love it out at Griffith Gulch."

Verity turned and gazed sternly at her mother. Then her lean, rather austere face softened, and the gray-blue eyes warmed. "Mom. You know working for rich folks is volunteering for a pain in the butt. Do we really have to do this job?"

"Sweetie, I could charge five hundred a day for the pair of us. For a week—I wouldn't commit to any longer. And the money would give us a good start on a new counter and new shower stall for the studio."

"Oh, joy, no more squinting at black spots and wondering whether they're bugs or mildew." Verity brought her glass and the chardonnay bottle to the table and sat down, pulling her long red-gold braid over her shoulder to tug at it as she always did when thinking. "So tell me about what's worrying Daphne."

"Probably nothing more than a grieving old man's delusions," Patience said, and outlined the problem as Daphne saw it.

"Give me a rundown on the family." Verity, who had left a bad marriage and a powersuit-and-briefcase San Francisco banking job a year earlier, now lived in the studio adjoining the cottage on her mother's north-of-town five acres and did the small-town scramble to make a living, putting in at least half of her time as investigator's assistant, the rest as cook. From the look of her—long tanned legs stretched under the table and wineglass in hand—she was easy with the change.

Patience opened the folder she had brought from downtown. "There's David Griffith—we've covered him. Penelope Griffith is David's younger daughter; Daph says she's silly but harmless.

"Then we have Jack Androvich, Penny's third husband. He's ten years younger than Penny, didn't get tenure at Sonoma State College, where he was teaching English—mostly, my friend on the English faculty told me this afternoon, because he ignored stringent new rules against dating students. So he has retired to Griffith Gulch to write his novel."

"Bastard," suggested Verity.

"That's Daphne's view. Then there's Jon-David Williams, called Jon, Penny's son from her first marriage. Jon is twenty-five, a blond California hunk, graduated from Southern Cal."

"Yuck."

"Hush. Not everybody is temperamentally suited to Stanford. Anyway, Jon has worked the stock exchange, and real estate, and is 'thinking about' various MBA programs. Then there are two children from the second marriage, Mark and Tessa Leconte." Patience held out her wineglass and Verity poured.

"Thank you, dear. Mark is nineteen, had a bad freshman year at Humboldt State, and is now a struggling rock guitarist trying to put together a group locally. Daphne says he's skinny, fumble-footed, and not very bright. But not a bad kid."

"Faint praise."

"Perhaps," said Patience. "Tessa is eighteen, was accepted at U.C. but chose to spend the year at the local community college. In Daphne's words, she's the pick of the litter."

"How do the kids get along with poor old Grampa?"

"Daphne thinks, from her few talks with her father, that he's fond of Tessa. Penny complains that he's very stingy with the boys; David Griffith apparently believes that any healthy male over the age of twelve should have a job."

"Does Penny work?" asked Verity.

"Only at keeping some man happy and productive."

"Sounds like a charming bunch, Ma," said Verity, getting to her feet at the buzz of the timer. "And one of them might be a murderer. Was Angie David Griffith's heir?"

Patience shook her head. "David told Penny, at the time of the marriage, that he'd had Angie sign a pre-nup. She got a given lump sum of money every year, so long as they stayed married, but she was to have no claim on the estate."

"Terrific. I hope it was a big lump and she had fun spending it."

Griffith Ranch, some ten miles south of Port Silva, occupied a broad, humped headland between Coast Highway One and the Pacific Ocean. Because of the way a small creek had cut the land on its winding route to the ocean, local people called the place Griffith Gulch.

Monday morning Patience slid a coded card into a slot on a post and then piloted the Ford pickup through high iron gates that swung shut behind them. They followed a meandering road through a landscape of wind-carved Monterey pines and cedars and now and then a young redwood. They caught glimpses of the creek, saw paths probably made by deer, passed a wider, man-made trail curling around a hill. And finally reached open grassland and a sprawling structure of cedar and glass perched at ocean's edge, several smaller buildings of similar design huddled around its flanks.

"Impressive," said Verity in flat tones. "But I bet it's always cold, always windy. And seriously lonely."

"It *would* be the better for a gnome or two," said Patience. She tucked the Ford in among the Jeep wagon, newish Jetta, and geriatric Toyota Corolla on the graveled parking apron to the north of the house.

"From the Jerome Agency," said Verity to the small blonde woman who answered her ring. "Verity and Patience Mackellar."

"Penny Androvich," said the woman, peering up at six-foot Verity from eyes that were the same ice-blue as Daphne's. "I was dubious about a woman gardener, but you certainly look strong enough. Let's put you to work at once, since this dry spell can't last forever."

"Wait!" said Patience. "*I'm* the—"

"You'll work up those old flower beds," Penny Androvich went on, stepping out to the edge of the deck and gesturing Verity to follow, "and plan new landscaping for the front of the house; but first I want all those nasty diseased fuchsias pulled out. Perhaps I can get someone—ah, here's my daughter."

"Mrs. Androvich, wait," said Patience, but the other woman ignored her.

"Tessa, this is our new gardener, Verity. Would you show her around, please?"

The girl had lank, light brown hair, not recently combed and a skinny body draped in a gray sweatshirt, faded jeans, and a carpenter's apron. But her narrow face was smooth and tanned, Patience noted, and she'd missed those pale blue eyes; hers were a nice clear tea color, fringed with dark lashes. "Hi," she said. "Mom, I thought I'd go up to see Granddad, show him this piece of wood I'm working on."

Her mother shook her head. "I'm afraid he's not feeling well this morning, dear. Maybe later."

Tessa sighed and said, "Okay, c'mon." Verity, with the tiniest shrug for Patience's benefit, set off after the girl. "Now . . . Mrs. Mackellar, is it?" said Penelope Androvich. "Come in and let me show you our wonderful kitchen."

Fate sealed, Patience suppressed a sigh and acknowledged to herself that it was probably for the best. Verity was a good investigator in the field, tireless and inventive. But lurking, prying, and eavesdropping called for Patience's kind of irreverent and bottomless curiosity—what her husband had called plain basic snoopiness. Besides, Verity was in better shape for grubbing out woody old plants.

"Ms. Jerome told me we were lucky to get you," Penny chirped. "A mother-and-daughter team is unusual, isn't it?"

"We enjoy working together," said Patience.

"That's nice. Oh, here are my men, waiting to see their new cook. My husband, Jack Androvich—Mrs. Mackellar."

Jack, tall and vaguely Kennedyesque with thick dark hair and green eyes, gave his wife a sexy smile and the new cook a distant nod. Servant invisibility, Patience noted; it would probably prove handy.

"My elder son, Jon," Penny said, touching the beefy shoulder of a crew-cut, blond young man who blinked stubby-lashed blue eyes and nodded. "And this is Mark." Taller than his brother, so skinny his Levi's hung at hazard on his narrow hips, the boy ducked his head and blushed. "If you boys have any special requests, you just tell Mrs. Mackellar."

She gave each of her sons a loving little pat, got a quick peck on each cheek in return, and the two young men hurried out, Jon herding Mark before him like a Border collie with a recalcitrant sheep. "And you can go back to your study, dear," Penny told her husband. "I'll show Mrs. Mackellar the kitchen and explain her duties."

"I don't eat red meat except occasionally very lean pork. And no dairy products," he said to Patience. And then, to his wife, "Have you talked to your father again, about the Merc?"

"Later, love. I promise," she said, and reached out to squeeze his arm. She was a toucher, this fluffy little woman in pink jeans and silky-white shirt. And she was clearly fond of her "men." Patience filed this impression while wondering whose "Merc"—presumably Mercedes—was at issue here.

But this touch seemed to infuriate her husband, who snatched his arm away and glared. "Look, my Corolla is falling apart and meanwhile that 500 SL sits in the garage gathering dust as some kind of damned memorial to his slut of a wife, known to have screwed every male in sight, including his own grandson, for Christ's sake!"

Every male in sight but you, I bet, thought Patience as Penny said "Jack!" in anguished tones and took his arm again to pull him away. The invisible servant turned her back on the pair and surveyed her surroundings.

The slate-floored foyer opened into a vast room with a twenty-foot-high ceiling and a west wall made almost entirely of glass. A stone fireplace and hearth occupied the wall to the left, bookcases climbed the one on the right. Furniture varied from country-cottage wicker to mission oak and clubby leather, all of it insignificant against the backdrop of gray and surly ocean.

"Kitchen through here," said Penny, returning pink-cheeked to lead the way into a stainless-steel cave: tall double refrigerator and adjoining freezer, hulking great stove with two ovens and six burners.

"A Wolf range; you'll love it," said Penny.

Right. Patience took note of a central island with what looked like a granite top, pans hanging above. A presumably magnetic strip festooned with knives. Slate floor. More like a morgue than a kitchen.

"I do only plain cooking, for the family. No cocktail parties or dinner parties."

"These days we don't entertain," Penny said, "because of my father's—"

There was a rumble, a thump, and a two-note chime from the wall beside Patience: a dumbwaiter.

"Excuse me." Penny slid the door open and reached inside to pick up a tray bearing food-smeared dishes and dirty glasses. Patience caught the acrid brown odor of whiskey

and had a good notion why David Griffith wasn't feeling
well this morning.

"My father has separate quarters upstairs, the master
suite," Penny said over her shoulder as she carried the tray
to the sink. "He's old and . . . sad. His wife died in an accident recently, and he's taking her loss hard. Angie was a
nice girl, and we all miss her."

Patience found this a fairly graceful cover-up for both
husband and father. "I'm sorry," she said, and picked up a
piece of notepaper from the floor of the dumbwaiter. "Oh,
he's sent down a list of menu suggestions for the new cook:
meat loaf, pot roast, green beans with bacon, spaghetti and
meatballs none of that 'pasta' crap, chicken fried steak and
biscuits and gravy."

"Oh, for heaven's sake," said Penny. "If he stuffed himself on any of that he'd be up sick all night, and me with
him."

· "I see." Patience handed the note to Penny. "Does your
father ever go out?"

Penny tossed a look upward, toward David Griffith or
perhaps God. "He's frail—arthritis, failing vision, falling-
down dizzy spells. In recent years Angie always drove him,
because he'd lost his license for too many moving viola-
tions, but he just hates to ride with any of us, except sometimes Tessa."

"Doesn't he go out to walk, or just for a breath of fresh
air?"

Penny's chin lifted and her eyes narrowed, fluffy little
lady suddenly gone sharp-edged. "He has his own deck
overlooking the ocean. And he likes to sit in his hot tub
with the roof pushed back, to look at the stars and listen to
the surf. Not that it's any concern of yours."

Oops. "Of course it's not," Patience said in humble
tones. "He's lucky to have a loving family to take care of
him."

Penny was mollified. "It's as if he's lost his will to live.
He refuses to be consoled, even by his grandchildren,

who've certainly tried, poor dears. Actually I suspect senility or even Alzheimer's; he turned eighty last month."

"My mother is the same age," said Patience. Hope Smith, she did not add, was at eighty a fire-breathing Baptist preacher who still climbed into the baptismal font to dunk sinners.

"Then you understand. Don't worry, he'll soon forget what he asked for, and you can go ahead preparing nutritious low-fat meals for all of us, with maybe a little melted cheese or something over his."

Steamed fish and broccoli gratinee—that should cheer the poor old guy right up. Never mind, she'd think of something.

"He didn't come down even for dinner!" Long after the fact, after dinner and the cleanup and her drive home, Patience was still twitchy with exasperation. " 'Just put it in the dumbwaiter,' says Penny—exactly what we'd done with his lunch. And so far as I could see, nobody in that house went near him all day."

"Maybe that's his choice, Ma." Verity had called it a day at gardening when the fog rolled in around five, phoning Harley to pick her up instead of waiting for Patience. Now, wrapped in a fleecy robe with a glass of zinfandel at her elbow, she was working on her fingernails with rosewood stick and file.

"Penny did say he was refusing to be consoled by his grandchildren. Anyway, I made a couple of friendly gestures in his direction—skillet corn bread to go along with the fish and rice and broccoli, and an apple pie."

"Apple pie yet." Verity got to her feet to fetch a glass of wine for her mother. "Maybe you should give up this snoop stuff and get born again as a pastry chef at Purely Fresh."

"Hush," Patience advised firmly. "Let's see—small discoveries and plans. One: Jack Androvich sits in his beautiful study playing solitaire on his computer but flips to text when interrupted by a servant. The manual on the desk was

for "Word for Windows," so I'll be able to look at his files
when chance permits. Two: Penny makes telephone calls
and writes checks in a little room off the kitchen that looks
interesting; I think there's a file cabinet in the closet."

As Verity nodded, untroubled, Patience gave a moment's
guilty thought to her own Baptist upbringing. Her sin was
probably less in what she planned to do than in the pleasure
she'd take in the doing. But something was cold and wrong
in that house.

"Three: David Griffith likes Mozart and Beethoven,
played loudly. And that's the sum of my success today.
What about you?"

Verity settled back into her chair and put her feet up.
"Mark's a pothead—you can smell it six feet away. Tessa,
who acts more like his mother than his younger sister, says
he's a talented musician; their father was Rick Leconte, a
great rock guitarist."

She paused for a sip of wine. "Jon has money; that Jetta
is his and I bet even his underwear has names on it. Hard to
figure why he's living out here. Also, he's a prick. He had
an argument with Tessa and punched her shoulder in a way
that looked friendly but wasn't. I wanted to hit him with my
shovel, but figured that wouldn't do much for my dumb-
gardener role."

"Hank left me a message on the office machine," said
Patience. Captain Hank Svoboda of the Port Silva Police
Department was her very good friend. "No one at the Gulch
has an alibi for the night of Angie's disappearance. Well,
except for Jack—the sister he was supposedly visiting in
Santa Rosa. David, Penny, and Tessa were asleep. Mark
was in the spare cottage practicing, Jon was upstairs watching whoever's late show. Nobody left, nobody heard anyone else leave.

"However," she added, getting to her feet with a sigh, "it's
hard to see why any of them would have killed Angie."

"To make the old man miserable?" suggested Verity.

"Suicidal, you mean? That seems very roundabout. But be cautious, sweetie, and stay in character."

"You too, Ma. I don't like these people."

David Griffith was eating the meals she sent up, but he was not sending down any compliments to the cook nor, alas, asking to meet her. The quality for which Patience was named had worn very thin by midafternoon Tuesday, when the house was finally empty except for David and Penny, who had settled herself in the kitchen-wing office with a pot of tea, a tape player, and the announced intention of working on household accounts. This arrangement wouldn't permit Patience to creep upstairs to see the old man, but she could have a quick run at Jack Androvich's study in the south wing.

The box on the desk contained one hundred pages of a manuscript entitled "Novel." Patience passed that by and turned to the computer. "Word" indeed, and praise be, not the newest version. On the "Word:documents" folder of the hard drive she cued "find file" and saw the "Novel" chapter files, none of which had been edited since the previous July. Jack was not making much progress with his great work.

She got up and moved to the door, to listen: no sounds of movement, Penny's Bruce Springsteen tape still playing.

A file listing by date showed Patience what Jack had written most recently: verse, short pieces with titles like "To D—— at Twilight," or "To a Coy G——." If the titles suggested a latter-day Marvell or Herrick, the poems themselves struck her as appropriate for lavatory walls. And amid innocuous business letters she found pungently personal missives to three different women. Was the man out of his mind, to leave this in his machine in his wife's house?

At the sound of a car, Patience quickly closed down files and system, put the chair as she'd found it. Slam of car door and she sped on sneakered feet through the hall and into the main room. Jack's voice, from the north wing; he must have come in the kitchen door. When he passed through the big room moments later she was at the window wall observing the ocean, and he didn't speak or hesitate. Whew.

After a minute or two of deep breathing she headed for the kitchen, where she belonged, and surprised Penny there at the open door of the dumbwaiter. Inside lay six bottles of wine; the box Penny was holding contained two big bottles of Wild Turkey, one of brandy, one of gin.

Penny, cheeks pink, shoved the box in beside the wine and punched the button. As the load of booze moved upward, she gave an embarrassed little smile and shrugged her shoulders. "He drinks a lot but he's a grown man and believe me, he doesn't take kindly to advice. Besides, who's to say a sad old man can't drown his sorrows?"

"Not me," said Patience.

Patience drove the truck carefully along the dark and fog-shrouded private road. "So what could I do?" she asked Verity, who had stayed late to help her clear the kitchen.

"Nothing. It's *her* problem, *her* father. Maybe she's doing the best she can as she sees it. Maybe she's afraid he'll kick her and her crew out if she challenges him."

Patience's breath hissed as she drew it in through clenched teeth. "But the plain fact is that a grief-stricken eighty-year-old man, arthritic and dizzy and not seeing very well, spends his days and nights all alone with a hot tub and plenty of booze. And for a breath of air he goes out on a second-story deck that drops straight down over the bluff. I went out and got a look at that."

"Will you call Daph?"

"I need to know more, Verity. If he's living the way he is because that's what he wants, I'm not sure I think anyone's entitled to interfere. Penny has a beauty-shop appointment tomorrow midday, and Jack is supposedly having lunch with his sister in Santa Rosa, so I plan to get upstairs to talk to that old man. Is that the road you're wondering about?" She flipped on the truck's high beams.

Verity sat forward and peered out at the track that circled the hillside to the north. "Right. It's been driven on quite a lot, and recently. When I called Daph she told me that there was an old bootlegger's cave behind that hill, looking down on the creek. Years ago her father had it fitted up to use as a wine cellar, but then he lost interest. However, the door is solid and it has a new lock. Not, fortunately, a very expensive one."

"Oh," said Patience. They drove on in mutually thoughtful silence.

Next morning Patience pulled onto the Griffith parking apron, dug into her big shoulder bag, and handed Verity a slim leather case. "Just remember," she said, "that simply having those in your possession is against the law."

"Yes, Mother." Accepting this for the general caution it was, Verity pocketed the case, got out of the truck, and headed for the garden shed. Patience sighed and set off for the morguelike kitchen, sure to be a mess from careless breakfasters. She had finessed last night's dinner in David Griffith's direction by producing a meat sauce for his spaghetti while everyone else was having pasta primavera. Tonight she planned a nice lean Swiss steak, with a chicken breast as alternative for Jack the non-red-meat-eating philanderer. It would be only sensible to trot upstairs and ask the old man whether he was satisfied with her efforts.

Balancing the tray against her hip, Patience knocked on the door. "Mr. Griffith? It's Patience Mackellar, the cook. I've brought your lunch."

"About time. Come in," said a raspy voice. She stepped inside, nudging the door shut behind her.

"Patience. Good name for a cook. Just set that on the table over there." David Griffith, wearing a blue running suit and heavy socks but no shoes, was stretched out on a chaise, his long body indenting its puffy surface. His pewter-colored hair was thick and uncombed, his face grooved and weathered around a thrusting beak of a nose; eyes like glacier chips gleamed from under sagging lids.

The table, with two chairs, was set against the inner wall, next to a small refrigerator and wet bar where a half-full bottle of Wild Turkey stood uncapped. Above the table hung a picture frame containing four snapshots of a broad-shouldered, strong-featured woman with a mop of black hair and, in three of the shots, a grin.

"So, Patience," he said, "you bring me more of that spaghetti?"

She turned to face him. "Yes, Mr. Griffith, and a turkey sandwich."

"Next time put in some meatballs, got that?" As he spoke, he lifted his right hand from the deep upholstery beside his leg and propped a long-barreled black revolver on his thigh, muzzle pointed straight at her.

Two seconds for stern directives to her face, her mouth, her bladder. Then she shoved her hands into the pockets of her denim skirt and said, "If you pulled that on the last cook, I bet you had to give her a hefty severance check."

He frowned at her, then looked down at the revolver. "Don't be cute. It's loaded."

"I can see that. Besides, you don't look like a man who'd carry an unloaded gun."

He responded with a pleased grin, which faded after a moment as tears welled in his eyes. "Goddamn it. Goddamn stupid old fart," he muttered, and wiped his eyes with the back of his left wrist. Then he laid the gun on a table to one side of the chaise, pushed himself upright, and swung his legs over the other side. He picked up a cane from the floor and began to struggle to his feet.

"Don't look at me, dammit. And don't help—I don't need help."

"Fine with me," said Patience. This was clearly a sitting room, with bathroom and bedroom beyond, hot tub at the very rear. Big windows, lined floral draperies, pale Berber carpeting. Thirty-some-inch television set, music system, rack of CDs and videotapes. Two easy chairs. Bookshelves, crowded.

Griffith was on his feet now, standing straight with obvious effort, one hand on his cane while the other made a smoothing pass at his hair. "You look like you enjoy food. The spaghetti was pretty good; do me a pot roast with gravy, I'll raise your salary."

"Mr. Griffith, I've been hired to cook for the household. I don't think your daughter will eat pot roast."

"She'll eat what I pay for, silly damned female. . . ." He clamped his mouth shut and shook his head, tears filling his eyes once again.

"Mr. Griffith, if you'll come downstairs to eat with your family, the others will probably agree to a wider range of foods. One of your grandsons could help you down."

"I said I don't need help," he snapped. "Specially not from my grandsons; the two of 'em together couldn't come up with a real muscle or a matched pair of balls." He set his cane in front of him and clasped his hands on its top as he inspected Patience from narrowed eyes. "Okay, it's a deal, I'll come down there and sit at the head of the damned table. For dinner, anyway."

"Good."

"And maybe afterward you could come up and relax in my Jacuzzi with a glass of wine. Good for what ails you."

She had a momentary glimpse of the pure male energy that had won him a twenty-year-old wife when he was seventy. Patience bit back a grin that would have taken her out of character and said, rather primly, "I'm sorry. I have a good friend and he would not approve."

"I bet you do. I bet he wouldn't." David Griffith's grin faded, his eyes glittered with moisture, and he moved toward the table, stumbling once but catching himself by grasping the back of the chair. "I'm tired. Go away and let me eat my lunch in peace."

She was turning to leave when the photos caught her eye again. "Are these pictures of your wife, Mr. Griffith?"

He sighed and lowered himself carefully into the chair.
"Yeah. That's Angie."

"I heard about her accident; I'm very sorry. She was an
attractive woman."

"Angie was a good girl. My daughter will tell you she was
a slut. And for all I know she might've been, sometimes. But
she was always—how is it the kids say now? She was always
there for me." He turned his attention pointedly to his food.

"Enjoy your lunch, Mr. Griffith," Patience said quietly.
"And I'll see you at dinner." On her way to the door she
eyed the pistol, considered appropriating it, decided she had
no right and besides, he probably had others. What she
would do was tell Daph, tonight.

Downstairs again, with an ear cocked for the sound of returning cars, Patience shut herself in the kitchen office and
opened the louvered bifold doors of the closet to find a desk,
an array of shelves, a small computer, and a file cabinet.

None of this looked new; probably David Griffith had
used the room as the household office before Penny and her
family moved in. Patience gave the desk drawers and
shelves a cursory going-over and then turned to the file
cabinet. Unsure of just what she was looking for, she figured she'd know it when she found it.

"You missed lunch, Mark. I bet Mrs. Mackellar would fix
you a sandwich."

Mark Leconte smiled his sweet, stoned smile. "Not hungry. Gotta go to town with Jon."

Tessa glared at Jon, who gave her a mean white grin.
"Mark, the new bass player is coming at three. For the band."

"Oh, yeah? Well. Maybe . . ."

"Mind your own business, baby sister," said Jon.

"Mind yours, dickhead!" snapped Tessa.

"Watch your dirty mouth!" Jon lifted an arm for a back-
hand swing at the girl, but Mark stumbled against his
brother, grasping the lifted arm to support himself.

"Oops. Sorry. Tessa, later, okay?"

Verity, watching from some distance away in the shadow of Tessa's cottage, relaxed. The skinny kid was smarter than he looked.

"Shit shit shit *shit!*" Tessa stood with fists on hips and watched the two move off, Jon talking fast and Mark just shambling along. After a moment she spotted Verity and said, with a shrug, "Sorry. Every family has its rat, right?"

"It's a rule," said Verity.

Tessa gave a snort of grim laughter and looked at her watch. "Oh well. See you later."

The Jetta was moving out smartly with Jon at the wheel. And Tessa had a class at two. When girl and Jeep left half an hour later, Verity put her tools away and set off at a good pace for her midday run. Past the wine-cellar trail, where nothing seemed to be happening, on to the highway and then back. From this side she could see that no vehicle was parked on the other side of the hill.

She wasn't very experienced with picklocks, so it took her several minutes, but the lock finally yielded. A deep breath, and another, for a clear head; then she pulled the door open and slid quickly inside, closing it behind her.

The odor that enveloped her was not the rotting-flesh stench she'd anticipated and feared, but something dark and green, thick with humidity, fecundity. Raised planter boxes marched back in orderly fashion, each under its own bank of lights, each with its own drip-irrigation arrangement; the leafy plants reaching for the lights were not yet large, but seemed to be growing as she watched. These were not tomatoes.

"The little bastards," she said softly. She had no idea of the market value of this much potential bud, which was clearly not a crop just for personal use. She had no current notion, either, of the penalties risked, except that they were painful.

The side walls sloped down into darkness and a thicket of cords and hoses. At the rear of the room, also dark, old wine racks were stacked with bags of soil and fertilizer. Verity's penlight found spiderwebs, tools for gardening and other purposes, empty bags, extra or discarded hoses and wire, and light tubes.

When the sound of an engine penetrated the earth-insulated building, she swore softly and turned the light on her watch: only 2:15. Maybe just a generator kicking in? she thought, looking frantically for a rear exit and finding only a too-narrow vent pipe. When the slamming of car doors squashed that faint hope, she dived behind the loaded racks and buried herself among the debris and bags of manure.

David Griffith came down the stairs on his own, one hand clutching the railing, the other gripping his cane. When he reached the bottom, he pulled a bottle of red wine from the pocket of his tweed jacket. "Smelled meat," he said. "When do we eat?"

"Daddy!" Penny rushed to offer him an arm, but he waved her away. Patience moved to the head of the table and pulled out the chair there; Griffith hobbled over, seated himself, and surveyed his family, lined up as if for presentation.

"Sit down, for chrissake."

Everyone was here, Tessa in a long cotton skirt and the boys slicked up a bit, although Mark kept his head down in an effort to hide a blackening eye. Penny wore navy wool trousers and a pink sweater, Jack cords and a sports shirt. Paying close attention to this edgy tableau as she brought dishes of food to the table, Patience had a niggling worry in the back of her mind: she had not seen Verity since lunchtime.

Unless she'd come in while Patience was upstairs with David, Verity had not phoned Harley for a ride. The truck was still parked where they'd left it this morning. Once the last serving dish was on, she slipped out for a look around; the fog was in and thickening, Verity nowhere in sight, the door to the garden shed ajar. No one in there but three cats.

Patience went back inside to her job—or jobs. Through the glass panel high in the swinging kitchen door, she could see the dining table. David Griffith sat in his arm chair like a potentate. Penny looked small and flustered, Jack seemed to be grinding his teeth. Mark cowered, Jon sulked; only Tessa was enjoying herself, talking brightly to her grandfather about something Patience couldn't hear.

Patience was dishing up dessert—pound cake and sliced early strawberries—when the outside kitchen door opened and a filthy, grim-faced Verity slipped inside.

"What happened?" breathed Patience. Remembering Mark's black eye, she reached for the overhead rack and pulled the big chef's knife free.

"Go easy, Ma." Verity spoke very softly and managed a smile. "I'm not hurt."

Patience took a deep breath, laid the knife aside, and went back to spooning strawberries over cake. "Tell me."

"I got in without much trouble, but they caught me there. Tied me up and locked me in, but I convinced them somebody'd left the door unlocked, and they didn't find my picklocks. No dead bodies there, okay? But let me tell you what the 'boys' have been up to."

After serving dessert and coffee, Patience moved to David Griffith's side and said, quietly, "Mr. Griffith, my daughter has some information for you."

Griffith looked at Patience, looked past her as Verity came into the room, stiffened and stared. "What the hell happened to you, young woman?"

Jon's coffee cup shattered as he dropped it, and Mark moaned, "Oh, shit!"

"I found the marijuana plantation your grandsons have working in your wine cellar. So they tied me up and locked me in."

"Marijuana . . . dope growing on my property, by God? Stay where you are, you sneaky little sons of bitches!" A blow from his fist set dishes rattling. "If this is the truth . . . Sure it is, I can tell by your faces, and I'm gonna have your hides for it!"

"Daddy!" wailed Penny.

"Shut up, Penelope. Jon, Mark. On your feet, you pissant bastards. Tessa?"

As the girl stared at him wide-eyed, Mark moved to stand behind her chair. "No, sir. She wasn't involved. Just me and Jon."

"And do you—all of you!—understand that if the cops and the feds find out about your goddamn dope factory, they will send you little pricks to jail for the rest of your natural lives and confiscate this place and probably any other assets of mine that happen to catch their attention?"

Patience watched, content to let the old man work this through; perhaps he'd even get to the other piece, the connection she'd found in the file cabinet.

Penny was wailing and dripping tears over prayerfully clenched hands. Jack looked distant: nothing to do with me. Tessa pressed a hand over her mouth and looked as if she might be biting her fingers.

"And what about this girl here? What did you two geniuses have in mind for her? Maybe . . ." Patience saw the thought hit him like a fist.

"Or maybe. Or maybe," he said softly, and looked at his two grandsons, Mark standing straight and Jon slouched with hands in pockets. "Maybe you've already got that worked out, eh? Maybe it's a plan you used before, when my Angie came across your little victory garden?"

"Oh, no!" said Mark, voice catching in his throat.

"No way!" said Jon. "Absolutely not! Look, maybe I talked rough about Angie, sir, but I really respected her. Even if she had found out—and she didn't—I honest to God wouldn't have done her any harm. We wouldn't."

"Of course you wouldn't." Penny got up from her chair and scuttled around the table to stand beside Jon. "Daddy, of course they wouldn't."

"You're not being smart, Penny. Never were very smart," Griffith said sadly. He slid his right hand into his jacket pocket and pulled out the big revolver. As Penny shrieked, he propped both elbows on the table and took a two-handed grip on the gun. "Who's first?" he asked, thumbing back the hammer.

Tessa thrust herself up from her chair, to stand in front of Mark. Jon stood where he was, a dark stain spreading down the leg of his gray trousers.

Patience remembered her chance at the gun, chalked it up as a bad decision, and hoped the old man carried an empty chamber under the hammer.

Penny clasped her hands before her and gave a ghastly, girlish smile. "Daddy, they didn't do it. Truly they didn't. I did it, and I'm really sorry, but . . . I had to take care of my family, didn't I?

"I found a copy of the prenuptial agreement that was supposed to protect us, and it had a ten-year limit. And you weren't renewing it; your attorney's secretary is a friend and she told me. Everything would be community property. Or worse. And then what about us?"

David Griffith lifted the revolver and sighted along its barrel. Penny, still smiling, reached for Jon's arm, but he moved aside and she nearly fell.

"Mr. Griffith, don't." Patience took a step toward the table as she spoke; from the corner of her eye she saw Verity moving to circle behind David's seat, her feet silent on the carpet.

"What, you're going to tell me it won't bring Angie back? Just shut up."

"I wouldn't tell you anything so obvious. But I can promise that shooting your daughter won't make you feel better."

David Griffith sighed, lowered the gun, and laid it on the table next to his plate. He turned his head to look up at Verity, right behind him now. "Take it. Christ, you're a big one; no wonder my wimpy grandsons couldn't stop you.

"Somebody shut her up," he added as Penny sank to her knees and began to sob. "Tessa, deal with your mother."

"Mr. Griffith," said Patience, "your older daughter, Daphne, is a friend of mine. Would you like me to call her for you?"

"Daphne. Hell, yes, why not? She's a better man than anybody here. Including me." Griffith gripped the table edge, looked around the room, and pointed a shaking finger.

"You! Mark!"

"Yessir."

"You and your brother and . . . and you, too, Androvich. The three of you get out there and clean out that wine cellar, got me? *Remove all traces!*"

As the three of them moved, Griffith looked at Patience. "You got any trouble with that?"

"With what?"

A short time later Patience and Verity trooped in not quite companionable silence to their truck.

"Want me to drive?" asked Verity.

"Yes, if you don't mind. I feel old and tired. Did those rotten boys hurt you much?"

"No worse than I'd get in a fast basketball game. And I pounded Jon where it counts," said Verity with satisfaction. "I really hate it that they're being let off with no . . . okay, okay, that's a stupid law. But I'd like them to suffer."

"I think they will." Patience leaned her head back and closed her eyes.

"I suppose. And so will Penny, one way or another."

"True."

"Hey, Mom? You know what those guys are saying right now?"

"I have no idea."

"They're looking at each other and going, 'Hey, who the hell *were* those masked women?' "

Without opening her eyes, Patience giggled.

Murder for the sake of love is one crime that often seems easy to reconcile. But even when the purest intentions are involved, the truth must be found out, one way or another. In this tale of the American colonies, a shrewd woman helps get to the bottom of a crime of passion, only to discover the case is more complicated than it seemed at first glance.

The Cat-Whipper's Apprentice

Margaret Lawrence

I

"Welcome back, Tuck!" cried Josh Lamb, and flung wide the double doors of the inn parlor to admit the jovial bulk of Mr. Philemon Tucket, Cat-Whipper, whose journeys took him up and down the northern tier of the newly independent American states. "Welcome back to Maine! And you, young Martin! Come in now, lad, and put your cobbler's bench by the hearth there. It's a chill evening for June; I'm half sorry we've no more fires. But the price of a cord of wood here in Rufford nowadays—"

"Aye, that's true indeed," chuckled the cobbler, trotting in with a clip-clop of his shiny buckled pumps. For his first arrival in a town, Tuck always made a point of dressing in his best. "Forest every place you look," he said, accepting a foaming mug of ale from Joshua, "and cut wood so dear since the war you must freeze your backside to save a shilling! Ha! If we dwelled in the desert, Landlord, some rich devil would find a way to charge us a dollar a day for the sun! Ha, ha!"

He collapsed with delight at his own joke and sank onto the nearest settle, and there was an answering ripple of mirth from the regulars who lounged about the bar counter.

Beyond the open door to the comfortable living quarters at the back of Lamb's Inn, Mistress Hannah Trevor and her aunt, Julia Markham, Mistress Dolly Lamb's redoubtable mother, were stitching away at their quilt blocks, a new pattern of Hannah's called "Rose in the Wilderness." Old Matthew Sprodge's young wife, Winifred, was with them tonight, pale and silent as a white rose herself. There was always a quilt in progress somewhere in the village, and the work moved from house to house depending upon the season.

It made a fine excuse for visiting, but for Hannah the cutting and fitting of scraps and bits into a coherent and rational whole was more than a handsome diversion and an exercise of thrift. It was how you made sense of the jagged ends of living, and kept the mind stitching true and clean.

Winnie Sprodge was the first to glance up from her work at the sound of old Tucket's laughter, and Hannah saw a brief smile, fleeting as moonlight, cross the girl's face. It was the first time, she thought, that Sprodge's wife had ever looked her proper age, which was still only a year or two past twenty. At New Year's she had lost her first child, a son, to one of Gaffer's recurrent beatings, and now the girl was lame in one foot and deeply troubled in mind.

Hannah, the midwife who had delivered Winnie Sprodge's stillborn son three months before his time, could do little now but bring comfrey tea and poultices of boneset for the badly healed ankle. The hurt mind was beyond her powers and had to be left to God. Hannah knew the way of such things, for she had buried three children of her own, and she grieved for them yet, after fourteen years.

Still, a laugh or two might do much to heal the mind, she thought, and you could not be sad at the sight of Philemon Tucket.

Whipping the Cat was what they called the stitch a cobbler used to sew the heel and top of a boot together, but Cat-Whipper was a hard kind of name indeed for such a sweet and mellow soul as Tuck.

Now in his early sixties, the traveling shoemaker was still pink-cheeked as a schoolboy, but the rest of him had long outgrown a boyish shape, for he was fifteen stone if he was a pound. He was no taller than Hannah herself and when he walked he seemed to roll from place to place without moving his legs at all. He could barely breathe inside the bright green coat whose dozen or more shiny brass buttons he insisted on doing up, and his buff-colored nankeen breeches were in danger of splitting whenever he moved.

Only his snow-white stockings seemed to have room in them, for they drooped in chicken-neck folds all the way to the tops of the silver-buckled pumps. There were but two parts of Tuck's costume that fit him: the shoes—for he had made them himself and was a good workman—and his elderly white bob wig. Powder floated down from it in a kind of blizzard when he laughed, to land in pristine drifts upon his bulging chest.

Martin Vise, Tucket's humpbacked apprentice, had to smile at his master as always, glancing up from under his heavy load of tools and equipment as he came in at the door. He had been with Tuck from childhood, a stray picked up along the roads and taken home as an apprentice to Salcombe, the county town, where Tucket had a home, or as close to such a thing as any traveller had.

Martin had thought it a good enough bargain, and except for the hump that marred his stature, he had grown into a handsome young man. He had a broad, squarish face to steady the quicksilver of his pale blue eyes; a wide mouth, full-lipped, with deep dimples at the corners when he

laughed; and thick, straight, red-brown hair carefully
brushed and tied at the nape of his neck with a rusty black
ribbon.

A young fellow some girl might have loved, thought
Hannah wistfully, as Martin, silent as always, moved cautiously into the inn parlor. A humpback soon learned the art
of becoming invisible in public.

But just as he passed them, trouble broke out among a
knot of men clustered round the shove-penny board.

"You pushed that penny in with your sleeve, Sprodge!"
cried Phineas Rugg. "I seen you!"

Nobody spoke for a moment, and some of the men
looked away, pretending they hadn't heard. They all knew
Matthew Sprodge had cheated, for he did it every time. But
he was a man you did not confront lightly about the error of
his ways. Phinney was a fool to try it, drunk as he was.

Young Martin Vise, still heavily laden with the Cat-
Whipper's traveling bench and last, stopped in his tracks
like a deer, smelling danger on the wind.

"Damn me, I *seen* you shove that penny sideways," insisted the scrawny Mr. Rugg. If Gaffer was known for
cheating and getting away with it, Phinney Rugg was
equally well-known for being a sore loser.

Gaffer Sprodge was a thickset farmer in his middle
fifties, red-faced from too much rum, and hard-eyed. On
the floor at his feet lay a pikestaff, five feet long and two
inches thick, and cruelly sharpened at the end. Gaffer could
do more damage with that pike than most men could with a
sword or a musket, and he was never without it.

But Josh Lamb saw the trouble simmering and moved to
keep it off the boil. "Dolly!" he cried, bustling behind the
bar counter and pouring out mugs of his home-brewed
cider for all the men. "Dolly, my dear! Mr. Tucket's come
and wants his supper! We've venison roast and a fine trifle
to finish! Gentlemen! Come! Have a drink of cider to the
Cat-Whipper and his lad! I'll haul my old fiddle out, and

we shall have a tune, eh? What'll it be? 'Old Colony
Times?' 'Yankee Doodle'?"

"I still say he cheated," muttered Phinney, but he quickly
got up to help Dolly hand round the mugs—well out of
range of the wicked pikestaff.

"Go fish in hell, you worthless bastard," growled Gaffer
Sprodge after him, and scooped a small heap of battered
coins into his flat-brimmed hat.

The moment of crisis was past, or so Hannah thought.
Mugs in hand, the men began another game, and young
Martin Vise felt it was safe to move at last. To reach the
cold, scrubbed hearth where he and Tuck would set up their
traveling cobbler's bench, he had to pass very near the
shove-penny table, stepping as softly as he could so as not
to attract attention.

But it was not soft enough. Sprodge had been robbed of
reprisal against Phinney Rugg, and now he saw a closer
victim. He tilted his chair back and aimed a hard, mud-
crusted boot at the seat of Martin's breeches. It was no
mere shove, but a cruel kick to the base of the spine, and it
sent the boy down hard, sprawling on his belly with a shrill
cry as the cobbler's bench and its awls and needles and
spools of waxed thread clattered helter-skelter across the
sand-sprinkled pine floor.

Jonathan Markham, Dolly's younger brother and Rufford's new constable, out riding the village bounds for the
last time before the Night Watch took over, came in at the
door just in time to hear the drunken laughter, and Gaffer
Sprodge's loud voice addressing old Mr. Tucket.

"If you come round my place, Cat-Whipper, you must
leave your hunchback monster somewhere else, for I'll not
have the likes of him on my ground, with his eyes on my
woman."

"Aye," said somebody, no more than half in jest, "the
sight of a hunchback will sour a nursing woman's milk, and
dry up any cow he comes nigh."

"And they do say," said somebody else, "as how the Devil lives in a hunchback's hump."

"Then we must beat the Devil out of him!" cried Sprodge.

In an instant he was on his feet, the brutal pike in his hand. The apprentice was up on his knees now, trying to gather his master's scattered equipment from the floor.

"Martin!" cried Hannah from the doorway. "Mind yourself!"

It was too late. The pikestaff cut the air and it struck the boy's back with a sickening thud. The blow was brutal, but this time Martin was prepared for it. He took it staunchly, his face set and eyes sightless; he did not cry out, nor make any sound at all.

"Hold, sir!" shouted Mr. Tucket. Malice like Sprodge's seemed to put him in a panic, and he rolled wildly from side to side. "Do not strike again, sir! What harm? Ha? What harm is he to you?"

Sprodge paid no heed. This time Martin tried to duck away, but the pike came down again across his misshapen shoulder. Again the boy gave not the slightest cry of pain.

It was only Gaffer who cried out, for the next instant Johnnie Markham landed a blow of his own that sent the bully sprawling straight onto the shove-penny board. It broke under his weight and set the loose coins rolling.

No one dared to laugh. For a moment, the only sound was the steady ticking of the tall clock in its black walnut case.

"It's growing late," said the soft voice of Winnie Sprodge, and one or two of the men jumped as though their hair had stood on end.

Hannah herself was startled. She had not noticed Winnie come into the parlor, had no idea how long she had been there. The girl stooped to help Mr. Tucket pick up some of his things, barely glancing at any of the others, especially Martin and her husband. Then at last she stood up and faced them. "Will you take me home now, Husband?" she said quietly.

With a crash, Gaffer Sprodge kicked free of the table and the ruined playing board and picked up his pikestaff from the floor. He raised it slightly, and would have struck the girl down where she stood, but for the constable and his brother-in-law.

"I'll have that stick, if you please," said Jonathan quietly. He took it and threw it into the cold fireplace with a vengeance.

"And I'll not serve you at this counter again, Sprodge," said Josh Lamb. "I welcome no bullyboys at Lamb's Inn. You may give your trade to the Red Bush, and good riddance. Though your wife is welcome at my door whenever she so pleases."

"I don't care a piss for your welcomes! Be damned, then, the lot of you," Gaffer hissed, and strode angrily out.

Winifred bid no good-byes to Hannah and the other women, only limped out after him, dragging her lame foot painfully.

"He'll find another stick, Johnnie," said Hannah softly, as Josh began to play "Jenny Jenkins" on his fiddle. "Is there nothing the law can do to stop him?"

"Nothing," said Jonathan. "Not till after she's dead."

II

The Journal of Hannah Trevor
21 June, the Year 1786
Two Mills Farm, Rufford Township, the County of Sussex
On the River Manitac, Maine

Today is the first of summer. We do not keep fires this month or more, but in Maine, the morning air carries cold in its fist all the year.

Mr. Philemon Tucket, the Cat-Whipper, and his young apprentice, Mr. Martin Vise, arrived last night at Lamb's Inn

*and will tarry with us at Two Mills this week to make three
pair of shoes from our calf-hides and a new sole for my Uncle's boots and mine.*

*The young man grows more clever each year at his
trade, but he is hump-backed. The children laugh and set
dogs on him as they do my daughter, Jennet, by reason she
is deaf and mute. For she has more spirit than the lot of
them, and they know it, though she has no proper words.*

*Jennet takes greatly to Martin Vise. I almost think she
will laugh aloud when she is with him, or make some sound
at last.*

*I am resolved this day to visit Mrs. Sprodge, with a gift of
honeycomb cakes from our hearth. For she suffers too
much in silence, and her heart is buried deep as the grave.
But she is yet young, and sweetmeats I pray will please her.*

    My Aunt's Receipt for Honeycomb Cakes
*Take half a pound of cone sugar, beaten fine, and two
spoonfuls of rose water. Two spoonfuls also of orange-
flower water and two or three of spring water, boiled to a
candy, with a little minced orange-peel. Pour it out onto
small papers well slicked with grease and leave till they are
set.*

III

Hannah fancied she could hear the singing long before she
saw Winnie Sprodge the next morning. It was a broken
tune, something like a hymn and something like the old
ballads, like "Lord Ronald" or "Patrick Spens" or "Barbara
Allen."

But when she caught sight of the stone-walled burying
ground at the edge of the yard where the child's grave was,
the tall, pale-haired figure of Winifred Sprodge was
nowhere in sight.

Perhaps she had imagined it. The wind was blowing the morning fog out to sea, and it played tricks with sound. Yes, surely she had only thought she heard it. Hannah, bareheaded as always, shook herself slightly to banish her ghosts, making her mop of short brown curls dance.

Then she straightened her back and marched on, keeping an eye out for Gaffer. For though she would never have admitted it to anyone, Hannah feared the man. He was the secret thing in the world you must beware of, the face that peered in from the darkness. Oh, why had she not brought the musket?

Too late now. Use your tongue instead, Mistress Trevor, she told herself, *and talk the Devil to death. If words fail you, then use your boot. You have studied the male anatomy at closer range than most, and know what spot is best to aim at.*

Ahead of her, young Martin Vise and little nine-year-old Jennet, Hannah's daughter, swung along hand in hand, the boy's long, reddish hair tied with a new blue ribbon. Martin could be little more than nineteen, and must have had few enough companions, traveling as he and his master did from place to place.

The ribbon was Jennet's gift to him. Hannah had bought it for her the last time Dick Covington, the peddler, came to call. Ninepence it had cost, a fine satin ribbon meant to finish the frilled sleeves of the child's new gown. Ninepence! Hannah sighed, looking down at her own plain brown homespun skirt and worn yellow bodice. No ribbons there, nor any likely.

Ah well, she thought, hiking up her basket to balance it better on her hip. *"A free gift freely taken blesseth the giver twice." God give them both joy of it.*

Martin had only just returned from some early errand in the village in time to come with them. A good thing, too, for Jennet would have been heartsick if he had stayed away. She seemed to notice his hump no more than he her deafness and her silence. Together, they were perfect and whole.

The three walked on until they reached the narrow stone bridge over Foxtail Creek where it crossed the village high road, the child and the hunchback playing at touch-and-tag and Hannah keeping her steady pace behind them.

The early fog that had kept the fishing boats late in harbor had lifted at last, and the morning was cool, scented by the stand of white pines that broke the brisk north wind from the river. Underneath the trees, lady ferns already grew as tall as Jennet, who had darted off the pounded dirt track now, with Martin in pursuit, and gone to investigate a family of foxes that lived among the trees.

From the far side of the bridge, with Winnie's keening still whispering at her—more in memory than in mind—Hannah glanced back again the way they had come, up the river path. Cabot Cove met the River Manitac just as it began to narrow and draw toward the forest beyond Rufford village, beyond Uncle Henry's softly turning mills on the South Bank and Maplewood Grange on the North. It was a still place, the sickle-curve of dark water barely rippled by the downstream current, ringed by huge spruces that grew nearly into the river on both sides, and scented by pine and bayberries and elder bushes—an island, almost, with a narrow strip of clean sand beach that stayed sun-warm for hours in the summer dark.

The Cove was a place for lovers, and when old Jotham Cabot had owned the land, he had winked and smiled and let them be. But now the land was Gaffer's, and he had no tolerance for lovers. He went prowling out each night with his pike and sometimes even his pistol to hunt them, and the lovers made a game of teasing him, ducking and dodging and laughing as they ran, shirts and shifts and naked bodies shimmering white in the darkness. Hannah had patched up more than one broken head or grazed buttock that had not quite escaped Gaffer's wrath.

Jennet was back on the path now, playing the game she had of treading on shadows, but Martin Vise had disappeared. The meadow below the woods, where a dozen black-faced sheep were already out to graze, was head-high with grass in places, tumbled with meadow rue and Indian paintbrush and alive with butterflies and the hectic circling of a family of gulls. They moved fitfully, soaring away with nervous cries, then diving back again to a spot in the long grass at the edge of the wood. *They must have nested there,* thought Hannah, *and be worried for their young. Wherever the hunchback is, he must be troublesome to them, for he is full of mischief.* Hannah could see a trampled pathway through the long grass where he must have gone.

A loon gave its wild, sad cry and dived below the fast-flowing dark water. Out in the current, a fishing boat with red-brown sails made downstream for the sea. It was Joseph Cool's boat, the *Turtle;* Hannah could hear the deep, clear voice of his deckhand, Black Jasper, singing at the helm as he put out for the Banks.

"I had a love and warn't she pretty/ She sailed away for London city/ Never got there, oh, more's the pity . . ."

I shall never see London, she thought. *Nor sail upon the wide sea. I shall die small and alone and be taken for less than I am, as women are if they grow weary of battling.*

"Hot-water soup and gravel barley/ I'll die for the love of my sweet Charlie . . ."

In a wild, hard country, such moments washed over a woman without warning. Some women drowned in them.

But Hannah Trevor would not be such a one. Her hands found the rough stones of the bridge curb and gripped it till they ached, and her brown eyes closed behind the square-rimmed spectacles.

It was at the moment she opened them that she caught sight of Winnie Sprodge, moving through the trees that circled the Cove, dragging her lame foot clumsily. Her cap had been snatched off by a branch and her pale blonde hair slipped its pins and streamed out behind her, drifting across the darkness of the trees.

"Martin!" she cried, the high clear voice caught and half-smothered by the wind. "Come away now!"

She broke through the ring of spruces and started up the path toward the house. Her skirts were sodden and tangled and her face and arms badly scratched. One eye was blackened and Hannah could see dried blood on her swollen lips. Winifred Sprodge stopped in her tracks and stared. "Dead," she said softly, and ran on, plunging into the high grass of the meadow.

At the edge of the woods below the house, the gulls were screaming like mad things now, diving down again and again at the same spot in the weeds. The sheep, frightened, hugged the wattle fence at the far side, bleating and stumbling over one another.

"Martin?" cried Winnie. She stumbled and fell, disappearing in the tall grass, then clambered up again, her lame foot scraping as she ran toward where the family of hysteric gulls shrieked and dived. "Martin, my heart!"

Hannah left Jennet with the basket of sweetmeats and followed the trail of trodden grass Winnie Sprodge had taken. But she knew long before she reached the place what she would find, just as the gulls had known.

In the center of a ragged circle of trampled grass and flowers, Gaffer Matthew Sprodge lay flat on his back, a great club of gnarled pine still clutched tight in his right hand, and a shoemaker's awl driven up to its handle into his windpipe.

Beside him sat Martin Vise, the Cat-Whipper's apprentice, rocking Winifred Sprodge in his arms.

"Best call your cousin Johnnie," he said quietly, looking up at Hannah. "For I've killed my love's husband, though I hang for it."

IV

Piecing the Evidence:
Questioning of Mrs. Winifred Sprodge, Widow
Made by Jonathan Markham, Constable,
22 June, the Year 1786

Question: Mistress Sprodge, how did you come by your injuries? Let the record show that Widow Sprodge's left eye is blackened and swollen shut and two of her teeth have been but lately broken out.

Mrs. Sprodge: "On Friday morning he did go
        Down to the meadow for to mow . . ."

Q: Do you know that Martin Vise has confessed to your husband's murder? He says you are lovers. Is that so?

MS: "He mowed and mowed around the field
    Till a poison serpent bit his heel."

Q: Clerk! Send for my cousin Mrs. Trevor. She is waiting outside.

MS: "His cries were heard both near and far,
    But no friend to him did appear . . ."

Q: Who killed your husband, Winifred?

MS: Why, I did, Johnnie Markham. For he did love nothing human in the world, and it must be better for the lack of him. And so I killed him.

Q: He was stabbed with the shoemaker's awl. It has Mr. Tucket's trademark on it, three stars and a new moon. How did you come by it?

MS: I was visiting at Lamb's Inn last evening, sewing a quilt with Mistress Lamb and the rest. You saw me there yourself, for you took his pikestaff from him. You cast it away from him and when we came home through the trees there, by night, he took up a great branch and beat me with it. I determined to bear it no longer, and I knew what I must do. In the morning, then, I went with him to put the sheep out in the meadow. I put my arms round his neck as though to kiss him, for he was vain and wished to think I could not

do without him. I made to kiss him there. And so I killed
him.

Q: But the awl, Winnie. Where did you get the awl?

MS: The Cat-Whipper and his boy were there, weren't
they? At Lamb's. Husband beat the boy and he dropped the
cobbling bench. I picked up the awl where it rolled, and I
kept it. Husband did kill my child with that wicked staff before ever it was born or breathed. He owed a death for that.

Q: Winifred, I must ask you: How long were you the lover
of Martin Vise? Did your husband discover you together?

MS: "Twas the month of May in seventeen sixty-one
    That this sad accident was done . . ."

Q: Hannah, my dear, can you induce the lady to answer my
questions?

HT: She is distracted, Cousin. I shall give her a decoction
of valerian, and once she has slept some hours, her mind
may come clear.

MS: "Let this a warning be to all,
    To be prepared when God doth call."

Q: We shall try again tomorrow, then. Take her to Two
Mills and keep her close.

V

"Need he lie chained, Constable?" asked the cobbler, pacing unhappily around Jonathan's small office in the Town
Jail. Hannah, who had come with him, could hear the rattle
of the irons as Harry Bly, the old jailer, went to bring the
boy out. "He is not by nature violent, sir. Not my Martin.
Surely he need not have been chained."

"It is a capital crime, Mr. Tucket," Jonathan told him
soberly. He was new to the work, but he seemed to have
found his vocation at last. "A man accused of murder must
be chained in his cell till he is tried. Unless we can clear
away the blood from him, he must go before Magistrate Siwall tomorrow and be arraigned."

The door opened, and Martin came in, gray-faced and silent. There were tears in Philemon Tucket's round hazel eyes, and he scrubbed at them with his sleeve.

Jonathan drew a breath. "Unlock him, Harry," he said softly. The jailer did so, and went shuffling off about his work.

The four were only a moment alone in the room when they heard unsteady footsteps on the split-log sidewalk outside, and then the door that faced the Common opened to admit Winnie Sprodge. She was wearing Hannah's best summer gown of gray linen and one of Aunt Julia's ruffled caps, and though her eye was still swollen, she was calm, as if her husband's death had healed the last of her grief and left her whole.

"What's she doing here?" Martin demanded.

"I begged Mr. Markham to bring me here," said Winnie. "For my heart may not rest till I am punished for Husband's death. As I deserve."

"'Tis not true!" cried Martin. "The bastard beat me and I waited till he was alone in the meadow as it grew light, and then I killed him. I tell you, 'tis *my* awl, and I done it."

"I think Mrs. Sprodge should sit down," said Hannah. "And Mr. Tucket, too. He's had no sleep since this began. I heard him pacing half the night, till it was almost daylight."

"I shall never sleep again, I think," whispered the cobbler, and sank down on a bench under the window. The girl moved close and sat with him. When Hannah looked back at them again, Winnie's hand had slipped gently into the Cat-Whipper's and held it tight.

"Both of you may be lying, or one of you may be bound for a noose," said Jonathan, "but whichever it is, I mean to get at the truth of this. Mr. Tucket, Martin says you sent him early to buy a spool of strong linen thread from the Boston packet boat. At what time would you make it?"

"He left Two Mills at half past seven," said Hannah. "For I heard the clock bell strike the half."

"Aye," Tucket agreed. "We'd measured and cut two pair of shoes for the ladies last evening, and I could see we should soon run shy of proper thread if the packet had none to sell us. So I sent Martin on horseback first thing to look some out." He reached into a scrip at his waist and pulled out a big wooden spool. "See! Here is the very thread. You may ask Captain Munday, who sold it him!"

"I have asked him already," said Jonathan. "Munday says Martin bought the spool, then stopped with him at the Inn for a mug of tea. He came away not long after nine, according to Josh Lamb." He turned to Hannah. "You've seen many dead men, Cousin. Is there any certain way of telling when Sprodge died?"

Hannah glanced at Martin Vise, and then at Mr. Tucket and Winifred, still hand in hand on the bench, as though they might otherwise drown. *Lost and drifting,* she thought, *you must catch hold of some peace you have known, some thing you have loved and keep it close in the mind, for even the memory of loving keeps you human and forces you to live.*

It was the thing Hannah had seen in Winnie's face when she caught sight of Tuck and his apprentice arriving at the Inn. Winifred Sprodge may have been the hunchback apprentice's lover, but old Philemon Tucket held some bit of her heart's memory in his own warm, stubby hand.

"When I touched him, Mr. Sprodge was already cool," Hannah told the constable. "And his jaw and neck had stiffened hard. You may ask Dr. Clinch when the body is dissected, but I should guess he had been dead nearly six hours by the time I reached him."

"And what was the hour then?"

"Joseph Cool's boat was just putting out, for I heard Jasper's singing. There was fog until near ten, and all the boats stayed in."

Jonathan got up and began to pace round and round his rough oak writing desk. "If Sprodge was found at ten, and dead six hours earlier, then he was killed near four in the morning, when it was barely growing light. Where was your Martin at four o'clock, sir?" He looked at the cobbler. "Did you share a bed at Two Mills?"

"Aye, sir. But the household rose at half past four, and—"

Jonathan was too preoccupied to listen. "So at four, when Gaffer Sprodge met his death, Martin here was—"

"Still in his bed," said Hannah quickly, glancing at Mr. Tucket. He looked away from her, staring at the floor. "For my uncle swears he wakened the boy at a quarter past four, and Martin helped with the milking and drove out the ox to pasture. And there would scarcely be time enough to walk or ride from Sprodge's to the Mills in a quarter hour and be discovered snug in bed again."

Jonathan's official mask was shattered by a heartfelt sigh of relief. "So Martin Vise is no murderer after all! And am I to believe that this girl, lamed as she is, and having suffered a beating only a few hours before, could grapple with a brute like Sprodge and fell him?" He turned to face her. "Do you persist in your story, madam? Surely not."

"Winifred," said Hannah Trevor in a quiet, level voice. "We know you did not kill Matthew Sprodge."

"I did so. I have told you how 'twas done," said the girl.

"But now you must tell us the truth. Martin followed you home last night when you and Sprodge left the Inn, did he not? Hoping to protect you?"

"That I did," said Martin Vise. "For I did know Winnie before she married him, and I loved her, only I've nothing to offer besides a back like a camel's hump, have I? But how could I let her be so ill-used and have no kindness at all in the world?"

"And so you gave her comfort, and were her gentleness, and when you left Rufford last spring, Winnie was with child by you. The time is right, for you were here at the end of June last year, just as you are now. It *was* your son, the child stillborn three months early, after that terrible beating at New Year's. The child Sprodge killed."

"'Tis so," whispered Winifred. She turned to the boy. "Husband did not credit the child was his own as it grew in me. He said he would kill it, once he had seen it had no look of him. Only he did not wait till it was born." She looked up at her lover. "I would have run away to find you, my heart. Only there came a bad snow and wind, and I could not."

"And when Martin came to you last night, when you left your husband drunk in his bed and slipped away to the Cove to your lover, you told him what had happened and who had killed his son and lamed you. Did he threaten to murder Sprodge then, for vengeance? Oh, surely he did, for who would not, in such bitter, helpless grief?"

Hannah's two hands rested on the boy's misshapen shoulder and she could feel it tremble at the unaccustomed touch.

Jonathan took up the story now. "Only Martin is no killer. But when you went out with the sheep this morning and found Sprodge lying in the meadow, dead, you were certain he must have done it in the night, and so you confessed to keep him from the rope."

"But you did nothing, my love, no more than I did." Martin's arms slipped round Winifred and held her close. "Now you know I am clear of it, and you must tell them the truth, that you've done nothing—"

"I hated Husband and wished him dead with every word and every touch, and every time he used me," cried the girl, breaking free of her lover. "I'd have burnt him alive, only—"

"Only you are too much your father's gentle child," said Hannah suddenly. "Is that not so, Mr. Tucket? Winnie is your daughter. Is she not?"

The shoemaker stared at her for a moment before he sank down on the bench. In an instant, Winifred was beside him, Martin at his elbow.

"It is true. She is my daughter, ma'am," he said. "As you have guessed."

Johnnie was astonished. "I'm damned. But how . . ."

Hannah smiled. "Last night when Tuck and Martin came in at the door, I saw ten years drop away from her with the pure pleasure of seeing them. I thought until she came in at the door just now that it was for Martin's sake alone, but when she found the Cat-Whipper here, she scarcely had a thought for anything else. It is for her father's sake she has persisted in the lie even now, because the awl was his, and bore his mark."

Tucket groaned. "And a poor enough father I have been to her, to let her wed such misery."

"It was my own doing, Father, to marry," said Winnie. "You left me free to choose, and Martin was but fourteen then, and still a lad. Though I did love him even then, I thought it was but as a girl loves a brother. Then when he came to me here, and I was alone with only Husband . . . I could not bear it any longer. I could think of nothing but you, Martin, my heart. And of home."

Her voice drifted off and she seemed for a moment to go with it, into some other place and time.

"Last night, when I saw the man in his cups and raging, I made up my mind to face the wretch out and take my girl back with me," said Tucket. "I determined to charge him at law if I must, with abusing her. So I rose early, before it was light, and set off, meaning to be back by the time the household woke at Two Mills. Martin was still fast asleep in his bed, I took care of that."

"And you found your son-in-law had been drinking all night," said Hannah. "Where was Winifred?"

"When Martin left me," said the girl, "he bid me sleep in the woods by the Cove and not go back to the house till morning. 'Twas as I went back by the meadow at first light that I found Husband, dead."

"He said he would sell her back to me," cried Tucket. "*Sell* her! A price of a thousand pound! Even if I would stoop to buy my dear girl as though she were a poor slave on a block, where would the likes of me get a thousand pound, I ask you?" The cobbler's movements were jerked and broken, as though he had snapped into pieces and the pieces no longer would fit. "When I told him I could not pay and would not, he began to strike at me, and drove me out of doors into the fog. He had a great cudgel from the woods, a great pine bole, that he kept by the house door."

"Husband could find a killing weapon anywhere," said Winifred softly. "He often did brag of it."

"We found the club still in his hand," said Jonathan. "But you had no such weapon."

"Nor would've known what to do with one, if I'd had it," Tucket told him ruefully. "I have no stomach for fighting."

"So you ran into the sheep meadow, and Sprodge after you."

"I felt in my coat and found my awl there, that I had picked up from the floor at Lamb's," Tuck continued. "I'm a heavy man and cannot run far, and if I fell and he struck me with that great bole, I knew he would strike me dead, and what would become of my poor girl then? And of Martin? For I knew what was between them."

The cobbler sat down again, his head in his hands, the wig slipped back to reveal a soft fine growth of gray-blond hair that must once have been as pale as his daughter's. It was a few moments before he could collect himself enough to go on.

"I slowed my pace to let him get close enough, for at more than the length of my arm, the awl would not reach him. I meant only to strike at his forearm, you see, or his shoulder, to make him drop the cudgel. I turned on him, quick. He did not expect it of me, and he stopped in his tracks and did not move for a minute, only stared at me. Then I saw his arm lift a bit, to smash me. So I struck at him first." He looked up. "Such men creep through the world like poison, sir, and care for nothing but greed and harm." Philemon Tucket mopped his face with a square of cream-colored linen, and went on. "I could feel his breath on my face as I struck. And the blood of him, heart's blood on my fingers."

"Ah, but he had no heart," whispered Winifred. "No heart."

Tucket was finished now, and sat silent for a moment more. Then he stood up straight and faced Jonathan. "Put on the chains, sir. I am a confessed felon, and that is the law, so you say."

Jonathan sat tapping a quill on the tabletop. "As you tell it, it is no murder, Cobbler, but only defense of your life. But if there is no witness, there must be a trial. I suppose you have no witness?"

The Cat-Whipper was silent. Hannah looked at the two young people, and the rosy old man who might still hang with no one to witness to the truth of his story. If Gaffer Sprodge had been the dark thing that lives hidden in the world, then Philemon Tucket was the light the dark too often drives under the ground.

If he were hanged, it would be law. But it could never be justice.

"I saw Mr. Tucket," said Hannah, and fixed her cousin with a steady gaze. "Saw him plainly, just as it grew light. I was called out early to see old Mrs. Bailey at Gilly Pond, but when I got there, she had bettered and had no need of me, so I came away home, back to Two Mills. And as I passed Sprodges' and crossed Foxtail Creek by the bridge there, I saw the pair of them come out of the fog at me. Sprodge had the same club in his hand we found him with, swinging it to make Mr. Tucket fear him. I saw Mr. Tucket run away, and Sprodge after him with the cudgel raised. And then the fog came up and I saw nothing more of them."

Jonathan's eyes narrowed and he studied her face. "It was still little more than dark by four o'clock, and you said yourself there was heavy fog on the river. How could you see so plain?"

"I have excellent spectacles," she said, smiling softly. "And I see like a cat in the fog."

"And you did nothing? Raised no alarm? Did not call the Watch?"

Hannah closed her eyes and removed the famous spectacles. "I am but a woman, sir. I was afraid."

Jonathan raised one dark eyebrow and sniffed resignedly. Then he looked at Mr. Tucket and at the two young people. "Well then," he said with a sigh. "There will have to be a hearing tomorrow, when the dissection's done and Mr. Siwall's court sits on the evidence. But self-defense is what I must tell the magistrate, and I think he will believe me. Providing Mrs. Trevor sticks to her story, you're free to go about your business here, so long as you stay within the bounds of Rufford until all is cleared away."

The young constable turned back to Hannah, and laid a hand on her arm. "'But a woman,' indeed! You no more saw Sprodge threaten old Tuck in that meadow than I did," he said, too low for the others to hear. "Do you persist in this perjury, Cousin?"

She smiled. "Now, Johnnie. Have you ever known me to waver from my duty where justice is concerned?"

VI

The Journal of Hannah Trevor
4 July, the Year 1786

We celebrate this day the Liberty of these struggling States, and also of Winifred Vise, that was Winifred Sprodge, who is married this day to Martin Vise, the Cat-Whipper's apprentice. Aunt and I baked a Great Cake with currants, figs, and candied peel, and flamed up with brandy when the Bride was Hailed Home.

Martin is made journeyman. Mr. Tucket very well, but says he will travel no more.

My uncle Markham read us at prayers this night the verse of Isaiah the Prophet, which I treasure to recall.

The Lord hath anointed me to bind up the Broken-hearted, to proclaim Liberty to the Captives, and the opening of the Prison to them that are Bound.

I fear I took much sin upon me for Mr. Tucket's sake. I pray the mercy of God upon us all.

And yet, I have done worse sins in my time than tell a lie in the service of life.

*I know the old saying about boys will be boys and all that, but
sometimes I still don't understand children nowadays. It's as if
they speak another language, a language that can get them into
trouble, as happens here.*

The Recluse

Betty Rowlands

THE SCHOOL BUS pulled up at the bottom of the hill and
four teenagers tumbled out, calling good-bye to their
friends. Normally, they went their separate ways, but today
they stayed together and wandered the short distance to
where the lane crossed a brook. In silence, they dumped
their schoolbags on the ground and rested their elbows on
the stone parapet of the little bridge, staring moodily down
at the swiftly flowing water.

A pair of mallards appeared, paddling close to the bank.
One of the group, a ponytailed youth of about fifteen,
picked up a stone and threw it at the birds. It landed close
behind one of them and they both took off with startled
squawks and a noisy flapping of wings. All three lads broke
into foolish, braying laughter, but the only girl among the
four rounded on them.

"Why d'you do that, Billy Daniels?" she demanded.
"They wasn't doin' you no harm!" Indignation puckered
her face, pale and pretty beneath a neat cap of glossy,
chestnut-brown hair.

"Fun," sniggered Billy.

"You're stupid!" she shouted, bunching her fists. "All of you, stupid!"

"Shut up, Becky Tanner, or I'll clout you one," said Dave Potter. He was a skinny lad with a tangle of elf-locks hanging round thin features, a mean mouth, and hard, pale eyes.

Becky flinched, even though she knew he would not dare touch her in front of her elder brother. "Don't let him hit me, Gary," she whined, moving closer to the tallest of the three youths. He had the same finely cut features and coloring as his sister, but his hair was cropped close to his head.

"Leave her be, she's only a kid," he said, stepping between Becky and Dave. A halfhearted scuffle in the middle of the road ended abruptly at the hoot of an oncoming car. The driver, a middle-aged woman, smiled and waved as she passed, but the youngsters were too concerned with their own affairs to notice.

"She's too bloody cheeky," muttered Billy as he resumed his study of the sparkling water.

"She's right, though, we are stupid," said Dave.

Billy looked at him, dumbfounded. "You gone soft in the head or somethin', stickin' up for a girl?"

"Not stickin' up for nobody, just statin' a fact. We came here to think how to get ticket money, not chuck stones at bloody ducks."

"All right, clever dick, since you're so smart, where's your idea?"

"I just had one." Dave jerked his tousled head and his companions followed the line of his gaze to a dilapidated cottage with a single chimney, half-hidden amongst a clump of trees bordering the stream. "Sammy Judd."

"What about 'im?"

"My dad reckons he's a miser," said Dave. "He draws his pension every week and he does odd jobs around the village, but he never goes to the pub or buys tobacco nor new clothes nor nothin'." The other two lads turned to look at him, the same idea half-formed in their minds. Only Becky kept her eyes fixed on the cottage.

"My dad reckons Sammy hides his money somewhere indoors," Dave continued.

Now they were really interested. "Maybe under the floor in front of the fire," suggested Gary. "Like that old git in the book."

"Yeah, you could be right!" said Billy.

The boys were reading *Silas Marner* at school and Becky had seen it on television, but it had never entered their heads that old Sammy Judd, who had lived alone in his isolated dwelling for as long as any of them could remember and who went around winter and summer in the same tattered clothes and broken boots, might be hoarding treasure like George Eliot's solitary weaver.

"Maybe he gets it out and counts it every day," said Dave, his pale eyes glistening at the thought. "I vote we go and look."

"Yeah, why don't we," chorused the other two.

"I reckon that's a daft idea," said Becky. "You won't find no money hidden there." The lads stared at her; they had forgotten her presence.

"How would you know?" Gary jeered. "You been there first, I suppose?" The others joined in his scornful laughter.

"'Course not," Becky flushed under their mockery, but she stood her ground. "If you're thinkin' of breakin' into Sammy's cottage, forget it," she said defiantly.

"What's it to you?"

Her scowl made her look like an angry kitten. "You'll get caught, an' our da'll leather you, and then we'll never get to no rave."

"We?" Dave stared at her contemptuously. "You're not goin' with us."

"Who says?"

"You're only a kid; they'll never let you in."

Becky forgot her pique and assumed a coquettish expression. "I can pass for sixteen when I'm wearing makeup."

She tilted her head at a provocative angle, pouted, and waggled her hips. Under her school sweater, her young breasts made two soft mounds.

Billy and Dave looked at her with new eyes. Ever since she was a toddler they had thought of her as Gary's kid sister who insisted on tagging along and making a nuisance of herself when they wanted to be alone to do boys' things. Suddenly, an unfamiliar quality in the thirteen-year-old girl appealed to their adolescent sexuality—a quality that vanished as her brother, looking aghast, grabbed her by the arm.

"You reckon our da's goin' to let you wear makeup?" he said. "He'd leather *you* if he knew you had any in the house."

"I'd not let him see me," insisted Becky, trying unsuccessfully to shake herself free. "I'd sneak out after he's abed, like you're plannin' to do."

"And where d'you reckon to get the money for your ticket? We ain't payin' for you."

"I can pay for myself." A cunning look crept into Becky's dark eyes. "An' if you don't think of a way to get money, I'll be goin' without you."

"You got money?" Gary eyed his sister suspiciously. "Where d'you get it?"

"Doin' odd jobs—baby-sittin' and stuff."

"What stuff?"

"Oh, for God's sake, stop wastin' time on the kid," said Dave crossly. "We got more important things to talk about."

"You're right," Gary released his sister's arm and gave her a shove. He glanced at his wristwatch. "It's time you went home anyway—you've got your lesson from Mrs. Craig in ten minutes."

Sulkily, Becky picked up her schoolbag and went up the lane, dragging her feet, while the three lads settled down to some serious plotting.

In the kitchen at Oak Tree Farm, Jake Tanner was making tea for Melissa Craig, who came twice a week to give his daughter Becky extra coaching in French. The arrangement suited them both very well. Melissa was glad of the excuse to switch her mind for an hour or so away from the business of plotting crime novels, and the walk to the farm gave her an opportunity to stretch her legs and get some fresh air. Jake was only too happy to pay the modest fee that she charged in order to give his adored younger child every possible educational advantage. He was a tall, heavily built man, not yet fifty, but cares and bitter experience had chiseled deep furrows from nose to chin, making him look ten years older.

Jake poured tea into two thick china mugs and put them on the table. He pushed a bottle of milk toward his guest and she helped herself with a smile and a word of thanks. She had a lot of time for Jake; she knew the family history, understood his problems and sympathized with his determination to do his best for his motherless children.

"So how's the lambing been this year?" she asked as she stirred milk into her tea.

"Could be worse."

Melissa drank some of her tea to hide her amusement. All the reports spoke of an excellent season, but no farmer she had ever met would admit that everything was wonderful.

Jake glanced at the old-fashioned clock on the wooden dresser with an anxious frown. "The kids should have been home by now—wonder where they've got to. Ah, that'll be them," he added at the sound of the metal gate in the yard opening and closing. "Been expecting you these past ten minutes," he said as the back door opened and Becky entered.

"Sorry, Da. Bus was late." She dropped a kiss on his forehead and greeted Melissa with a polite, "Good afternoon, Mrs. Craig."

"Where's Gary?" asked Jake.

"Talkin' to Billy and Dave. He'll be along directly. Had a good day, Da?"

"Not so bad, thanks, love. Run along and get ready for your lesson now." The girl vanished and the father turned to his guest with a fond, proud smile. "She's a good girl, is my Becky," he said. "Do well in life, she will. Got plans for her . . . and her brother, of course. He's a good lad in his way."

"They're both good kids," Melissa agreed warmly, knowing that it was what he wanted to hear. She finished her tea, picked up her briefcase, and followed Becky upstairs. There was something she wanted to say to her before the French lesson.

The track to the cottage led through dense, neglected woodland. From May to September, brambles on either side threw out thick, thorny stems that left to themselves would during a single season form an impenetrable barrier. From time to time, Sammy Judd was seen using an ancient sickle to clear the narrow pathway that hardly anyone but he ever trod. If asked, the inhabitants of Upper Benbury would be hard put to it to remember the last time anyone had driven a car along it.

Until today. Today, the undergrowth on either side lay flat, crushed by the wheels of police vehicles and an ambulance. A small knot of villagers, most of them women, some with dogs fidgeting and whining at their heels, had gathered in the lane to watch and speculate.

The door of the cottage opened directly into the single downstairs room, which served as both kitchen and living room. It was crowded with scene-of-crime personnel, gingerly picking their way round one another in the confined space. Detective Chief Inspector Harris wrinkled his fleshy nose in distaste as he stepped over the threshold and surveyed the squalid interior.

"Christ, what a tip!" he muttered. "Not fit for a pig to live in." He stared at the bloodstained heap on the floor, all that was left of Sammy Judd, and called over his shoulder to the uniformed officer guarding the door. "Who found him, Matthews?"

"The district nurse, sir."

"Where is she?"

"Waiting in the patrol car. Sue—Constable Jennings—is with her. She's a bit shook up."

"I'm not surprised. What was she doing here?"

"The old man was supposed to attend the clinic for treatment to his arm." Constable Matthews indicated a grubby bandage round the left wrist. It was heavily spattered with fresh blood, as if it had been raised in a final, futile attempt at self-protection. "He didn't show up, so she called by during her round to see what was wrong."

"How long d'you reckon he's been dead, Doc?"

The pathologist, a gaunt figure whose head almost touched the rotting beams in the ceiling when he straightened up, pursed his lips and gave a judicious frown. It was a harmless mannerism that Harris, for no sensible reason, found intensely irritating. "At least twelve hours, maybe longer. Death apparently due to multiple injuries caused by a sharp instrument, probably that sickle. Can't be more precise till I get him to the morgue for further tests—I've done all I can here." The pathologist repacked his bag and left.

Matthews held up a transparent plastic envelope. "Found lying by the body, sir."

Harris glanced at the blood-encrusted tool, gave a curt nod, and looked at his watch; it was gone one o'clock. "That means he was killed sometime during last night or yesterday evening." He took a couple of steps forward to look more closely at the empty cavity in the floorboards in front of the ancient kitchen range. A square piece of wood with two roughly cut finger holes lay beside it. "Any idea what was in there?" he asked Matthews.

"No sir. Something valuable, presumably, since it's not there now. Most of the boards are pretty rotten—they've been patched up in several places—but here they've been quite carefully cut out and the edges of the cavity reinforced.

I guess the old rug the body's lying on was used to cover it up."

"Anything else disturbed?"

"No, sir. I've had a look round upstairs." Matthews grimaced. "Not exactly a four-star hotel, but there doesn't seem to be anything suspicious."

"So the killer knew what he was looking for, and where to find it."

"Looks like it, sir."

Harris grunted and called to his sergeant. "You take over here, Waters. I'm going to make some inquiries in the village."

Melissa Craig was in her study when the front doorbell rang. At first, she ignored it. She was seated at her word processor, working on a key episode in her latest crime novel, firing herself up in her efforts to find the right words to convey the tension and suspense of the situation. At the second ring, she got up and peered surreptitiously out of the window. Seeing the familiar car parked at her door, she gave a resigned sigh and went to answer.

"You were ignoring me, Mel," accused DCI Harris as he followed her into the kitchen.

"Nothing personal, Ken," she assured him. "I didn't really want to be disturbed, but as it's you . . . coffee? Beer?"

"I'd love a beer." He settled his bulky frame onto a chair and leaned back like a man at ease in familiar surroundings. "I don't suppose you could rustle up a sandwich?" he added hopefully as Melissa set an unopened can and a glass on the table. "I look like missing lunch."

"I suppose so. Cheese? Ham?"

"Yes, please." A grin illuminated the lugubrious countenance. "With pickle."

"What brings you to Upper Benbury?" Melissa asked as she rummaged in the refrigerator. "Has there been a break-in?"

Harris did not reply for a moment. He took a pull from his drink, exhaled in appreciation, and set the glass on the table. "That tumbledown cottage by the stream," he began.

"The one near the bridge?"

"That's the one. What do you know about the occupant."

"His name's Sammy Judd. He's lived there for years—everyone knows him, of course, but he's something of a recluse. He's not in trouble, is he?"

Harris finished his beer and said quietly, "The worst kind of trouble. He was found dead in his cottage a couple of hours ago. It looks as if someone attacked him with a sickle."

Melissa paused in the act of spreading chutney on a thick slice of brown bread and stared at him in horror. "How awful!" she gasped. "Whoever would want to kill a harmless old man like Sammy?"

"Was he harmless?"

"I've always thought so." Melissa passed a hand over her eyes, shaking her head in bewilderment. "I've never heard anyone speak against him—he just lived alone and minded his own business."

"Tell me what you know about him."

She put the plate of sandwiches on the table and fetched another can of beer. "Help yourself. I need some coffee."

He watched her as he ate, admiring her brisk, economical movements as she filled the kettle and took things from cupboards. Despite being caught in her working clothes, she looked fresh and well-groomed. Her leisure suit was an old gold color that flattered her clear complexion, and her glossy brown hair was tied back with a matching velvet ribbon. As she sat down opposite him with her mug of coffee, he caught a whiff of her perfume.

"What do I know about Sammy Judd?" she mused, half to herself. "He worked on one of the Benbury Manor farms for years—his cottage belongs to the estate. When he retired from full-time work they let him carry on living there rent-free and he does—did—odd jobs on a casual basis, helping local farmers with lambing and calving and at harvest time and so on."

"You said he was a recluse. Didn't he have any friends or associates . . . or enemies?"

"Not that I know of. He never went to the pub, or joined in any village activities. He bought most of his food in the village shop, but he never stayed to gossip—just passed the time of day. He goes—used to go—into Stowbridge now and again on the bus."

"There's a bus through the village?"

"It runs a couple of days a week—a few elderly folk without cars use it to go shopping. They might be able to help. And I suggest you have a word with Jake Tanner at Oak Tree Farm. I believe Sammy has been giving him a hand with the lambing." Melissa watched as the detective jotted down names and addresses. "What on earth was the motive?" she asked. "He couldn't have had anything worth stealing, surely?"

"We think he may have." Harris told her about the cavity under the floorboards. "Have you ever seen anyone hanging about near the cottage?"

"Not hanging about exactly—not acting suspiciously, I mean. The school bus drops some of the village kids near the bridge and they don't always go straight home. In fact, I saw several of them larking about there earlier this week."

"They might have spotted something or someone. Where can I find them?"

"Yeah, we did go in, but we never took nothin' and we never hurt Sammy. He weren't there, honest." Billy Daniels, all his bombast evaporating under the laser stare of DCI Harris, looked nervously from the detective to his worried mother and back again.

"What were you doing, then?"

Billy shuffled his feet. "We thought he'd got money hidden there."

"Hidden where?"

"Under the floor."

"Why under the floor?"

"We peeked through the window the evenin' before. We saw the hole, but we couldn't see what was in it."

"Did you see Sammy?"

"No, but we knew he was there, 'cos we heard him."

"What do you mean, you heard him? Was he talking to someone?"

"Not talkin' . . . just makin' funny, moanin' noises."

"Was he ill, do you think?"

Billy looked uncomfortable. "Don't reckon so," he muttered, then rushed on, "he musta' been okay 'cos we saw him go out next day."

"What day was that?"

"Tuesday."

"You mean, you bunked off school. . . ."

"We never bunked off, it were a holiday. . . ."

"That's right," Mrs. Daniels chimed in. Harris had the impression that she was glad to be able to confirm that on this point, at least, her son was telling the truth. "The school was closed on Tuesday."

"All right, you decided to hang around till Sammy Judd went out, so that you could go into his cottage and rob him. And maybe you went back again another time, and maybe he came home unexpectedly and . . ."

Billy turned to his mother in desperation. "It weren't like that," he said beseechingly. "We never saw Sammy, and we never hurt him, honest," he repeated.

"But you did go in?" Harris continued implacably. Billy nodded miserably.

"How many times?"

"Just the once."

"All right. So, what did you find? Come on, lad," Harris coaxed. "You want to help us catch the person who killed the old gentleman, don't you?"

Billy shrugged and stared at the floor. "S'pose so."

His mother dug him sharply in the ribs. "Tell the officer what you found," she snapped. "And I'd like to know too," she added, "and your father certainly will."

The color in Billy's face deepened. "Books with dirty pictures in 'em," he muttered with evident reluctance.

"You mean, girlie magazines?"

"Worse'n that. Real dirty, these were."

Harris exhaled slowly. "And of course, you were hoping to find money." There was no reply. "And then what happened?"

Billy continued to study the floor. "Nothin'," he said after a pause.

Harris leaned forward until his face was level with the lowered head. "Look at me, Billy," he commanded. Reluctantly, the lad raised his eyes. "What did you think, when you saw those pictures?"

"We thought, 'dirty old sod' . . . ," the lad began, then jumped as his mother cuffed him smartly on the ear and exclaimed, "Billy, just you watch your language!"

Harris, unmoved, pressed on, "So perhaps you decided the dirty old, er, man needed a lesson?"

"No!" Billy's eyes widened in alarm at the implication.

"Maybe you told someone about it . . . someone in authority . . . your parents, for example?"

"That he did not!" This time it was Billy's mother making the denial. Her face was white with anger. "He never said a word to me or my husband about any of this. I'll swear it on the Bible."

"All right, Mrs. Daniels, I believe you," said Harris. He turned back to her son. "Did you tell anyone at all?" Billy shook his head vigorously. "So tell me exactly what happened after you found the books."

"We put 'em back and went away."

"You put all of them back?"

"Yeah—well, nearly all," the lad admitted, and burst into tears.

• • •

The following day, Harris was back in Melissa Craig's kitchen, morosely contemplating a mug of untouched coffee.

"We're not getting anywhere," he said glumly. "We've questioned the three lads very closely, but they all tell the same story. We can't shift them."

"Do you think they might be protecting someone?"

"It's hard to tell. They've admitted taking some of the magazines and selling them at school to raise money for some rave they're planning to go to, but they claim they don't remember the names of everyone who bought them. And they swear blind they never told a soul where they got them. I'll tell you one thing, though: Whoever killed Sammy must have got their clothes heavily bloodstained, so someone's covering up for someone."

"It shouldn't be difficult to find out who they sold the magazines to. Have you spoken to their head teacher?"

"Naturally. He's been very cooperative and we've been able to question a number of students, but they all tell the same story—they admitted buying the magazines but denied knowing where the boys got them from, and they'd never heard of Sammy Judd till they read about him in the papers."

"What about the other teachers?"

"They all say they had no idea what was going on. It seems the boys conducted their business outside the school gates." Harris took a swig from his coffee and pulled a face. "Hell, I've let it get cold."

"Give it to me, I'll reheat it." Melissa put the mug in the microwave and pressed buttons. When the pinger sounded, she took it out and passed it back to Harris. "Do you suppose," she began thoughtfully, "that any of the boys' fathers . . . or maybe elder brothers . . ."

Harris sighed deeply. "Thought of that too," he said wearily. "All the boys—and their parents—are adamant they never mentioned it at home until after Judd's murder."

"The three who broke in, you mean? What about their customers? Maybe one of them was careless . . . some nosy kid brother or sister could have found a magazine and told tales. . . ."

"If they did, they're not saying. No, it looks as if we'll have to appeal to the public for help. Someone, somewhere, must know something."

"Speaking of kid sisters . . ." Melissa glanced at the clock. "I'm due to give Becky Tanner her French lesson in an hour and I haven't prepared it yet."

"Becky Tanner?" Some of the gloom lifted from Harris's heavy features. "Pretty kid, isn't she? Precocious little madam, though—judging by the saucy look she gave me when she opened the door, I'd say her dad'll find her a handful when she's a bit older. Young Gary's a handsome lad, too. One interesting thing about him, incidentally—he admits to being involved in the robbery, but says he never sold any of the magazines or took any of the money for them. The others confirm that."

"I'm glad to hear it."

"What happened to Mrs. Tanner? The old man clammed up when I mentioned her."

Melissa gave a rueful shrug. "It's a sordid little story, but not unusual—a city girl who got bored with being a farmer's wife and began fooling around with members of the local 'landed gentry.' She ran off in the end with a wealthy polo player when the kids were toddlers. Jake's still bitter about it. It's made him very protective toward them, especially Becky—she's the apple of his eye. I'm afraid you're right about her being a handful," Melissa added wryly. "I've a feeling she takes after her mother in more ways than one. Have any of your officers questioned her about the break-in, by the way?"

"Not directly—the father wouldn't agree—but the lads swear she knew nothing about it and I've no reason to disbelieve them."

"How did Jake react, by the way?"

"He didn't say a lot at the time, but I got the impression he was pretty angry inside. I imagine young Gary had a hard time once I was out of the house."

Melissa nodded. "That's Jake all over—he never shows his feelings, except where his daughter's concerned."

Harris drained his mug and stood up. "I must be off. Thanks for the coffee."

An hour later, the sight and sound of the school bus grinding up the lane that ran close to Melissa's cottage was a signal that it was time for her to leave for Oak Tree Farm. She put on her coat, picked up her briefcase, and set off, as usual, on foot.

It had been a pleasantly mild April day, but a lively breeze had sprung up, sending fluffy white clouds scudding across a china-blue sky. The fresh green of new growth was spreading over the hedgerows and clumps of primroses blossomed at their feet. Melissa strode briskly along, telling herself—as she so often did at this time of year—that nowhere in the world was the spring more beautiful than in the Cotswolds. She inhaled deeply and caught a whiff of smoke on the wind; someone must be having a bonfire.

As she crossed the farmyard, she noticed what appeared to be flakes of charred paper fluttering in the air. Others were clinging to some bales of hay stacked on a trailer, evidently waiting to be fed to the livestock on the farm. Suddenly, a stronger than average gust blew a larger, only partially burned fragment into her face. Instinctively, she grabbed it and was about to throw it aside when she caught sight of what was printed on it. Initial shock and revulsion was followed by creeping apprehension.

The sound of footsteps made her jump and she spun round. Jake Tanner was standing within a few feet of her. His features were as set and expressionless as if they were hewn out of stone. Only his eyes were alive; as they traveled from Melissa's face to the telltale scrap of paper in her hand, they blazed with a terrible, avenging fire.

For a moment, neither of them spoke. Then he said, in a voice that she hardly recognized, "He wasn't fit to walk this earth. He used pictures of my innocent baby to gratify his filthy lust."

"We found the camera hidden in the old bread oven in Sammy Judd's kitchen," said Harris. "The Vice Squad couldn't wait to get their hands on it—they've been hunting a pedophile ring for months and this could be a break-through for them."

"How did Jake Tanner find out about the photographs?" asked Melissa.

"Gary told him." Harris accepted the cup of coffee that she handed him and took a gulp from it. "He found them in an envelope at the bottom of the cavity. The others were so busy with the magazines that they never noticed, and he certainly wasn't going to betray his sister to them. The packet was too bulky for him to hide in his pocket, so he put it back and covered it up. It took him a while to pluck up the courage to tell his father. You can imagine the effect it had when he did."

"I'll say I can—his innocent baby taking her clothes off for that old lecher. D'you suppose Sammy Judd actually abused her physically?"

"According to the women officers who questioned her, she's adamant he never laid a finger on her. She's absolutely devastated at what her father did on her account, but up till then she seemed to have regarded the whole thing as a bit of a lark."

"I suppose the old pervert gave her money to pose for him." Melissa screwed up her face in disgust. "I can understand Jake feeling outraged, but I'd never have thought him capable of murder."

"He swears he never intended to kill Judd, only give him a good thrashing to teach him a lesson—and recover the pictures, of course. But when he got to the cottage—the door wasn't locked so he was able to barge straight in—he found him masturbating over his daughter's photographs and simply went berserk."

"Understandable," said Melissa grimly. She put down her drink, having suddenly lost her taste for it. "It must have broken his heart to realize that she's not Little Miss Innocent after all. I've known for a while that she's an accomplished fibber—in fact, I've spoken to her about it several times and once I hinted as much to her father, but he'd never hear a word against her. He'll have to face up to the truth now."

Harris shook his head, a little sadly. "That's the tragedy—he won't. In his eyes, she's still pure and innocent and he believes everything she tells him."

"So how does she account for the photographs?"

"Simple. She denies knowing anything about them. Says Judd must have taken them secretly one day when she was caught in the rain near his cottage and he invited her in to dry her clothes. Claims he went out of the room while she took them off in front of the fire and never came back until she gave him the all-clear. You only have to look at the pictures to know it's a cock-and-bull story, but Tanner believes it because he can't bear the thought of what really happened."

Feeling sick at heart, Melissa went to the sink and emptied the contents of her cup down the drain. "For the sake of his sanity, I guess that's just as well," she said.

It's amazing just how many people there are who will believe whatever they're told, even when their gullibility has led to disappointment in the past. While it is said hope springs eternal, there are times when it's better to face reality.

The Subject of Prosperity

D. R. Meredith

ALTHOUGH NO ONE claimed that Highwater, Texas, was or ever had been prosperous, at least not within the memory of any except the oldest of its four hundred and fifty-five residents, the subject of prosperity was the one most often discussed over coffee at Buddy's Cafe at ten o'clock most mornings except Sunday. None of the ranchers and farmers and small businessmen seated at the round table nearest the cafe's front window could agree on exactly when the town's decline had begun, or what event had precipitated it, but every man defended his own opinion. Rarely did this debate escalate into an acrimonious exchange, and then only in response to a perceived change in the status of Highwater, although why its citizens chose to argue among themselves rather than uniting for the common good had never been adequately explained. The fact remained that no one doubted that the town's survival and prosperity depended on solving the puzzle of its decline, that the future was dependent upon the past. Highwater had its own way of thinking, and only a fool or an outsider questioned it.

Or a woman—but no one at Buddy's asked Elizabeth Walker her opinion.

Which was just as well, since Elizabeth considered High-water's debate over the subject of prosperity as useless as asking which came first, the chicken or the egg. If she had learned anything in her forty-three years, it was that such philosophical questions fascinated men because of, or per-haps despite, its lack of practical answers. In Elizabeth's experience, men were less practical than women, more in-clined to argue over abstracts, more visionary, and some-times more romantic. Men followed a vision West; women figured out how to make a home in a Conestoga wagon pulled by oxen. Men argued over how many angels could stand on the head of a pin; women wondered why they didn't instead use their time to teach children to count. Men opened the gates of Troy to the wooden horse; a woman ar-gued for a closer look at that gift horse. For that matter, Troy fell because a man fancied a pretty face above charac-ter.

Therefore, at heart, if not always in practice, men were philosophers and visionaries and, very often, fools, and never more foolish than when philosophizing on the subject of prosperity, or Highwater's lack of it. The only woman in this circle of men, Elizabeth sipped her coffee and kept her opinion to herself. Her companions had not invited her to join them as an active participant—that had probably not occurred to them—but to receive necessary indoctrination into the sacred nature and history of Highwater, since lack of an opponent ensured her election as Bonham County's first woman justice of the peace. Although she suspected her male constituents preferred to think of her as a *lady* jus-tice of the peace. More gentle. Less threatening. But woman or lady, political expediency demanded she listen politely to today's lesson on Highwater's decline.

The first lecturer was Jake Palmer, a middle-aged rancher whom Highwater always described as having "a hangdog look in his eyes." Elizabeth called it an expression

of melancholy. Both she and Highwater agreed that an unfortunate first marriage had brought on Jake's poor spirits.
The first Mrs. Palmer left Jake with a year-old son and a
broken heart; the present Mrs. Palmer raised the son but
never cured the broken heart.

"In the beginning, Highwater wasn't a town, technically
speaking," said Jake Palmer, his long face set in its custom-
ary solemn lines. "It was a division headquarters of the XIT
Ranch, and everybody, by God, knows that a division headquarters ain't the same thing as a town even if it is the
county seat and has its own post office. When the XIT
started selling off its three million acres around the turn of
the century, it was like the Rocky Mountains just weren't
there no more. The XIT Ranch was who we were in the
western half of the Texas Panhandle. It was the reason the
railroad came, and it was the reason our grandpas came,
and it was the reason the cattle traders came. It was a giant
and when it went, there was nothing but pygmies left. Once
the XIT was history, then Highwater was an independent
town, and that's when it went into a decline. Highwater lost
its identity and we ain't never got it back."

"That ain't true at all, Jake," argued Calvin Howard, a
rancher with graying hair and a ruddy-colored, leathery
face. "Highwater was doing fine after the land sale was
nearly over. The town was booming—until the hotel
burned down in 1928 and was never rebuilt. That meant
there wasn't no place for the visiting investors and cattle
traders, so they went to Amarillo instead."

Elizabeth smothered a grin. Calvin's lecture on the hotel
was another chicken-or-egg story. Did the proprietor burn
down the hotel because the cattle traders stopped coming,
or did the cattle traders stop coming because the hotel
burned down? The answer depended on whether you favored Jake's or Calvin's version of the Highwater story.

Butch Jones, who owned Highwater Grocery and considered himself the town's most prosperous businessman, not
that there was much competition, favored the Depression as

the cause of Highwater's mortal illness. "I remember my
daddy talking about how hard times were, with ranchers
slaughtering their cattle in the pastures and leaving the carcasses for hungry coyotes 'cause they couldn't afford to
feed the cattle and couldn't make nothing selling them. And
the Depression wasn't hardly over when along comes
WWII and every man who wasn't blind or crippled goes
marching off to war. The ones the Nazis didn't kill, the as-
sembly lines in Detroit got. Anyhow, most of those boys
didn't come home."

"You boys ain't nowhere near right!" announced Buddy,
a man whose opinions were generally respected if for no
other reason than that he owned the only restaurant in town,
and was thus in a position to hear—or overhear—all the
gossip in Highwater. "It wasn't the Depression or the XIT
or the war. No siree! The final nail was hammered in Highwater's coffin when the town tore down the hitching rails
around the courthouse in 1956."

Elizabeth joined the communal groan of dismay that
greeted Buddy's statement. Buddy's obsession with hitching rails was a joke that Highwater had long ago ceased to
find humorous.

"We never shoulda done that," continued Buddy, wiping
his hands on the long white apron he wore over his Levi's
and denim work shirt. "We spit in the face of our past when
we tore up the last landmark that made us stand out from
the rest of the towns in the Texas Panhandle."

"You're beating a dead horse, Buddy!" exclaimed
Calvin. "I remember them hitching rails from when I was a
kid. Full of splinters and leaning worse than a drunk cowboy on Saturday night. They were unsightly and made
Highwater look behind the times, like everybody still drove
a buckboard to town instead of a Ford pickup. Nothing
stays the same, everything's got to change—even towns."

Buddy raised his arms in the air. Elizabeth thought he
looked like Brother Edwards giving the benediction after
the Sunday morning service down at the First Baptist

Church. "That's my point! Highwater changed for the worse in 1956! We tore up her roots and she's been withering ever since. The town's gonna blow away with the next high wind."

"Good God Almighty, Buddy, the town started drying up long before '56!" exclaimed old D. B. Debord. "Excuse my language, Elizabeth, but it was that damn Roosevelt and his bank holiday. The First State never opened back up after that, and what's a town without a bank?"

At eighty, D. B. DeBord was the oldest member of the coffee klatch, and the only one who actually remembered banking in Highwater. Sometimes he even remembered the check he cashed sixty years ago better than the one he cashed last week, but otherwise his mind was as keen as ever.

Elizabeth smiled at the old man. If the truth were known, she could probably cuss as well as any man sitting around the table. Any woman who worked her own cattle soon gained a proficiency in the use of four-letter words equal to her proficiency in other skills such as roping, branding, or castrating. Maybe somewhere there was a woman satisfied to respond with a simple "darn it" when kicked by a thousand-pound steer, but Elizabeth was not that woman. She could rip off a string of profanities that would scorch the hair off that steer's hide faster than a branding iron. But some truths were better left unsaid in Highwater, and principal among those truths was that any lady interested in being elected to a public office had better not cuss—or admit to it if she did.

"We ain't heard your opinion, Jim," said Buddy. "What do you think hurt the town most?"

Along with the men, Elizabeth looked at Jim Hayworth. Jim had already been sheriff of Bonham County for twenty-five of his fifty years, and most folks agreed the office was his for life if he wanted it. Still whipcord-lean with the flat belly and strong arms of a younger man, he resembled an aging Gary Cooper, and in the opinion of most Highwater women, welcome to hang his pants on their bedpost any

night. Highwater men liked him because they trusted him to
stake out his own bedpost and leave theirs alone. Every
community had a lodestar, a point of reference from which
everybody took their direction. Sheriff Jim Hayworth was
Highwater's lodestar, and eventually every issue, every debate, every argument came down to a single question:
What's Jim got to say about this?

Elizabeth watched Jim glance out the cafe's front window at what he could see of the west side of Highwater's
Main Street. The view didn't amount to much: an old two-
story brick school, a few frame houses, the First Baptist
Church, a block-square, weed-choked lot where the hotel
once stood, and the three-story brick courthouse, minus the
hitching rails. What Jim couldn't see—the east side of
Main Street—didn't amount to much more: the filling station remodeled into Buddy's Cafe on the south end of
town, and Highwater Grocery on the north. In between
stood Phil's Hardware and Variety store, Sue's Beauty
Shoppe, Benny's Liquor Store, the XIT Bar, Highwater
Feed and Seed, and several boarded-up buildings, including
the long-closed First State Bank.

"Knowing the exact time and cause of death doesn't
change the need for a funeral, Buddy," Jim finally said,
glancing at the cafe's proprietor. "The fact is Highwater's
the next best thing to a corpse, and to be honest I've seen
livelier-looking corpses."

"I don't think that's any way for our county sheriff to
talk, Jim," said Buddy, his frown of disapproval reflected
on the faces of the other men at the table.

Elizabeth didn't think so either—not after the lecture Jim
had given her last week on not offending the voters. At the
same time, she admired his answer. Which was why she
sometimes invited him to stay over for breakfast when he
came to dinner. At her age she enjoyed a practical man
more than a romantic one. They tended to be more comfortable to be with and downright competent when it came to
taking care of the basics.

Jim shrugged his shoulders. "I've lived here all my life, but that doesn't mean I don't recognize that towns like Highwater can't survive much longer. Jawing about what happened and when it happened won't make a bit of difference. We're just talking to hear ourselves talk, because we can't go back to change a damn thing."

"That's where you're wrong, Jim," said Buddy, jabbing his index finger in the air to make a point. "We can put things back to the way they were—new hitching rails around the courthouse, fix up the vacant buildings on Main Street and rent them out to new businesses."

"Wait a minute!" exclaimed Calvin Howard. "We never said nothing about new hitching rails."

"If you and Butch can rebuild the hotel with verandahs and all, then I can put up hitching rails," said Buddy, folding his arms and glaring at the other man.

Jim Hayworth pushed back his chair and stood up. Elizabeth felt a prickle of uneasiness as she suddenly realized that whatever the other men were planning, he disapproved of. In all the years she had known him, both as her husband's best friend and as her own now that she was widowed, Elizabeth had never seen a project proposed or completed without Jim's approval. It simply didn't happen. That it was happening now unsettled her as much as a heat wave in January when she expected a blizzard.

"What are you men plotting?" asked Elizabeth.

Buddy swallowed, Calvin looked at the floor, and Butch Jones studied the old clock on the wall behind the cafe's lunch counter. Jake Palmer cleaned his fingernails with a pocketknife, a breach of manners he never would have committed under ordinary circumstances, and several other men traced circles and squares on the table's red-checked oilcloth cover. Other than the tick of the clock and the thin shriek of the wind as it threatened to burst through the cafe's front door, there was no sound—or none a stranger could hear if he had walked in at that moment. But Elizabeth was no stranger, and she heard guilt in that silence as surely as she heard the wind.

"Leave me out of this," said Jim finally. "You want Elizabeth's cooperation, you persuade her yourselves; tell her about your cockamamy plans. I recognize the necessity of what you're doing, but I don't have to like it, and I'm not going to talk anybody else into liking it. I'm going back to my office. I've got a bottle of bourbon in the bottom drawer of my desk, and I'm going to do a little drinking on county property and county time. Maybe I'll do a lot—get rid of the bad taste in my mouth."

He grabbed his Stetson off the hat rack and jerked open the door. The wind whirled in, bringing with it the scent of dust, of seared brown prairie, of spicy sagebrush and pungent cattle. Jim turned back to glance at the watching men and Elizabeth. "This plan won't work, Buddy. It won't bring back the Highwater your grandpa talked about—or the one you remember. And it sure as hell won't save the one we've got now."

The glass in the front door shivered when Jim Hayworth slammed it behind him.

"Well, is someone going to tell me, or are you all going to sit here like bumps on logs?" asked Elizabeth, staring at each of the men in turn.

Finally D. B. DeBord pushed his coffee cup away and, folding his hands, looked up at Elizabeth. "Highwater has received a proposition, one that will bring back prosperity and put this town back on the map where it ought to have been all these years. Jim's a tad upset 'cause we didn't say nothing to him until we had most of the details settled, but he's only got himself to blame. You know how finicky he's been about the last two businesses that the Industrial Development Board talked to—"

"He certainly was, and he should have been," interrupted Elizabeth. "A waste disposal company that wanted to spread toxic industrial sludge over ten thousand acres of grazing land, and a recording studio that pirated audiotapes and sold them in China."

D. B. wiped his balding head with a large bandanna. "Well, we won't argue that maybe we got carried away and didn't look close enough, but this time we know the folks we're dealing with—one of them anyhow. And technically speaking, the sheriff ain't got any call to be sticking his nose in anyhow. He ain't on the Industrial Development Board."

Elizabeth sucked in a breath, shocked at D. B.'s disrespect toward Jim. Her prickle of uneasiness grew into a foreboding as dark and chill as a grave. "Is this about Troutman wanting to be the county seat? That's about the only time we hear about the Industrial Development Board—when Troutman circulates a petition to move the county seat."

"Don't have nothing to do with moving county government," said Buddy quickly. "This is something else entirely. This is an opportunity Highwater has to grab onto before Troutman does. Not that it has been offered to Troutman, but it will be if we turn it down. We got to act fast while the offer's on the table; got to strike while the iron's hot, so to speak."

"That's when you're most apt to burn yourself, too," retorted Elizabeth. "I swear, waving Troutman in front of your faces like a red rag in front of a bull makes you men act crazier than a gelding I once owned that got hold of some locoweed. I raised that horse from a colt, but that didn't make any different once the poison was in his blood. He turned on me. You men been poisoned? Is that why you're turning on Jim?"

"Elizabeth!" exclaimed Buddy. "We ain't turning on Jim. He's supporting us—just not very happy about it is all. Now I know that you're a friend of Jim's, and you feel you have to jump to his defense, and I want you to know that we don't hold that against you."

"I hope you're not suggesting that my loyalty to Jim might be a reason not to vote for me," said Elizabeth.

Buddy flinched as though Elizabeth had skewered him. "What kind of dirty dogs do you think we are?"

"The kind of dirty dogs that would go behind Jim's back."

"There's no need to be talking like that," Jake protested.

"I don't plan on talking any sweeter until I know what you men have done that bothers Jim Hayworth so much."

"Highwater's gonna be on TV, Elizabeth," said Buddy, a grin on his face. "Jessica Fletcher's moving to town. They're gonna film a bunch of episodes right here in Highwater! Then the production company is going to take a thirty-year lease on ten sections of Jake's ranch to build warehouses and soundstages and whatever. And Calvin and Butch bought the vacant lot where the old hotel was. They figure to rebuild it 'cause all them actors are gonna need a place to live. D. B. is looking into getting one of the Amarillo banks to open a branch in Highwater. You got to have banking services if the town's going to be a major film location. In six months this will be a boomtown. Prosperity is finally coming to Highwater."

Elizabeth sank back in her chair. "I don't believe this—any of it. *Murder, She Wrote* in Highwater, Texas. How come I never heard any gossip?"

"Marta wanted to keep it real quiet so nobody would start trying to work their own deals with the TV people. Those Hollywood people like to work with one representative instead of every Tom, Dick, and Harry in town. We had all the meetings over in Amarillo instead of Highwater, and Marta said we had to make decisions quick and get papers filed so she could start the negotiations right away," said Calvin. "We didn't even tell Jim until the contract was all signed, sealed, and delivered—which might have something to do with why his nose is out of joint. But anyhow, we're calling a meeting down at the schoolhouse tonight so Marta can explain to the town what's happening. We want

you there, Elizabeth, because we figure that having a lady
JP will be good publicity. You'll be Highwater's own Jessica Fletcher."

"Who is Marta?" asked Elizabeth.

"She's Jake's wife," said D. B.

"Jake's wife's name is Imogene," said Elizabeth. "And
when I saw her at Sue's Beauty Shoppe last week, she didn't
say anything about Jake trading her in on a new model
named Marta."

"My first wife," said Jake, raising his eyes to look at
Elizabeth. "She's come home to Highwater."

"Best I remember your first wife was named Mavis . . . ,"
began Elizabeth.

"Well, she changed her name," interrupted Jake. "She
thought Mavis sounded too countrified for a professional
woman."

"A woman who deserts her baby son is trash no matter
what she calls herself," said Elizabeth.

"She was a little confused, said she had a bad case of the
blues after the baby came and just didn't know what to do."

"That's got to go down in the record books as the longest
case of postpartum depression in history. What's it been,
Jake? Fifteen years since she left a note telling you to feed
her poodle ground round and a raw egg once a week?
Which according to the gossip is more than she bothered to
say about baby Travis."

"Now, Elizabeth, if Jake can forgive and forget, then you
can, too," said Buddy.

"Jake can do what he wants, but since it appears that
Mavis has sold the Industrial Development Board a bill of
goods, and since I'm fixing to be elected justice of the
peace of this county, I think it would be downright irre-
sponsible for me to follow his example. An elected official
ought to look into the reputation of anybody wanting to do
business with the county, and Mavis Palmer's reputation
smells worse than the manure pile back of my barn!"

"You're confusing Jake's domestic situation with public business," said Butch. "I guess that's easy enough for you to do, being a woman and all, but if you're gonna be in county government, Elizabeth, you got to look at the bigger picture. You got to have a vision!"

"This is a chance for Highwater to prosper again," said Calvin.

"I might have known the subject of prosperity would come up at least six times in this conversation," said Elizabeth. "So would you tell me how Mavis Palmer and prosperity go together—other than the usual way when a bunch of men negotiate with a woman of uncertain morals?"

Jake Palmer kicked over his chair in his haste to get to his feet. He leaned over the table, his hands curled into fists. "Don't be bad-mouthing my wife, Elizabeth! I don't intend to put up with it!"

Elizabeth gritted her teeth. "I don't recall every saying a bad word against Imogene."

"I wasn't talking about Imogene!"

"Neither was I!"

Jake was motionless, then straightened and whirled toward the door. "Marta and I will drive in from the ranch a little early tonight in case the board has any questions."

If Elizabeth had been the kind of woman to swoon, she would have swooned at Jake's words. "Jake Palmer, do you mean to stand there and tell me that you have your ex-wife who abandoned you and your son staying in the same house with your present wife? How does Imogene feel about this? And what about Travis? How does he feel about a mother that sashays into his life after not saying boo to him for fifteen years? Have you talked to Travis about this? It has to be a terrible shock to him."

"Mind your own business, Elizabeth," said Jake, slamming the door behind him.

Elizabeth turned back to the other men. "Don't you see anything wrong with what's going on here?"

"Now, Elizabeth, according to the Bible, we got to be without sin before we start throwing stones," said Buddy.

"I don't think Mavis Palmer is any Mary Magdalene, so don't quote Bible verses to me. Where is that contract, Buddy? I want to see exactly what she gouged out of this town."

"She didn't *gouge* anything," said Calvin, pulling a folded legal document out of his coat pocket and handing it to Elizabeth. "She paid us ten thousand dollars, plus one percent of whatever she gets when she signs an agreement with the film company. I think it's a real good deal."

"This contract's not signed," said Elizabeth after skimming the document.

"Of course not," said Buddy. "That's just a copy. All the members of the board got one. Marta kept the original and filed it with the county clerk soon as the courthouse opened this morning. Jake took her over there."

Elizabeth grabbed her old black leather purse and rose. She took several deep breaths. "There are times when I think a fence post has more sense than the average man. This is one of those times."

She might not have slammed the door hard enough to crack its glass if D. B. DeBord hadn't been a little deaf and consequently couldn't hear how loud he spoke. Then she would not have heard what he said to Calvin Howard when she turned to leave.

"Ladies her age act peculiar sometimes. The change of life, you know."

"Hello, Imogene."

The woman who answered Elizabeth's knock was plain: brown hair without highlights of any color; skin clear but wind-roughened; figure average; eyes brown and empty; expression, none.

Imogene Palmer held open the screen door. "Come in, Elizabeth. I need the company, and you're the only woman in Highwater that I'd let in the house today."

Elizabeth stepped inside. She had come to the back door, as the kitchen was where any ranch family lived. The living room was for show; the kitchen was for friends. "How are you holding up, Imogene?"

The other woman pushed her hair back from her forehead, a nervous gesture that Elizabeth suspected she was unaware of making. "I'm about in the shape you'd expect a woman to be when her husband moves a slut into the guest bedroom. But I can forgive that. Mavis is a good-looking woman—better-looking than me—and I always knew he felt more for her than for me. She got the first helping and I got the leftovers. But I can accept that, too. Jake Palmer's a weak man in a lot of ways, too weak to put her behind him. I knew that when I married him, but I married him anyway. Took him for better or for worse, and it's worse."

Elizabeth checked her impulse to hug Imogene. The other woman was held together with spit and baling wire, and a sympathetic touch just might make her fly apart. "You're more saintly than I would be, Imogene. I don't believe I'd be feeling as kindly toward him as you are."

"Oh, I'm not feeling kindly. I'm *acting* kindly, but that's different. It would just make it worse if I acted out how I feel, so I don't. But I hate him, Elizabeth, hate him nearly as much as I do her—but I'm not leaving him. No matter what happens, I'm not leaving!"

Elizabeth admired a practical woman above one who indulged herself in teary self-expression. "What does she want, do you know? I don't believe her story about the TV show, so she's here for something else. I need to know what it is, because I think she's a threat to Highwater, and those men on the Industrial Development Board don't know it. They're so busy chasing a vision that they can't see what's in plain sight. Unfortunately, I don't see it either—but before I'm done, I will."

Imogene's eyes took on life where there had been none. "I don't know what she wants and I don't care. She can have this house, this whole damn ranch and every cow on it, so long as she leaves Travis to me. I had female troubles and never could have babies of my own, so Travis is all I got. I raised that boy, Elizabeth! It was my heart he stepped on when he was growing up, not hers. She deserted him with no more thought than if he'd been a pup she tied up in a gunnysack to drown in a river. Well, he's mine now, and I'll kill her if she tries turning him against me."

Elizabeth thought Mavis would be a fool to try reclaiming her child from this woman. She might even be a dead fool. "Where is she, Imogene? I've got to talk to her."

"Last I saw, she was down by the barn sweet-talking Jake until he didn't know which way was up, and Travis hanging on every word. Go talk to her, for all the good it'll do you. Woman would lie even when the truth would serve her better."

Elizabeth thanked her and slipped out the door. She could feel Imogene's eyes following her as she walked toward the tall, slim woman leaning against the galvanized steel building that served as Jake Palmer's barn. Next to her, his shoulders hunched and hands pushed in his pockets, stood a thin, gangly boy who seemed to be all knees, elbows, and hobnail boots. At sixteen, Travis Palmer was a year or so shy of knowing exactly where his feet would land when he took a step.

"Mavis."

Mavis Palmer tossed a mane of auburn hair over one shoulder and lit a cigarette, exhaling a whitish cloud of smoke as she stared at Elizabeth. "Now that I see you close up, I remember you. You don't see green eyes very often. You've aged well, considering the climate."

Mavis herself looked a little worn around the edges, but Elizabeth saw no need to mention it. "Travis, would you excuse us? I've got some official business to discuss with Mavis before tonight's meeting."

Travis Palmer swallowed. "My dad says you been stirring up trouble in town, trying to ruin Highwater's deal

with the TV show." His face turned red and he had diffi-
culty getting the words out.

Elizabeth felt sorry for him. Imogene hadn't raised a
rude boy, and Travis couldn't just shuck off her rules
overnight in order to please his father—who, in Elizabeth's
opinion, needed his behind kicked for involving the youngster in his quarrel in the first place.

"Isn't he the cutest thing," said Mavis. "Protecting his
mother just like a grown man."

Mavis was another one who needed a butt-kicking, hu-
miliating her son by talking about him like he wasn't present. "Imogene could use some company, Travis," said
Elizabeth. "Don't hurt her when she's been good to you
just to prove your loyalty to someone else. Don't let anybody put you in that kind of bind."

Travis hesitated, the struggle between nurture reflected
in his eyes, then loped toward the ranch house and a fierce
protector. Elizabeth turned to Mavis. "Not interfering when
I sent that boy back to the house is the second decent thing
you ever did for him."

Mavis watched her son walk away. "What was the first?"

"When you left him for Imogene to raise. I think she did
a better job of it than you would have done."

Mavis laughed. "I think you're right."

"Not that it was your intention, since I don't think you
gave a thought to what would happen to him when you
left."

"Right again. But you didn't come out here to talk about
my deficiencies as a parent, so shall we get to the point?"

"I think that *is* the point. Fifteen years ago you walked
out and left a mess behind. I want to make sure that you
don't do the same thing again. Highwater is counting on
you, just like Travis counted on you. Now, I read Buddy's
copy of that contract, and so far as I can tell, you paid ten
thousand dollars for nothing!"

Elizabeth saw the other woman's nostrils flare as if she were a mare scenting a lurking predator, and knew her gut instinct was right. Mavis was a snake oil salesman.

"Between all the whereases and wherebys and parties of the first, second, and third parts, you represent Highwater in the event the folks at *Murder, She Wrote* demonstrate an interest in the town. There's nothing in writing about your initiating any contact. If they don't get in touch with you, then you're out a lot of money, and if I was a betting woman, I'd bet those television folks never heard of us. If any strangers had been looking over Highwater, everyone would know it. The last stranger anyone saw represented industrial sludge, not a film company, and the sheriff ran him out of town."

Mavis Palmer shrugged her shoulders. "Maybe you ought to come to the meeting tonight and listen to my presentation."

"What am I going to hear? Hot air? Are you going to tell folks exactly who you know at the TV show? Are you going to tell them when we can expect trucks full of cameras to roll into town?"

"You ain't on the board, Elizabeth, so you ain't got any more of a right to be interfering than your friend the sheriff."

Elizabeth had been so intent on Mavis that she'd missed hearing Jake Palmer's footsteps behind her. She flinched when his voice sounded in her right ear, and whirled around. "I'm a taxpayer and in another two weeks, God willing and the creek don't rise, I'm likely to be an elected official. Either way I'm entitled to answers."

Jake Palmer's eyes held a distinctly unfriendly expression. "You ain't elected yet,and right now you're trespassing. You come on my property and accuse Mavis of being a liar and a thief and a cheat—I was in the barn and I heard you—but you don't offer no proof at all. When has she lied and what has she stolen and who has she cheated? Answer me that, Mrs. Big-Shot Elizabeth Walker."

"I'm not in court, and I don't have to *prove* anything, Jake. I just want to raise enough reasonable doubt for you and the other fools in Highwater to look this particular gift horse in the mouth."

"Get off my property, Elizabeth. You're nothing but a nosy woman with a foul mouth."

"I'm going," said Elizabeth impatiently. "I just need another minute. Why did you keep the only signed and notarized copy of the contract, Mavis? That's not the usual way of doing business—even in Highwater, where we tend to take a person at their word. But then, of course, you're not really doing business, since you never filed that contract with the county clerk. I checked."

Jake's face went blank, and for a second Elizabeth thought she saw fear in Mavis's eyes. Then the woman flicked ash off the end of her cigarette and laughed. "You're just full of questions, aren't you, Elizabeth?"

"And you better be full of answers, Mavis, starting with what's in it for you," said Elizabeth before turning and stalking back to her pickup for the five-mile drive back to town. Her last sight of Mavis Palmer was in her rearview mirror, and she looked every bit of her age—which, if Elizabeth recalled, was only a year less than her own.

The brick, three-story Bonham County Courthouse squatted on the north end of Main Street, a brooding concrete expression of abstract prosperity—or the hope thereof. It had marble floors, mahogany paneling, brass hinges and doorknobs, twelve-foot molded ceilings, and a crystal chandelier hanging in the foyer for which any whorehouse would gladly had paid its Saturday night receipts. But prosperity had never measured up to its expression, and the courthouse fell into disrepair, and edifice of cracked mahogany, empty offices, and echoing halls where ghosts of abandoned hopes walked.

The Bonham County Sheriff's Department was on the third floor next to the district courtroom. In addition to fourteen cells, almost always vacant, there was an enormous squad room with four desks, and Jim's private office, where the marble floor was no less cracked than in the rest of the building, but the brass hinges were polished.

"Elizabeth, can I pour you a drink?" asked Jim, standing up and waving his hand toward one of the sturdy oak chairs in front of his desk. "Your cheeks look a little pale—probably the shock of hearing from the ad hoc government down at Buddy's that Highwater is fixing to be on prime-time television."

"No thank you," said Elizabeth. "Drinking when I'm mad always gives me heartburn—and I think you better put the cork back in the bottle yourself. Looking at you trying to stand up, I figure you're about ten percent off plumb, and I need you perpendicular to the floor."

Jim rubbed his forehead as he studied her with bloodshot eyes. "Elizabeth, honey—I'll call you that even though you don't like me doing it during office hours, but I'm just a tad drunk and I figure you'll let me get by with it out of consideration for my condition. So Elizabeth, honey, pour me some of that coffee I brewed this morning early. It ought to be strong enough by this time to sober me up real fast, and judging by that look in your eye, I figure I need to be sober before I hear whatever you're fixing to say. You had that same look the day you went chasing out to Ed Hays's place to accuse him of murdering his wife. I didn't take you seriously then. I don't intend to make that same mistake."

"I was right, wasn't I," asked Elizabeth, pouring coffee into an oversized mug and passing it to Jim.

"You might say being right contributed to Ed Hays's trying to kill you," agreed Jim. "You're damn lucky I'm not taking flowers out to the cemetery to put on your grave. So what are you thinking this time, Elizabeth?"

"Highwater won't be the next Hollywood, U.S.A., but if we don't find out what the truth is, I'm afraid we may have a real *Murder, She Wrote*."

Jim stared at Elizabeth over the rim of his mug as he took a long drink of coffee. Finally he lowered the mug without moving his eyes from her face. "You going to leave the rest of the story to my imagination, or do you plan on telling me?"

Elizabeth got up and walked behind Jim's desk. She rested her hips against the edge of his desk and, folding her arms, looked out the window at Highwater, its few buildings reduced to insignificance by the vast, empty land that stretched out to meet the horizon on all sides of the town. She sensed a threat to Highwater just as her pioneer ancestors had been able to sense Comanches waiting in ambush. But what was it? What in the name of God did Mavis Palmer want?

"Elizabeth?"

She blinked and turned her attention to Jim. "As the sheriff of Bonham County, has it occurred to you how dangerous this whole business is? From a practical point of view, Mavis and Jake and Imogene and young Travis all staying together on that ranch is tempting fate. All that plot needs is Jessica Fletcher as a houseguest."

"You're telling me that you believe it's likely Mavis and Imogene will shoot each other before the meeting tonight?" asked Jim.

"That's one possibility," said Elizabeth.

"I suppose you think there are others?"

"There may be, Jim, because I believe the contract is a hoax. Mavis Palmer has the only signed and notarized document—but she never filed it with the county clerk. I don't think she ever intended to finalize that contract, and without any signed copies, there is no proof that one ever existed. And I bet the board hasn't seen that ten-thousand-dollar check either."

"But why do that, and why such an elaborate story?"

"Because sometimes the bigger the lie, the easier to sell it. And Mavis knew Highwater, Jim. She knew we would be so busy disagreeing with one another over the past while planning how to re-create our own vision of it that we wouldn't be paying much attention to what was going on right under our noses. But she didn't count on me. I'm not from the chicken-or-egg school of philosophy: I'm too practical to argue over questions with no right answers. So instead of worrying about the past, I asked the obvious question about the present: What's in the contract? The answer is nothing."

"You only answered half my question," said Jim.

Elizabeth shrugged. "I only know half the answer. I don't know why she did it—and she refused to tell me when I talked to her this morning."

"I might have known you'd do something foolish like that. You think the situation with the four of them is dangerous, so you go running off half-cocked to stir it up a little more," said Jim in a resigned tone of voice.

"What are we going to do, Jim?"

"About Mavis? I don't know. I can't arrest her, because she hasn't broken any law. She never promised in that contract that *Murder, She Wrote* would actually film in Highwater, and I'll bet she never promised it verbally either. She conned my entire town, and I never noticed. I sat around on my butt, drinking rotgut bourbon and whining about how Highwater would turn into a tourist trap where we'd sell cheap souvenirs made in Hong Kong and strangers would laugh at our ways. Someone was laughing all right, but it was Mavis Palmer! And I can't do a damn thing about it. She's the slickest confidence man—woman—that I ever saw. The only problem is no one got swindled."

Elizabeth idly traced circles on the top of Jim's desk. "She conned the town—but she's not swindling the town. So why did she do it? Answer: Because she had to. Because she couldn't separate her mark—that's the right slang, isn't it?—from the rest of Highwater. But she didn't file the contract because she didn't need to continue the con game. Why not? Because Mavis Palmer had won the confidence of her mark!"

Elizabeth stiffened as she saw the final scene of a petty domestic tragedy. "Oh my God, Jim! She's swindling Jake Palmer."

Jim knocked over his chair getting up. "Good God Almighty! I better warn her to get off Jake's land before he figures out he's been had!"

Elizabeth swallowed. "It's too late. He knows. I told him, and I didn't even realize it."

The subject of prosperity is still the one most often discussed over coffee at Buddy's Cafe at ten o'clock most mornings except Sunday. But the farmers and ranchers and what few businessmen there are in a town of four hundred and fifty-five residents are careful never to mention the events that occurred just before Elizabeth Walker won election as Bonham County's first woman justice of the peace. Elizabeth herself only spoke of the tragedy once, and to the best of anyone's recollection, has never referred to it again. There is a disagreement among the coffee drinkers as to whether it was the day after the murder or the day after the funeral that she broke her silence that one and only time. Buddy, who has the best memory for such occasions, says it was the morning after the funeral that Elizabeth slipped into a chair at the round table nearest the front window, and began to speak.

"I knew before Jim and I pulled up in front of the Palmer ranch house that Mavis Palmer was dead. I guess anybody who knew the circumstances could have guessed that. When Mavis conned Jake into giving her power of attorney on ten sections of his land, she might as well have slit her own throat, because she was a dead woman. Once he learned from me that Mavis never filed that contract with the county clerk, once he figured out there was no film company coming to Highwater, then he knew the answer to the last question I asked of Mavis: What's in it for you? Jake knew Mavis had come for his land. It didn't take a smart man to figure out the connection between a waste

disposal company that had wanted empty land only a few
months before, and a woman who suddenly had land to sell.

"If Jake Palmer had shot her, I wouldn't be so down-
hearted."

Elizabeth had looked through the window at that point,
and Buddy always tells folks that her face kind of glowed,
as if a light were shining on her alone. He says the men
around the table hardly breathed for fear of missing her
next words.

"Imogene killed her so Jake wouldn't have to. She told
me that Travis never really had his mother, and wouldn't
miss her much. But he loved his dad, and Imogene didn't
want him doing without both his blood parents."

Although I do so enjoy the countryside around Cabot Cove, there is a lot to be said about other parts of America. Beautiful northern California is one example. Unfortunately, not everything in the country is peaceful or relaxing. Especially not a murder.

The Body in the Redwoods

Katherine Hall Page

THE MOON WAS waxing in the crystal-clear night. A single gull flew across its face, silhouetted against the light, which was as silver and shimmering as the goddess herself. Cypress trees below cast gnarled shadows on the dunes. Nothing was stirring, the air impossibly still. It was the kind of night when things could be expected to happen and sometimes did.

Inside a rustic cabin a fire crackled merrily in an old stone fireplace, but not loudly enough to prevent Faith Sibley Fairchild from hearing the Monterey Bay surf pounding the California shore. She was visiting Redwood Ridge—"The Ridge," as it was affectionately termed by the loyal guests who returned like lemmings year after year and who, from the look of some of them, were on the doorstep when the impressive gates had first opened eight decades ago.

Redwood Ridge represented a unique combination of one for all and none for all. The high prices kept it exclusive, but its conferences diversified the guest population. Situated on over one hundred acres of woodlands and frag-

ile dunes, fiercely protected by boardwalks, it attracted
those with a naturalistic bent—or those who thought it was
chic to assume the pose. Thoreaus with thousand-dollar
binoculars gazed at the horizon; Carsons with pedicures tip-
toed around tide pools. Meals were served "family style" in
a cavernous redwood-beamed dining hall, reminiscent of
the turn-of-the-century Adirondack retreats built by
wealthy New Yorkers in similar pursuit of the simple life.

Faith was not complaining. Far from it. Her husband, the
Reverend Thomas Fairchild, was at The Ridge for a three-
day conference, "Heretics: Heroes and Heroines? Conver-
sations About Sects," sponsored by the denomination. Tom
was delivering a paper on his speciality, the Albigensians in
France, twelfth-century ascetics who rebelled against
church and state, losing life, limb, and property in the
process.

Besides non-affiliated guests, The Ridge was playing
host to three other groups this week: a footwear sales force,
a watercolor society, and the International Association for
Human Sexual Response Research and Therapy (IAH-
SRRT). With sex and sects, it should be a lively and poten-
tially confusing couple of days, Faith had commented to
Tom when they'd checked in and she'd read the welcome
board.

After the conference, the Fairchilds would also have two
days in the decidedly nonrustic St. Francis Hotel in San
Francisco, where the only family-style meal Faith intended
to consume was dim sum in Chinatown.

She gazed into the blazing fire, mesmerized by the
flames. Tom was out on the Redwood Ridge beach collecting enough driftwood to prevent the fire from dying down
anytime in the near future—say three or four years. He'd
already stacked a load of wood worthy of Paul Bunyan on
the deck outside the spacious room. Faith believed fire
tending revealed a definite gender difference, like knife
sharpening. Not that she didn't keep her kitchen cutlery on
the cutting edge—her job as a caterer depended on it. But

Tom raised the whole process to new heights with his special Arkansas stone, just the right honing oil, and so on. It took hours, and he loved it.

And fires. It was burn, baby, burn all the way—no pleasantly glowing embers, but the equivalent of yule logs and Promethean bonfires roaring whatever the time of year.

The time of year—Faith pulled on the colorful Adrienne Vittadini sweater sent by her sister for her last birthday, a birthday that still put her squarely in her early thirties, and was glad she'd packed it. She knew that the moment she left the hearth area the room would be cold.

The time of year—oh yes, it was the end of June, characterized by another California phenomenon, or at least one in this locale. It was beach weather during the day, but the warm, sunny blue skies emerged from a cold morning fog and retreated to nights reminiscent of the cool temperatures that were the norm three-quarters of the year in Faith and Tom's Aleford, Massachusetts, home.

She got up from her comfortable position and walked over to the sliding glass doors that led to the deck. She drew the drapes back and peered out. The Ridge had tasteful walk lights, but they were unnecessary with the moon's own bright steady beams. A bird cried, or at least Faith thought it was a bird. There was no sign of Tom. She wasn't worried, but she wasn't not worried. Near the window she could hear the waves crashing more clearly. There were signs everywhere on the beach warning people not to swim—"Extremely Strong Currents."

It was beautiful and she was tempted to walk down to find him. He'd probably need help carrying the forest he'd collected. It was a romantic night, especially since their two children—Ben, four, and Amy, nine months—were many miles away in Aleford being totally spoiled by Tom's parents, who seemed to count the days until they could get their hands on the grandchildren . . . and then count the days until they could hand them back over again.

Yes, a romantic night, a night of—

She was abruptly shaken from her mood by a frantic knocking at the cabin door. With a passing thought as to why Tom had decided to come back that way, she ran to let him in.

It wasn't Tom.

"Please, you've got to help me! Please hide me!"

She was a beautiful blond in her mid to late twenties with a deep tan that set off her lacy turquoise gown and peignoir. She was barefoot, and the look on her face made Faith instantly reach to pull her inside. This was no joke.

"What is it? Are you in some kind of danger? Do you want me to try to call someone?" As Faith spoke, she remembered one of the "quaint" customs at The Ridge—no phones in the room. The nearest one was down by the dining hall.

"No, no! Don't tell anyone I'm here!" The woman was getting hysterical. "Just hide me. Hide me quickly!" As she spoke they both heard a faint male voice calling, "Carolann! Carolann! Where are you?"

The woman looked as if she was going to faint. Faith pushed her into the bathroom. "Don't worry. The only person coming in will be my husband. You're in safe hands." The woman nodded and silently closed the door.

The voice was getting louder, and after a while Faith heard heavy, deliberate footsteps outside the door. The Fairchilds' was the last cabin in the row. There was plenty of room between them and whoever it was had been taking his time searching the area. He would call out every once in a while, his voice concerned, loving. A marital spat? What in the world could be happening? He called once more. He was on the boardwalk near the deck. Faith could hear him clearly. The steps stopped, then started again; he was moving away.

Faith had seen the woman sunbathing at the end of the beach that afternoon. Neither her suit nor her nightwear left much to the imagination, but a great deal to fantasy on the part of some onlookers. A California Girl, maybe even a

Valley Girl. She'd been alone on the beach, splayed out on her back, her body glistening with oil, like some sacrificial offering to the sun god.

The glass door slid open and Faith jumped.

"Tom!"

"And you were expecting whom? Brad Pitt? Paul Newman? Given this place, Roger Tory Peterson?" Tom, tall with deep brown eyes and reddish brown hair, windblown and flushed from his exertions, had his own appeal.

"Sssh, there's a young woman in her nightgown hiding in our bathroom. She appeared at the door a few minutes ago absolutely terrified and begging me to help her."

"You and Pix have been reading that *Total Woman* book again, haven't you? It's a great shtick, honey, but with Ben and Amy safe and sound at home, I really don't need any fairy tales to get—"

"Tom! There really *is* a woman in the bathroom. Go see for yourself. She's in some kind of trouble and we've got to help her."

"Just so long as it's a *live* woman," Tom played along. If Faith wanted to kid around, so be it. But she had managed to stumble into a fair number of murder investigations over the years, usually by stumbling across the corpse itself.

"Oh, she's very much alive—and I am not hallucinating."

"All right, I'll go look. Meanwhile, why don't you open the cognac and pour me a tad."

He was back in a flash.

"Faith! There's a woman cowering in our bathtub! She looked like she was going to flip out when I opened the door, then she put her finger to her lips and pulled the shower curtain shut! What the hell is going on!"

"I told you," Faith said with a justifiable trace of smugness. "She knocked on the door, asked me to hide her, and I did. A man was outside calling for 'Carolann'—that must be her name."

"I heard him when I came up from the beach. He was going down the stairs at the far end."

"That means he's left. If she knows that, she might come out and start talking."

The Fairchilds went to the bathroom door and Faith knocked softly. "He's gone now—why don't you join us by the fire," she suggested. When there was no reply, they opened the door.

The room was completely empty, save for the moonlight streaming through the open window. Carolann had seen herself out.

Faith opened her eyes and rolled over. Tom was already gone. The serious business of sects started early and he'd told her the night before he would be breakfasting at seven if she cared to join him. She did not, but noting that it was after eight and there would be no food after nine, she jumped out of bed, showered, dressed, and headed off for sustenance.

They had talked about the mysterious woman in turquoise until well after midnight, but the only explanation seemed to be a quarrel with her husband, soon regretted.

Breakfast was semi-cafeteria style. You chose what you wanted, then someone brought it piping hot to your table. Apparently neither flab nor cholesterol worried anyone at The Ridge. There were eggs in many guises, sausages, bacon, ham, home fries, pancakes, muffins, toast, and huge pecan sticky buns—and as a sop to the health-conscious, melon and mounds of strawberries. Faith chose fruit and a bun, planning to walk it off. There were few late risers and she was sitting in solitary splendor at one of the big round tables with the whole lazy Susan to herself. It was crowded with fresh orange juice, coffee, milk, cream, and an endless variety of jams and jellies. Occupied with the serious business of food, Faith didn't see, until they passed her table, the woman from the previous night with a man who matched her in age, tan, and hair color.

"Hello," said Faith, weighing her next words. It might not be tactful to say, "Everything patched up between you two?" or "Have any trouble getting out of my bathroom window?" Before she could decide, the couple had moved toward the kitchen, the woman returning the greeting— without even a flicker of recognition on her face.

Faith had a good view of them when they came back and sat a few tables away. Whatever was wrong the night before *had* been resolved. They could have been honeymooners—and maybe were. Both wore wedding bands. He kissed her hand when she passed him the salt and Faith was sure there were kneesies going on under the chaste, white tablecloth while they ate. When he rose to go to the kitchen, Faith seized her chance and made her way over to their table. She had no intention of leaving until she had an explanation for the night before. If the husband came back, she could pretend to be passing the time of day on her way out.

"Is everything all right? You were so distressed last night, then when you disappeared, we didn't know what to think."

The woman was startled and answered hastily, "Yes, yes, everything's fine." Faith was struck by the confusion on her face. Was it a question of Faith's knowing too much? The way a friend who has unburdened him or herself of some problem often becomes a mere acquaintance afterward? The man was walking toward the table now, but Faith stayed put. It would have been awkward to leave.

"I couldn't help myself. I ordered some more of those pancakes. The food here is fantastic." It was the same voice that had called "Carolann"—a hearty, used-car-salesman-type voice.

While Faith's sticky bun had been edible, she wouldn't have called it "fantastic," and she'd had no trouble in leaving it unfinished. Maybe lunch would show the chef's true colors.

"Hi, I'm Jim Hadley. My wife, Carolann, and I stay at The Ridge whenever we're up here. Been coming for years." He put out his hand. He had a strong grip.

"Hello, I'm Faith Fairchild. This is my first visit. My husband is attending a conference."

"Which one?" Jim sniggered slightly, and Faith was tempted to satisfy his prurient interest and declare Tom one of the world's leading authorities on participatory sexual research.

"The one on heretics."

Jim was not disappointed. "Oh, the sects, not sex." His self-congratulatory grin indicated he'd obviously been waiting for the opportunity to get that one off since his arrival.

"Oh, darling, you are terrible! What will Mrs. Fairchild think?" Carolann said with mock severity—and absolutely no fear.

Faith said good-bye. She had serious beach plans for the rest of the morning.

As she slathered herself with the highest numerical sunblock in existence, she pondered the absurdity of lying in the sun while doing everything possible to avoid a tan. Soon the sound of the waves, considerably calmer this morning, and the warm, gentle rays worked on her senses, and her eyelids drooped.

"Now, don't go falling asleep. That's a sure way to get a burn, especially with your complexion." A shadow fell across her.

Faith sat up. It was Carolann—and from the tone of her voice, the world's leading authority on tanning.

"You have to do this gradually." She spread her towel companionably close, Faith noted in dismay. She was treasuring solitude on this vacation—a rare thing in her everyday life. Still, with Jim nowhere in sight, Carolann might talk about the previous evening.

But she didn't. What she did do was talk about everything else under the sun. Their home in Beverly Hills that

was on the market for a million-five, because they wanted
to move to Carmel. "It's more normal up here," Carolann
confided. "You don't see so many homeless people." She
also managed to work in their Mercedes and an account of
the house they had looked at the day before, right on Pebble
Beach and only $650,000. "But, of course, it's a teardown."

"Of course," Faith murmured, looking surreptitiously at
her watch. It wasn't lunchtime.

When one of the other clerical wives came along with
children and sand pails in tow, Faith nearly leapt at her, insisting she join them. The woman, slightly bewildered by
the intensity of Faith's invitation, spread out a blanket and
began to unpack. The sight of all those juice boxes, kites,
shovels, small hats, flip-flops, and granola bars gave Faith a
fleeting pang of guilt—guilt for not missing the kids more.
It really was wonderful simply to get up from a beach and
go, without the frantic cries to stay just a little longer and
the accompanying tears as they left. She also didn't miss
the dump truck-loads of sand that invariably accumulated
on various parts of a child's body or the role of mother as
packhorse—a child on each hip and a fifty-pound sack of
toys on one's back.

"Perhaps I'll see you at lunch," Faith said fifteen minutes
later, escaping gratefully. Carolann could give her tanning
lecture to a new victim, who—if Faith remembered cor-
rectly from the barbecue dinner of the night before—had a
few lectures of her own up her sleeve. Mrs. Tucker was one
of those women who asks extremely detailed questions—in
the hopes of catching you out in a lie, or worse. In fact, after
she'd gotten settled on the sand, her first, slightly ac-
cusatory, words to Faith had been, "We didn't see you at
breakfast. Where were you?" As a method of information
gathering it was unsubtle but effective, Faith realized as she
struggled for a more impressive excuse than "sleeping in"—
something like a run on 17-Mile Drive or early-morning
bird-watching. She'd have to remember the method for her

next investigation. The drawback was the necessity of developing the personality to match.

At lunch she regaled Tom with an account of her morning, complete with a description of the sex researchers on the beach. The Japanese and many of the Europeans wore suits and ties with their IAHSRRT name tags prominently displayed on neat lapels. They'd spent a great deal of time taking photographs of each other in front of the ocean, looking completely incongruous among the sunbathers. Their California colleagues were a bit more relaxed—Birkenstocks, khakis, and open-necked shirts, even a tie-dyed T-shirt. Like the vintage cars that looked like new without the depredations of winter, there was a timelessness to California fashion.

Tom was relieved to hear that all was well with "the toothsome morsel in our shower."

"I'd be happy to risk skin cancer if you like, Tom, and maybe there's a Victoria's Secret in Carmel." Faith was slightly miffed. "Anyway, my blonde hair isn't out of a bottle." She tossed her shoulder-length, shining locks, glad she had decided not to cut them before the trip.

"Toothsome as in cotton candy, fluff. You, my love, are the real thing—the mousse au chocolat, the soufflé Grand Marnier, the—"

"I get it." Faith was appeased. "But please stop talking about food!" She was pushing some runny turkey pot pie and broccoli steamed to a pulp around on her plate. Wasn't Castroville, with all those luscious artichokes and other veggies, just down the road? Redwood Ridge was obviously not acquainted with California cuisine, and all Faith's hopes for Alice Waters's or Jeremiah Tower's imprimatur had been dashed by the menu that greeted them at the dining room door. Pineapple tapioca was listed for dessert.

"We have got to go somewhere else for dinner, honey."

Tom nodded vehemently and then said loudly, "What a terrific place this is."

A voice at Faith's shoulder said firmly, "Is something wrong with your lunch? You do not like the food?"

It was Elsa Whittemore, The Ridge's formidable director. She had delivered a short speech of welcome to their group at the barbecue before marching off to more important things, like reclaiming the dunes single-handedly. She had reminded Faith of the woman in one of those James Bond movies with the knives in the toes of her shoes. Click, click. Faith could almost hear Elsa's heels now. The knives were out.

"Actually I had such a big breakfast, I'm not very hungry," Faith lied shamelessly. She was starving. For some reason, doing nothing all morning had given her quite an appetite.

Tom was slavishly cleaning his plate. Faith glowered at him. Elsa left, shoulders back, chest out. Her graying Dutch bob did not dare to move a strand.

"Yum, yum. Yes, sweetheart, I agree: We have to get out of here for dinner."

"You are such a fraud."

"First of all, as you well know, I eat everything, and second, I can't let down the troops. We may want to meet here again. You have to admit, it is an ideal spot. And I hear Elsa pretty much controls who comes and who doesn't."

On the way out, Faith noticed that "the shoe people," as she had come to call them, had what looked like baked Alaska for dessert and wine with their meal. The watercolorists had had garden salads in addition to their pot pies. It was an interesting pecking order.

"What are you going to do this afternoon?" Tom asked as he kissed her before leaving for the next intriguing lecture, "Martin Luther at the Schlosskirche Doors: Did He Really Want In?" "I'll be finished by four, then there's a social hour from five to six and after that we can slip away." He hadn't eaten the tapioca.

"Perfect. I'll make reservations at that fish place we heard about in Pacific Grove. Or we could try Fresh Cream in Monterey. That's supposed to be good. I think I'll go there to the aquarium this afternoon and I can check it out."

Although prepared, Tom had still been nonplussed to discover that Monterey's Cannery Row was not the one of his, or John Steinbeck's, imagination. "Maybe the fish place." He wasn't sure he was ready to see Doc burgers or Palace Flophouse flounder on a menu.

An hour later Faith was standing in front of the Kelp Forest at the Monterey Bay Aquarium peering in fascination at a diver who was feeding varieties of fish from sardines to sharks swirling about in the giant seaweed. She honestly wished Ben were at her side. He would have loved it. But the face reflected next to hers was Jim Hadley's, not Ben's. Carolann was a few steps behind.

"Great place, isn't it? You've got to go upstairs and see the Planet of the Jellies," Jim enthused.

Faith had planned to see the special exhibit and decided there was no time like the present. The aquarium was a large attraction and it was reasonable that the Hadleys would also be there, even if they had stayed in the area before. And there was no way they could have known Faith was coming. *And*, she asked herself as she climbed the stairs to the jellies, why would they want to follow her anyway? After last night's encounter, it was more logical that they would try to avoid her.

She was staring at a large tank filled with moon jellies, some the size of Frisbees, enchanted by their translucent delicacy. The exhibition rooms were dark and people spoke in whispers. It *was* a bit like stepping onto another planet.

"Hard to imagine that something so pretty could hurt you. I had to have another look. Carolann's off powdering her nose." It was Jim.

Faith looked him squarely in the face. The Hadleys' ubiquitous presence was developing into quite a string of coincidences. Maybe they thought the Fairchilds were swingers. Maybe they were embarrassed about the other night and didn't know how to introduce the subject. Maybe it was just her dumb luck.

"So, what do you do, Jim?" Faith asked, and strolled to the next tank. It was a small one filled with tiny bell jellies that floated past her eyes, trailing chains of thin, silver tentacles.

"I'm in insurance—supervise branch offices, do some sales. I'm on the road a lot," he replied. She was not surprised. He had the handshake and the voice—confident, with undertones of genuine, money-back-guaranteed interest. He demonstrated it by asking in turn, "And what about you, Mrs. Fairchild? I know your husband's line of work, but not yours."

"I'm a caterer," she told him, and hoped he wouldn't start asking her about her coverage—or worse, start figuring the exact minute, hour, and date of her demise as a prelude to a life insurance pitch. Death was a fact she hoped would come as a painless, far distant surprise.

Carolann's face appeared in the tank, the jellies' tentacles writhing about her head and transforming her into some mythological creature.

"I have to be going," Faith said. "I want to get my children some of these Planet of the Jellies T-shirts. Do you have kids?" Faith wasn't sure why she asked. After the letdown of last night's potential drama, the Hadleys, busy clawing their way to the top with all their shallow symbols, held very little interest for her.

"None—yet," Jim responded, and put his arm around his wife. She was wearing a backless sundress and there wasn't a trace of a tan mark anywhere. His hand moved from her shoulder to the nape of her neck and continued down. Faith didn't wait to see where it ended up.

Tom was in the cabin when Faith returned.

"I could get very used to this way of life," Faith told him. "If only you didn't have to go to all these talks."

"How about we skip the social? I hear Walter Wade, a worthy reverend from someplace in North Dakota, plans to entertain us with a medley of sing-along songs."

"But you love 'Michael Row the Boat Ashore'!"

"I know, but it might not be in his repertoire . . . and besides, I can think of a better activity for the time, an activity decidedly not antisocial."

So could Faith.

The fish restaurant was jammed and Faith was glad she'd made reservations. Even so, they had to wait on the pleasant, flower-filled patio. They were sipping a nice Geyser Peak Chardonnay and helping themselves to tasty chunks of smoked albacore proffered by a waiter when Faith suddenly grabbed Tom's arm, nearly spilling his drink.

"I can't believe it! They're here! No, don't turn around. Maybe they won't see us."

It was the Hadleys, of course, and at that very moment a smiling young woman came walking through the crowd calling, "Fairchild, party of two. Your table is ready. Fairchild, party . . ." Faith quickly waved to her and dragged Tom to the table before the Hadleys could suggest a foursome.

"Honey, I think you're getting a little paranoid about all this," Tom said as they sat down. "These are simply chance meetings. Obviously they were not up for Swiss steak either—why it is called that I hope you will explain to me someday—and this is one of the closest restaurants."

"I know, I know. It doesn't make any sense. It's just the way they look at me. They seem to be measuring me for something—and Carolann doesn't strike me as the type who is handy with a needle."

"Well, neither are you. Now why don't you forget about them and concentrate on more important things, like the menu and your husband. If they have any interest in us, it's probably to sell us insurance. I'm having the cioppino. What are you going to have?"

Knowing that her husband liked to share, Faith ordered sailfish. When the food arrived, it pushed all thoughts of the Hadleys, and most everything else, from their minds. The sailfish had been marinated in what Faith judged was a combination of dry white wine, lemon thyme, and perhaps a touch of lime juice, then grilled over mesquite. It was accompanied by a fragrant saffron rice pilaf and an enormous, succulent steamed artichoke. Tom had refused the bib the waitress offered and was happily attacking the mussels, cockles, Dungeness crab, lobster, and other piscatorial pleasures floating in the delicious broth in his tureen-sized bowl. From time to time, he dipped a piece of the sourdough garlic bread thoughtfully provided into the soup and also popped some morsel into Faith's mouth. He liked the sailfish, but cioppino was something a man could really wade into, getting legitimately messy at the same time.

They shared a serving of Key lime pie and felt well and truly fed for the first time since arriving on the West Coast.

Faith was in such a good mood that even the Hadleys' appearance at the end of the meal did not dampen her spirits.

Jim took one look at the tablecloth. "You had the cioppino, right? They do a good one here. We really love this place, don't we, Carolann?"

The check arrived, but still the couple did not move on. Faith stood up. It was time for the ladies' room. She hadn't counted on Carolann joining her, but then she seemed to need to powder her nose often. Faith stepped back to let her lead the way and they soon found themselves in the kitchen.

"I have such a poor sense of direction," Carolann apologized. "It's over there, of course." Back on track, they soon found the right door, the one labeled "Gulls." Carolann did spend some time refreshing her makeup, but as Faith washed her hands, she thought the woman painstakingly applying eyeliner in the mirror looked anxious again. Another fight brewing? Should she offer their shower again?

"Have you and Jim been married long?" Faith asked.

"Four years. Why do you ask?" There was no mistaking the coolness in her tone.

"Oh, you seem a bit like newlyweds, that's all," Faith commented, then added, in an oblique allusion to the previous night, "It's nice to see people so much in love they can straighten out any difficulties that come up." She hoped Carolann would take the bait, but all she said was "Uh-huh," as she reached for some lip gloss.

The Fairchilds drove back to The Ridge by way of Carmel for a look at its pretty beach and posh shops. Tom's conversation with Jim had been only marginally more scintillating than Faith's with Carolann. The men had talked baseball.

"I may be getting as bad as you," Tom said, "but one thing was funny. He said something about it being a shame that we weren't staying longer. Did you tell them when we were leaving?"

"No, but the conference dates are probably posted somewhere." Faith was devil's advocate now.

"True, but many of the participants are staying on. Remember, we could have done that, but decided to go to the city instead."

It had been such an automatic decision that Faith had forgotten the option.

They pulled in the Redwood Ridge gate, defined by stone pillars topped with faintly oriental-looking iron pagoda shapes, and started down the redwood-lined drive. They were almost to the reception center when a figure popped out in front of their car and firmly gestured them to stop. Tom hit the brakes, the tires squealed, and the car stopped short of the imperious hand raised in front of them.

"Jumping Jehoshaphat! What does *she* want?" Faith had never heard her husband use this expression. She figured he must be as shaken as she was, although the words leaping to her mind were a great deal pithier.

It was Elsa.

Tom rolled down the window. "Good evening, Miss Whittemore. Is there something I can do for you?"

"Just checking, Reverend Fairchild. We did not see you, or your wife," she added pointedly, "at dinner and no one seemed to know of your whereabouts. We had some concern. That is all." Her voice managed to suggest that police from several counties were searching the area with helicopters, bloodhounds were sniffing the grounds, and divers were combing the ocean floor for the Fairchilds' lifeless bodies.

"I'm sorry you were troubled. We took the opportunity to see a bit more of this lovely area." It was the wrong thing to say. Clearly for Elsa, nothing matched The Ridge.

"In case you're concerned about the Hadleys, we saw them at dinner," Faith said, driven by some flashback to childhood. Maybe she wouldn't have to miss recess after all.

"*The Hadleys* informed us of their plans this afternoon." No need to ask who would be getting blackberries and milk and who would be sent straight to bed.

After that, there wasn't a whole lot to say other than "Good night." Elsa graciously stepped back and motioned them on with her powerful flashlight.

"I feel like I just got caught sneaking a girl, or a beer, into my room!" Tom laughed. Faith tried to laugh too, but discovered that she was extremely annoyed.

"What ever happened to good old-fashioned privacy? We are paying to stay here, aren't we! Every time I turn around someone's following me!"

There were deer, a doe and a fawn, feeding a few yards from their deck and the night air was still warm. Faith was partly appeased. "I guess she's annoyed because we don't like the food. She's probably been waiting there for us since dinner." The thought further lifted her spirits, and by the time they were drifting off to sleep, she had conceded that she would come back to The Ridge again for the setting and facilities—if allowed.

"I think I'll do one of those crafty things tomorrow."
Redwood Ridge had an energetic activities director, Sal Pedrone, who was constantly pushing everything from aquatic
aerobics in the pool to enamel jewelry making.

"This is so unlike you," Tom mumbled, already half
asleep.

"Maybe you just don't know me as well as you think,"
Faith retorted, equally sleepy. Her last conscious thought
was that it *was* unlike her, but seemed to go with the whole
camp atmosphere of the place. She'd like to have at least
one thing to bring home to mother.

Something woke her at three o'clock in the morning. It
was a bird cry, or something else equally unidentifiable to
Faith. It sounded a little like a baby crying, but she hadn't
seen any babies at The Ridge. It wasn't her baby, at any rate,
but she found that she could not get back to sleep, and after
fifteen minutes of tossing she got out of bed, put Tom's
jacket on, and slid open the door to the deck. The night air
hit her full in the face. It was cold and damp. She went back
and got one of the extra blankets. She felt like staying outside. The moon was a bit more full than the night before and
again it was light out. She couldn't see the beach or the main
buildings, because of the fog, but some of the other cabins
were visible, dark shapes scattered about the dunes. There
were apparently no other insomniacs. The only light visible
was the moon's. She wound the blanket around herself and
sat on a bench, leaning up against the side of the cabin.

So far it had been the vacation she'd hoped for only in-
termittently. Like a sore tooth, the Hadleys kept appearing
to remind her that something was wrong. Very wrong. It
was a thought she'd kept in the back of her mind since the
night before, unwilling to take it out for closer examination,
but there was no way to avoid it.

The woman the night before—Carolann—had been terrified. It wasn't a squeezing-the-toothpaste-tube-in-the-middle-
or-from-the-end kind of spat, it was fear. Fear for her own
safety. When she had begged for help, begged to be hidden,

her face had been filled with terror. At the sound of Jim's voice—and now Faith knew it had been Jim—the woman had almost passed out.

After every encounter with the Hadleys, Faith had tried to erase the memory of Carolann's frightened face. She'd told herself that her involvement with various criminal investigations had made her overly suspicious. Yet things did happen. Horrible things.

But nothing was wrong. No crime had been committed, or none that was visible. Maybe Jim was skimming some off the top. Maybe their house, up for sale in Beverly Hills, had termites. Maybe . . . Maybe what? Faith shook her head. It was freezing and she was getting stiff. Stiff. Stiffs. No stiffs in sight. Carolann was as hale and hearty as Miss June.

Faith got up and went inside. It felt as warm as a sauna, and she crawled next to Tom gratefully. She was getting drowsy. Tomorrow afternoon they'd head off for San Francisco. She'd eat a gargantuan breakfast and tell Elsa about every last mouthful. Tom's was the last scheduled talk of the conference. She hoped not too many participants were planning to cut out early, but men and women of the cloth tended to be charitable—or perhaps might have memories of how they felt when parishioners slipped from the pews in the middle of the sermons.

And then they'd leave the material Hadleys far behind. "Material Girl"—and boy. The words kept repeating until she was sound asleep.

Faith got up with Tom the next morning. She didn't feel much like facing either the Hadleys or that inquisitive clerical spouse over breakfast. But she picked Mrs. Tucker, the lesser of two evils, fully prepared to hear "We didn't see you at dinner?" and so forth until Faith's entire life would be laid bare.

Secure in the knowledge that their reservations at Star's were not until nine o'clock, Faith ordered two eggs over

easy, Canadian bacon, and English muffins plus fruit. Tom
had the same plus waffles. They were rewarded by a slight
nod from the director. There was no sign of the Hadleys.

"I have to go now, sweetheart," Tom gave her a quick
kiss. He wasn't nervous about his talk, just preoccupied.
"Have fun at your basket weaving or whatever."

"Sand casting," Faith corrected him. "I'll meet you in the
cabin. I'm going to pack up now, so we can leave right
away." He nodded and walked off in the wrong direction,
recollected himself, and went the right way.

The wrong direction. It reminded Faith of Carolann heading for the kitchen instead of the bathroom in that restaurant
she knew so well. Faith shoved the Hadleys firmly and figu-
ratively away as she returned to the cabin. She concentrated
instead on the numerous varieties of wildflowers growing
on the dunes to either side of the boardwalks constructed to
protect the reclamation project. Her favorites were small
golden poppies that seemed to be made of the finest silk.
There was a patch of them just by the door and they were
swaying in the morning breeze. The fog was starting to lift
and Faith could see the deep teal color of the ocean. Later it
would be turquoise, just as the sky would be clear blue and
empty of anything save brightly colored kites anchored in
the sand, stretched to the length of their strings.

She packed quickly and changed from jeans to shorts.
The class started at nine-thirty and lasted two hours. She
pulled her hair back—it wouldn't do to get it mixed up in
plaster—put her keys in her pocket, and set off. When she
came to the conference center where the group was to
gather, she saw Carolann absorbed in conversation with
Elsa. They seemed to be each other's best friend and as
Carolann left, she patted the other woman on the arm affectionately. Of course, in California, Faith had noticed, there
was a lot more of that sort of amiable gesture than in New
England. Still, Elsa did not seem eminently pattable.

"Well, good morning. What are you up to today?"

Faith couldn't think of an escape. She'd already signed up for the class and Sal Pedrone was coming toward her, his "Welcome, crafty lady" smile firmly in place.

"I'm taking a workshop this morning, then we're off."

"The sand casting one?"

Faith nodded. She knew what was coming.

"Me too." Carolann looped her arm through Faith's. "I know whatever I make is going to look awful, but it's fun to try new things."

Sal introduced them to their teacher, who looked to be nineteen and dedicated to her art. She was wearing sand-cast jewelry and had a display table featuring the objects she'd made. Her name, she told them with a straight face, was Sandy. Which came first? Faith wondered.

Soon the participants, all female, were ready to start. Everything was set out under the trees. Faith headed for a place, Carolann at her heels. It was inevitable.

"It's sad you have to leave so early," Carolann commiserated, "You just got here." Faith realized it was true. They'd been at The Ridge less than three days. It seemed much longer. "You're sure you have to go?"

"Yes, we have reservations in San Francisco and then we have to get back home." Wild horses wouldn't drag the name of either the hotel or Aleford from Faith's lips. She glanced over at Carolann. There was no mistaking it: She definitely looked relieved.

Faith was startled. As Tom had said that first night upon discovering the woman in the bath, what the hell was going on?

Sandy clapped her hands together, "Now, ladies, the first thing I'm going to ask you to do is take off your rings, watches, bracelets, anything that might get in the sand or plaster. Believe me, it will be too late after you get all gooky." She sounded as excited as a child.

Faith slipped off her wedding band and engagement ring, putting them securely in her pocket. She watched Carolann do the same. First the rock on her left ring finger, too large to fit with her wedding band. Then the band. She wiggled her fingers in the air.

"I can't believe I'm doing this. I just had my nails done!"

Nails seemed to be big business on the West Coast; establishments that wrapped, polished, and replaced were as plentiful as car washes.

Sandy was bringing each person a basin of wet sand. Carolann held her hands above hers. She seemed to regard the prospect of molding the grains with as much enthusiasm as she'd have had for molding cow patties. Faith wondered why she was doing it. Faith wondered—and then Faith knew.

She turned to her neighbor. "I'll be right back. I should have stopped at the bathroom before I left the cabin."

"Don't worry. I'll tell Sandy you'll be back in a minute."

But it wasn't a minute. It was two hours later and the class was almost over when Faith Fairchild returned, accompanied by several members of the Pacific Grove police force, who walked up to Faith's sometime shadow and partner in crafts, read her her rights, and arrested her for the murder of her twin sister, Carolann Hadley.

"Here's looking at you, kid." Tom Fairchild raised his glass to his wife. Particularly striking in pale celadon green silk, she sat opposite him in the bar at the Top of the Mark with the lights of San Francisco spread like a bejeweled flying carpet behind her.

Faith sighed with pleasure—and fatigue. It *had* been a rather tumultuous day, starting with her desperate attempts to convince the Pacific Grove police that she was not a lunatic and that in all probability a woman had been murdered. Finally, they agreed to call Faith's old friend—and, she liked to think, partner—Detective Lieutenant John Dunne of the Massachusetts State Police. She'd decided against Aleford's Chief MacIsaac as possibly too small-town, besides his possessing an anathema toward the phone that sometimes led to dire miscommunications. Dunne had vouched for her—quickly, to her passing surprise—and they were off and running.

The crime was so obvious it had almost worked, and she was annoyed that she hadn't figured out that the two women might be identical twins earlier. "Twins," Faith said to Tom later, "that desperate ploy of mystery writers everywhere."

Once the police established that Carolann Hadley did in fact have a twin sister, Carolee Reese, living not too far from Monterey in San Jose, events accelerated. Two officers in plainclothes were dispatched to Redwood Ridge to make sure the Hadleys or whoever stayed put. The authorities in San Jose were notified and, sure enough, found a very dead woman wearing a turquoise nightgown lying in bed at Carolee Reese's address. The house had been ransacked and a window broken to create the appearance of a robbery. Neighbors said that Carolee Reese had told them she would be on vacation for a few weeks. It was not unusual for her to take trips, one woman added. The San Jose police even obtained a description of Jim Hadley, a frequent guest. "I'm on the road a lot"—his words at the aquarium rang in Faith's ears.

And the two must have been on the road the night before last. Carolann had been strangled, probably shortly after leaving the Fairchilds, trapped in the redwoods as she tried to escape once more. Carolee and Jim would have put the body in the trunk or propped it in the backseat, then take a quick trip up Route 101 to her loving sister's house and back to Redwood Ridge for Mr. and "Mrs." Hadley's grand performance.

Faith took a sip of the Kir Royale she'd ordered and shuddered slightly. "Her own sister, that's what keeps coming back to me!" Faith and her sister, Hope, had had their differences, but even as kids, their feelings toward each other had never been remotely murderous. "I keep imagining Carolann's last moments. She knew her husband was after her, but what a horror it would have been to see her twin sister's face!"

Tom nodded. "Evidently Carolee had purchased a large life insurance policy, with Carolann as sole beneficiary. Carolee—or rather she and Jim—were smart enough to have done it over a year ago and not used his company. The girls had no other siblings and their parents are dead, as are Jim's. It was almost the perfect crime—the discovery of the tragic murder, the inheritance, and all the Mercedes and 'teardowns' they wanted—except that somehow Carolann got away from them and came to our cabin."

"And they *have* been watching us, especially me. To see if they were pulling it off. That must have been a tense moment at breakfast when I asked Carolee—really, these names are so confusing; why do parents of twins do this?— if she was all right."

Breakfast reminded Faith of Elsa Whittemore, who had practically started the Fairchilds' car for them, so eager was she to hurry them off the grounds. Murders didn't happen at Redwood Ridge. And if they did, they weren't committed by nice people like the Hadleys, who had been coming for years, except that the Hadleys weren't nice and weren't the Hadleys, at least not both of them.

"You know, honey, I can't believe this, but I keep forgetting to ask you how you knew Carolann Hadley was Carolee Reese? Did she let something slip at that class?"

"In a way." Faith smiled. "When she took off her wedding band, there was no tan mark. The ring on her right hand left a stripe as white as snow. I think she was so busy keeping an eye on me, she got sloppy. Agree?"

Tom reached for his wife's left hand, raised his glass once again, and said, "I do."

If there's one thing I love about summer, it's going to visit one of the many orchards near Cabot Cove. There's nothing like being able to enjoy the fruits of your labors after a pleasant day of picking. Of course, for some people, even the sweetest fruit can leave a bad taste in their mouth. In this story, the Valance family discovers this in a most unusual way.

Poison Peach

Gillian Linscott

" . . . care must be taken not to bruise any part of the shoot; the wounds made by the knife heal quickly, but a bruise often proves incurable."

—The Gardener's Monthly Volume:
"The Peach." George W. Johnson
and R. Errington. October 1847.

January was the time for pruning. In the peach house the journeyman gardeners untied the branches from their wires on the whitewashed wall and spread them out as delicately as spiders spinning webs. The fruit house foreman stepped among them with his bone-handled knife, trimming off the dead wood that had carried last year's fruit, choosing the shoots for this year's. Behind him an apprentice moved like an altar boy with a small basket, picking up every piece of branch as it fell. Few words were said, or needed to be said.

In the eighty years since the peach houses had been built by
the grandfather of the present owner, this same ritual had
gone on, winter after winter. Victoria ruled an empire and
died, apprentices took root and grew into head gardeners,
the nineteenth century turned the corner into the twentieth,
and always, just after the turn of the year, with the solstice
past but the days not yet perceptibly lengthening, the trees
were pruned in the peach house at Briarley.

From the door between the peach house and the grape
house, Henry Valance watched as his father and his grandfather had watched before him, all of them decent, careful
men, accepting their role of guarding, cautiously improv-
ing, passing on to sons. What was different this January
was that Henry's wife, Edwina, stood beside him, staring
out through the sloping glass at the brassicas and bare soil
of the kitchen garden. In the five years they'd been married,
Edwina hadn't taken a great interest in the garden, being
more concerned with the house and the duties of a hostess—although not yet of a mother. She didn't seem very interested now, but in the last few months had accepted her
husband's timid suggestions on how to spend her time as if
they were commands, following him dutifully but without
the animation that had once sparked in her every word or
movement. Her hair under the turban hat was still as glossy
as the shoulder of a chestnut horse, her tall figure graceful
in the long astrakhan coat she wore because it was cold,
even inside the glass houses. But her hands, smoothly
gloved in silver-gray kid, were clasped tightly together and
her face was as blank as the winter sky.

Her husband moved closer to her so that the men working
on the peaches couldn't hear them.

"I've had a letter from Stephen."

Over the past few months they'd fallen into the habit of
talking about the things that mattered in almost public
places, with the servants not far away. It limited the scope
for damage. She moved her head a little, still looking out at

the vegetable garden, as if the stiff rows of brussels sprouts might creep away if not watched.

"It seems he's written a book."

"What kind of book?"

"A novel."

"Why would he do that?"

Her voice had always been low. Now it was scarcely alive.

"He says he needs to make a career for himself." She said nothing. He glanced at her face, then away at the peach pruning. "I've written offering to pay him. I've told him I'll double whatever he's expecting to make from it, if he'll agree not to publish."

"He won't accept."

She said it with flat certainty. They stood for a while, then he gave her his arm and they walked away through the glass galleries of the grape house and the empty melon house scrubbed clean for winter, their feet echoing on the iron gratings. In the peach house, the foreman watched as two journeymen used strips of cloth to tie to the wall, fan-shaped, the tree he'd pruned back. He signaled them to stop, stepped forward with his pruning knife, hesitated over a fruiting spur, and then, without cutting, nodded to them to carry on. The shape was right after all and the shoot should live to carry its peach. Behind the fruit houses men were cleaning and riddling the great boiler that fed hot water into the pipes under the floor gratings. Soon, when the pruning was finished and the stopcock turned to start the artificial indoor spring, the sap would begin to rise up the narrow trunks, along the spread branches, and into that spur, along with the rest. For a day or two longer the peach trees could rest.

By April the peach house was warm and full of pink blossoms, although the air outside hadn't lost the edge of winter. Amongst the petals, the gardeners fought their campaign against small pests that might threaten the setting of the

fruit. An apprentice with a brass syringe walked the aisles
between the trees, spraying the leaves with tobacco water to
control the aphids. A journeyman with a paintbrush worked
a mixture of sulfur and soft soap into every joint and
crevice to kill off the eggs of red spiders and kept an eye on
the apprentice at the same time.

"Careful with that bloody thing. You nearly knocked that
spur clean off."

In fact, the apprentice's momentary carelessness had
scarcely dislodged a petal and the journeyman's attention
was not wholly on the killing of spider eggs and aphids.
Things were happening that even the apprentices knew
about and the waves that had started in the family rooms of
the house had spread out through the upper staff down to
the kitchens, out through the scullery door to the gardeners
who carried up baskets of vegetables every day. A collection had been organized among the journeyman gardeners
and a discreet order placed at the bookshop in the nearest
town. The groom was to collect the result of it when he
went down to the station, along with the other copies ordered by the upstairs staff, the kitchen staff, and the stables.
The butler, who had connections in London, was believed
to have got his hands on a copy already but wasn't showing
anybody. At lunchtime the journeyman gardeners gathered
in their bothy behind the wall at the back of the fruit
houses, made themselves as comfortable as possible on
sacks and buckets, and elected a reader. His attempts to
make an orderly start at the beginning of chapter one were
immediately voted down.

"That's not what all the trouble's about. Start at the business between him and her and we'll go back to the beginning later."

"If we want to."

Laughter, but muted. They were allowed half an hour in
the bothy for their bread and cheese, but what they were
doing was no part of their duties and could lead to trouble,
and even dismissal for impudence, if discovered. The door

had been firmly shut in the noses of the apprentices but was no protection against foreman or head gardener. The reader asked, plaintively, how he was supposed to know where the business was.

"They don't put it in the margins like they do with the Bible."

"I heard it was chapter ten."

The reader rustled pages, scanned silently, then whistled between his teeth.

Several voices told him to get on with it and not keep it to himself.

"It's where she calls him in to give him a piece of her mind because he's been getting too friendly with one of the maids."

"Is that how they put it—too friendly?"

"Oh, get on with it."

Now it had come to it, they were all a little embarrassed. The man trusted with the book read it in a fast mutter so that they had to crane forward to hear him. The lady calls the gentleman into her boudoir. She is stern. She does not usually listen to servants' gossip, but he must realize that the young housemaids are in her care and as employer she has a moral duty to them and to their parents. If the gentleman can assure her that these rumors are baseless then she will take severe action against the people spreading them. A sound outside. The men froze, but it was only two apprentices trying to listen and they were seen off, nursing cuffed ears.

"Go on."

The gentleman cannot give her that assurance. He compliments her instead on her good taste in employing such very attractive housemaids. She is unbelieving at first, then furious. He remains calm, then asks her if she is not, perhaps, jealous. She loses control and actually tries to hit him. He grabs her by the wrist and she falls back across the sofa, her furious black eyes gazing up at him. He stands looking down at her, smiling a little inward smile.

"Well, what happens after that?"

"Nothing. It's the end of the chapter."

He turned the book toward them to show the blank half page.

"Well, go on to the next one then."

He turned the page.

"It doesn't go on. Not with that, anyway. It goes back to the husband at his club."

"Well, what does he—"

The bothy door opened suddenly. In the doorway was the square, bowler-hatted figure of the head gardener himself, who could dismiss all of them with a snap of his fingers, quick as pulling an earwig in half.

"What do you men think you're doing? You've been nearly an hour in here."

Then he saw the book and snatched it out of the reader's hand.

"I'm ashamed of you all. You should know where this filth belongs."

With the journeymen trailing shamefaced after him and the apprentices peering from behind the pot shed, he marched across the yard to the barrel that held liquid fertilizer, pats of cow dung seething in rainwater. He nodded to one of the men to remove the lid, tossed the book into it, and waited while it globbed into the viscous depths. Another nod, and the lid went back.

"If I catch anybody in my gardens dirtying his hands with that again, if I catch anybody even mentioning it or looking as if he's thinking about it, he'll be applying for a new post without a character. Now get back to your work, all of you."

Dispiritedly they went, two of them toward the fruit houses.

"Tell you what, though, he got one thing wrong."

"What's that?"

"Her eyes aren't black—they're brown."

They laughed at that but sobered up when they found Hobbes, the fruit foreman, waiting for them and couldn't meet his eyes.

". . . neither peaches nor nectarines acquire perfection, either in richness or in flavour, unless they be exposed to the full influence of the sun during their last swelling."
—*An Encyclopaedia of Gardening*.
J. C. Loudon. 1835.

By late June the peaches were close to perfection. Cosseted and watched over from the time the first green knobs formed behind the blossom, scrutinized and selected until there was just one fruit to every spur, all they waited for now was their final ripening. In case the midsummer sun should be too strong and scorch them through the glass, early every morning Hobbes would stand among the orderly rows of leaves, looking up, then say a few words, quietly as in church, to his assistant. The assistant would operate a wheel to open rows of ventilating panes, inch by inch, until they were at the exact angle to give a gentle circulation of air, and the process would be repeated every few hours as the sun climbed. Once the ventilators were open the peach house was tidied as carefully as a drawing room, every fragment of loam swept off the path, every tree checked for the slightest sign of insect damage, because by this time the season was at its height and the peaches were out in society. Briarley was famous for its fruit houses and a stroll between breakfast and lunch past the swelling grapes, under green and golden melons hanging among their heavy leaves, was almost a social duty for guests. In fact, there'd not been many guests at Briarley that season, but the fruit houses were always kept ready for them, as they always had been. Today Henry Valance came on his morning visit alone. Alone, that is, apart from the train that followed him at a respectful distance, first the head gardener, then Hobbes the foreman, then the two journeymen with particular responsibility for fruit.

Occasionally he'd pause, palpate and sniff a melon, finger a grape. When this happened the head gardener would catch up with him and a few serious words would be exchanged. The procession made its slow way to the peach house and stopped between the rows of trees.

"Nearly ripe then, are they?"

A nod from the head gardener signaled to Hobbes to come closer. It was a sign of the respect he had for Hobbes as a master in his own field that he allowed the foreman to answer the employer's question directly. Hobbes stood there in his dark suit and hat among in the green-dappled shade, gardening apron discarded for this formal visit, watch chain gleaming.

"The Hale's Early should be ripe by next Monday, sir, and the Early Beatrice not long after. Then the Rivers and the Mignonnes are coming on very nicely."

"Excellent. We'll look forward to that."

Henry's father and grandfather had stood in the same place and used much the same words. The difference was in the flatness of his voice that said everything he might have looked forward to was already in the past. Then, with an effort:

"You'll make sure we have plenty ripe for the second weekend in July, won't you? We have a lot of people coming, house quite full."

The two journeymen exchanged glances. It would be the first house party since it happened. The staff had been speculating that there wouldn't be any this year.

"We'll make sure, sir."

His question had not been necessary. It was the work of them all to see that there were ripe peaches all through the summer, whether there were guests to eat them or not. Still, there was no resentment that he'd asked it. He was, on the whole, liked by the gardening staff—and pitied.

"Nets . . . are perfectly useless in keeping off wasps and other insects, as they will alight on the outside and, folding their wings, pass through those of the smallest meshes."

—*An Encyclopaedia of Gardening.*

There was the sound of footsteps coming through the glass galleries from the direction of the house, too light and quick for a gardener's, too confident for a maid's. Hurrying steps. The man went tense.

"Henry."

His wife's voice, with scarcely controlled panic in it. He met her in the doorway.

"A letter for you. It's just arrived."

She held it out to him. At first he'd looked simply puzzled. Dozens of letters arrived every day, and it was no part of Edwina's duties to chase him round the estate with them. Then he saw the handwriting. Took it from her and read.

"He's heard about the house party. He's inviting himself."

"No!"

The gardeners were in an impossible position. To eavesdrop on employers' private conversation was unthinkable. On the other hand, it was equally unthinkable to melt away through the door into the kitchen garden, since they'd been given no sign to go. They made a great business of scrutinizing the peach leaves, which they already knew were perfect.

"Write to him. Tell him he can't come."

"I can't do that. He is my brother, after all."

"He can't come if you don't let him."

"He'd come in any case, and what could I do then? Call the police to bring a van and drag him away? Tell the men to throw him in the lake, with the house full of visitors? It would mean that people would go on talking about it for years."

"That's what he wants."

"Yes, and the only way we can prevent him from getting it is facing it out, letting him come here."

"No."

But it was a different word now, numb and dispirited. He put out a hand to her but she moved away and her slow steps back toward the house seemed to go on for a long time.

The head gardener said kindly: "The figs are doing very nicely, sir. Would you care to look at them?"

"Figs. Yes, certainly, figs."

As they were moving off, the head gardener stopped suddenly .

"Excuse me, sir, but look at that."

He pointed at one of the peaches. An intake of breath from the gardeners.

"A wasp. Early for them, isn't it?"

The insect was sitting, wings folded, on the down of a peach. Hobbes stepped forward, mortified.

"I'm sorry, sir."

One of the journeymen ventured, unasked: "The lad was saying he'd seen a nest of them at the back of the pot shed."

The head gardener glared at him.

"Well, why didn't you do something about it? See to it, will you, Hobbes." His instruction to the foreman was less brusque than it might have been, considering the shame of the wasp's invasion. Hobbes nodded and the party moved on.

> *"A gentle squeeze at the point where the stalk joins the fruit will soon determine whether it be ripe enough."*
> —*The Gardener's Monthly Volume:* "The Peach."

July, and the scent of ripe peaches hung on the air like a benignant gas. Every morning the foreman would pick the ripest and lay them gently onto a padded tray held by the apprentice, ready for the house party at lunch. All but a few. It was a custom at Briarley that some of the best fruit should be left on the trees for the look of it when the visi-

tors walked round, glowing through green like the eyes of a
sleepy animal. But the party hadn't reached the peach
house yet, lingering on the way to admire the ripe purple
clusters on the grapevine. Murmurs of admiration and
white-gloved hands reaching out, almost touching but stopping just before making contact, unwilling to smudge a
bloom on the fruit like the first morning in Eden. But one
pair of hands, male and gloveless, kept moving, breached
the invisible barrier, picked a grape. A little shiver, half
shocked, half pleased, ran through the party. Relishing the
attention, the picker put the grape in his mouth. His lips
were full, for a man's, and as he munched he let the under-
side of his lower lip show, slick and smooth.

"Is it good?"

The woman guest who asked the question had dark piled
hair and wide eyes. She smelt of carnations and her dress-
maker had been perhaps a shade too attentive in cutting her
dress so exactly to the curve of her full breasts. Instead of answering in words, the man picked another grape and held it
half an inch from her lips. Her eyes flickered sideways to
where her host and hostess were standing, then she opened
her lips in a little round pout just wide enough to let the grape
in, dipped her head, and took it from his fingers like a bird.

"Yes, very good."

A silence, then from the side of the group, their host's
voice: "Shall we go and look at the peaches?" But he
couldn't stop himself adding: "If you've had enough,
Stephen."

"Oh, enough for now, don't you think?"

The party moved on in silence.

*"It is common practice to lay littery material beneath the trees to
save from bruising the fruit which falls, and sometimes those
which fall are extremely luscious."*
        —*The Gardener's Monthly Volume*: "The Peach."

On Sunday morning the day started later. Only a few guests came to the fruit houses between breakfast and lunch. Host and hostess went to church as usual. A few of the house party went with them, but it was a hot day and most preferred to stroll by the lake or in the lime avenue. After lunch, with the weekend drawing to its close, the strolls became lazier and polite slow-motion competition developed for places on rustic benches under the trees. Afterward, nobody knew who had proposed another tour of the fruit houses. It might have been a suggestion from the host—certainly not one from Edwina, because she had a headache and had retired to the drawing room after lunch, with an old friend in attendance. The suggestion might have come from Stephen, as he'd been the focus of the younger set in the party for most of the weekend. A stranger might have taken him for the host instead of his brother, although his behavior toward Henry and Edwina had been entirely correct throughout. He'd let it be known that he enjoyed being back at the old place so much that he thought he might stay for the week. Whoever suggested it, the proposal collected a little following and about a dozen people joined the tour, including the woman who smelt of carnations. Some of the older guests felt that for a woman whose husband was working abroad she'd been a little too eager for Stephen's company over the weekend. Late at night, among some of the men lingering in the billiard room after too much port, there'd been jokes about Stephen doing research for his next novel, only not in Henry's hearing. Only one more night to go and she'd be leaving on Monday morning. The men in the billiard room had even been placing bets.

Sun, food, and wine swept away the touch of solemnity that usually went with the fruit house tour. Stephen was triumphant, unstoppable. He ranged along the fruit-smelling avenues like a big child, greedy to see, touch, taste. The younger element in the party had caught his mood. The woman who'd eaten the grape had competition now as they

all fingered, dared, ate. A melon was parted from its stem
and thrown from hand to hand until golden flesh and pips
splattered on the red-tiled floor. Henry watched, impassive.
Farther back, not part of the party, the head gardener
watched, equally impassive. He stayed ten yards behind
them as they laughed and pattered through the grape house,
leaving the bunches blemished with bare stems and torn
tongues of purple skin.

When they got to the green-dappled shade of the peach
house Hobbes was at work there, and it looked for a moment as if he were going to commit the sackable sin of
rudeness to his employer's guests in defense of his cherished peaches. He actually stood for a moment in the path
of the party until the head gardener caught his eye and he
stood reluctantly aside. This little stutter of opposition
seemed to increase Stephen's pleasure. He challenged one
of the women to eat a peach without picking it. She moved
her lips toward a red and golden fruit that trembled on its
stem with ripeness. Hobbes started toward her, perhaps in-
tending to hand it to her with proper respect for lady and
peach. The head gardener looked alarmed at the impending
breach of etiquette and might have stopped him, but at the
last minute the woman drew her face away from the peach,
giggling.
   "You can't. It would fall. Nobody could."
   "Yes you can. All you need is a soft mouth. Look."
   In silence, with them all watching him, Stephen ad-
vanced on the largest peach in sight. It hung conveniently
on a level with his chin, standing out from the leaves on its
spur. He bent a little at the knees and turned his head back
so that the fruit was almost resting on his mouth. His teeth
closed on it. Juice ran down his chin, dribbled onto the
lapel of his white jacket. A little gasp from one of the
women, hushed at once. The peach shifted a little, rotating
on its stem, but still didn't fall. His neck muscles tensed
and he took another, larger bite. Then there was a little

cracking sound and he was falling, falling backward with the peach clenched in his jaws. This time the gasps weren't hushed but turned to screams. Because of the way he'd been standing, the back of his head hit the iron grating with a crash that sent every leaf in the place quivering. Then voices.

"Choking. For heaven's sake, get it out of his mouth."

"Air. Get some air in here."

"Get the ladies out."

"Isn't there a doctor?"

Henry was at the front of the group, along with the head gardener and the foreman. They turned Stephen over, wrenched the peach from his teeth. From the look of his contorted face it seemed likely that he'd choked on the fruit before his head hit the grating, but since he couldn't be dead twice over that didn't seem to matter. Henry got to his feet coughing, staggered backward against the wall, then was violently sick.

"Get him outside. Get him into the air."

"Everybody outside."

"A piece of cloth fastened to a stick, soaked in a saturated solution of cyanide of potassium, is immediate death to all wasps within or returning to the nest."

—*"The Fruit Grower's Guide.*
John Wright. 1892.

It took some time for the doctor to reach Briarley and while they waited for him doubts were already setting in, mainly because of the smell. Several of the men besides Henry were coughing as they came out of the peach house, and a woman collapsed and had to be revived. When Henry and most of the party were on their way back to the house, the head gardener, Hobbes, and a few of the male guests covered the body with clean sacks. Then they shut the door firmly and waited on the other side of it in the grape house, the guests smoking, the two gardeners standing a little apart from them. When the doctor arrived at last they followed him in but stood at a safe distance, although most of the smell had worn off by then. He peeled back the sack from the face.

"What did you say happened?"

"He was eating a peach and he choked."

He examined the body briefly, then told them they should cover it up again but not do anything else until the police arrived. He was a comparatively new doctor in the village, Scottish and conscientious. The old doctor might have managed things more tactfully.

The verdict was never in doubt: Stephen Valance had deserved what he got. If you seduce your brother's maidservant, then his wife, and—for a profit—tell the world about it, you can't complain if your peach turns out to contain cyanide. Even those who had quite liked Stephen and watched his career with interest felt a kind of satisfaction that there was a limit after all, although there had been some sporting interest in seeing how far and fast a man could go before he hit it. Stephen had chosen to ride his course that way and by the natural law of things he was heading for a fall. No more needed to be done and very little said, except in private when the servants were out of the room.

That, at any rate, was the immediate verdict of society. The verdict of the country's system of justice was another matter and at first seemed likely to throw up more difficulties. That Stephen had died by cyanide poisoning and that the carrier of the poison had been the peach was never seriously in doubt. The hopeful theory of suicide in a moment of well-earned remorse was abandoned instantly by anybody who had the slightest acquaintance with Stephen or his reputation. Which left . . .

"Well, I suppose if it comes right down to it, it has to be murder."

The discussion was going on very late at night in the billiard room. Not that anybody had actually tried to play billiards, which would have been totally inappropriate on a Sunday, with the hostess prostrate upstairs, the host at her bedside, and the host's younger brother in the mortuary. The men who had influence had naturally congregated there—not the giddier sort who had followed Stephen but the more sober ones who had known Henry's father, who sat as magistrates and chose men to stand for Parliament.

"You can't blame him. I'd have done the same thing myself."

"Not very nice, poison."

"Quick, though. Practically painless, I'd have thought. Anyway, what can you do? I mean, you can't challenge a man to a duel in this day and age."

"I suppose the next thing's the inquest. They can bring in murder by person or persons unknown. . . ."

"Or they can even name the person they think did it, if they think there's enough evidence."

Silence, while they considered it.

"Of course, there's always accidental death."

"There was a glass vial of cyanide in that peach. How does that get in there accidentally?"

"They use cyanide to kill wasp nests in glass houses. At any rate, my gardener does, and I don't suppose Henry's are any different. You get a lot of wasps after peaches."

More silence, finally broken by the oldest man amongst them.

"I think I'd better have a word with his head gardener in the morning."

"Only professional men can use it safely."
                                                    —*The Fruit Grower's Guide.*

Hobbes stood in a shaft of sunlight in the coroner's court, dark-suited in his Sunday best, new bowler hat on the table in front of him, and gave his evidence. By that point the court had already heard from the brother of the deceased, from two doctors, from a police officer, and from the head gardener, who clearly remembered telling the fruit foreman to do something about the wasps in the peach house. The coroner had been respectful to the brother's grief, businesslike with the doctors and the head gardener. To the fruit foreman his tone was colder, and Hobbes answered respectfully. He had been in Mr. Valance's employment for twenty years. Yes, he had used potassium cyanide on a wasp's nest; they kept a drum of it for the purpose in the pot shed. No, he did not know how it had come to contaminate a peach. Yes, he had been warned to be careful with it and knew that it was poisonous. If any of it had somehow come onto the fruit, from his gardening gloves or some tool, then that was very great carelessness. Could he think of any other way that the cyanide might have come onto the peach? No sir, he could think of no other way. There was a rustling and sighing in the court, like heavy leaves in a breeze. The coroner paused to let the answer sink in, then turned to another aspect of the matter. The doctor who had certified death and the police officer had noticed small fragments of glass in the peach.

"It was put on the floor, sir, by one of the gentlemen, when they took it out of his mouth."

"You're suggesting that was when the glass became attached to it?"

"Yes, sir."

"Are you accustomed to leaving glass fragments lying on the floor of your employer's fruit houses?"

"Not accustomed, no sir."

"And yet glass fragments were there?"

"Yes sir."

"Should we assume that this was another example of carelessness?"

It took Hobbes some time to realize that an answer was required. When he did he said "Yes sir" again in the same respectful voice. At last he was permitted to stand down. The head gardener—who would hardly allow a petal to settle on the floor of the glass houses for more than a second or two—looked straight ahead throughout the foreman's evidence, face expressionless. In his summing-up the coroner had some hard things to say about carelessness by men who should know better. Hobbes took them all, head bent over the bowler hat that rested on his knees. The verdict was accidental death.

Outside the court, one of Henry Valance's friends went up to Hobbes as he stood on his own among departing cars and carriages.

"Well, Hobbes, always best to own up to things."

"Yes sir."

"I gather Mr. Valance is letting you keep your position."

"Yes sir."

"A very generous man, Mr. Valance. I'm sure you're grateful."

"Yes sir."

And although he'd been one of the chief movers in arranging things so satisfactorily, the friend really did feel that Henry was acting generously. The coroner's rebuke had wrapped itself around Hobbes and his deplorable carelessness with cyanide was now a fact of history, officially recorded.

"Anyway, I don't suppose it will happen again."

"No sir."

Both men took their hats off as the Valances' motor car drove slowly past, with Edwina sitting very upright beside her husband, pale under her heavy veil.

By October the peach season was almost over. A few Prince of Wales and Lady Palmerstons still gleamed among the leaves but there hadn't been much call for peaches from the household, or many tours of the glass houses. Henry made his dutiful rounds from time to time and exchanged a few words with Hobbes about indifferent things, but that was all. One morning when there was already a frosty feel to the air outside the head gardener came in while Hobbes was retieing labels on wires. There was nobody else within hearing.

"All well, Hobbes?"

"Yes."

The head gardener looked out through the panes to where the men were digging over a potato plot.

"Some people are saying you got left with the dirty end of the stick. Still, you said your piece very well and you didn't lose by it."

No response. The head gardener's attention seemed to be all on the men outside, then he said: "Funny, the things you find when you dig."

The wire under Hobbes's hand suddenly tightened and began vibrating. He kept his head down.

"What are you thinking of?"

"End of July, I was in the herb garden and I noticed this little freshly dug patch right at the back of the angelica. Now I hadn't told anyone to dig there. I went and got a spade from the shed and turned it over to have a look. What do you suppose I found there?"

Hobbes's grip on the wire was now so tight that the tree branch it supported was quivering too.

"Peaches, that's what I found. I backed off quickly, I can tell you. There's a paving slab over them now, in case of any more accidents."

The tree branch was near to breaking when Hobbes released his grip of the wire and straightened up. The head gardener took his arm, not roughly.

"Of course, you couldn't be sure he'd take that one peach so you'd have to do a few of them. And you were going to stop the lady when she looked like biting into one of them instead."

Hobbes nodded. "How did you know?"

"That it was you? Well, Mr. Valance might have done the one of them, but to do more than one like that you needed to be neat-fingered and you needed to have time. Nobody has more time in the peach house than you do, and nobody's got neater fingers. I've watched you grafting fruit trees."

Hobbes took the compliment with another nod.

"And another thing I know—I know why you did it, and I don't blame you."

The foreman looked at the head gardener's face, then the words surged out of him.

"They were all talking about what he'd done to her, to Mrs. Valance, as if my girl didn't matter. All this about the book, everybody reading about what he'd done to the housemaid, to my girl, and the lady calling him in to talk about it and then he . . . When I knew he had the face to come back here, laughing at us, I started thinking—supposing I did so and so. And, well, I did it."

The head gardener's hand stayed on his arm. Anybody looking into the peach house from outside would have seen nothing but two men enjoying the autumn sunshine on their employer's time.

"How is your girl?"

"Gone to her aunt in Wales. They've put it about that the father's a sailor lost at sea. She won't be coming back here."

Silence. They were two men used to patience, but Hobbes gave way first.

"Let's be going and get it over with."

"It *is* over. You've been careless. The coroner said so."

"But—"

"Be quiet. I'm thinking."

"I thought you'd already done the thinking."

"That space over there. Do you think another couple of Rivers or maybe Lord Napiers instead?"

Hobbes stared first at the blank white wall, then at him.

"You're asking me that—now?"

"Why not? None too soon for you to start planning for next year, is it?"

"For next year . . ."

It took him some time to understand. When he did he said thank you and turned back to the fruit trees. A spur, fruitless now, snagged at his cuff, but he freed it with a hand still shaking a little and went on with his work.

About the Contributors

DAHEIM, Mary. "Tippy Canoe." In this story, Mary Daheim takes a closer look at the earlier life of her heroine Judith McMonigle's beau Joe Flynn. McMonigle and Flynn are featured in Daheim's series of bed-and-breakfast mysteries, including *Nutty as a Fruitcake, Auntie Mayhem, Murder My Suite,* and *Bantam of the Opera.*

DENTINGER, Jane. "The Last of Laura Dane." Former actress Jane Dentinger once again returns to the theater world, which provides so much rich fodder for her series of mystery novels. Her most recent book, featuring actress Jocelyn O'Roarke, is *Who Dropped Peter Pan?* (1995).

ECCLES, Marjorie. "Anne Hathaway Slept Here." Marjorie Eccles lives in the Chilterns, but sets much of her work in the English Midlands, where she lived for many years. Her most recent mystery, featuring Detective Chief Inspector Gil Mayo, is *Pandora's Box* (1996).

GUNNING, Sally. "Framed." Sally Gunning, a resident of Cape Cod, is the author of the Peter Bartholomew mystery series, which includes *Hot Water, Under Water, Troubled Water, Rough Water,* and *Still Water.*

HAGER, Jean. "A Deadly Attraction." Jean Hager is the author of three mystery series, two of which feature Cherokee detectives, and the third, the Iris House series, with amateur sleuth Tess Darcy. The latest title from Mysterious Press is *The Fire Carrier,* a Chief Mitch Bushyhead Cherokee mystery. Hager has won numerous Oklahoma Tepee awards and was nominated for an Agatha Award for Best Short Story in 1992.

HARRIS, Charlaine. "Deeply Dead." Charlaine Harris' librarian sleuth, Aurora Teagarden, appears alongside Jessica Fletcher in an unexpected development at a book talk. The most recent Teagarden book is *The Julius House* (1995); an earlier one, *Real Murders* (1990), was nominated for an Agatha for Best Novel. Harris launches a new series in 1996 with *Shakespeare's Landlord*.

HART, Ellen. "Sight Gag." This story from Ellen Hart centers on another character in her series of mysteries featuring lesbian restaurateur Jane Lawless. Other Lawless mysteries include *Faint Praise, A Small Sacrifice, A Killing Cure, Stage Fright, Vital Lies,* and *Hallowed Murder. A Small Sacrifice* won the Lambda Literary Award for Best Lesbian Mystery and the Minnesota Book Award for Best Crime Fiction. Hart lives in Minneapolis with her partner of eighteen years.

KINGSBURY, Kate. "A Nice Cup of Tea." Kate Kingsbury checks out briefly from her Pennyfoot Hotel mysteries to examine malice among siblings. The most recent Pennyfoot Hotel mystery is *Grounds for Murder* (1995).

LaPIERRE, Janet. "Patience at Griffith Gulch." Janet LaPierre's mysteries, centering on the chilly and foggy California north coast, include *Children's Games, The Cruel Mother, Old Enemies, Unquiet Grave,* and *Grandmother's House.*

LAURENCE, Janet. "Come to Tea." In this story, Janet Laurence features tea and a love triangle. Drawing on her culinary background, Laurence's series of mysteries features cook Darina Lisle. Her most recent effort is *To Kill the Past.*

LAWRENCE, Margaret. "The Cat-Whipper's Apprentice." With this story, Margaret Lawrence initiates a new series of women's heritage mysteries. Mystery readers will recognize her other pseudonym of M. K. Lorens and her series featuring Shakespeare professor and author Winston Marlowe Sherman.

LINSCOTT, Gillian. "Poison Peach." Gillian Linscott takes a break from Edwardian England with this tale of questionable fruit at a house party. Well-known for her series of books featuring suffragist sleuth Nell Bray, Linscott is a former BBC reporter.

MASON, Sarah J. "Safe Deposit." Trewley and Stone—like Spenser, Morse, and Quiller—are known only by their surnames. Their creator is more richly nominated, answering at the same time to Sarah J. (for Jill) Mason and (pseudonymously) Hamilton Crane. Hamilton Crane continues the late Heron Carvic's Miss Seeton series. Sarah J. Mason's fifth full-length Trewley and Stone mystery, *Sew Easy To Kill,* was published in 1996.

MEREDITH, D. R. "The Subject of Prosperity." For this story, D. R. Meredith returns to the Texas Panhandle setting of her two series featuring Sheriff Charles Matthews and lawyer John Lloyd Branson. Her full-length mysteries include *The Sheriff and the Folsom Man Murders, The Sheriff and the Branding Iron Murders, The Sheriff and the Panhandle Murders,* and *Murder by Impulse.*

MILLHISER, Marlys. "Body in the Bosque." Marlys Millhiser's psychically gifted sleuth Charlie Greene returns in this story. Charlie appears in *Death of the Office Witch* and *Murder in a Hot Flash.*

PAGE, Katherine Hall. "The Body in the Redwoods." With this story, Katherine Hall Page continues her popular series featuring caterer and minister's wife Faith Fairchild. Page won the Agatha for Best First Novel for *The Body in the Belfry* (1990). The most recent full-length Faith mystery is *The Body in the Basement* (1995).

PICKARD, Nancy. "The Potluck Supper Murders." Nancy Pickard departs from her Jenny Cain series to provide another delightful glimpse of Virginia Rich's Eugenia Potter. An earlier Rich/Pickard collaboration appears in *The 27-Ingredient Chile Con Carne Murders* (1993).

ROWLANDS, Betty. "The Recluse." Betty Rowlands, a resident of Gloucestershire, England, brings her crime-writer-turned-sleuth Melissa Craig to this story. Craig appears in four novels, including *Exhaustive Enquiries* (1995).